WESTERN

Rugged men looking for love...

Expecting A Fortune
Nina Crespo

The Doc's Instant Family
Lisa Childs

MILLS & BOON

Nina Crespo is acknowledged as the author of this work
EXPECTING A FORTUNE
© 2024 by Harlequin Enterprises ULC
Philippine Copyright 2024
Australian Copyright 2024
New Zealand Copyright 2024

First Published 2024
First Australian Paperback Edition 2024
ISBN 978 1 038 90578 9

THE DOC'S INSTANT FAMILY
© 2024 by Lisa Childs
Philippine Copyright 2024
Australian Copyright 2024
New Zealand Copyright 2024

First Published 2024
First Australian Paperback Edition 2024
ISBN 978 1 038 90578 9

MIX
Paper | Supporting
responsible forestry
FSC® C001695
www.fsc.org

Published by
Harlequin Mills & Boon
An imprint of Harlequin Enterprises (Australia) Pty Limited
(ABN 47 001 180 918), a subsidiary of HarperCollins
Publishers Australia Pty Limited
(ABN 36 009 913 517)
Level 19, 201 Elizabeth Street
SYDNEY NSW 2000 AUSTRALIA

Cover art used by arrangement with Harlequin Books S.A.. All rights reserved.

Printed and bound in Australia by McPherson's Printing Group

Expecting A Fortune
Nina Crespo

MILLS & BOON

Nina Crespo lives in Florida, where she indulges in her favourite passions—the beach, a good glass of wine, date night with her own real-life hero and dancing. Her lifelong addiction to romance began in her teens while on a "borrowing spree" in her older sister's bedroom, where she discovered her first romance novel. Let Nina's sensual contemporary stories feed your own addiction to love, romance and happily-ever-after. Visit her at ninacrespo.com.

Visit the Author Profile page
at millsandboon.com.au for more titles.

Dear Reader,

Welcome to Chatelaine, Texas, home of the Cowgirl Cafe. If you have been here before, welcome back!

In *Expecting a Fortune*, Devin Street is a single dad, owner of the *Chatelaine Daily News* and a dog lover. Bea Fortune is a businesswoman realising her dream to open a new restaurant featuring her mum's recipes. Their one night together opens the door to the unexpected. I'm sure we can all relate to changes that happen in an instant!

But Devin and Bea decide to embrace their curiosity about what the unexpected can bring. This takes them on a journey with twists, turns and challenges. But they also discover wonderful rewards like acceptance, joy and love.

Speaking of love, I'd love to hear from you. Visit me at ninacrespo.com. Say hello and connect with me on Facebook, Instagram or sign up for my newsletter. There, I share details about my books, upcoming appearances and my favourite things.

Thank you for choosing *Expecting a Fortune* as your new romance read. May this book provide an enjoyable escape that causes you to smile as you turn the pages.

Wishing you all the best,

Nina

CHAPTER ONE

THE BEAUTIFUL SPRING day mirrored Bea Fortune's mood as she hurried down the sidewalk. She wanted to shout out in glee to the residents of the small sleepy town of Chatelaine, *Tonight's the night!* Her long-held dream of opening a restaurant, the Cowgirl Café, was just hours away.

On some level, she still couldn't believe it was happening. Over the past few years, she'd shadowed chefs and restaurant proprietors as well as completed a degree in restaurant management. But financially, the goal had remained out of reach until her life had changed overnight.

A few months ago, she'd been summoned to Texas with her sister, Esme, and their brother, Asa. Their deceased uncle, Elias Fortune, had left an inheritance in his will for them and his grandchildren. Elias's widow, Freya Fortune, had explained how he'd wanted to make each of their wishes come true.

Bea didn't consider herself a small-town girl, but something about Chatelaine had felt right, and she'd stayed to launch a restaurant there using the windfall she'd received. Now she could finally share her take on down-home family food inspired by her mom's recipes. Fried green tomatoes on a bed of fresh basil with remoulade. Bourbon-glazed pork chops and sautéed kale. Gulf shrimp and green chili–cheddar grits, and baskets of buttery homemade biscuits served at every table. Those selections were just some of her favorites on the menu.

Growing up, the food her mother, Andrea, had prepared had been made with love. Even now in her thirties, Bea still remembered the warmth and goodness filling the kitchen as her mom had cooked—and playfully admonished Lars, Bea's dad, when he'd come in and sneak a taste from a pot warming on the stove.

More than anything, she wanted her customers to leave with that same sense of contentment after enjoying a meal at her establishment. And for the café to be something her parents would have been proud of had they still been alive.

Anxious to get to the restaurant, Bea picked up the pace. An afternoon breeze ruffled her long auburn hair. As she smoothed strands from her forehead, she spotted Devin Street, the owner of the *Chatelaine Daily News*, walking toward her. Bea's heart did a little flip-flop in her chest.

Dressed in dark boots, black jeans, and a light blue button-down shirt, he fit in with the rest of the casually dressed pedestrians. But his height—and the way he wore a cowboy hat—put him head and broad shoulders above the rest. The tan Stetson was pulled low over his deep sepia eyes, and his gaze reflected keen observation along with a confident, relaxed nature not every guy their age possessed. Add in the dark beard that was a hint more of a shadow on his angular, brown jawline, and he was worth-a-second-look sexy.

And she'd given in to the temptation to look more than a few times since her future brother-in-law, Ryder Hayes, had introduced them after she'd moved to town.

He gave a nod and a smile. "Hello, Bea."

His voice, rich and smooth, flowed like the warm golden-brown honey served with biscuits at the café.

Slightly breathless, she pushed out the words "Hi, Devin." *Jeez.* She sounded like she had a case of laryngitis.

"Ready for tonight?"

"Absolutely." Her tone rose an octave higher than normal. "Everything is great." And now she sounded like a cheerleader at a pep rally. Thankfully, Devin didn't seem to notice.

As he strode past, a wonderful masculine scent with notes of cedar, citrus, and musk followed him. Unable to resist, she glanced over her shoulder. The pair of Levi's he had on suited him well.

Before she looked away, Devin glanced back and met her gaze.

Oops...busted. On a reflex, she waved at him.

With a slightly questioning expression, he waved back.

No, that wasn't awkward at all... As Bea faced forward, the heat creeping into her cheeks turned into a blazing fire, making her feel overly warm in the outfit she'd chosen for the restaurant's opening. The lightweight peach sweater, white blouse, jeans, and flats gave her a professional look, but the ensemble also allowed her to move around quickly during dinner service.

Instead of drooling over Devin, she should have asked him if the freelance food critic was coming to dinner tonight.

The anonymous person wrote a column for the paper and rated establishments in Chatelaine and the surrounding area. Rumors swirled over where the columnist was from. Corpus Christi? Austin? Maybe Houston? But even if she had asked Devin if the person was showing up, he wouldn't have told her. He and his staff were tight-lipped about the critic's plans along with his or her identity.

Whoever it was had recently given a glowing review to the new menu at the Saddle & Spur Roadhouse, a local casual restaurant known for their desserts and the option of steak as a side dish. If all went as expected, there was a good chance they would see her restaurant in the same light.

Nervousness expanded in her chest, and she released it in a long exhale. Everyone was prepared for the mid-week opening night, thanks in part to her younger sister, Esme, who was also acting kitchen manager, and Freya, who was filling in as the temporary waitstaff supervisor. The older woman had been a big help, stepping in to fill the void after the person Bea had hired for the job had suddenly bailed out.

They and the staff had worked hard yesterday preparing for the big night. And if the soft opening for the café the week prior with just friends and family was any indication, success was on their side. Everyone had raved over the food.

A few steps later, Bea reached the blue-doored entrance to the corner restaurant and went inside.

The space with light gray walls and white trim was modern, but the tan brick fireplace, Western-inspired metal wall art, and vases of brightly colored wildflowers on each table gave the place a type of intimacy that invited people to relax and savor their meals.

As she locked the door behind her, Bea's gaze landed on the nonfunctioning alarm-system panel. It was the last major task that needed to be completed in the building. The security company was doing the installation tomorrow. An appointment with them had been set up by Esme for last week, but the company had claimed someone had called and canceled it.

A smudge that needed to be wiped away from one of the windows near the panel suddenly caught her eye. As did a basket of rolled silverware. Instead of sitting on a table, it should have been under the host stand. They were small details, but ignoring them today would just make it easier to let go of the high standards that would set the Cowgirl Café apart from other places. She would mention the issues to Freya.

As she ran through a mental list of other items she wanted to review before they opened, Bea flipped the light switch.

None of the overhead lights came on.

That was odd. Had a power surge happened again in the dining area? That situation had occurred the day after the rewiring of the building, shutting down part of the circuit panel, but the problem was supposedly fixed. Bringing the electrical system up to code in the older structure had been a major expense along with the plumbing.

On the way to the circuit panel in the kitchen, her phone rang. It was Esme.

"Hello."

"Hey." Her sister's happy mood reflected in her voice. "I'm running a few minutes behind. Sorry. But Tanya and the staff are good to go on food prep. They just have to set up the stations."

Esme's wedding day was in just a few days, and Bea was amazed at how calmly her sister was juggling planning the big day and working at the café, along with motherhood.

Esme and Ryder each had baby boys the same age, Chase and Noah, and their children were the reason they'd met a few months ago.

On the day the boys had been born, the staff in Labor and Delivery at the county hospital had accidently mixed up their identification bracelets. No one had realized the switch had occurred until Esme had taken an ancestry test.

The news had been a shock to everyone, but as Esme and Ryder had tried to find the best way forward, another truth had been abundantly clear: they were meant for each other. And since they'd become engaged, they'd been inseparable.

Bea had tried to convince Esme to at least take time off before the wedding, but she'd refused, not wanting to miss the grand opening. Admittedly, it was a comfort to have Esme and Tanya watching over the kitchen. Tanya was not only a talented sous chef, but she was good with the staff and highly organized like Esme. The two women made a good team.

"I'm sure everything will be fine, but hmm, let me take a wild guess," Bea playfully replied. "Does Ryder have anything to do with you being late?"

"Only because we were discussing the wedding and getting in some much-needed cuddle time with Chase and Noah."

"*Just* cuddle time with Chase and Noah, and nothing else? Now why do I find that hard to believe?" Bea chuckled. She flipped the light switch in the kitchen, but again, none of the overhead lights illuminated. "Are you kidding me? What's going on?"

"With me and Ryder? Honest—nothing else happened." Esme laughed. "Not that we weren't tempted."

"No, not that. The electricity is out."

"Maybe something tripped the main switch."

"I'm checking it now." Bea went to the utility closet in the hallway just off the kitchen. Inside of it, she examined the circuit panel on the side wall. "It looks like something did trip the main switch. But why didn't the generator kick in to compensate?"

"Good question. I'll add making an appointment for an inspection of the generator to my to-do list. You have enough to worry about. Just stay focused on having a successful grand opening."

Esme was right. She was letting worry mix up her priorities. What would she do without her sister and Freya
to keep her straight? Bea flipped the main switch on the
panel.

"Is everything good?" Esme asked.

Bea stared into the darkened kitchen. "No." She turned
other switches off and on in the circuit box as well, but
nothing happened. Dread started to sprout. "I've got to
figure out what's going on now. We can't do anything
without power!"

"Do you want me to call the electrician?"

"No, I'll do it, but maybe I've missed something." Bea
walked out of the closet. "I'm going to take a look at the
generator."

"Okay," Esme said. "I'll step on it. I should be there
soon."

"No. I don't want you speeding to get here. Just drive
safely."

Minutes later, Bea had triple-checked everything to do
with the circuit panel, the generator, and searched online
for outages in the area. Finally, she called the electrician
and explained the problem.

"We're still finishing a job just outside of town," the
woman said. "It'll be at least a couple of hours before we
can get there."

Doing her best to stay in crisis-management mode versus heading straight into panic, Bea paced the dining room.
"Is there any way you could get here sooner? Tonight's the
grand opening of my restaurant."

"Well, I could send my apprentice. He might be able to
spot the problem."

"I'd appreciate that. Thank you." At this point, Bea
would take any help she could get.

As she hung up, urgent knocks sounded on the back door, which was also the staff entrance.

Bea used the flashlight on her phone to light her way past her office to the door at the end of the hall.

Before she got there, something crunched under her shoe.

A piece of shrimp? How had that gotten here? As Bea shone the light around, she spotted more of them smashed on the floor along with leaves of romaine and what looked to be some kind of sauce.

Yesterday, she'd gone out the front entrance, but surely someone who'd exited through the back must have noticed the mess. Why hadn't anyone stopped to clean it up? Disappointment pushed out a sigh. But right now spilled food was the least of her worries.

Bea opened the door.

Freya stood outside. The tall, eighty-something woman with a stylish ash-blond bob had a pep in her step as she walked in.

The waitstaff's signature uniform was a black, checkered button-down shirt, black jeans, tennis shoes, and a camel-colored bistro apron, but her fashion-forward great-aunt had upscaled the look. She had on a pair of black kitten-heeled slides, slim-legged black slacks, and she'd added an artfully knotted beige silk scarf around her neck.

"You must have a lot on your mind," Freya said cheerfully. "You forgot to unlock the door." As she peered at Bea's face her expression shifted to concern. "You look upset, honey. Has something happened?"

"The electricity is out, and the generator isn't working. I've called the electrician, but they won't be here for a while." Admitting the situation aloud made Bea a tad nauseous.

"Oh, that's terrible!" Empathy filled Freya's emerald-green eyes as she patted Bea's arm. "And everything was going so well with the plan for tonight's opening. What can I do to help?"

"Would you mind making a sign instructing the staff to use the main entrance? It's too dark for them to come in this way. And then if you could monitor the front and let the staff in as they arrive. Ask them to take a seat in the back of the dining room. I'll be out soon to give everyone an update."

"Of course."

Bea retrieved paper from the printer in her office along with a marker and a flashlight. She gave them to Freya, and the older woman hurried off.

As she sat down at her desk, looking for a second flashlight in the drawer, her heart rate amped up as her aunt's words kept echoing in her mind.

Everything was going so well...

The alarm system not being installed. Now the power was out. Bea normally wasn't superstitious, but what was that saying about bad luck happening in threes? She had broken one of her favorite coffee mugs that morning. Did that count? *Stop.* This wasn't about bad luck. The electricity issue was just an opening-night hiccup that needed to be handled...quickly.

On the positive side, the food would remain at a safe temperature in the walk-ins and prep refrigerators, as long as they didn't open them while the electricity was out. They just needed enough time to cook the food and be ready to serve customers once the café opened.

Later on, as the electrician's apprentice worked on the problem, Bea addressed the staff: "We'll have less time to get ready, but the good news is we've already had the soft opening and we know what we're doing."

Taking a pause, she glanced around the room and met

Tanya's gaze. The anxiety Bea felt was written on the young Black woman's face. This was her sous chef's first time helping to open a restaurant. She was probably nervous about that already, and this situation was making it worse. Maybe others in the group felt the same way. And honestly, could she really blame them?

Bea's own anxiety started to rise.

She looked into Esme's green eyes. Her dark-haired sister gave her a nod and an encouraging smile.

As the boss, she had to remain just as confident as Esme. Bea paused a few seconds longer, searching for the right words to assure Tanya and the rest of the staff. "I have faith in all of you. You've worked hard to make this day possible, and I'm grateful for all you've done. Once the issue is fixed, I know we'll pull together and make tonight's launch amazing!"

As if on cue, the lights came on.

Relief rushed through Bea as everyone cheered.

Esme gave her a hug. "See? Everything is all good. Don't worry—we'll be ready."

But they were opening in less than three hours. Would they make it? "We should check on how many early reservations we have."

Just as Bea and Esme started walking to the host stand, Tanya hurried toward them.

"We have a huge problem," she whispered. "I can't find any of the food we prepped for tonight."

"What?" Bea and Esme both asked at the same time.

"It has to be there," Esme said as they hastened to the kitchen. "Maybe one of the cooks moved things around?"

"I asked." Tanya replied nervously. "But they said they didn't."

Inside the kitchen, the three of them along with the cooks searched the walk-ins, looked in storage rooms, and frantically rechecked every shelf. Even if they could thaw out what remained, there wasn't enough of anything to serve a restaurant full of hungry customers.

Freya came into the kitchen. "I can hear you all the way in the dining room. What's all the commotion about?"

"The food is gone." As the truth became clear, Bea's stomach sunk to basement level. "We have to cancel the grand opening."

CHAPTER TWO

DEVIN STREET QUICKLY locked up the downtown office of the *Chatelaine Daily News*. He had a very important date. He was meeting his daughter, Carly, at the Cowgirl Café for dinner.

Most nights during the week, he worked late and ate his meals at his desk. As the owner, main reporter, and editor for the paper, his schedule was full. He *did* have to do a little work on the side tonight—it couldn't be helped. He was the anonymous restaurant critic, but spending quality time with Carly was his main focus.

It had taken a lot to convince her to join him instead of going to a friend's house to eat pizza. A chance to be one of the first in her friends group to check out the new spot in town had swayed her decision.

Lately, so many things had become a struggle with his thirteen-year-old daughter. He and his ex, Lauren, were co-parenting Carly through her seemingly endless mood swings. Last year, when she'd "officially" become a teen, almost overnight her communication style had shifted from intelligible words to huffs, eye rolls, and constant groaning over the rules they laid down to keep her safe and prepare her for adulthood.

What was that saying about how your teenager's actions were payback for giving your own parents hell when you'd been growing up? Devin sighed. But had he really been *that* challenging when he'd been her age?

A vision of his father sitting behind the desk in the office he'd just left made Devin smile. Carl Street, who Carly had been named after, was probably looking down, laughing at him right then.

Carl had raised him as a single father after his wife had passed away when Devin had been just five years old. His dad had possessed the right balance of healthy skepticism, optimism, and a balanced view of the world. They were important qualities to have as a parent, journalist, and a boss. And now that he was following in his father's footsteps, he made it a priority to emulate him.

As Devin walked to the restaurant, he reviewed a text from the pet shelter asking him if he had time to foster a dog. The pet's elderly owner was moving into a senior-living apartment building and wouldn't be able to take his beloved companion with him. The shelter was trying to find the dog a permanent home before the move. If they couldn't, they would need Devin's help. Without a second thought, he responded yes.

For many years, his father had also assisted the shelter. Carl had used the experience to teach him responsibility and the importance of helping others when they needed support. Hopefully Carly was learning the same thing from him as he continued that tradition as well as giving the shelter free space in the newspaper to feature animals up for adoption.

She'd done a great job helping him take care of Chumley, a Great Dane he'd fostered last month. He'd even considered adopting him for her. But a couple who'd been searching for that specific breed had reached out to the shelter about the dog, and from the way Chumley had immediately bonded with them, it had been clear where he belonged.

As Devin finished answering messages, his phone chimed with a familiar ringtone. It was his ex.

On a reflex, he checked the time on the screen before answering. *Shoot.* He was running a little late.

"Hey, Lauren. I'm a minute or so from the restaurant. Just drop Carly out front and tell her to wait for me."

"Oh, I guess you missed the big news."

The hint of light sarcasm in his former wife's voice made him pause. "What happened?"

"The Cowgirl Café is postponing their grand opening."

"Since when? They've been advertising it in the paper for weeks."

"Since not too long ago. I suspect that no one saw this coming considering the amount of people they're turning away."

He quirked a brow. "Did they say why?"

"I have no idea, but why the restaurant isn't opening is the least of your worries."

Carly... Her having bragging rights for being the first of her friends to eat at the new hotspot was no longer a possibility.

He started walking again, picking up the pace. "I know she's probably bummed. But let her know we can go anywhere she wants tonight."

"Oh, no—I've already gotten my dose of attitude for the day. One of her teachers called this afternoon. Your daughter's been goofing off in class. I told Carly if she doesn't get her behavior in order and bring her grade back up, I'm changing her curfew to six on a school night *and* the weekends to make sure she studies." Frustration tinged Lauren's tone. "Now her hate-my-mom hormones are on full blast and I'm on the verge of losing my patience with her."

Your daughter? Devin quietly huffed a chuckle. It was interesting how Carly became all his when she was acting up. But having been in Lauren's shoes when it came to *their* daughter, he understood the exasperation she felt. "I'll be there in a sec to handle things."

A moment later, he arrived at the café.

More than a few disappointed people mingled near the entrance where Freya Fortune stood with one of the hosts.

"I'm so sorry," the older woman said to everyone. "Something unexpected has happened, and we don't have any food to serve you tonight. But we can put your name and number on our email list. We'll contact you when we have an update."

Some folks added their information to the list while others walked away, frustrated over their ruined dinner plans.

No food—that was why the opening had been canceled?

Resisting the urge to find out more, Devin jogged to Lauren's tan SUV parked farther down the street.

As he got closer, his dark-haired ex-wife met his gaze through the windshield. He went to the driver's side, and she opened the window.

Carly sat beside her in the front passenger seat, head down, texting on her phone. Their daughter had inherited his brown eyes and the color of Lauren's deep chestnut-brown hair as well as her light brown complexion.

After exchanging a look of acknowledgment with his ex, he spoke to Carly. "Well, little lady, it looks like we have to hang out somewhere else tonight."

"I guess," Carly mumbled. As she stared at her phone, her face lit up. "But Michaela said I can still come to her house and make pizza. Her dad just built a pizza oven in their backyard."

"But what about our father-daughter date? You're not standing me up, are you? We can order pizza from your favorite place and watch a movie or go to the Saddle and

Spur Roadhouse for some burgers and those triple-fudge brownies you like."

"*Father-daughter* date? Seriously, Dad, I'm not ten years old."

No, she wasn't. At that age, she'd always been eager to spend time with him.

As if reading his mind, Lauren gave him an empathetic look before turning her attention to Carly. "You can hang out with Michaela and make pizza at her house another time. Your dad cleared his schedule for you."

"But I told everyone I would be eating at the Cowgirl Café." World-ending unhappiness filled Carly's face as she slumped in the seat. "Just ordering pizza or going to the Saddle and Spur is embarrassing."

Embarrassing? A small pang of sadness hit Devin, but he forced a smile. "I know eating at the Saddle and Spur isn't as exciting as trying out a new place, but..."

"So I can go to Michaela's?" Carly's expression was hopeful as she looked between Devin and Lauren.

The last thing he wanted to do was force his daughter to spend time with him. And Lauren could probably use a couple of hours to herself. Figuring that accepting a compromise was the best solution, he gave his ex-wife a nod. "That's okay with me if you're good with it."

"All right, then." Lauren sighed. "You can go to Michaela's. But you owe your dad a thank-you hug before we go."

Smiling, Carly bounded out the SUV. She threw her arms around his neck. "Thanks, Dad. I love you."

He hugged her back. The love swelling inside his chest almost choked him up. "Love you, too. Have a good time."

He waved goodbye as Lauren and Carly drove away. Standing alone on the sidewalk, he stared at the front of the Cowgirl Café and the surrounding area. It was like a ghost town. A sense of desolation set in as he walked back to his car parked near the office.

The feeling was still there as he microwaved last night's leftover enchiladas in the kitchen at his house on the outskirts of Chatelaine.

The ranch-style home had all the necessities. In the living room, a beige couch, side chairs, a solid-wood coffee table, and a media console underneath a wall-mounted widescreen television partially filled the space. The dining room with a window overlooking a small deck in the backyard was empty. A king-sized bed and dresser furnished his main bedroom, and he'd converted one of the guest bedrooms into an office.

The second guest bedroom was Carly's.

In the kitchen, one of her purple hair ties sat on the counter. Not feeling up to the effort of walking down the hall and putting it in the bathroom, he stuck it in a junk drawer. It also contained a half-empty bottle of glitter nail polish, lip balm that was also close to done, and other odds and ends his daughter had left in his truck or around the house.

He'd learned a long time ago not to get rid of anything she owned, no matter how long it sat unused or how empty it looked to him. Because as soon as he did, she would come searching for it, claiming the item was something she couldn't live without.

As he shut the drawer, he released a deep sigh. He'd really been looking forward to watching her eyes light up as they tried out several items on the menu. Her guard always came down when she was truly enjoying herself, and in those moments, he saw his little girl again.

Seriously, Dad, I'm not ten years old...

But wasn't it just yesterday that Carly had been a toddler crawling on the rug between him and Lauren in the living room of their tiny apartment in Dallas?

As Devin stood at the kitchen counter eating dinner, nostalgic memories flooded his mind.

Back then, he'd been employed at a newspaper as an entry-level reporter and Lauren had worked at a clothing store. Money had been tight, but they'd made enough to pay the bills and take good care of Carly.

Within a few years, their priorities had shifted as promotions at their jobs had opened up a better life for them. But a house and all the possessions in the world couldn't mask the obvious. He and Lauren had been growing apart. Busier schedules. Different interests. It had been a combination of a lot of things. Their love for Carly had become their main bond.

Wanting to give their marriage a second chance, they'd moved back to his hometown of Chatelaine seven years ago, and he'd started working with his dad at the paper. But even with more balanced schedules, he and Lauren had still struggled to find their way back to each other.

Just as they'd been considering a trial separation, his dad had gotten sick. He and Lauren had rallied together to take care of Carl.

Managing the paper in his father's absence had given Devin a good look at the financials. The *Chatelaine Daily News* had been barely breaking even. But it was the one thing that had kept Carl going through the harsh chemotherapy treatments.

The image of his father, frail yet trying to remain upbeat for everyone until the end, came into Devin's mind. Lauren had been a huge help as he'd coped with the loss. But a year later, they'd been more like strangers than husband and wife. The ending of their marriage had been an amicable decision, and they'd worked out the details of their divorce with a mediator instead of attorneys.

They'd also both agreed to remain in Chatelaine. Lauren had gone back to school at the local community college, and he'd kept the newspaper. Making it profitable again had required him to whittle the staff. He, along with the managing editor, Charles, who also contributed articles, and their staff assistant, Quinn, produced the newspaper that went out online every Thursday and in print on Sundays.

When the budget allowed, he used freelance journalists and photographers to fill the gaps.

They'd been saving space in tomorrow's online edition for his review of the Cowgirl Café. But he wasn't sure what he wanted to write yet.

Done with dinner, he went to his home office and reviewed his emails and messages.

A woman named Morgana was interested in looking through the newspaper's archives. Everything from the past ten years could be accessed from their website. Anything beyond that Quinn was working on organizing and uploading to their cloud-storage account. But whatever this woman was looking for they could provide in one form or another.

After answering Morgana's email, he went to the paper's online social media page, the *Chatelaine Daily News* Community Corner. As the moderator, he reviewed the remarks from residents on posts regarding happenings in the town or teasing upcoming stories in the paper.

Usually there were just a few praises, concerns, or opinions, but the multiple comments under the post about the Cowgirl Café's grand opening snagged his attention.

New restaurant in town is a huge disappointment...

The Cowgirl Café ruined my sister's birthday...

New restaurant owner needs a lesson on customer service...

No food? Way to screw up opening night...

The chatter was brutal...but honest.

Devin pulled up the Cowgirl Café's website. A statement was on the welcome page.

Due to an unforeseeable incident, the Cowgirl Café's grand opening has been postponed. We apologize for the inconvenience and hope you will join us when we reschedule this celebration...

Freya Fortune had said they didn't have food to serve customers. But when he'd asked Bea earlier that afternoon if she was ready for the grand opening, she'd given him an enthusiastic confirmation. What type of unforeseeable incident could have caused a cancellation? Incompetence? Poor planning?

He worried his lower lip, mulling it over. Bea's response didn't fit with either of those scenarios. But the statement the Cowgirl Café had issued wasn't disputing Freya's explanation. And as a restaurant critic, it was his job to give an unbiased opinion.

But he didn't want to make Bea look bad either.

The memory of Bea walking past him on the sidewalk flashed into his mind. Along with the tingling sensation along the back of his neck that had made him look over his shoulder.

He'd been surprised and pleased to see her glancing back at him. Had he really glimpsed a sparkle of interest in her eyes? Or had he imagined what he'd wanted to see? That if he could ask her out, there was a chance she would say yes.

As he let the wonderful daydream of that moment run through his mind, a slight smile tugged at his mouth.

Another comment appearing under the social media post for the Cowgirl Café pulled him back to the present.

Having food on opening night is Restaurant 101 in the industry. Maybe the owner needs to find a different hobby to occupy her newfound wealth and time...

Devin sat back in the chair. That was harsh. But was the commenter right?

CHAPTER THREE

WEARINESS WEIGHED ON Bea as she trudged down the carpeted steps of her two-story condo dressed in a faded blue sleep shirt. When she'd awakened, she'd hoped last night's canceled grand opening of the café had just been a bad dream. Unfortunately, it was a nightmare that had actually happened.

After the successful soft opening, she'd felt exhausted but elated and ready to conquer the world. She'd anticipated experiencing the same high with the café's official launch last night. Not this sense of failure, embarrassment, and utter confusion.

Of all the things that could have happened with the grand opening, the last thing she'd expected was for someone to steal the food. They'd broken in through the back office. Everyone had been so focused on the problem with the electricity they hadn't noticed the shattered window until after they'd realized the food was missing.

The police had asked if there was someone Bea was aware of who might have a grudge against her or the restaurant. Maybe a current staff member or an applicant she hadn't hired had decided to get even about something? But she couldn't think of anyone. Even the managers of the other restaurants in the area had wished her well. And all the workers seemed genuinely upset over the turn of events.

Just as she reached the bottom step heading for the

kitchen, the doorbell rang. She took a detour in the opposite direction and answered the door.

It was Esme. Dressed in jeans, an oversized navy sweater, and heels, she looked a little tired but more refreshed than Bea.

On the way in, she gave Bea a tight hug. "You don't look like you got much sleep. Are you okay?"

Bea hugged her back. "I think I'm still in shock."

"I am, too." Esme followed her through the adjoining archway.

In the kitchen, professional-grade stainless-steel appliances and dark granite counters were balanced with whitewashed wood cabinets and lots of natural light from the bay window in the breakfast nook.

Herbs thriving in pots on the windowsill and a bowl of fresh fruit on the table gave the space a homey appeal.

"Coffee?" Bea set up the Keurig on the counter with water and grabbed two coffee pods.

"Please." Her sister took two mugs from an upper cabinet and handed them to her. "Have you heard anything new from the police?"

"No. Not yet."

Confusion shadowed Esme's face as she shook her head. "I was up for most of the night trying to think of anyone who would want to sabotage the grand opening or even carry out the plan as a practical joke gone wrong. It's so unbelievable."

Bea took a plate of lemon-coconut muffins she'd made the other day from the refrigerator. "The police *did* say that there's a good chance we'll never know who's responsible. Without video footage from security cameras or witnesses, they don't have any leads."

A short time later, they sat at the kitchen table with full mugs of coffee and the food.

As Esme unwrapped a muffin, she asked, "Are you up for going over what's happening at the café today, or should we skip it?"

A vision of crawling back into bed and ignoring the world came into Bea's mind. "As long as it's not bad news—sure."

"It's not." Her sister sucked crumbs from her finger as she peered at the calendar on her phone. "The technician from the security company will be at the restaurant between ten and one, and the generator is being serviced at eleven. And they're fixing the window in the office at noon."

Bea sipped her coffee. If the alarm-system install had happened when it was supposed to occur, they wouldn't be discussing any of this. Had the cancellation really been a mistake on the security company's part like they'd all assumed, or had someone actually made that call?

Sighing, she set the questions aside and focused on the present. "Okay. I'll be there."

"No. Freya, Tanya, and I will take care of things," Esme said. "You need a break. And we can handle tomorrow morning's online staff meeting, too."

"I appreciate the offer, but you're getting married next Saturday. You have to get ready for your wedding, and as the boss, I have to be at tomorrow's meeting." Bea squared her shoulders. "The staff needs to hear directly from me that they're getting paid while we're closed. And I still might stop by the restaurant this afternoon. I can't just sit around scrolling through social media and watching cute animal videos all day."

An expression of dread passed over Esme's face so quickly Bea almost missed it. "Yeah, scrolling through social media today probably isn't a good idea."

"Why? Has something been posted about the café?"

As Esme paused to take a sip of coffee, she didn't meet Bea's gaze. "Not really. A few comments were made on the *Chatelaine Daily News* Community Corner, that's all."

Oh no… If bitching and moaning were an art, the people who commented there would win a prize.

Before Esme could stop her, Bea snagged her sister's phone from the table.

"Bea…" she warned. "Seriously, it's not worth reading what they said."

"I need to know what I'm up against." A couple of taps later, Bea pulled up the post about the café. The comments seemed endless.

A complete fail…

This place is permanently off my "must try" list…

The review in the Chatelaine Daily News's online edition is spot-on…

Her heart thumped hard in her chest. "The restaurant critic posted a review?"

"They did? I haven't seen anything. What did they say?"

"I'm afraid to look."

The last time an unfavorable review had been written about a place, it had remained one of the hot topics in town for weeks, and *Don't eat there* had practically become the restaurant's new tagline.

Esme gave her an understanding nod. "Do you want me to read it?"

"No." Bea took a deep breath. "Whatever it is… I can't run from it." She clicked the link, and the review came up on the *Chatelaine Daily News Online*.

Savory pot pie. Steak with chimichurri sauce.
Grilled tilapia with mango salsa. Bourbon-glazed
pork chops. Apple fritters topped with ice cream and
caramel sauce.

The Cowgirl Café's menu promised mouthwa-
tering goodness, but after so much hype over the
past weeks, all it managed to deliver was disappoint-
ment with a failed grand opening featuring no food.
Should we give them a second chance?

The last line struck like a knife in her chest. Bea handed
the phone to her sister.

As Esme read the review, frustration and empathy shone
in her eyes. "I'm sorry. I know this isn't what you'd hoped
everyone would say. We could reach out to the paper and
explain how the opening was sabotaged—"

"We can't. One, it will sound like an excuse, and two, a
restaurant mentioning sabotage could make people wonder
if the food is safe. But maybe the critic has a point. Why
should anyone give me a second chance?" A sad chuckle
escaped from Bea. "Are you sure you want me in charge
of the food for your wedding? I might ruin that, too."

"First of all, you're *not* responsible for what happened.
Whoever broke into the restaurant is to blame. And as
far as the wedding? Ryder and I couldn't imagine anyone
else catering our reception." Esme grasped her hand. "And
more importantly, you deserve all the chances in the world.
Opening the Cowgirl Café is important to you. Don't let
some anonymous restaurant critic crush your dream."

Hope and determination sparked inside of Bea. "Thank
you. I really needed to hear that. But enough about the
café. I want to talk about the wedding. You've finalized
everything, right?"

"Yes. Working with Lily, as you know, has been amazing." Esme's cheeks glowed with happiness. "I can't wait for next weekend to get here so I can see everything we've talked about come together."

Esme and Ryder's wedding ceremony and reception were being held at the Chatelaine Dude Ranch. It was owned and managed by their brother, Asa, and his wife, Lily.

Lily was organizing the ceremony happening on the lawn behind the spacious event lodge on the property, and the reception taking place afterward inside the lodge.

As Bea listened to Esme gush about all things bridal from dresses to anticipated jitters, a feeling of excitement and joy for her sister made her sit back and smile.

Esme had been there for her with the café. Now was the time to set her own troubles aside and prepare for her little sister's big day.

"THAT'S PERFECT." THE wedding photographer, a brunette dressed in a yellow jumpsuit, snapped candid photos of Esme, Bea, and Lily in the bridal suite located in the lodge at the ranch.

The late afternoon sun shone through a window overlooking a lush green pasture with horses. It gave the cozy bridal suite with a sitting area, makeup table, and curtained-off changing areas a soft glow. It also enhanced Esme's natural radiance and sparkled in her silver jeweled earrings.

Dressed in a pearl-white lace-and-satin gown with an asymmetrical hemline, she beamed the brightest smile out of all of them.

Memories crept into Bea's mind about her own wedding day. Like Esme, she'd been happy. But she'd also had a strong sense of doubt.

No. This wasn't the time for unhappy thoughts.

As Bea pushed the recollection aside, she adjusted the thin shoulder strap on her light coral chiffon knee-length dress. Lily wore the same semiformal attire, and they both had their hair in an artful messy bun.

Lily pretended to fix the white-and-pale-pink flowers adorning Esme's updo. The slender woman with light brown hair, hazel eyes and freckles beamed a smile. "You look so beautiful."

"Thank you." As Esme smiled back at her sister-in-law, she nervously pressed a hand to her stomach. "I can't believe the day is finally here. This all feels like a wonderful dream. Someone might need to pinch me."

As if on cue, Bea and Lily gave Esme's bare arms gentle pinches. The photographer caught the moment along with them laughing about it. As the three Fortune women stared at their reflections in the floor-length mirror on the wall, their expressions shifted to soft smiles.

In her mind's eye, Bea easily imagined Andrea standing with them, beaming a smile and lovingly fretting over if Lars was ready to walk Esme down the aisle. Their parents would have loved Ryder and the grandbabies.

Bea met Esme's gaze in the mirror. From the look on her little sister's face, she'd probably been thinking almost the same things. As Bea rested a hand on her shoulder, they both blinked back tears.

A tragic plane crash had taken Andrea and Lars from them, along with their Aunt Dolly and Uncle Peter. But the love their parents had for them remained.

"Don't you dare cry," Lily warned Esme. "You'll ruin your makeup."

"I know." Esme sucked in a shaky breath as she grasped each of their hands. "But I'm so happy. Thank you for making all this possible."

"You're welcome." Bea held her sister's hand a little tighter.

"And thank *you* both for letting me be a part of this," Lily said.

"You had to be a part of it." Esme smiled brightly. "We're all sisters."

"That's the perfect toast." Bea turned to the side table near the couch where three flutes and a bottle of champagne in a metal ice bucket sat on top of it. She filled the glasses, then handed them to Lily and Esme. "To sisters— family forever."

"Forever," Lily echoed. "And to Esme and Ryder finding true love."

They clinked their glasses, then sipped champagne.

Lily set down her glass. "It's almost time. Bea and I should get out there." Hurrying to the couch, she picked up the beautiful cascade bouquet adorned with purple-and-white flowers and pale pink roses from a long white box and handed it to Esme. "Asa will be here to get you soon. Are you all set?"

"I'm ready." Esme's eyes sparkled.

Bea and Lily each picked up one of the two smaller round bouquets from the box. After a quick hair and makeup check in the mirror, the two women walked to the door.

On the way out, Bea blew Esme a kiss. "Love you. See you soon."

Moments later, Bea and Lily stood on the lawn a few yards away from a natural jute-burlap aisle runner dividing rows of white wooden chairs in *bride's side/groom's side* configuration.

At the other end sat a white wood gazebo. Pale chiffon and ivy were wound around the columns. Baskets filled with roses, clematis, and hydrangeas in hues mirroring Esme's bouquet hung near the front facing columns forming an arch.

A guitar, cello, and violin trio sitting in the gazebo played a gentle melody.

As Bea looked out at the friends and family there to witness Esme and Ryder's union, her mind drifted back to her own wedding day, over a decade ago in Denver. She and her now ex, Jeff, had met, gotten engaged, and married in a span of less than two months. Their small ceremony with the justice of the peace had been a spur-of-the-moment thing.

None of their family had been able to attend on such short notice, and it had felt so wrong not to have the people she cared about surrounding her on such an important day.

But Jeff had insisted on getting married before they'd relocated for his job, and wanting to please him, she'd gone along with it. He'd been the man of her dreams.

Shortly after they'd said *I do*, the excitement of new-lywed bliss had begun to fade and reality had begun to sink in. Communication wasn't one of Jeff's strong suits. That coupled with Bea, as well as their relationship, coming last in his list of priorities had made it painfully clear their marriage was in trouble. After two years of trying to make the impossible work, she'd divorced him.

Luckily, Esme had gotten it right with Ryder. As a couple, they were all in on continuing to build a strong relationship and family. And it was good to see so many people supporting them. The only ones missing, aside from their parents, were their cousins Bear and West Fortune.

Esme hadn't mentioned it, but she was probably disappointed that Bear hadn't responded to the wedding invite. In fact, no one had heard from him in a long time. Hopefully he was okay and just couldn't make it. And West...

Bea's gaze went to West's former fiancée, Tabitha Buckingham. The young blonde woman in her late twenties sat on the end of a row, tending to her twin babies, Zane and Zach, in their strollers.

West had been a prosecutor. A little over a year and half ago, one of the criminals he had sent to jail had taken West's life. No one in her family had realized Tabitha and the twins existed until the funeral. Now that she lived in the area, they all tried to keep in touch with her. Over the last few weeks, Bea had been meaning to call and check in on her. Tabitha was raising the twins on her own.

Bea glanced down at her dark-haired nephew Chase asleep in the stroller she gently rocked in front of her. He and his brother, Noah, were dressed in midnight-navy suits with pale blush ties like the groomsmen. They looked absolutely adorable.

But unlike his brother, Noah was wide awake in the stroller behind Bea. He was also becoming a little fussy, and Lily was trying to soothe him with a pacifier.

While adjusting her bouquet tucked under the handle, Bea sent up a silent prayer for Chase to remain peaceful while she walked with him down the aisle.

Freya and a temporary nanny seated up front on the bride's side would take over the strollers. They would be watching over the little ones during the ceremony and the reception.

As Bea glanced at the lodge behind them, her attention momentarily halted on the large windows. Inside the building, servers in black-and-white uniforms checked over the tables. Some of them were staff members from the Cowgirl Café, and the rest had been hired from a temp service.

Ryder and Esme had chosen a straightforward sit-down menu: Classic romaine Caesar, choice of grilled flat-iron steak with thyme-and-blue-cheese cream or a seared chicken breast. Both were served with herb-roasted green beans and tomatoes, seasoned rice, and homemade biscuits and honey butter.

Aside from the wedding cake, there were also peach, apple, and pecan tartlets to be served with vanilla cream for dessert.

Having gone over the menu so many times with Tanya, Bea could easily imagine what was happening right now in the lodge's kitchen. All of the food had been safely delivered—she'd double-checked before going to the bridal suite to get dressed for the wedding. By now the cooks should have plated up the salads and prepped their cooking stations.

With this menu, timing was everything, especially with the flat-iron steaks. If they were cooked too long, by the time they were served to the guests, they would be well done and tough. But if they were taken off the grill too soon... What if the cooks couldn't keep up? Esme had trusted her to come up with a great menu. Maybe she'd been too ambitious and should have gone with roast beef instead.

Anxiety twirled in Bea's stomach. No. The menu was solid, and Tanya and the cooks from the café adored Esme. They would do everything in their power to make the meal special.

The musical trio paused, and Bea pushed all other thoughts aside as the minister walked in front of the gazebo.

Moments later, Esme's husband-to-be joined him along with his brother, Brandon, and, Esme and Bea's cousin, Linc Mahoney Fortune. The blond-haired men made a striking trio.

Dressed impeccably in a tailored midnight-navy suit with a pearl-white tie and shirt, Ryder looked just as amazing as Esme. And by the way he kept smoothing his hand down his low-cut vest, he was also nervous.

Brandon briefly rested a hand on his back and murmured something. All three of the men chuckled and Ryder's shoulders relaxed as he took a deep breath.

The trio began playing Pachelbel's "Canon in D."

"That's our cue," Lily said.

After a quick glance down at Chase, Bea went down the aisle, and then Lily followed with Noah.

As planned, they handed off the babies to Freya and the nanny, then took their places. Seconds later, the familiar strains of Wagner's "Bridal Chorus" floated in the air.

Tall, dark-haired Asa, handsome in a suit, walked Esme down the aisle. As she came closer to the front, Esme's gaze locked with Ryder's, and their faces grew luminous as they smiled.

Bea's heart swelled with joy as she held back tears.

The couple shared special passages from books they loved as part of their vows. As they exchanged rings, Chase released a short squeal as if voicing his approval, and everyone laughed.

Their first kiss as husband and wife inspired applause from the guests. On impulse, they scooped up their sons from their strollers. Smiling happily, they walked back down the aisle along with the bridal party to Mendelssohn's "Wedding March."

Following the ceremony, the bridal party greeted the guests on the lawn.

After what seemed like endless hugs and kisses, the line dwindled to the final few.

Devin Street was the last person to congratulate the happy couple. Dressed in a gray suit with a blue tie, he looked scrumptious as usual.

As he chatted with Ryder and Esme, his gaze briefly

connected with Bea's. Just like the day of the grand opening, he caught her staring at him and a puzzled look briefly crossed his face. He smiled at her.

Bea glanced down at the bouquet in her hands. She could only imagine what he thought. Either her attraction to him was that obvious or he was thinking about the critic's review of the Cowgirl Café. He was probably trying to figure out how her answer of *Absolutely* when he'd asked if she was ready had been so horribly off the mark.

Suddenly feeling self-conscious, Bea's palms started to sweat. She couldn't face him. Slipping out of line, she spoke to Lily as she handed over her bouquet. "I should go check on the food."

Bea headed for the lodge, certain the tingling along her spine was from Devin watching her as she hurried away.

CHAPTER FOUR

CONVERSATION AND LAUGHTER reverberated in the lodge, and Devin made mental notes of all that was happening from his perspective, seated at a round table for eight in the center of the room.

Luckily he didn't have to remember all the details. The wedding photographer was also freelancing for the *Chatelaine Daily News*. Esme and Ryder had agreed to allow some of the photos to be published along with a brief article he was writing about the wedding.

The lodge was nothing less than impressive. The oak-floored, white-walled space with multiple windows and wood-beam accents had been totally transformed into the perfect venue for the reception.

Guests were seated at tables covered in cream linen and low centerpieces with greenery and white roses. Small trees strung with white lights were nestled near lattice dividers artfully placed in the corners and framing the cake table featuring a three-tiered confection.

One end of the lodge had been delineated as the dance floor, and a DJ played a seamless mix of instrumentals from country to oldies to pop ballads at a low volume.

Esme and Ryder relaxed at a sweetheart table for two, and the bridal party as well as family members sat at nearby tables around them. But Bea wasn't there.

After the ceremony as he'd spoken to the bridal party in the receiving line, their gazes had locked. She'd looked so gorgeous. He hadn't been able to take his eyes off her and had lost his train of thought while chatting with Ryder. But before he'd gotten a chance to talk to Bea, she'd run off.

Lily had explained that Bea had gone to check on the food for the reception, but a part of him wondered if she might be upset about the review of the Cowgirl Café published in the paper. He'd written the damn thing three times, striving for honesty but not wanting to come across as harsh. That exercise in near futility only proved what he'd tried to deny for a long time. He had a thing for Bea.

He'd wanted to ask her out more than a few times, but he'd hesitated. He was a journalist, after all, and she might think the only reason he was trying to get to know her was because of a potentially big story related to her uncle, Wendell Fortune.

Back in 1965, members of the Fortune family had owned a silver mine near Chatelaine that had collapsed, killing all of the workers. Speculation had always existed about the involvement of Wendell's brothers, Elias and Edgar, in the incident. And recently a question had been raised about the actual number of miners who'd perished. Fifty had been the documented number, but mysterious notes had been found claiming fifty-one lives had been lost.

The arrival of Freya Fortune in Chatelaine with Elias's will—and the claim of him wanting to make amends with his family—had also reinvigorated local interest in the topic.

Who was the fifty-first person, and why point to an additional death now? A couple of months ago, Devin had asked Wendell those questions.

He glanced over at the lean eighty-something older man with a grizzled beard sitting a few tables away with his sister-in-law, Freya. Wendell had said he had nothing to add to the record about the mining disaster, but Devin couldn't shake the feeling that the man was hiding something. And possibly Freya, too.

Mrs. Cofield, an older woman with a silver streak in her dark hair who was seated across from Devin, paused in eating her chicken entrée. She and her husband lived on one of the larger ranches in the area.

She addressed the middle-aged couple next to her. "Wendell Fortune doesn't look well at all. I hardly recognized him when he sat up front before the ceremony."

"You're right—he doesn't look good," the blonde with high-arched brows responded. "I haven't seen him in a while. From what I understand, he's been hiding out in that monstrosity he owns…"

Monstrosity? That was harsh. Wendell's home in town, Fortune's Castle, was elaborate and a little crazy in its medieval design, but Devin didn't think it was an eyesore. And besides, it wasn't in a very populated area where people had to look at it every day.

Holding back the comment, Devin focused on his delicious steak instead of the banter taking place.

"Mr. Street," Mrs. Cofield called out to him, "do you know what's going on with Wendell Fortune?"

He gave her a polite smile. "I'm sorry. I missed what you were saying…"

"Wendell Fortune—have you heard anything about his health?"

"I'm afraid I don't know anything about that." Devin took a sip of iced tea. And even if he did, he'd never reveal that information. He ran a respectable newspaper, not a gossip magazine.

Fortunately, just then, Brandon Hayes tapped his glass diverting attention as he rose from his seat at a table near Esme and Ryder.

He faced the guests. "As part of my speech, I'm supposed to sing my brother's praises and tell you all about his many good points." He looked to the couple with a humorous smile. "Or I can dish the dirt so my new sister-in-law has a really clear picture of what she's gotten herself into..."

He delivered some good-natured teasing, then ended with a heartfelt wish for Ryder and Esme's long and happy future.

During the applause after the toast, Bea came from the back of the room and joined Brandon and the rest of the bridal party.

Devin took note—everyone at the table had a plus-one seated next to them except for Bea. She was smart and beautiful—how could she not have a date for the wedding? Was she on her own because she was busy supervising the catering for the reception?

As the room grew quieter, she rose from her seat and spoke to the newlyweds. "There's a saying about love looking outward in the same direction. When I look at you two, that's what I see..." Bea continued to share a loving, heartfelt recognition of the couple. At the end of her speech, she encouraged everyone to raise their glasses. "To Esme and Ryder."

After the toast, servers delivered trays with an assortment of fruit tartlets to the table.

Mrs. Cofield put one on her plate. "Aren't these on the menu at her restaurant?" She pointed to Bea, who was moving from table to table, chatting with guests. "Considering what happened with the Cowgirl Café, I'm not surprised she's been hiding from everyone. I heard some ridiculous rumor about someone stealing the food."

The blonde sniffed. "She should just own up to whatever really happened. If the place does finally open, I'm not sure I'll ever eat there. She ruined my sister's birthday celebration." She raised her voice, seemingly wanting others to overhear the conversation. "I'm completely on board with the restaurant review in the *Chatelaine Daily News*. I'm not convinced her café deserves a second chance."

That wasn't what he'd said...exactly. Irritation sparked in Devin. Although the restaurant hadn't confirmed anything officially, from what he'd pieced together, whatever had happened wasn't entirely Bea's fault. But this wasn't the time or place to mention the review or the failed grand opening...unless the woman intentionally wanted to hurt Bea's feelings.

The DJ called out, "It's time to bring Mr. and Mrs. Hayes back to the dance floor..."

Esme and Ryder's first dance as a couple had been to a slow song at the start of the reception. Now an upbeat country track played through the speakers.

Bea paused at a nearby table and then headed toward his.

The thought of her smiling at Mrs. Cofield and the blonde woman without a clue of what they'd been saying about her, and the café, irked him even more.

Devin rose to his feet and intercepted her. "This is the song you mentioned, isn't it?" He grasped Bea's hand. "The one you really wanted to dance to tonight?"

As she glanced up at him, her expression grew perplexed.

He gave her hand a squeeze, willing her to follow along.

To his relief, Bea squeezed back. "You're right. Let's go."

Devin led her to the dance floor. As soon as he took her into his arms, they moved in time to a country two-step.

Bea leaned in, making it easier for him to hear her. "I'm assuming I read the situation right—you needed a save?"

Devin considered his answer. There was no point in telling her the truth and risk ruining her night. "I did. If you hadn't come along, I would have had to fake an injury so I could leave the table."

She quirked a brow. "What type of injury were you going to fake?"

"I don't know. I hadn't gotten that far yet. Maybe a sudden reoccurrence of an old elbow injury from my college football days."

"An old elbow injury?" As she leaned back to look up at him, humor filled her blue eyes and a light flush came into her cheeks. "Aggravated by what? Sitting there eating dinner?"

"Hey, it could happen."

As Bea's laughter radiated into him, he couldn't help but chuckle. The happiness on her face caused his heart to jolt with an extra beat. Damn, she was pretty.

Momentarily distracted, he missed a step. If he didn't keep his mind on what he was doing, he'd stomp on her coral-painted toes peeking out of her strappy sandals.

Unfazed by his clumsiness, Bea synced her steps with his and settled comfortably in his arms.

More couples came onto the dance floor, and they were pushed closer together. Devin fought the urge to confirm his suspicion that she'd fit perfectly against him.

As she leaned near his ear, the alluring perfume wafting from the curve of her neck intoxicated him. "You're not faking wanting to dance with me, are you?"

Her whispered words, only for him, raised goose bumps on his skin. Devin's heart thumped harder in his chest. "Not a chance."

CHAPTER FIVE

BEA FELT LIKE she was dancing on air. Was she really this close to Devin right now? Wow. He was gorgeous.

Normally she was tongue-tied around him, but now she couldn't stop flirting with him. It was probably because of the champagne and that she was deliriously happy for Esme and Ryder. And she might've been delirious from hunger, too. She hadn't eaten anything since breakfast. But Bea's need for food faded as her and Devin's hands clasped a bit tighter.

One song moved into the next, and the distance between them started shrinking to mere inches as they moved through the maze of the dance. Devin spun her around, and Bea couldn't wait for the turn to end, anxious to feel his warmth and the solid strength of his arms around her again.

The DJ cued up a slow song, and they didn't hesitate in getting close. As she wound her arms around his neck, he slipped his hands around her waist.

Each gentle sway was a tease as they brushed against one another, until finally she was pressed up against him. Desire warmed inside of her like the first sips of champagne. Savoring the heady feeling, she closed her eyes and reminded herself to breathe.

Devin's shaky exhale feathered along her cheek, and she felt a small shudder move through him.

It was good to know that she wasn't the only one affected.

The melody ended far too soon, and the DJ picked up the pace with a faster song.

Bea and Devin stopped moving, but she remained in his arms at the edge of the floor, out of the way of enthusiastic dancers.

"I'll escort you back to your table." He stepped back and took hold of her hand.

"No…wait. I haven't eaten yet."

Concern furrowed his brow. Before she could explain, he led her off to the side of the room. "You should have said something. I wouldn't have held you up."

"You didn't hold me up. I liked dancing with you…a lot," she confessed. And even though they'd stopped, she wasn't ready for the moment to end.

Going out on a limb, Bea glanced out the window at the gazebo. "We could sit outside." She rushed to explain, "It will feel strange if I'm sitting at the table eating when no one else is." As if it had a mind of its own, her hand tightened a bit more around Devin's.

He brushed his thumb over the back of it, and her heart skipped a beat. "Fix yourself a plate. I'll wait for you outside."

In the lodge's small kitchen, the area was already cleaned up. Most of the staff had departed except for Tanya, who was making one last check for any of the café's supplies, and the scaled-down waitstaff crew.

It was hard to believe that just a few hours ago they'd been in the thick of it, preparing plates for the guests.

"Thank you for doing such a great job. And for this." Bea pointed to the plate in her hand piled high with food.

"I'm so glad we pulled it off." Tanya smiled. "Now people will know what to expect when the Cowgirl Café opens."

I'm not sure I'll ever eat there. She ruined my sister's birthday celebration…

Bea had overheard the remark from the woman at Devin's table. She'd just decided to ignore it and greet everyone with a smile. But then Devin had stood up. As soon as he'd taken her hand, she'd forgotten about the woman's snarky comments. Well…maybe she hadn't completely forgotten. She just didn't care. Dance with Devin, or talk with people who thought it was okay to gossip about her at her sister's wedding? The choice hadn't been that hard to make.

"Oh, and I can't take full credit for the plate," Tanya added. "Make sure you thank Esme for that. She noticed you hadn't eaten and asked me to set aside some food for you."

Warmth flooded through her. Even on her own wedding day, her little sister was looking out for her.

As Bea headed toward the door to join Devin, she passed by the dance floor. She spotted Esme and Ryder, holding each other close. They swayed slowly to their own beat, oblivious to the fast timing of the song and the energetic dancers around them.

They were so lucky to have found each other. A longing for something just as wonderful in her own life hit Bea. Maybe someday…

Outside, the chairs were still set up, and Devin stood in front of the stairs leading to the gazebo.

As she walked toward him, a hint of strange, giddy excitement hit her. She hadn't walked down the aisle at her first wedding. Was this a small glimpse of what that felt like?

He pointed to the structure. "I set up chairs for us. I thought you could use one as a table."

"That's perfect—thank you." She strolled up the stairs, took a seat, and did just as he'd suggested.

Devin put his suit jacket on the back of the chair beside her before taking a seat.

She offered him the extra rolled silverware she'd brought along.

He held up his hand in refusal. "After all the running around you've been doing today plus me making you dance, I know you're starving."

"There's way too much here for one person, and you didn't make me dance with you."

"I kind of did. I ambushed you."

"Yeah, you did." She winked at him. "And the only way I'll forgive you is if you help me eat some of this."

A smile tugged at his mouth. "Well, if it's the *only* way, I guess I don't have a choice." He accepted the silverware. "Actually, you don't have to twist my arm. The food was excellent. I'm looking forward to eating at your restaurant."

"Thank you." The thought emerging in her mind slipped out. "I wish your restaurant critic and your tablemates felt the same way as you do."

"So you *did* hear those women talking. I was hoping you hadn't. You shouldn't have to engage with negativity about the café, especially at your sister's wedding." He paused. "About the restaurant review…"

"No, you're right. Let's not spoil this." On a reflex, she briefly laid her hand on his arm. "I don't want to talk about the grand opening. I'm having a good time right now. I'd rather find out more about you."

What looked to be discomfort flickered in his eyes. Maybe she'd misread their chemistry and Devin was just politely sharing a meal with her. Disappointment set in. Bea prepared to give him an out.

But genuine interest came back into his expression. "Do I get to find out more about you, too?"

"Are you asking me as a journalist?"

"Nope. As me," he replied.

"Then ask away."

His gaze held hers. "Ladies first."

Talking and sharing a meal flowed as easily between them as dancing together.

Favorite songs. Hot or mild salsa. He liked his off-the-charts spicy. Wait. Had she really just confessed her go-to movies were holiday films…all year long? Devin was just so easy to talk to, and watching his smile turn into an unconscious sexy grin was an experience of its own.

He leaned closer as he relayed a story about a Great Dane he'd recently fostered. "I'm sitting on the couch watching the game, eating vanilla ice cream with crumbles of salted-caramel chocolate chip cookies—"

"Hold on. Not just cookies, but *crumbles* of cookies?"

He shook his head. "No. Not just any cookies. Salted-caramel chocolate chip cookies. Crumbling them is the only way for them to perfectly blend with the ice cream. Everyone knows that."

She feigned seriousness. "I didn't, but of course that makes perfect sense…"

He kept a semi-straight face as humor gleamed in his eyes. "Glad I cleared that up for you. So, Chumley starts chasing his tail, like dogs do. Just as I put my bowl on the coffee table to check something on my phone, I see disaster coming. Before I can stop it, he loses his balance and his paw—or maybe it was his tail—hits the bowl, and it flies across the room, slams into the wall, and shatters. Chumley does a duck-and-cover move, then glances up at me with a what-did-*you*-do look on his face. I swear he thought it was my fault."

As Bea laughed with Devin, his sexy grin reappeared, and all she could do was stare at him.

"Something wrong?" he asked.

"No."

In fact, everything felt just right. Maybe a little *too* right. She couldn't remember the last time she'd felt this good with a guy. Or wanted a kiss so badly. The desire to feel his mouth on hers grew into a persistent longing.

As she dragged her gaze upward, she met his gaze. Who leaned in first? She didn't know.

When their lips met, it didn't matter.

One all-too-brief press of their lips turned into a second one. He cupped her cheek, and heat curled inside of Bea as she waited in anticipation. When he angled his mouth back over hers, she opened to him. The heady decadence of the kiss pulled a moan out of her as she grasped onto his forearm, his bicep, then his shoulder, fighting the urge to crawl onto his lap.

Devin eased back. As he let go of her, he stood. "Dance with me."

The switch from kissing to him wanting to dance again confused her. As she stepped into his arms and he brought her close, the mix of need and barely reined in control she spotted in his eyes explained everything.

But she didn't want him to hold back.

As if reading her mind, he rested his forehead to hers. "Bea...it's not that I don't want you, but we shouldn't go beyond that kiss."

"Why?" She leaned away and looked up at his face. "Because you're friends with my brother-in-law? Or because you're a journalist, and my family and I have had some newsworthy events come into our lives?"

Devin smoothed back a strand of red hair that had wandered in front of her eyes. As he took his hand away, a trail of tingles remained where he'd caressed her cheek. "That's a big part of it..."

As he took hold of her waist with both of his hands, she

searched for the words to make him see her point of view. She'd taken a bold risk to follow her dream of opening a restaurant in Chatelaine. But when it came to her personal life, she'd kept it on hold for so long. Waiting for what? She didn't know. But she wanted to move forward with what she felt...what she *wanted*.

Bea called upon the boldness that had fortified her choices over the past months. "Whatever that 'big part' is, it doesn't have to affect us being together right now. Why can't we set that all aside, just for tonight?" she asked. "We don't talk about it. We don't worry about it. We just focus on being together and enjoying the moment."

He looked into her eyes. "And after that?"

"Tomorrow, when the sun rises, we get back to reality."

CHAPTER SIX

DEVIN HELD BEA'S waist a little tighter, fighting the temptation to bring her flush against him and kiss her. If he did, he might not be able to stop.

Lyrics from the song they were dancing to filtered into Devin's thoughts. It was about a guy who'd encountered a woman who'd unexpectedly grabbed his attention, and now he was so caught up in her, he couldn't let her go.

Those words definitely mirrored how Devin felt in this moment with Bea. He hadn't come to the wedding anticipating any of this—especially this connection with her that kept growing by the minute.

She studied his face. "What are you thinking?"

That if he gave in to what he was feeling, he *would* need until sunrise to get Bea out of his system. Maybe one night wouldn't be enough. But on the other hand, if he walked away now, he would have regrets. He really liked Bea. And if one night was all they could have, he would take it.

He caressed up and down her back, and she leaned more against him. "I was wondering how much longer you have to stay at the reception."

"Esme and Ryder should be cutting the cake soon. Shortly after that, they'll leave for their honeymoon," she told him. "Once that happens, there's not much more for me to do, and if there is, I'll figure out a way to move things along. I'll text you before I leave."

He retrieved his phone from his suit jacket and gave it

to her. After Bea added her information to his contacts, he called her number.

"Bea…" Esme shouted from across the lawn. "It's time to cut the cake."

"Okay," Bea answered, then looked back to Devin. "Are you coming?"

"Not yet." He needed to cool off.

As Bea started to walk away, he caught her lightly by the hand. She wasn't from Chatelaine, and she'd only gotten a taste of what gossip was like in a small town from what had happened with the restaurant.

He couldn't resist one last reality check. "I'm sure people have noticed us together and they're already speculating about what's going on between us. If you're hurrying to leave the reception, they might figure it out."

Bea came back toward him, rose onto her toes, and gave him a lingering kiss. Just a fraction away, her whispered words warmed his lips. "I know."

Just as she'd predicted, after the cutting of the cake, events at the reception moved along at a steady pace.

Soon, the guests stood in a pasture near the lodge as Ryder and Esme exchanged hugs and kisses with family and close friends. A helicopter waited to whisk them away to the airport to catch a flight.

As the craft lifted off, the couple waved. Everyone waved back, watching until it became smaller and smaller in the sky.

Devin met Bea's gaze across the lawn. Certainty was still in her eyes, and his heartbeat amped up. He couldn't wait to be with her.

LATER ON, AS he knocked on the door of her condo, taking it slow was the plan. But then Bea opened the door. She was still wearing the coral dress. As he took her in, from her long, red hair now loose around her shoulders down to her bare feet, he was more than just caught—he was lost.

He walked inside, and Bea shut the door behind him.

In the next instant, they were in each other's arms, and he gave in to the need to feel her soft, full lips under his. Oxygen became secondary to the ever-deepening kiss that conveyed what they craved for just one night.

Each other.

He'd left his tie and jacket in the car, and Bea took over where he'd left off, unfastening buttons at the top of his shirt. Her moan of frustration vibrated into him, and she gave up, tugging his shirt from his slacks.

With his sleeves already rolled to his forearms, Devin used the advantage and pulled his shirt over his head.

As he tossed it aside, her gaze roamed over his torso.

He worked out and had a toned physique, but maintaining a six-pack had taken a back seat to keeping up with his schedule and raising his daughter. But as Bea glided her hands over his bare skin, her touch ignited a sharp breath, resurrecting a swell of tiny muscles in his abdomen as hard as the solid ridge pressing against the front of his slacks.

Need fired through his blood. But as he brought her close, he took the pace down a notch with long, slow kisses and even slower caresses as he pulled down the zipper on the back of her dress.

Devin eased the straps from her shoulders, and Bea shimmied out of the dress. Coral-colored lace highlighted the combination of her smooth, silky skin, full breasts, and soft curves.

Kissing her, he murmured, "You're beautiful."

As Bea led him up the stairs, the mesmerizing sway of her hips was like a Siren's call, beckoning him to follow.

Urgency fueled them as they took off the rest of their clothing. The breathtaking view of Bea almost made him forget to take condoms from his wallet and lay them on the bedside table.

Moments later, she lay under him, skin to skin. He savored every moan and deep sigh as he pleased her with more caresses and hot, branding kisses.

Holding on to his shoulders, Bea trembled. "Devin... please. I need you."

Pausing briefly, he grabbed protection and put it on.

When he returned to Bea, she reached for him, widening her legs to accommodate him. As he grasped her hips, the wonderful sensation of being inside of her almost overwhelmed him, but he held on to control.

Eyes locked on each other, they moved as one. Entranced by the play of blissful emotion on her face, Devin became driven by as single-minded mission to bring her pleasure.

Bea reached her peak. And soon after he joined her, finding his release.

Later on, instead of leaving, Devin crawled back into bed and held her close. "You good?"

"Very good." Facing toward him, Bea fit like a puzzle piece finding its place.

He shouldn't get too comfortable, right? That's not how a one-night stand worked. He should get dressed and say goodnight.

But being with Bea, holding her...it was too hard to convince himself to leave.

JUST AFTER DAWN, Bea awoke in Devin's arms. As erotic memories from last night and earlier that morning played through her mind, she couldn't stop a smile. She hadn't experienced anything like being with Devin since...well, she had nothing to compare it to.

"Hey..." His voice was husky from sleep. He wrapped

an arm around her and caressed up and down her bare back. "Are you getting up already?"

"Not yet." She snuggled closer to his side and laid her head on his shoulder. As she rested her hand on his chest, the warmth from his skin seeped into her palm.

Just as she was about to ask him if he liked pancakes, a buzz and a ding reverberated from the floor.

"That's my phone. Sorry—I better see who it is." Devin slipped his arm from around her, leaned down, and fished it out of his pants pocket.

She settled back on the pillows. So much for pancakes.

Devin lay back down and checked the screen. "It's my daughter, Carly. She can't find her earbuds, and she's wondering if she left them at my place. She wants to look for them this morning." Sighing, he laid his phone on the nightstand. "Teenage priorities. She never gets up this early for school."

Bea knew he had a daughter but hadn't realized she was a teenager. "How old is she?"

"She'll be fourteen in a few months."

Lying on her side, she faced him. "Raising a teen—I hear that's an interesting experience."

Devin chuckled wryly. "You could say that. But it's also amazing and baffling at the same time. She's growing up and learning how to figure things out for herself. That's the amazing part. But sometimes, trying to understand how a teenage girl's mind works is like trying to solve a puzzle without clues. Almost everything I say or do, these days, is the opposite of what she wants."

Hints of frustration were in his tone, and Bea's heart went out to him. Despite his frustration, the soft rays of sunlight streaming between the slats of the window blinds illuminated parental pride on his face.

She rested a hand on his arm. "When she's older, I'm

sure that will change. At least that's what I've heard happens with teenagers."

"I hope it's true." Devin sat up on the mattress. He leaned over and kissed her forehead. "I better get going. Mind if I take a quick shower?"

"Not at all." As she sat up, she tugged at the sheet, holding it to her chest.

Devin's gaze dropped from her face to the curves of her breasts still peeking above the covers, and he swallowed hard.

A part of Bea was tempted to let the sheet drop and go for round three. But he probably wanted to get home and change out of yesterday's clothes before meeting his daughter.

Pulling the sheet up higher, she asked, "Do you want coffee?"

Devin cleared his throat. "That would be great."

She gave him a clean towel and one of the pre-pasted toothbrushes she kept on hand for travel. After finding out how he wanted his coffee, she put on a sleep shirt, made a pitstop in the other bathroom, then went downstairs.

A short time later, Bea climbed back up the stairs carrying two full mugs of dark Colombian brew. As she slowed down, making sure not to spill hot coffee, she glanced down at the mugs and smiled. She and Devin weren't just sexually compatible. They even liked their coffee the same way—a couple of teaspoons of sugar, no cream.

That would have been a good sign…if they were at the start of a relationship. But they weren't. She had a restaurant to run, and he had a teen daughter to raise. They were on different paths.

Still, Bea's mind started to wander, imagining what might happen next if those different paths converged, even for just a few more days. Would they meet up later and spend the rest of the day together? Then would they explore possible plans to see each other for the rest of the week or maybe a bit longer? As long as they both knew an end was in sight…

As she walked into the bedroom, Devin walked out of the bathroom wearing just a blue towel around his waist.

Her thoughts short-circuited as want curled in her belly.

As he walked toward her, drops of water glistened on his muscular chest. She couldn't tear her gaze away as a few droplets slid down his abdomen toward the edge of the towel.

"Bea…"

His voice snapped her out of a trance, and she looked up. Blatant need was in his eyes.

Devin slipped the mugs from her hands, set them on the dresser, then came back to her. Taking her by the waist, he brought her close.

"But your coffee…" The three-word question was all she could manage to say.

"It can wait." Devin leaned in. "This can't."

He slanted his mouth over hers.

In short order, his towel and her sleep shirt were on the floor. As he cupped her bottom, Devin brushed open-mouthed kisses along the sensitive skin of her throat. The evidence of his desire nestled against her belly. Holding tightly to his shoulders, she wound her legs around his waist as he swiftly carried her to the unmade bed.

Every touch, kiss, and caress reflected all she felt. Impatience and pure need. By the time he entered her, she was trembling and nearly lightheaded with anticipation. Each swift, hard stroke delivered more and more pleasure until she splintered apart in ecstasy.

Depleted from his own orgasm, Devin rose to his elbows supporting his weight. "You okay?"

Floating in contentment, Bea smiled as she stroked a hand up and down his back. "I'm wonderful."

He stared into her eyes. "I'm sorry I can't stay longer."

"Me, too." But maybe it was better this way. If he hung around for coffee and breakfast liked she'd imagined, it would have been harder to watch him leave.

Devin moved away from Bea and sat on the edge of the bed with his back to her. He moved to get up but stopped, staring between his legs. "Damn," he whispered.

Hearing concern in his tone, she grasped the sheet to her chest once more and sat up. "What's wrong?"

He glanced over at her. "The condom broke."

STILL PROCESSING WHAT had occurred earlier in the bedroom, Bea stood with Devin at the kitchen counter holding on to her coffee mug. For her, having the cup in her hand was a nervous gesture more than a need for caffeine.

They'd waited until coming downstairs to discuss what had happened. She'd never fully understood the saying about cutting through tension with a knife until now. It filled the room along with a heavy silence.

Devin sat down his full mug. "I'm sorry. I should have noticed…"

She couldn't let him take all the blame. "We were caught up in the moment. It's not your fault."

As she reached for his hand on the counter, he reached for hers, too.

Devin released a heavy exhale. "This isn't how I imagined this morning would end."

"Me neither."

His fingers tightened around hers as he looked into her eyes. "Whatever happens next, I'm here."

CHAPTER SEVEN

BEA, FREYA, AND Tanya sat at a table in the empty café. The topic of their Tuesday-morning meeting was the rescheduled grand opening happening next week.

But Bea's mind kept wandering back to her off-the-charts sexual encounter with Devin a little over a week ago...and how it had ended.

If her cycle wasn't so irregular, she might have been able to count days to get an idea if she'd been in the pregnancy window. But with the added stress of opening the restaurant, her cycle had been even more erratic than usual. And based on her history, there was more than just a good chance she *wasn't* pregnant. Maybe she should have told that to him. He'd looked so concerned before he'd left to meet his daughter.

The next day, he'd sent a text checking in to see how she was doing, and again a few days later. Both times she'd texted back that she was fine. They hadn't communicated since then. But why would Devin reach out again? He was probably waiting to hear news from her. After all, their intent *had* been a one-night stand.

"The key is to not focus on what didn't work but concentrate on what did," Freya said.

The comment brought Bea back into the conversation. That was a good point. Focusing on what hadn't worked would only lead to worry. Why not just remember how good things had been between her and Devin before the moment had gone sideways?

But her hookup with Devin wasn't what Freya was talking about.

"You're right." Bea slipped off the lightweight gray cardigan she'd paired with a blue shirt and black jeans. "We have to do all we can to promote this opening in a way that will encourage people to rebook their reservations."

"And our plan of offering a free item to the first fifty who do will help with that," Tanya added. "But maybe the options should just be a dozen biscuits to go or a dessert. I think the biscuits will be popular, and food-cost wise, they're a lot cheaper than our appetizers."

Freya smoothed a strand of ash-blond hair from her cheek. "I think either will work as long as we aren't sabotaged again." She frowned. "That's such a terrible thing that happened. I couldn't imagine even conceiving something like that. Could you?" She looked between Bea and Tanya.

"None of us could," Bea replied. "But like you said, we should focus on the positives. And that means we probably shouldn't use the word *sabotage* to describe what happened." Earlier, she'd heard Freya using the word liberally while booking reservations on the phone. "We've come up with a good plan. That's our focus, and now we just have to implement it."

"True." Freya tapped on her tablet. "Lily's idea to have everyone share their photos of Esme and Ryder's wedding has really paid off. She's uploaded them to a site. I know we're supposed to be talking about business, but you have to take a peek."

The wedding was definitely a bright spot. And from Esme's text message a few days ago, she and Ryder were enjoying their extended honeymoon at a resort in the Maldives. And they were looking forward to the nanny bringing Chase and Noah to join them.

Bea accepted the tablet from Freya. Many of the photos showed the couple gazing lovingly at each other, even the candid ones when they weren't aware someone was watching them. And there were several cute pics of their baby boys as well.

Freya pointed. "This one of you and Devin is really nice."

The person taking the photo had captured Devin as he was about to spin Bea around. They were smiling at each other. Memories of happiness along with remembered desire curled through her.

She'd told Devin that she didn't have time for a relationship of any kind. But honestly, if things had ended differently after their night together, she would have been tempted to see him again.

A knock sounded at the front door.

Tanya stood. "That's probably Mrs. Lansing. I'll let her in."

"I'll do it." Freya gathered up her things. "I'm on my way out anyway. I have errands to run."

"Okay, thanks." Tanya turned to Bea. "There's a delivery coming in. I'll be in the kitchen if you need me."

Moments later, Bea sat at the table with the thirty-something brunette dressed casually in blue active wear. She'd spoken to Esme a few weeks ago about the possibility of booking the café for a private event.

"Please, call me Sophia." The woman's cheeks flushed pink as she became the equivalent of an octopus, giving her baby a pacifier and setting up her five-year-old son, Easton, with a coloring book all while wrangling her daughter, a toddler named Amelia. "Apologies for bringing the kiddos along. My sitter woke up sick this morning and couldn't look after them. I just didn't want to cancel our meeting."

"That's perfectly okay. Can I get you anything?"

"No, I'm good. Thank you." After settling Amelia on her lap, Sophia snagged an adult water bottle for herself and a matching kiddie water bottle for the toddler. "So, I'm planning a fiftieth wedding anniversary celebration for my in-laws…"

They chatted about several ideas for the Sunday late-morning event.

Bea drew out a rough sketch of the room layout for the party on her tablet. "Not going with a plated meal actually opens quite a few options. We can set up a buffet line, and we can also set up separate omelet and Belgian waffle stations here and here. And even a dessert station if you like." She looked up from her tablet to smile at her client. "You mentioned all the grandkids would be attending. Make-your-own ice cream sundaes could be fun."

"We get to have ice cream?" Five-year-old Easton flashed a grin, revealing a missing front tooth.

Amelia squealed at him.

"Maybe." Sophia smiled. "Ice cream sundaes are actually a great choice. My mother-in-law used to work at an ice cream shop in high school. My father-in-law was the stud quarterback, and he used to stop by to flirt with her. All these years later, they still act like teenage sweethearts."

"Aww. That's wonderful."

"It is." Sophia leaned away as Amelia waved her arms, spraying drops of water from the attached straw on her bottle. "And they had six kids." Giving in to Amelia squirming around, she let the child slide from her lap. "Honestly, I don't know how Joan did it. My husband and I barely had a handle on things with two kids when Corbin snuck up on us."

"Snuck up?" Bea smiled brightly at the toddler who came over and grasped on to her fingers.

The weight of Amelia's hand in hers was almost nothing, but the light in the little girl's hazel eyes declared, *I'm here. I know you see me. I see you.*

"*Snuck up* is probably the wrong choice of words." Sophia laughed. "Hubby and I went to Acapulco for a long weekend to celebrate our anniversary, and the result was Corbin." She glanced at the baby sleeping in the stroller. "He was absolutely unexpected. A word from the wise— even the best protection fails."

A short time later, they wrapped up their meeting and Bea walked Sophia and her children to the door. But Sophia's warning about her Acapulco trip remained on Bea's mind.

Her morning with Devin couldn't have resulted in the unexpected? *Could it?*

The question haunted her the rest of the day. On the way home, she gave in to the impulse and drove to Great-Store. The big-box retailer sold everything from groceries to clothes to home goods and personal items...including pregnancy tests.

Inside the store, she grabbed a handheld shopping basket and headed for the personal-care section.

She perused the myriad of test boxes. The packaging on some of them had changed from years ago, but they were still familiar. Rapid results, countdown clocks, pregnancy test strips, a triple-check test proclaiming it offered even more reassurance about the result.

A fleeting recollection played through her mind of buying multiple tests years ago. At times, when she'd used them, it had almost felt as if she was playing the pregnancy lottery, hoping for the winning result. But it had never happened.

A customer passing by jostled Bea from her thoughts. She didn't recognize the woman curiously staring at her, but what if she had? Or what if Freya or Asa and Lily or one of the staff at the café walked by and saw her looking at pregnancy tests? What would she tell them?

Heart thumping from a sudden surge of anxiety, she grabbed a "six days or sooner" test kit along with another kind as a backup and quickly left the aisle. On a reflex, she snagged two pairs of neon-colored moisturizing socks and piled them on top of the tests along with packages of deodorant and a large value-size bodywash from the next aisle.

Moments later, she stood in the "twenty items or less" self-checkout line, praying she wouldn't run into anyone she knew.

After what felt like forever, she finally reached the register. Nervousness made her hands a tad unsteady as she dug out the tests first and scanned them on the reader.

If Esme were around, Bea would have called her for support. She didn't know Lily well enough to tell her, but she wouldn't want to burden her with keeping this type of a secret from Asa. If he found out, he'd leap into big-brother protective mode and maybe even call Devin, demanding to know his intentions.

Farther down, a familiar-looking guy entered the store. The bodywash she was scanning almost slipped out of her hands. Had thinking of her one-night stand conjured up his presence? No, of course not. It was just a small town.

Devin paused in the main aisle and glanced at his phone.

Whatever happens next, I'm here…

Recalling what he'd said brought a sense of comfort. If she told him how nervous she was about taking the test, would he empathize with her? Or maybe even be there when she took it? A large part of her believed he would. But she couldn't just walk up to him in the store and ask. But she did have his number. She could call him from the parking lot.

As Bea hurried to pay for her things, a teenage girl joined Devin. He smiled at the girl as they walked in the opposite direction.

Was that Carly?

A sense of isolation hit Bea. Devin had other important priorities. She would have to face this next step on her own.

CHAPTER EIGHT

DEVIN INCHED HIS black truck forward in the trailing line of cars headed to the front of the middle school. As he flipped down the visor, blocking out most of the morning sun, he stifled a yawn.

Carly sat beside him in the front passenger seat of the crew cab, munching on cinnamon French toast sticks while texting on her phone.

Yesterday she'd stayed after school for a club meeting. Lauren had had to work late and couldn't pick her up, so he'd taken his daughter to his place for the night. At Great-Store, while they'd been shopping for the items to make spaghetti for dinner, she'd put the box of toast sticks into the basket.

Lauren was a health nut and wouldn't approve of Carly eating what she deemed the equivalent of junk food first thing in the morning. But from the way the thirteen-year-old was gobbling the toast sticks, she'd needed a break from the choices of muesli, quinoa, raisin bran, or Greek yogurt with fruit for breakfast.

But he *had* fed her a balanced meal last night. Spaghetti with meat sauce and a salad. Carly had sliced up the vegetables for the salad, and he'd made everything else. While they'd prepared the meal, she'd talked to him about her homework. One of her last assignments of the school year was to write an essay on a social issue affecting teens. She hadn't chosen a topic yet.

The impact of social media on mental health, peer pressure, bullying, addiction... While he was proud of her knowledge on those subjects, their conversation had made him acutely aware of the things she was facing at her young age.

Despite questioning his and Lauren's parental wisdom at almost every turn, Carly was staying on the right path, choosing independence and responsibility instead of caving to the wrong influences. He was proud of her.

It was hard to believe that soon she would finish eighth grade. And that coming fall, when he drove her to school, he would have to drop her off on the other end of the campus at the high school entrance.

Carly caught him looking at her, and teen wariness reflected on her face. "Why are you staring at me like that?"

"Like what?" he said.

"Like you're wondering about me."

"And that's a bad thing?"

Carly's silent raised brow before she turned her attention back to her phone conveyed her answer.

Moments later, they were at the designated drop-off zone.

She grabbed her backpack from the floor. "Bye, Dad."

Not wanting to embarrass her by making a "big deal" about the quick kiss she gave him on the cheek before she got out, he held back a grin until after he'd driven off.

Next stop was the Saddle & Spur Roadhouse to pick up the pastries and sandwiches he'd ordered from the restaurant. He and his staff were putting together the Sunday edition that was due to the printer, and they would be tied to the office until the late afternoon. An endless supply of food and coffee was a must.

As he exited the school's campus, he turned up the

radio. The last song he and Bea had danced to under the gazebo played through the speakers.

Maybe he should reach out to her again? But when he had, she'd said she was okay, and hearing from him now could be an unwanted distraction. After all, Bea *was* in the midst of preparing for the rescheduled grand opening.

He'd been debating whether he should show up for it as the anonymous critic. Giving an unbiased review of the café would be a challenge for him now. Especially since he felt guilty about her not knowing he'd written the review. In hindsight, he should have insisted on telling Bea up front, but letting go of everything and spending one carefree night together had been too hard to walk away from…and so had the morning after.

But if he'd left like he'd intended right after his shower, things would have ended with the two of them remembering how much they'd enjoyed being together, instead of worrying about possible life-altering changes.

His phone rang through the car's speaker system. But it wasn't Bea. He answered the call.

"Hey, Lauren."

"Hi, Devin. Are you on your way to work?"

"Not yet. I just dropped Carly off at school. I have to pick up some takeout before I head to the office. But before I forget—Carly and I went shopping last night, and she picked out some clothes. The bags are in the car with me. Do you mind if I let myself into the garage so I can drop them off before I head to the Saddle and Spur?"

"Actually, I'm still at home. I was hoping you might be able to stop by this morning so we could talk. Do you have a few minutes?"

Lauren sounded a little off. Was something going on with Carly?

Devin headed for the busy four-lane road just outside of town. "Be there in twenty minutes."

He arrived at Lauren and Carly's house a short time later and backed into the driveway.

When they'd all moved to Texas, the three-bedroom house with wood floors, high ceilings, and a loft over the garage had been their perfect dream home. And Carly loved her space. Over the years, she'd helped paint the walls in her new favorite color of the moment ever since she'd been able to use a paint brush and not make too much of a mess. After the divorce, it had made sense for him to move into a smaller place and his ex-wife and daughter remain there.

As he walked up the stone path carrying the shopping bags with Carly's new things, Lauren opened the front door. She was dressed for work in a gray blouse, slacks and heels.

He left the bags in the entryway, then followed her to the kitchen. Devin sat on a stool on the living room side of the beige granite island.

Lauren selected two glasses from an upper cabinet. "Orange juice good?"

"Sure. Thanks."

She took a container out of the refrigerator, poured him a glass, then spooned up some quinoa from a pot on the stove into a bowl. She set both in front of him.

He wasn't into quinoa, and Lauren knew that. Yeah, something was *definitely* off. Devin nudged the bowl aside. "So what's up?"

Lauren took her time pouring a glass of orange juice for herself. "Last night at work, there was a conference call with the higher-ups in the company. They announced that they're downsizing."

Was she at risk of losing her job? As a claims-department supervisor at an insurance company, she'd been climbing the ranks to a management position. He could only imagine how Lauren felt after receiving the bad news.

But her company, located in the next town over, wasn't the only one making big changes. In fact, the paper was publishing an article in the upcoming edition about the economic impact caused by the unexpected exodus of businesses from the area.

"I'm sorry," he said. "I know this is something you hadn't anticipated."

"No." She released a dry chuckle. "It definitely came out of the blue."

Luckily the house was already paid off and so was Lauren's car. As far as he knew, food, utilities, and incidentals were her main concerns.

"If you're worried about paying the bills, don't be. If you lose your job, I can cover expenses here until you find another one. Just let me know how much you need."

"Actually, they offered me a lateral promotion with a raise." Lauren carefully put down her still-full glass. "I can stay here in my new position...or I can go to Dallas or Corpus Christi."

She'd mentioned all three opportunities. That meant she was weighing all the options. "What did you decide?"

"I chose Corpus Christi. I start there in three months."

She was moving? This was sudden, but it wasn't an unmanageable situation.

Devin took a sip of orange juice and a moment to collect his thoughts. "Okay. Not a problem. Carly has volleyball camp and some volunteer activities lined up for the summer. I can adjust my schedule. I guess the big question is what do you want to do with the house? If it comes down to it, I could sell my place, and that way Carly could stay put."

Lauren gave him a baffled look. "Carly's not staying

here, Devin. She's coming with me. Of course, you'll see her. We'll have to work out weekend visits and which holidays she'll spend with you."

"Hold on. Her friends are here. She's been with some of them since grade school, and all they've ever talked about is attending high school together. And she's planning to try out for the freshman volleyball team or maybe taking up cheerleading again." He met her stare with a hard one of his own. "You can't just yank her away from all of that. This is her *home*."

"I'm not yanking her away from anything." Lauren shook her head. "She'll still be in contact with her friends. And she can join the volleyball team or the cheerleading squad at her new school in Corpus Christi. In fact, their volleyball team has made the regional or state championships for the past five years."

"Her *new* school. So you've already made up your mind. Don't I have a say in it? And what about what Carly wants? Doesn't that count for anything?"

"Of course what Carly wants counts." Lauren threw up her hands. "But we have to be realistic. All those activities she wants to get involved in—if she stays here, who's going to take her back and forth to them? You say you're going to adjust your schedule, but how long will that last? You barely have time for her now."

Irritation prickled over him as he stood. "That's not true."

"How much time has she spent holed up with you in your office because you're working? Or babysitting another puppy you volunteered to foster while you're working? Or tagging along with you on researching a story you're writing? Even the father-daughter-meal outings you take her on are work related. Carly knows you're reviewing the restaurant."

"How?" he demanded. "Because you told her?"

"No. Carly's the one who told me. She started noticing a review from the 'anonymous' restaurant critic appeared in your paper right after she went to the place with you. And you don't have to worry about her telling anyone. She thinks your little secret is exciting."

Carly keeping his secret was the last thing he was worried about. He was worried about losing his daughter. "I can't change the past, Lauren, but if Carly was living with me, there wouldn't be any scheduling problems. I would make it work."

His ex crossed her arms over her chest. "And if you can't, then what? According to our agreement, she's supposed to spend two weeks and two weekends a month with you. That hardly ever happens."

"You make it sound like Carly isn't my priority."

"She is—along with running the newspaper and chasing the next headline story."

Déjà vu hit with her last comment. It was a near repeat to what Lauren used to say during their arguments before they'd decided to get a divorce.

From the look on Lauren's face, the same realization had crossed her mind. "I don't want to fight about this. I just want what's best for our daughter."

"And so do I." Devin released a measured breath. "But we won't be able to decide what's best for her if we're dragging our past into it. We have to consider *all* sides of this decision. And that includes exploring the possibility of her staying here with me."

"You're right…we have to work this out for Carly's sake. She shouldn't see us divided on this. We also need to work out our differences before we approach her about what's going on."

"I agree. This is our problem, not hers." Grimness entered his tone. "It upsets her when we're not getting along. The last thing we should do is stress her out."

"At least we're on the same page about that, but as far as the rest…" Lauren uncrossed her arms. Her expression shifted from stubbornness to resignation. "There's only one way for us to solve things."

DEVIN DROVE INTO the parking lot of the Saddle & Spur Roadhouse. As he pulled into a vacant spot, his earlier conversation with Lauren, along with her accusations, played through his mind.

He couldn't imagine not having Carly in Chatelaine and only seeing her on weekends or select holidays. And yes, according to the agreement they had now, despite equal custody, she often didn't spend the two weeks and two weekends a month with him. But that wasn't because he didn't *want* her with him.

They knew Carly saw Lauren's place as home. And that made sense considering the three of them had once lived there as a family. They'd adopted a *three weeks there, one week at his place* schedule, and everyone had been happy. But if their daughter wanted to spend a few extra days or weekends in one place or another or wanted to pop by to see him, neither he nor Lauren objected.

His ex-wife throwing in the informal agreement change like it was a negative was more than just a little unfair considering they'd made the adjustment for a good reason. And she shouldn't have just sprung her decision on him. But the fact that she already had a high school picked out for Carly made Devin wonder if this move to Corpus Christi had been in the works for a while.

Yes, she had a right to excel in her career, but when it came to their daughter's welfare, it was a joint effort, not a singular one. And as far as him being able to balance his work schedule and look after Carly, he already had the perfect blueprint on that. His father had done it while raising him as a single parent.

Outside the truck, Devin locked it with the key fob and headed toward the restaurant. At least he and Lauren agreed on one thing. Just like they had with their divorce and the original custody agreement, they were using a mediator to reach an amicable decision.

As he walked past a four-door sedan to the left, he did a double take. *Bea...*

She was just about to open the driver's side door when her gaze met his. "Devin...hi."

"Hello." He walked over to her.

Dressed in black jeans, a white blouse, and a short tan jacket, her appearance was casual yet professional. And she looked pretty as usual.

Standing in front of each other, she seemed as unsure as he felt about how they should greet each other. They leaned in at the same time for a hug.

He breathed in her light floral fragrance, and any awkwardness he'd felt before melted away. Familiarity and sense of rightness replaced it, tempting him into holding her a bit longer.

They released each other.

Meeting her gaze, Devin debated what to say. He couldn't ask if she'd taken a pregnancy test yet. "How are you?"

"Good, but busy." Bea's smile curved up her mouth, but it didn't light up her face. Adjusting the purse strap on her shoulder, she looked at the restaurant. "The owner here has some extra tray racks he wants to get rid of. He called to see if I was interested in them. They're practically brand new."

"So are you interested in them?"

"Yes. We need them. Some of ours were...lost." As she looked up at him, uncertainty briefly shadowed her face, and she looked just as lost. "I should go." She headed back to her car. "See you, Devin."

"Bye, Bea."

He hadn't known her long at all, but he could sense something was off with her. Was he just picking up on the stress she was under with the café, or was it something else?

His phone rang. It was Quinn. She and Charles were probably wondering where he was.

Turning toward the Saddle & Spur, he answered the call. "Devin, wait..." Bea called out. "I'm pregnant."

CHAPTER NINE

I'M PREGNANT... THE confession had just flown out of her mouth. Hearing herself say the actual words that had drummed in her mind all last night felt surreal.

As Devin turned to face her, he spoke into the phone. "I'll call you back."

And she'd not only just told Devin, but most likely whoever he'd been on the phone with had heard it, too. Along with the guy she hadn't noticed walking past them.

The realization of her announcement, including the fact that her life was about to change in a huge way, made it hard to breathe. *Oh, shit...*

He came to her side and wrapped an arm around her. "You're okay. Take a deep breath. Good. Take another."

Devin guided her to his truck. Once she was inside the front passenger seat, he went to the driver's side, got in, and snagged a small bottle of apple juice sitting in the middle console.

He cracked it open. "Here—drink some of this."

Bea accepted the bottle. She took a sip, and the feeling of lightheadedness started to fade. Fine sand-colored granules stuck to her fingers.

Devin noticed her staring at her hand. "It's cinnamon sugar from French toast sticks. Carly was eating breakfast in the car on the way to school this morning." He opened the glove box, took out napkins, and traded them for the bottle.

Making sure his daughter had breakfast on the way to dropping her off at school, apple juice and napkins at the ready... There was no doubt in her mind that the strong, confident man sitting beside her was a natural parent. But as for her? She had no idea where to start in becoming one.

"Feeling better?" he asked.

"Yes, thank you." She balled the napkin in her hand. "I didn't mean to drop the news on you like that—or for whoever you were on the phone with to hear it along with that guy walking through the parking lot. Please tell me you don't know him."

"I don't." Devin studied her face. "And even if I did, I don't care what he heard. Now will you please answer me truthfully. How are you? And where are you in your thinking about being pregnant?"

Bea sorted through her whirling emotions. "I feel like I've been put in a scrambler and shot back out of it. I'm shocked and overwhelmed." The sincerity in his gaze prompted her to be even more honest. "And I'm a little frustrated this didn't happen to me sooner." She responded to his questioning look. "Eight years ago, when I was married, I tried to have a baby...but I couldn't conceive. I'd given up on the possibility of ever getting pregnant."

"And now you are." Devin glanced away with a pensive expression.

"And what about you." Bea balled the napkin tighter in her fist. "How are you feeling about this...honestly?"

His chest rose and fell with a breath. "I'm shocked, too. I've been in this situation of becoming a parent before, but this is different."

Different... She read between the lines, imagining what he wasn't saying. Back then, he'd been in a committed relationship with someone he'd cared about. "I'm not expecting anything from you. I want this baby, but I know having another child isn't necessarily what you want."

Devin met her gaze. "I didn't say that."

"You just said this situation is different."

"Different in that I'm not in my early twenties trying to get a foothold in my career while becoming a new parent," he clarified. "I have experience. Which is why I won't let you go through this alone."

She shook her head. "I don't want us to feel forced to be together. Or for you to feel trapped. Let's be honest... we don't know each other."

Devin wrapped his hand around her closed one. "No, we don't know each other that well. And I don't know what it's like to be pregnant, but I *do* know going through the changes of pregnancy can be a lot, mentally and physically, especially for a first-time mom. And, of course, I want to know my child. And that includes getting to know you, Bea." As he turned more toward her, he held her hand a little tighter. "I don't want you to be alone or even feel that you're on your own in this—financially, emotionally, or on any other level. It will be easier if you let me be there for you."

Seeing his earnest expression lifted some of the heaviness that had started weighing on Bea that morning. She really didn't want to go through the experience alone. She'd gotten a taste of that in her past marriage.

She and her ex had tried for a long time to get pregnant. When it hadn't happened, she'd been open to other avenues, but Jeff hadn't been. If she couldn't have a baby "the old-fashioned way," he'd told her, then he hadn't wanted one. The past memory played through her mind. If *she* couldn't have a baby... He'd actually said that.

That comment had finally awakened her to what she'd refused to see. Jeff hadn't been physically or emotionally there for her—and not just with their fertility issues. She'd been the one who'd given everything. All he'd given was promises he'd never kept. He also hadn't understood what she'd needed from him as a husband. And he hadn't been willing to make changes to sustain their marriage.

What Devin offered was the opposite of that. But what if he couldn't keep *his* promises? What if she put her faith in him and he bailed on her, too? She couldn't go through that again, especially with a baby on the horizon.

Bea met Devin's gaze. "I have to be up front with you—I appreciate you wanting to be supportive, but I'm anxious about it, too. You already have a responsibility to Carly. You also run a business. Adding in me and the baby will add more to your already busy life. I don't want to set you up for failure by expecting too much from you."

"It's a legitimate concern. And since you were honest with me, I should be honest with you as well." Grimness shadowed his face. "I just found out this morning that Lauren—Carly's mom—accepted a transfer to Corpus Christi for her job. And she wants to take Carly with her."

Bea's heart went out to him. Devin had probably still been reeling from the news when she'd dropped her bombshell revelation on him. But despite that, he hadn't hesitated in looking after her.

Even though she'd had no way of knowing that her timing was bad, a hint of guilt still rippled through her. Sighing, she relaxed her grip on the napkin, allowing Devin to grasp her hand. "I'm sorry. I know that must have been tough to find out."

He huffed a breath. "Yeah, I definitely didn't see that coming. We've decided to go through mediation instead of the courts to come up with a decision. We've worked things out this way before. Hopefully we can do it again. We just have to remember what's best for Carly."

"That's an important focus." And one she didn't want to get in the way of.

"It is. I'll have to be available to attend sessions with the mediator. And when we tell Carly what's happening with her mom and the move, I'll need to be there to help her process the situation. But that doesn't mean I can't be there for you and the baby, too. I just have to balance my time."

But it wasn't just about time. How would his daughter take the news about the baby? And would the pregnancy negatively impact his position when it came to negotiating the new custody arrangement for his daughter?

Bea held back in asking the questions. Devin had just found out he was about to become a father again along with the prospect of spending less time with his daughter. He hadn't had time to figure all that out yet. And just like she needed support, he probably did, too.

"I appreciate you telling me what's going on with your ex and Carly. You and I being honest with each other puts us on the right course."

"There's something else I need to tell you." A look of regret came over Devin's face. "I'm the newspaper's anonymous restaurant critic."

CHAPTER TEN

IN THE *CHATELAINE DAILY NEWS* office's main conference room, Devin, Charles, and Quinn sat at the large rectangular table reviewing a draft of Sunday's newspaper on their tablets and laptops. The program they used allowed them to make changes in real time so they could all see and comment on adjustments.

As Devin scanned the pages, one thought shadowed the rest in his mind. *Bea was pregnant.*

After their night together, he'd realized that was a possibility, but hearing her say the words was a whole other reality.

She'd looked so anxious. Assuring her that everything would be okay had been important to him. And he would live up to his promise to be there for her. But was he ready to be a dad again?

His heart thumped a little harder as he released a pent-up exhale. He and Lauren had planned having Carly. And as a married couple, bringing a child into the world had been a natural next step for them.

He and Bea weren't even close to ready for this. And they had to find a way to get there. Starting with her forgiving him.

The hurt look on Bea's face that morning after he'd confessed to writing the review about the café played in his mind.

I'm not holding it against you for not telling me, Devin.

I was the one who suggested we set everything aside. But that doesn't erase the fact you encouraged people to question if they should give my restaurant another chance... I don't know how I'm supposed to feel about this. I need time...

That was what she'd told him before she'd gotten out of his truck. She'd also mentioned she'd contact him when she was ready. He could have mentioned that by not being transparent about what had happened at the café on opening night, she'd missed the opportunity for there to be a balanced view on her situation.

But that thinking was from the outside point of view of a journalist and restaurant critic. Not Bea's...what? Just the father of her baby? Had his admission relegated him to only that role in her life? Discontent and concern tugged in his gut. He didn't just want to know his baby, he wanted to get to know Bea.

When they'd been at the wedding reception, they'd shared a natural connection that hadn't been merely on a physical level. A part of him believed that even though they had put a one-night limit on being together, they still would have linked up again. Their connection might have grown into something more. Wasn't that part of their relationship worth exploring, especially now that they were expecting a child together?

The front door chimed in the reception area, jarring him from his thoughts.

Quinn got up and breezed out of the room. The brunette in her early forties never slowed down, even when she was seated. She just moved from task to task with a fluid ease.

Charles slid his glasses farther up his nose, took a sip of coffee, and kept working. In the midst of calm or chaos, the bald-headed managing editor always retained an intense focus.

Moments later, Quinn popped her head in the door. "Devin—someone's here to see you."

Was it Bea? Hope made him sit up straight in the chair. "Who is it?"

"A woman named Morgana—she said you two spoke over the phone?"

Masking disappointment, Devin sat back in the chair. "We did. But she's early. We're not meeting until later this afternoon."

"Go ahead." Charles chimed in. "Quinn and I can handle this."

Considering how his mind was wandering, it was probably best to turn it over to them. Devin looked to Quinn. "Show her to my office, please. I'll be there in a minute."

After briefly discussing a layout issue with Charles, Devin left the conference room and headed to his office two doors down.

Charles's office was located on the opposite side of the main floor, and Quinn's desk was in the adjoining reception area.

The remaining offices bordering the square-shaped space were empty, along with the four desks in the middle of the room.

Years ago, the office had been occupied by full-time reporters, advertising sales reps, photographers and assistants. An electric energy had buzzed through the building, especially during the pre-publication phase of the paper. But those days were gone forever. Printed newspapers were dying out in favor of online resources.

Now freelance reporters came in and temporarily occupied a desk when they were writing a story for the paper. Or when Carly was there, she would set up camp and do her homework while waiting for him to finish for the day.

Devin's gaze landed on one of the desks that was now

being used as a catchall for files, office supplies, past editions of the paper, and new packages of dog chew toys.

Moving to a smaller, cheaper office space outside of downtown Chatelaine had crossed his mind, but he wasn't ready to leave the good memories of being there with his father. Or Carly being there as well.

In his office, a tall, slender woman with brown hair dressed in casual clothes stood with her back toward him.

He walked in. "Morgana?"

She turned around. "Yes, hello."

At first glance, the young woman looked like a teenager, but her green eyes reflected a maturity that came with adulthood. He figured she was at least in her twenties.

Returning her smile, he shook her hand. "Nice to meet you, Morgana. I'm Devin. Have a seat."

She sat in front of the oak desk, and he settled into the chair behind it.

Just like his home, this office didn't have a lot of extras—just a desk, chairs, and a couple of filing cabinets and a couch along the wall.

But the space seemed a lot smaller without Chumley and all of the toys and other pet items Devin had bought to accommodate the large Great Dane. He'd given everything to Chumley's new owners, and they'd been grateful to have them.

Speaking of which...he'd received another message from the shelter. There was a strong chance that he would be fostering Francis until they found him a new home.

Out of habit, Devin flipped to a clean page in the spiral notebook in front of him. He always took notes during meetings and preferred the old-school way of writing things out when he was in his office. "So in your email, you mentioned you wanted to look through our archives. What time period are you interested in?"

Morgana adjusted the small backpack on her lap. "The mid-1960s through the early 1970s."

"Oh, you want to go *that* far back? We're still uploading the editions from those years into our system."

The young woman's gaze dropped as a look of disappointment came over her face. "So you can't help me."

"No—we can still help. It just might take a little time. Everything from those years is still stored on floppy disks."

Morgana perked up. "I don't mind searching through them. Can I start now?"

Her sudden shift to eagerness raised his curiosity. "I don't see why not." He stood. "Just let me check in with my staff assistant about the disks." Just before he reached the door, he paused. "Are you searching for anything in particular? It could help narrow the search for the files."

"No, but I'll know it when I see it." Morgana made steady eye contact with him, but she was clutching the backpack.

"Okay. Sit tight. I'll be back in a minute."

She exhaled with a smile. "Thanks."

He checked with Quinn. The disks were located in the spare office where she'd been working on the filing project.

"All of the disks from 1960 to 1970 are in separate boxes," his assistant said. "I just took them out of storage, and I haven't gotten around to putting them in order, so she'll have to search them. There's also another box with disks that have labels with just headers but no dates. Did she mention what she was looking for? That box might be a place to start."

"She claims she doesn't know but that she'll recognize what it is when she sees it."

"Do you want me to help her sort through them?" Quinn offered.

Devin shook his head. It didn't make sense to pull her

away from working on the paper with Charles, and he was curious to find out what Morgana was up to. He got the sense she was hiding something. "No, I'll do it."

A few minutes later, he stood in the spare office with the young woman. He opened a medium-sized box marked *1960* which he'd put on the desk. "Are you sure there isn't more to go on to help with your search?" he asked. "Like a year or a span of years or a particular subject, like birth or death announcements or real estate listings?" He was fishing for information, but it was worth a shot.

"I'm not looking for those types of records. I'm more interested in a time frame…" Frowning, she worried her lower lip with her teeth, almost as if she was afraid to say too much. "I should probably check out 1964 to 1965."

"That helps." He started taking disks out of the box and laying them on the desk. "Let's get to it."

"Oh, no—you're busy. I can do it."

"I don't mind. Things will go faster if you let me help you weed through them. After that, I'll set you up on the computer with a disk reader and you can start your search."

She flashed him a grateful look. "That sounds good. Thank you."

"You're welcome."

Minutes ticked by as they sorted in silence.

As Devin added a disk to the 1964 stack, he asked, "Do you live in the area?"

"I guess you could say that." Morgana set aside a disk she didn't need. "I just moved here. I don't have a place yet, so I'm renting a room at the Chatelaine Motel."

It made sense that she was staying there. The motel functioned as an overnight lodging destination for travelers and a rooming house for extended visits. And it was the only option for anyone who didn't have friends or family in town.

"Well, if no one has told you yet, welcome to Chatelaine."

"Thanks." Her deliberate movements and her silence gave a clear message. She didn't want to talk about herself.

Devin set the question he really wanted to ask aside— why *had* she moved there? No one relocated to Chatelaine without a reason.

They finished sorting through the disks. He left Morgana to search through them and went back to the conference room.

A couple of hours later as he headed to his office, he glanced toward where Morgana worked. She was still at it. He should probably check and see how it was going. Just as he reached the threshold of the spare office, Morgana barreled out, almost running into him.

"Oh." She gave him a polite smile. "I was coming to find you. I'm done. I wasn't sure what to do with the disks I was sorting through, so I left them on the desk."

"That's fine. Are you sure you won't be back? I can leave them out for you."

"No, but thanks for your help. I'm good."

But her expression reflected the opposite of good as she turned away. She looked kind of rattled.

Morgana left, and he went inside the spare office. As he went to put the disks back into the box, papers in the trash basket caught his eye.

He took them out and flattened them on the desk. From the way they were crumpled, they'd gotten caught in the printer.

Most of the main text was unreadable, but the headlines of the articles jumped out. *Worst Mining Disaster in History of Chatelaine... Bodies of 50 Victims Found in Silver Mine... Locals Demand Answers about the Mining Accident...*

She'd been researching the 1965 Fortune silver mine

collapse? That seemed pretty specific considering Morgana had said she didn't know what she was looking for.

Devin slid the pile of disks she'd searched through closer to the computer and sat behind the desk. A stack of invoices waited for him in his office, but he would get to them later. Logically, the last disks she'd searched were on top.

Following Morgana's trail, he found the articles with the headlines on the crumpled pages and printed them out.

The articles had a few things in common. Their focus wasn't so much on the accident itself but the aftermath and speculation. And aside from Edgar and Elias Fortune, another name was prominent on the page. The mine foreman, Clint Wells, who'd also died in the collapse. They all seemed to point the blame to him.

Going with his instincts, Devin switched to searching for death announcements after the mining disaster and found one for Mr. Wells. He was survived by his wife Gwenyth and an eighteen-year-old daughter, Renee.

Devin sat back in the chair. Interesting.

The alarm on his phone chimed. *Carly...* She was at an after-school club meeting, and he was supposed to pick her up. If he was late, Lauren wouldn't hesitate to point that out during their first meeting with the mediator tomorrow morning.

He quickly put away the disks, shut down the computer, then hurried out the building to his truck.

All the while, his mind raced with thoughts of Morgana searching for information on the silver mine. Did she know something about those notes that had been left about there being a fifty-first miner who had perished? Or was her interest in the accident just a coincidence?

CHAPTER ELEVEN

BEA CARRIED AN order of Gulf shrimp and green-chili cheddar grits from the bustling kitchen into the dining room of the Cowgirl Café.

The clinking of glasses and silverware reverberated along with the murmur of conversations. And there were lots of satisfied smiles from the customers enjoying their meals.

She caught the eye of the blonde server who'd needed the order on-the-fly. The young woman had accidently keyed in the wrong item for one of her tables.

As the server rushed over to Bea, a look of relief was on her face. "Thank you."

"You're welcome." Bea gave her a reassuring smile.

Mistakes were bound to happen. But luckily nothing major, like stolen food, had occurred with tonight's rescheduled grand opening. The dining room was full, and although they hadn't experienced a huge rush as anticipated, business had been steady since they'd opened for dinner two hours ago. She was just grateful that so many people *had* decided to give her a second chance despite the comments online and the question about whether she deserved one.

I'm the newspaper's anonymous restaurant critic... I'm sorry, Bea. You have every right to be angry with me. But as a restaurant critic, I couldn't show my bias no matter how I feel about you. This may be hard for you to believe right now, but my interest in you didn't just start the day of the wedding...

Devin's admission last week in the parking lot of the Saddle & Spur Roadhouse had floored her. And for some reason the content of the review had struck even harder knowing he was the source. Devin wasn't an anonymous stranger. He was someone she knew so intimately they were expecting a child together.

She'd received the results of the blood test yesterday from her doctor, confirming the pregnancy tests she'd taken and what she innately knew. But it still felt so surreal, especially since her first prenatal appointment wasn't for at least another six weeks. The biggest reminder that she was about to be a mom was the prenatal vitamins she'd started taking every day.

A server rushing through the dining room carrying empty plates briefly paused next to her. "Tanya needs you."

The next couple of hours were almost a blur as Bea moved from task to task, jumping in to expedite meals in the kitchen, clearing dirty dishes from tables in the dining room, and checking in with customers about their meals and the service.

Toward the front of the dining area, a dark-haired woman sitting by herself at a corner table drew her attention. She was trying to take bites from a biscuit in between soothing the fussy infant in her arms. Makeup adorned her face, but it didn't hide her harried expression. She finally gave up on eating and focused on the baby.

Bea wrestled with the vision of herself being in the same situation. A sense of loneliness weighed down on her, mirroring what she'd felt that day buying the pregnancy test.

A tall, dark-haired guy walked into the restaurant carrying flowers. Spotting the woman with the baby, he hurried over to her.

Relief crossed the woman's face. He leaned down, and they shared a quick peck on the lips. Moments later, he sat across from her holding the baby. With the flowers lying beside her, the woman smiled as she dug into her salad.

Bea felt happy for her. The young mom wasn't alone. She had someone to share in the responsibility of caring for the child. And to support her as well. The man sitting with the baby might have been there for prenatal visits. The first ultrasound where they'd heard their child's heartbeat. Childbirth classes and the moment their child had entered the world.

At least that was what she imagined had happened for the couple. And possibly wanted for herself.

Devin had mentioned not wanting her to be alone or even feeling that she was on her own when it came to the baby—financially, emotionally, or on any other level.

It will be easier if you let me be there for you...

His words floated in her mind along with his apology and explanation for the critical review of her restaurant. He'd been honest with her. Wasn't that important? And now that the grand opening had occurred, did it even matter? Maybe it was time to set all that aside and focus on what was ahead.

Toward the end of the night, when business had slowed down, she slipped into her office and made a call.

He answered on the second ring. "Hello, Bea."

"Hi, Devin." Before she changed her mind, she pushed ahead. "Is there any chance we could talk tonight? I'm still at the restaurant, but I'll be free in an hour or so."

"Sure. Do you want me to come to you, or do you want to come here? I'm at home."

Once the restaurant closed, she wouldn't want to hang around. But meeting at her house could remind them of the awkwardness they'd experienced right after their perfect night together had gone sideways.

"I'll come to you."

Later on as she drove to his house outside Chatelaine, Bea practiced what she wanted to say to Devin.

"I would appreciate your help through the pregnancy. And of course I want you in our baby's life. But we should discuss the parameters, especially for the future."

A future that would include co-parenting their child for at least eighteen years.

But even after their child was on their own, she and Devin would be linked forever. Even if they weren't together.

She was attracted to Devin but rushing things along because of the baby would be a mistake. Sobering reality made Bea swallow hard. She'd pushed full speed ahead in marrying Jeff. Looking back, she'd deluded herself into believing she was taking a leap of faith. She'd convinced herself they were meant to be together while ignoring all the red flags that clearly indicated they shouldn't have.

After the divorce, she'd promised to never set up herself or anyone else for disappointment in a relationship by not facing facts. It had been easy to keep that promise since she hadn't found someone who'd piqued her interest in spending time with them. *Until Devin.* After their one night together, she'd started to think what more time with him might look like. Well, now she'd gotten that and then some—just not in the way she'd envisioned.

Bea parked in front of Devin's home. The stucco-and-brick ranch-style dwelling with a neatly trimmed lawn was similar to other houses on the street. At close to ten at night, the neighborhood was quiet.

As she stood at the front door, despite the dryness in her throat, she felt ready to embark on one of the most important conversations of her life. However, when the door opened, she couldn't speak.

Dressed in a burgundy T-shirt that clung to his muscular chest and a pair of black sweatpants, Devin was the perfect advertisement for casual, sexy, and relaxed. But as she looked into his eyes, she could see hints of apprehension.

"Hello." He stepped back and opened the door wider. "Come in."

"Thank you."

Their polite, stilted exchange felt out of place. Especially since the clean, freshly showered scent emanating from him as she walked inside made her want to throw herself into his arms and get up close and personal with him.

But she probably smelled like the café's entire menu—with an extra helping of Italian dressing courtesy of when a server had lost their grip on a salad they were carrying and accidently dumped most of it on her leg. She'd dabbed the stain, but the smell of vinegar and spices remained.

Devin shut the door behind her. "I was working in the living room. We can talk in there."

She followed him.

A light fixture with a ceiling fan illuminated the space. Looking around, she noticed a crime drama playing on the television hanging on the wall across from a beige couch with camel-colored pillows that matched the side chairs.

Devin's laptop sat on the wood coffee table next to a plate with crumbs and a small pile of potato chips.

On the floor near the couch sat a new, plush-looking dog bed filled with packages of toys as well as harnesses and leashes.

"Excuse the mess. I bought a few things for the dog I'm fostering." He moved the pet supplies to the empty dining area.

"When are you picking him up?"

"This coming Saturday," he replied.

As she sat in one of the side chairs, the story he'd told her about Chumley came to mind. "Is it another Great Dane?"

"No. It's a terrier mix this time. His owner is moving to a senior-living apartment and can't take the dog with him."

"Oh no! That's so sad."

"It is. But the shelter is really successful in finding pets new homes."

"That's good." As Devin stood by the couch, she met his gaze. The speech she'd practiced felt like an awkward lead-in to the next topic of conversation. But what *should* they talk about?

As the pause stretched on, she looked away from him and her gaze landed on the plate of chips. The Cobb salad she'd nibbled on around noon was a distant memory. She'd tasted a few of the entrées before dinner service, but that had been only a few bites and not a complete meal.

Her stomach gurgled.

If she were sitting on the couch, she might have snagged a few chips to stave off hunger.

Devin picked up the plate. "Can I get you anything?"

Her stomach answered with a full-on growl.

He arched a brow. "When did you last eat?"

The way he pinned her with his dark brown gaze was like a dose of truth serum. "I tasted a few of the entrées with Tanya before dinner."

"Turkey or ham?"

"We don't serve turkey on the menu…and that's not what you're talking about."

"No. I'm going to make you a grilled sandwich, and I was wondering which one you wanted. Or you can have both."

A hint of amusement came into his eyes and a faint

smile shadowed his mouth. A recollection of the many kisses they'd shared—luxuriously long, intensely passionate, spicy yet sweet—passed through her mind.

Her mouth started to water. Could she have a sandwich *and* a smooch on the side? "Turkey would be great."

"What about cheese? I have cheddar or Swiss."

"Swiss, please, and a little mustard." Did that request sound like a demand? He wasn't running a restaurant. "Actually, I don't mind doing it. Just point the way."

She moved to stand, but he waved her off. "No. You've been running around all night. Relax... I've got this."

He left, and a short time later, she heard sounds echoing from the kitchen.

It was strange having a guy wait on her like this.

Restlessness almost brought Bea to her feet. She occupied the time by taking advantage of the moment to see what the simple furnished space told her about Devin.

Aside from the laptop and dog paraphernalia, the only other things that gave a peek into his life was a small stack of mail on the coffee table and framed photos of him with Carly at various ages on the media console.

Devin returned carrying a plate with the sandwich cut in half with chips on the side. He was also holding a glass of lemonade. He handed her the food, then snagged a piece of junk mail to put under the glass on the coffee table.

"Thank you. But I don't think I can eat all of this." She took a bite of the heated sandwich, and a grateful moan slipped out. "This is so good."

"You're welcome. Sit back and enjoy it. Don't worry about leftovers." He sat down and started watching television.

Bea took several more bites before remembering why she was there. But fortunately, she didn't feel self-conscious at all not talking and just eating. The awkwardness she'd felt earlier had transformed into a comfortable silence.

He looked relaxed as well. The space on the couch next to him looked like the perfect spot to be. It was too easy to imagine herself there with her shoes off and her feet curled underneath her as she rested her head on his shoulder.

Suddenly, she felt lonely in the side chair.

After finishing almost three-quarters of the sandwich and all the chips, she put the plate on the table and picked up the glass of lemonade. It was just the right combination of cold, tart, and sweet.

Devin glanced over at her. "Better?"

"Yes. And you don't have to say it."

"Say what?" he asked lightly.

"That I have to do a better job of taking care of myself…now that I'm pregnant."

"You should take care of yourself in general, but yes, now that you're pregnant, skipping meals isn't a good idea."

"I know." She sighed. "Today was just so busy. Now that the grand opening is over, I can focus on other things."

"Did everything go well tonight?"

"It did. We had a full house. And everyone seemed pleased with the food." Curiosity made her ask. "So will my restaurant receive a review?"

"It will. But not by me, of course. I'm more than a little biased about the owner. So aside from a little hungry, how are you feeling?"

"Correction—I *was* hungry. But honestly, I don't feel any different than I did a few weeks ago. But that will change." It was time to stop stalling and get to why she was there. Bea put the glass on the table. "Thank you for giving me time to think about everything. Of course I want you to be in our baby's life, but like I said before, I don't want you to feel pressured to be there."

"I don't." Devin rose from the couch. After moving the plate and the glass with the junk mail aside, he sat on the coffee table in front of her. "And like I said before, I don't want to just know my child. I would like to get to know you as well. I like you a lot, Bea. And I think you like me, too. Or am I wrong…?"

Denying she still wanted to jump him in a very good way wouldn't get her anywhere. "No, you're not wrong. But attraction doesn't make a relationship."

"But it's a start. I know you and I had agreed to one night together, but I can't lie. My plan had been to ask if you would consider going out with me again once things settled down for you. And yes, I would have confessed that I was the restaurant critic." He took hold of her hand. "All I would have wanted then and still want now is a chance for us to get to know each other."

The guy she'd been crushing on like a schoolgirl for months wanted a chance with her. It was like a moment out of romance movie. But this wasn't a scripted scene. This was *real life*…and there was a baby to think about.

She met his gaze. "We have to take it slow. No rushing into anything. And if it doesn't work for us to be together, we have to be ready to accept that."

"I agree with all of that, but I have a question."

"What?" she asked a bit anxiously.

"Does taking it slow include holding you?"

"Yes." His huge grin eased her nerves and made her smile. "What are you smiling so big about?"

He tugged her to her feet and led her to the couch. "I'm happy you didn't hesitate in answering me."

As soon as they sat down, Bea did what she'd longed to do. She kicked off her shoes and curled up next to him.

His chest rose and fell under her palm with a deep breath. "This is better."

"It is." She hadn't realized how badly she'd needed to be held. Bea laid her head on his shoulder. "So, we've agreed to get to know each other. What happens next?"

CHAPTER TWELVE

DEVIN LOADED THE pet carrier and leash into the back seat of his truck parked in front of his house. He'd spend the morning proofreading the final version of the newspaper before sending it to the printer. After that, he would pick up Bea at the restaurant around noon for their first date. They were going to the pet shelter to get Francis.

The first few days with a rescue animal were critical. Francis was probably missing his owner. The pup might want extra attention, or he could be withdrawn. All Devin could do was try to make Francis comfortable and convey that he was there for him. Given time, the dog would come to realize he was safe.

That sense of being there and safety was what he wanted Bea to feel in their relationship as well.

The one thing that was clear—chemistry existed between them. It had been there from the start. That part of their connection had led them to their one night together, but Bea becoming pregnant could lead to a relationship that went beyond co-parenting. Exploring that possibility didn't feel like rushing to him but a natural next step. But he had to respect that Bea felt differently.

When she'd mentioned that she hadn't been able to conceive eight years ago, he'd sensed that she hadn't received support or maybe even compassion from her now ex-husband. It was understandable that she might want to keep her guard up and not risk getting hurt again.

Done packing up pet supplies, Devin got behind the wheel, started the engine, and headed for work. Traffic leading out of the neighborhood was sluggish, and a few miles down the road he found out why. Construction was happening, and there was a detour before the main road.

Following the directions of the worker managing traffic, he turned left.

Looks like I'm taking the scenic route... Devin settled in for a longer ride to town.

Homes sat back from the side of the road. Every now and then, he passed a ranch and open pastures with cows or horses.

He didn't travel this way often, but he recognized the area. He was just a few miles from Fortune's Castle.

The detour ended.

Turning right would lead him back to the four-lane road that would take him to town. But if he went left...

Giving in to the impulse, Devin made a left turn. A short time later, he turned right onto a long tree-lined private driveway. Up ahead, a security gate stretched across the narrow road sat open, and he drove past through it. Yards away in the distance sat Fortune's Castle.

A short time later, he walked up the cobblestone pathway toward the replica of a medieval castle. The decades-old concrete structure boasted so many features, it was hard to decide what to focus on first—ornate pointed arches, flying buttresses, gargoyles, or the stained-glass windows.

He'd been there once with his father when he'd been a boy. Carl had been covering a special event. The grounds had been open to the public but not the castle.

Devin reached the large wooden door. A speaker was built into the wall on the left, but there wasn't an intercom button. He used the ornate knocker shaped like a lion's head in the middle of the door.

Wendell refusing to speak with him was the worst that could happen. Other than that, Devin had nothing to lose.

The older man's voice came through the speaker. "Hello?"

"Hello, Wendell. It's Devin from the *Chatelaine Daily News*."

"Who?"

He spotted a camera up high and off the side and looked straight into it. "It's Devin Street. We've met before. I own the local newspaper."

"I know who you are. What do you want?"

"I'm hoping you can clear up some new information I came across about the silver mine accident." Wanting to get Wendell's attention, he added, "There's a young woman in town looking into it as well. Maybe you know her?"

A click echoed from the door as Wendell answered through the speaker. "Come in."

Devin opened the door and walked into a grand entryway with black-and-white checkerboard floor tiles. An elaborate wrought-iron candelabra hung from the ceiling painted with a Byzantine-style mosaic of peacocks and birds.

Black torch-shaped sconces interspersed with paintings of medieval lords and ladies in outdoor landscapes lined the left side of the wall along with abbey bench seats.

A sweeping ruby-colored carpeted staircase led up to the landing of the second floor.

Whoa... The rumors were right. The castle was strange and oddly magnificent at the same time.

Devin walked to the middle of the entryway and stood by a round glass table. The base of it was three knights in coats of armor holding swords and shields while on bended knee.

From what he'd heard, there were a lot of references to the number fifty cleverly embedded in the paintings and the artwork. And trying to find them was equivalent to a scavenger hunt. That wasn't surprising considering how the older generations of the Fortune family were all a big mystery.

"Wendell?" he called out.

A door on the right framed by an arch opened.

Wendell stood in the doorway. "I'm here."

The older man's bushy gray beard almost swallowed his gaunt face. A gray cardigan, white button-down and jeans hung loosely on this thin frame.

Devin walked to Wendell. "Thanks for taking a minute to talk to me this morning."

As they shook hands, Wendell's grip was weak and his hand felt cold and frail. Weariness shadowed his blue eyes. "You drove all the way out here. You must have something important to ask."

Important? Wendell clearly wasn't well. Maybe Devin shouldn't have disturbed him. A hint of regret pinged inside of him as he followed the older man inside the room.

"Have a seat." Wendell shuffled across the black-and-silver rug and dropped into the leather chair behind a large, polished wood desk. Behind him, floor-to-ceiling shelves with books filled the entire wall.

Devin sat in the red upholstered chair across from him. He pulled up the Notes app on his phone. "The questions I have won't take up too much of your time. I've been looking through a series of articles written by the paper about the mining accident. One name keeps popping up— Clint Wells."

"That's not surprising." Wendell's face remained neutral as he settled himself in the chair. "He was the foreman."

"Yes. And he had a wife, Gwenyth, and an eighteen-year-old daughter, Renee. Do you remember what happened to them?"

"They left town soon after the accident. I don't know where they went, and it's been my understanding that no one's heard from them since."

"Clint was initially blamed for the accident. Did anyone attempt to let them know other parties may have been involved and that he possibly wasn't to blame?"

Wendell's eyes briefly narrowed as he cleared his throat. "By *other parties*, you mean my brothers, Edgar and Elias."

"Yes. The accusations were damning and most likely led to them leaving town."

"As far as I know, no one reached out to them with that information. And it might not have made a difference to them. Clint was gone along with the other forty-nine miners."

"Or possibly fifty-one miners, like the notes have claimed?"

Agitated, Wendell waved him off. "Clint's widow is in her eighties now, and their daughter is in her fifties. I'm sure they would just like to continue to go on with their lives. No one wants to remember that terrible time."

"Respectfully, I have to disagree. The person who wrote the notes does. And a young woman spent most of an afternoon in my office looking up this information."

"A young woman? Who?" Wendell demanded.

"Her name is Morgana. She's new to the area."

"I don't know who she is. And I don't have the answer to your questions."

The old man's implacable expression signaled the meeting was over.

Devin stood. "Well, I appreciate your time. And if you do remember something, I hope you'll reach out to me so we can get the real story on record and end the speculation."

Wendell opened his mouth as if to say something but paused. "I'll keep that in mind. Forgive me for not walking you to the door. I'm a little tired."

"Not at all. I'll show myself out." Devin went to the office door. Before he walked out he looked back.

Wendell was staring at a series of black-and-white photographs in silver frames hanging on the side wall. As he rested a hand on his forehead, he sank wearily back in his seat.

LATER THAT AFTERNOON, Devin was on the road with Bea headed to the Chatelaine Veterinary Clinic, where the pet shelter was located.

She looked casual and cute in jeans, a peach-colored sweatshirt, and tennis shoes.

They were just outside of town. Traffic on the four-lane road started to thin out as cars pulled into the parking lot of the Saddle & Spur Roadhouse and, farther up, GreatStore.

Devin glanced over at Bea. She hadn't said much since he'd picked her up. Last night, she'd told him things were going well at the restaurant. Had that changed?

Settling in for the half-hour ride, he set the cruise control for a little higher than the speed limit. Visiting Fortune's Castle had put him behind schedule. "Thanks for coming with me this afternoon. I know you're busy. Now that the opening is over, how are things going?"

"Good." A distracted expression was on her face as she smiled. "What about you?"

"The usual. The paper is with the printer now, and we're not anticipating any major distribution issues tomorrow. And I'm working on stories for the next edition." He cleared his throat, then went on to say, "Oh, and I went to see your uncle today. I wanted to talk to him about the foreman who'd worked at the Fortunes' silver mine when the accident happened."

"That was nice." Bea tucked a strand of hair behind her ear and looked out the window.

Nice? Had she even heard him? "Space creatures from Venus were involved."

"Venus?" She looked at him. "What are you talking about?"

"Just checking to see if you were with me. You seemed preoccupied about something."

"I am...just a little." She sighed. "Okay, maybe more than a little. I came across an article online with information for expectant moms, and I kind of fell down a rabbit hole."

"I'm guessing it was a deep one?"

"Yes. There were all these lists." She grimaced. "Actually they were lists within a list within another list."

He furrowed a brow. "What do you mean?"

"For instance, on the newborn-essentials checklist, there's baby gear, and all the stuff needed for feeding, and diapering. And then there were suggestions from real moms about what to do and what not to do. The diapering issue...wow. I didn't know there was such a huge debate about cloth or disposable. I usually like lists, but this was...intimidating."

The days of parental judgment and guilt in figuring out what to do with a newborn...he remembered them well. It wasn't surprising Bea was feeling overwhelmed. "From my experience, while lists can be helpful, everyone's childcare experiences are different. You'll find ways and hacks for circumstances that work for you."

Bea gave him a skeptical look. "Including diapering hacks?"

"As strange as that may sound, yes. I still remember a few. Things like using a practical onesie versus those ones with all the snaps and buttons. When you're changing lots of diapers—trust me, simple is the way to go. And having an emergency diaper stash in almost every room and the car is a must."

She laughed. "It sounds like you're remembering just fine."

"I'm sure more will come back to me. But at the same time, after thirteen years, I'm sure some of the practices have changed."

"I thought sorting through food recipes to find the right one was stressful." Bea worried her lower lip, then sighed. "There's just so much to take in."

Devin reached out and laid his hand over Bea's resting on her thigh. "But you don't have to take it in all at once. The key is don't be afraid to ask, especially when you need something from me."

"You're right," she replied softly.

Most of the apprehension left Bea's face, but from the look in her eyes, something was still on her mind.

CHAPTER THIRTEEN

As Devin gave her hand a squeeze, she conjured up a smile, but she couldn't entirely let go of the anxiety hovering inside of her.

The lists in general were overwhelming, but one in particular remained on her mind—the parenting questionnaire.

Homebase for the baby. Prearranging a childcare schedule. Health insurance. There were so many things she and Devin needed to discuss before the baby arrived. He was right about not having to do everything right away. But even so, she needed to know where his responsibilities would begin and end.

"If I sent you the lists, would you take a look at them? And there's a parenting questionnaire, too."

"Of course I will. Email them to me."

Bea released an easy breath. Her ex would have given her a thousand and one reasons why he couldn't read them.

"We're here." Devin pointed to a long white building with green trim surrounded by open land.

There was a simplicity to the place, and it had a sanctuary vibe.

"It's a veterinarian clinic," he added. "And it also has a pet spa, and they provide space for the fostering and adoption service."

He pulled in and parked.

They got out, and Bea preceded him down the sidewalk to the entrance.

Inside the building, in the tidy reception area with orange seating along the wall, owners and their pets waited to see the vet.

The receptionist at the front desk greeted them.

"Hello," Devin replied. "I'm here to pick up a dog I'm fostering for the shelter. My name is Devin Street."

The woman checked her computer screen. "Yes, they're expecting you. One of the volunteers will meet you in the play area. Do you know where that is?"

"I do. Thanks." Devin led the way down an adjoining hallway.

They exited at the end into an outdoor space with colorful ramps and slides in various configurations arranged on fake turf.

A teenage boy was cleaning up a square patch of real grass off to the side. From the scowl on his face, he was the very definition of boredom and unhappiness.

Chuckling, Devin murmured, "Guess his day isn't going well."

"Give him a break. Would you be smiling if you were spending a sunny Saturday picking up dog poop?"

"It's a character-building experience." He shrugged. "When I was his age, I spent a lot of weekends doing things that weren't fun."

"Like what?" Bea asked.

"I washed my dad's car. Mowed the lawn, and it wasn't a tiny patch like that one. It was a couple of acres. And I also folded most of the newspapers for Sunday's home delivery, and I even had my own paper route."

"You *were* busy." It wasn't surprising to hear that even growing up Devin had had a full schedule.

"Looking back, I guess I was—partly because I was an

only child and didn't have a sibling to share the load. But mostly because my dad wanted to keep me out of trouble."

"You caused trouble?" She feigned shock. "No, I don't believe that."

He laughed. "Wait a minute. You have doubts? Okay, what about you? Did you have chores growing up, or did you just play all day?"

"*Play all day?* I wish. I rotated through chores along with Esme and Asa. Laundry, mowing the lawn, taking out the garbage."

"What about cooking? Did you guys help out with that, too?"

"Asa and Esme, not so much. But I didn't mind. Helping my mom in the kitchen was our special time together. While we cooked, I could really talk to her about things." A twinge of nostalgia hit Bea. Her mom had always had the answers, even when it had come to the most challenging things. What she wouldn't give to hear her mom's advice now that she was an expectant mother-to-be.

A couple of tears leaked from her eyes. Bea was shocked to feel them on her cheeks. Were pregnancy hormones kicking in this soon?

Looking down, she quickly batted them away. "Sorry— I don't know why I'm crying."

"Because you miss her." Devin traced a tear from her cheek. "And that's okay. I miss my dad, too."

"Our child won't have grandparents..." The realization made her a bit sadder.

"But they'll have plenty of aunts and uncles—and cousins on your side of the family. And Carly as an older sister." He cupped her cheek. "And they'll have us."

The warmth of his touch enveloped her. It was so natural to move closer and lean into his one-arm embrace.

An older woman with black-and-silver hair styled in a casual updo walked out the door. A high school–aged girl followed her, leading a Jack Russell–cocker spaniel, mixed-breed dog on a leash. They both wore short blue aprons over their clothes featuring the name of the shelter.

The woman strode toward them. "Hi—you must be Devin. I'm Meg."

"Yes, hello." Devin shook hands with her. "Meg, this is Bea." As he turned toward Bea, he gently laid a hand on her back.

She returned the woman's smile. "Hello."

Meg looked to the teen and the small brown-and-white dog who was off the leash and sniffing near a bench. "This is Emma, one of our student volunteers, and that's Francis. He's three years old. As you know, his owner couldn't care for him any longer. He dropped him off a little over a week ago. I actually thought we had an adoption lined up for the pup yesterday, but it fell through. I'm so glad you can take him in."

"I'm happy to help," Devin said. "How's he been adjusting through the change?"

"As expected, he was withdrawn at first, but he's interacting with everyone more now. We think he'll do much better in a home setting. While you two get acquainted with him, I'll get his things. He has a dog bed he's partial to, and we're going to give you a bag of what we've been feeding him. Oh, and you'll need this." She took a worn-looking yellow ball from the pocket of her apron and handed it to Bea. "This is his favorite toy. Maybe he'll play with you a bit. It might help him feel more comfortable in leaving with you."

As Bea turned to give the ball to Devin, Francis shyly approached, eyeing the toy. He lay down a few feet away and dropped his head onto his front paws.

Devin held up his hands, refusing the toy. "I think Francis wants his possession back."

Unsure of what to do, she shrugged. "Do I just throw it?"

"No. Lay it on the ground. Let's see if he'll come to us to get it."

"Hi, Francis. Do you want your ball?" Bea leaned over, and as she set the ball down, the pup lifted his head. "Now what?"

"We talk to each other. Direct eye contact can be perceived as threatening to a dog, especially if he doesn't know you."

Bea turned to Devin. "So we just stand here?"

"For a little bit."

She chuckled. "This feels like an audition."

"Relax. You're doing fine," he assured her.

The wind blew a strand of hair near her eyes.

Devin reached up and smoothed it back behind her ear. As his hand lingered, his gaze dropped to her lips.

Bea's heart skipped several beats. Despite wanting to, she still hadn't kissed him yet. Memories of how their lip-locks had ignited like sparks to flame their one night together played through her mind. Kissing him would probably make taking things slow a really torturous experience.

He glanced to the side. "Looks like we have a visitor."

Francis stood at Bea's feet. His liquid brown eyes tugged at her heartstrings, and she offered him her hand. He sniffed it. His tail wagged a little, and she kept petting him.

Devin greeted Francis, and they both interacted with him. After a while, the pup became more comfortable, and when Bea lobbed the ball a short distance away, he returned it.

"I think he's ready to go now." Devin went to get the crate.

Bea scratched Francis behind his ears and cooed,

"You're going to a nice safe place, and we're going to take good care of you." Wait. No, not *we*—Devin.

Meg walked over to Bea. "I can tell Francis is going to be in good hands." She beamed a friendly smile. "Once he gets used to his surroundings, he'll be a charmer. And he's definitely baby-tester material for the right couple."

Baby? Bea barely stopped herself from laying a hand on her abdomen. But there was no way this woman could know that she was pregnant.

"I'm sorry." Meg's smile sobered a little. "My little joke didn't go over well. Sometimes couples adopt a fur baby in preparation for a real one."

"Oh, but we're not..." Bea stumbled over what to say. She and Devin weren't a couple, but they were expecting.

He returned with the carrier. "Okay, Francis, let's go for a ride."

Once the dog was settled, they were ready to leave. After saying goodbye to Meg, they retraced their steps down the hall, through the reception area and out the door.

They secured the carrier with Francis on the back seat.

As Devin shut the back passenger side door, he smiled at Bea standing beside the truck. "Thanks again for coming. You made the transition a whole lot easier for him."

"I'm glad I could help. It gives me hope." She laughed. "If I can handle a dog, then maybe I can handle a baby."

"You can. You're compassionate. You care. You're going to be a great mom, Bea."

The assurance in his eyes almost erased her doubts. "You really think so?"

He lightly grasped her shoulders. "I do."

Bea laid her hands on his chest. Devin was so solid and real with his intentions. It was hard not to lean on him.

As she moved closer, he glided his hands toward her back.

"Um…excuse me." Emma stood nearby, holding up a leash. She looked between the two of them with a curious, slightly judgy expression. "This belongs to Francis. He's used to using it. Meg said you should take it with you."

"Thanks." As Devin accepted the leash, Bea got into the truck.

He went around to the other side. After settling into the driver's seat, he put his phone in the open section of the center console.

Bea remained baffled by the girl. "Did you see the way she looked at us? I feel like I'm her age again and just got caught making out with my boyfriend."

"Teens are like that when it comes to PDA. Carly's the same way."

"So what will you tell her about us?" she asked.

"That depends on you. Do you want to wait a while before officially telling everyone about the baby?"

She pursed her lips, contemplating. "Maybe we *should* wait. It's still early."

"Okay, we wait." Devin turned to look at her. "And what about us? Are we telling people that we're seeing each other?"

"I guess there's no point in hiding it. In fact, I think it would be impossible."

He quirked a brow. "Why's that?"

"Because when we're together, we're not exactly keeping our hands off of each other."

"We're not?" He reached over and took her hand, intertwining their fingers.

She laughed.

He angled more toward her. "But I'm confused. Why is not being able to keep our hands off of each other a bad thing?"

From the look in Devin's eyes, he was far from confused, but Bea played along. "Because touching leads to kissing."

"That's just a theory."

"No, it's a fact." Giving in to what she'd wanted to do since last night, Bea leaned in and pressed her mouth to his.

As Devin cupped her cheek, she parted her lips and the kiss deepened.

Just as she'd suspected, the simmering embers of desire from their first night hadn't completely died away. A part of her crossed her fingers and toes, hoping their connection would only grow stronger. But practicality needled that hope. They would also face trials along the way.

The rattling of his phone buzzing in the console broke into the moment, and they eased out of the kiss.

Devin grabbed his phone, and as he checked the screen his expression sobered. "Damn," he whispered. "She already knows."

"She?" Bea glanced at his phone, then him. "You mean your ex-wife?"

Devin's jaw angled as another text came in. "No… Carly."

CHAPTER FOURTEEN

"So it's true?" Lauren's voice rose an octave. "What happened to our agreement about letting the other know about major changes in our lives?"

Devin took several steps toward the cluster of bushes on the back wall behind Lauren's house. She followed him.

They were yards past the deck and screened-in pool, but the window in Carly's room upstairs faced the backyard. She'd been in her room since hearing about Bea and the baby. And, not surprisingly, she was upset about what she'd found out.

Michaela and the damn pizza oven had struck again. Carly had been over at her friend's house when Michaela's older sister, Emma, had spilled the news. The same Emma who'd brought Francis to the outdoor play area and delivered the leash to him and Bea at the truck. She'd witnessed them together and overheard them talking about the baby.

Devin modulated his voice. "I didn't intentionally break our agreement. My relationship with Bea happened recently."

"And the two of you decided to have a baby already."

During the subsequent pause, as Lauren looked at his face, her eyes widened. "It wasn't planned? Well, that's definitely going to spice up the next birds-and-bees conversation I have with Carly. The good thing is you probably made the conversation about telling her she's moving to Corpus Christi a lot easier."

"Moving?" He worked to control his tone. "That's something we're still discussing with the mediator on Monday."

"Seriously? The main reason our marriage ended was because our relationship fell second or third to everything else. Do you really think you can balance having a baby, being the primary co-parent of our daughter, *and* running the newspaper?"

The main reason? Devin struggled to get past Lauren's claim about what had caused their marriage to collapse. They'd grown apart. At least that was how he saw it. But debating their points of view on why they'd divorced wouldn't change anything.

"I can't undo the past. But I can and will build a future that includes Carly, Bea, and the child she and I are having together."

As Lauren shook her head, exasperation filled her face. She opened her mouth to speak, then she shut it. "There's no point in discussing it now." She pointed to the house. "What are you going to tell our daughter?"

"The truth."

"If telling her the truth doesn't work, you're about to have an interesting week," Lauren told him. "I have to go to Corpus Christi for a meeting. I leave on Tuesday, and she's all yours until after her event on Saturday."

"What event?" he asked.

"The school fundraiser. I sent you the text the other day."

"Right. I'll handle it." Somehow he'd missed it. He'd search through his messages when he got home. But first he needed to straighten things out with his daughter.

Moments later, Devin sat with Carly at the patio table on the deck. Her arms were crossed over her chest. The stubborn look on her face as she stared out at the pool reminded him of Lauren.

"I'm sorry you found out about Bea and the baby this way," he said quietly. "We'd planned on telling you, your mom, and everyone else. We just wanted to wait a few more weeks."

Carly looked at him. Hurt shadowed the accusation in her eyes. "So you're getting married?"

He and Lauren had agreed it was important to tell the truth about his relationship with Bea. But they'd decided to still wait a while longer to tell Carly about Lauren's new job and working out a new custody agreement.

Devin rested his arms on the table. "Bea and I haven't discussed that. But we are committed to raising the baby." He leaned forward. "But none of that changes how I feel about you. I love you, Carly, and you are and will always be my daughter."

"But she'll be, like, my *stepmother*, won't she?" Carly hadn't put *wicked* in front of *stepmother*, but her tone more than implied it.

Of course, he hoped that Bea and Carly would grow closer. Having someone like Bea to turn to as well as him and Lauren could be a bonus for the teen. But he couldn't speak for Bea.

"The type of relationship you and Bea will have is something that will develop over time. My only hope is that when you meet Bea, you'll give her a chance."

"Are you sure inviting me to dinner was a good idea?" Bea straightened the placemats on the square table in Devin's kitchen for the second time. "Maybe we should have waited a few more weeks."

He removed silverware from a drawer then walked over to her. "I'm sure. You being here tonight *is* a good idea. Trust me."

Still, Bea couldn't shake off a feeling of doubt as he laid out the forks, knives and spoons.

Carly had just left to walk Francis a few minutes before she had arrived. If she left now, Devin could claim an emergency had happened at the restaurant and she'd had to leave.

Bea sunk her teeth into her lower lip, holding back on suggesting that to Devin. No. She'd agreed to join him and Carly for dinner, and she was going to see it through.

Schedule wise it worked out. It was Tuesday night, and things were slow at the café. Maybe that was a sign that she *should* be there. But realistically, they couldn't forget Carly had just found out about them that past Saturday. And that she had not only been upset about the news, but also how she'd heard about the situation.

Yesterday, Emma's mother had contacted her, apologizing for her daughter's behavior. She'd also said that if the teen or her younger sister Michaela repeated the news, by the time they got their phones back, the technology would be so obsolete they wouldn't remember how to use them.

Ouch. Bea almost felt sorry for the girls when their mom had mentioned that level of a restriction.

Devin turned Bea by the waist to face him. "I know you're anxious. And I have to admit, I'm a little nervous, too. But there's no point in holding this off. But when I asked Carly about you joining us for dinner, she was okay with it."

Bea glimpsed a hint of reservation in his eyes. "Is that really what she said?"

"No, she said, 'Whatever,' but in teen speak, that's as good as a yes. And honestly, I think that's the best answer we're going to get from her for now." He gave Bea a light squeeze. "She's not going to accept us overnight, but this is a start. And she has an event coming up that I told her you might be able to give her some advice on."

"What is it?"

"Nothing big. For extra credit in one of her classes, as a group, they had to organize a fundraiser. They're having a bake sale on Saturday. The proceeds will go to nonprofits in the area like the pet shelter and the Chatelaine Fish and Wildlife Conservation Society. She's not sure what to make. Talking about it with her could help break the ice."

"I hope so." Bea laid her hands on his chest. "The last thing I want is to come between you and your daughter. Or for our relationship to impact the custody agreement you're trying to work out with Lauren. You never told me how the meeting with the mediator went the other day."

He gave her a lopsided smile. "Well, Lauren and I definitely aired our grievances. But the mediator made valid points. Despite our differences, we both love our daughter and that has to be the guiding factor. He suggested we each draw up a day-to-day schedule as the primary co-parent. It would allow us to understand what the other wants and expects for Carly's care."

"So how do you see it working?"

"Well, when it comes to school, I don't see much changing, except for I'll be the one dropping her off. After school, she normally takes the bus home. When extra-curricular activities happen, we usually carpool with other parents. Day-to-day expectations and responsibilities won't change either."

Curious, Bea asked, "When will she see her mom?"

He released a breath. "From my point of view, I'm thinking two weekends a month and designated holidays. Which ones, I would like to leave that choice to Lauren and Carly."

And what about her and the baby? Concern rose in Bea

that he hadn't mentioned them in the plan. But surely, he was including them.

The front door opened.

"Dad!" Carly called out. "The food is here."

"Coming." Devin pressed a kiss near Bea's ear and whispered, "It's going to work. We've got this." He snagged the tip from the counter for the delivery person and went to meet them.

Jitters swirled in Bea stomach. *We've got this.* That meant he was thinking of them as a team, right? Maybe she was reading too much into what he hadn't said. It didn't mean he wasn't factoring her and the baby into the ultimate plan.

A moment later, Devin came back into the kitchen with the food. He set the bag on the counter. "Carly's washing her hands. She'll be here in a minute. I forgot to ask what you liked, so I got a variety. Fried rice, lo mein, egg rolls, and three different entrées. Hope you're hungry."

"I am." She'd had a full day and only eaten a muffin for breakfast and a salad for lunch. But she wasn't confessing that to Devin.

As he started putting containers on the counter, Bea caught a whiff of garlic. Usually, the pungent aroma raised anticipation for flavorful food, but the smell was like an assault on her senses. Had something gone bad?

Devin opened one of the boxes, and the smell grew stronger. "Mmm. Chicken in garlic sauce. Just the smell of this is making me extra hungry."

She surreptitiously covered her nose with her fingers and stepped back.

Carly walked into the kitchen.

Smiling, Devin placed his hand lightly on Bea's arm. "This is my daughter, Carly."

Bea could see Carly's resemblance to Devin. She had

his eyes and maybe his smile if she would have given a genuine one instead of what came with her slightly tart expression.

"Hello." Carly went to the refrigerator.

Devin spoke to Carly, "While you're in there, grab the iced tea." He gave Bea a reassuring glance as he gave her hand a brief squeeze.

They worked together bringing the food, drinks, and plates to the table, then sat down.

Devin nudged the container of chicken in garlic sauce toward Bea. "Carly and I have been known to fight over this, but as our guest, we'll give you first dibs."

"Oh, no—that's okay…"

Bea held her breath and quickly passed the container to Carly seated next to her. But the smell seemed to linger and her appetite started to wane. She put a little fried rice on her plate along with an egg roll.

Carly put some chicken and garlic sauce on her plate, then set the container between them. "You don't like the food?"

"No, it's great." Bea moved the container toward the middle of the table.

As Devin glanced at the small portion of food on her plate, she saw questions in his eyes. Earlier she'd told him she was hungry.

"So how are things at the café?" he asked.

Thankful for the change of topic, she told him briefly about the anniversary party they were catering.

"I'm sure the kids will enjoy the ice cream sundae bar," he said. "Too bad you can't do something like that at the fundraiser this weekend, Carly."

"It's a bake sale." Carly picked up the container of chicken and garlic. She added some to her plate, then plopped the container right next to Bea.

It tipped over, and some of the contents spilled out.

Bea's stomach roiled. If she didn't leave right now, she'd hurl. She stood. "Excuse me."

As she hurried from the kitchen and into the dining room, the sliding glass door with the view of the wide-open backyard caught her attention. Bea opened it, walked out on the deck, and sucked in fresh air.

Feeling a little shaky, she sat down on the porch swing. She'd never had that reaction to food before. How embarrassing.

Devin walked out onto the porch carrying a mug. "Are you all right?"

"Yes—I was just feeling a bit closed in." As he offered her the mug, she looked up at him. "What is it?"

"Ginger-and-lemon tea. I didn't put any sweetener in it. I have sugar or honey."

Bea inhaled the steam, then took a sip. The warmth of the beverage soothed her stomach. "This is perfect."

He sat beside her, and the swing rocked a little. "Why didn't you tell me the food didn't agree with you?"

"It wasn't all the food. Just the smell of the garlic in the sauce. You mentioned it was your and Carly's favorite. I didn't want to deprive you of it."

"You're pregnant, Bea. If certain tastes or smells get to you, you're allowed to speak up, especially to me." He laid his arm behind her on the swing.

"If this is the precursor to morning sickness, I think I'm in trouble." Following his lead, she rested her head on his shoulder.

"Hopefully the tea will help."

"Is there one that will help me give birth and learn how to be a parent? When the baby's here, I won't be able to cop out when I don't feel well." Reality broke through, and anxiety started to replace Bea's lightheartedness. "I'll be responsible for a small person who will depend on me for everything, but they won't be able to tell me what they need, and I'll probably get it wrong. And then they'll grow into a bigger person who will be able to tell me what they want, but I'll probably still get it wrong."

"You're getting way ahead of yourself." Devin kissed her temple. "Yes, parenting can be scary, and sure, sometimes kids are hard to figure out, but there will be good moments, too. And whatever comes our way, we'll go through the experience together. Okay?"

Bea looked at his face. Seeing the confidence in his dark brown eyes made it easy to believe him.

"Okay." She settled her head back onto his shoulder.

His solid strength, the tea, the sway of the swing. The bright hues of yellow and orange surrounding the setting sun. As Bea soaked it all in, she started to feel better… and her eyelids grew heavy.

Devin slipped the cup from her hand. "Do you want to stay the night? You can sleep in my bed, and I can spend the night in my office."

It would be so much better if he were in bed with her. Before the shocking moment of their birth-control fail, there had been that wonderful moment of waking up in his arms. They were taking it slow, but it would be nice to experience that again. But they couldn't tonight.

She eased into a sitting position. "No. I don't think that would go over well with Carly."

Sighing, he intertwined their fingers on his thigh. "I'm sorry she was so unfriendly."

A thought crept into Bea's mind. Had Carly kept putting the container of food between them on purpose? She almost asked the question. But if Devin didn't see it that way, it would sound like she was making an accusation against his daughter. And she and Carly had already gotten off to a rocky start.

Bea mirrored back the confidence Devin had shown earlier. "Like you said, she's not going to accept us overnight. We just have to give it time."

CHAPTER FIFTEEN

DEVIN STOOD IN the driveway watching Bea drive away. He'd offered to take her home, but she hadn't wanted to leave her car there.

She didn't live that far away, but he'd worry about her until he got the call or text that she'd made it safely to her condo.

Someday, hopefully soon, she'd feel comfortable enough to bring an overnight bag along when she visited and would just stay with him. But first, his daughter's attitude needed to change. If Carly would be living with him full-time, she'd have to get used to Bea and, later on, Bea and the baby being under the same roof as them.

Devin went into the house.

Carly sat curled up on the couch with a bowl of popcorn, happily watching television.

Once Bea had explained it was just the smell of the chicken in garlic sauce that had bothered her, more than a few things had fallen into place about why she'd had to leave the table at dinner.

Devin picked up the remote, turned off the television, then sat on the coffee table in front of his daughter.

"How's Bea?" Carly asked with an all-too-innocent look on her face.

"Better. So do you want to explain your behavior during dinner?"

"What do you mean?" she mumbled between bites of popcorn.

"You know *exactly* what I'm talking about. You noticed Bea had an issue with the chicken and garlic sauce, and instead of being sympathetic, you kept thrusting the container in her face. Why?"

"No, I—" Carly's expression was easy to read. Clearly she'd realized he wasn't in the mood for her shenanigans, so she wisely remained silent.

"I'm disappointed in your actions, and your mom will be, too. What you did goes against how we raised you. How would you feel if someone treated you the way you just treated Bea?"

A hint of guilt sparked behind the defiance in Carly's eyes. "You can't make me like her just because she's having a baby."

"Bea's not just having *a* baby. She's having *my* baby, who will also be your brother or sister." Devin tamped down parental frustration. Just like he was asking Carly to see things from Bea's point of view, he needed to view the situation from his daughter's.

"I love you, Carly. You're my daughter, and that will never change. But I also care about Bea and the baby, and nothing will change that, either. The only thing that can change is your attitude." He pinched the bridge of his nose, then took a slow, deep breath. "And there's something you should know. Bea was willing to assist you with your fundraising project before you treated her badly."

"She was?"

"Yes. And before she left, she still said she was willing to help. You can think about that while you do the dishes. And after that, you can go to your room. No screen time. You have to get up early so I can take you to school in the morning."

As he rose to his feet, Devin saw tears escape from Carly's eyes. He hated seeing her upset but wouldn't coddle her. And no, he couldn't make her accept Bea or that she would have a sibling. But she knew right from wrong.

Working at the desk in his home office, he kept glancing at his phone. Shouldn't Bea have made it home by now? Was she in trouble? He stopped his mind from wandering down the road of the worst possible scenarios.

Finally, she called, and he snatched up the phone to answer it. "Hello."

"Hi. I'm home." She sounded even more tired than when she'd left. And she hadn't really eaten anything, either. Just when he was about to mention that, she added, "Sorry for not calling you as soon as I got here. I heated up a bowl of soup first."

Hearing her voice was such a relief, but the reason for her not calling him right away was a good one. "What kind?"

"Homemade chicken noodle. I made it the other night. I think I have some bread left over, too."

Good. At least she was eating something fairly substantial. "Sounds perfect." He wasn't ready to end the call yet, but she was wiped out from a long day. "Make sure you get some rest, too."

"I will."

"Good night, Bea."

"Good night."

After hanging up, Devin sat back in the chair. If he were there, he would have heated the soup for her while she took a shower or a bath. Then he would have brought it to her while she relaxed in bed. And afterward, he would have held her as she'd fallen asleep.

A longing for her tugged at his heart.

Francis whining and nudging his leg brought Devin out

of his thoughts. The dog sat at his feet as if sensing his melancholy mood.

"I'm fine." Devin rubbed Francis's head and scratched behind the pup's ears.

But a small seed of self-doubt started to sprout. He'd thought he was ready for anything when it came to Bea, the baby and Carly. But could he balance being a dad of two? Was tonight's episode an indication that he couldn't?

That night, he restlessly dreamed of Bea reaching out for him. Just as he got to her, she slipped out of his arms and backed away.

When he woke up, he wished she was with him, and for more sleep. But he needed to walk Francis, and he wanted to make sure Carly had breakfast before he took her to school.

After returning from a longer-than-anticipated stroll with Francis, Devin woke up his daughter, then rushed through trimming his beard and a shower.

Oatmeal for breakfast would have been a nice healthy option. That was what Lauren would have made, but he also had to pack a bag for Francis, as he was taking the dog with him to the office. Cold cereal would have to do.

Devin set up everything on the table, then called out down the hallway, "Carly—breakfast."

She would be a while. The teen took forever to get ready in the morning.

He poured himself a mug of coffee, sat down, and started reviewing the *Chatelaine Daily News* online edition on his phone. It had gone live earlier that morning.

Carly trudged in wearing jeans and a pink sweatshirt. She'd pulled her damp curly hair into a ponytail, fully revealing her face.

Unable to gauge her mood, he fortified himself with a

sip of coffee before dealing with whatever state of mind she was in right then. "Good morning."

"Morning." She dropped into a chair at the table.

"Do you want toast?"

"No, thank you." Carly poured herself a bowl of cereal.

He switched from the online paper to his email. The first correspondence wasn't good news. A lead he'd been following on the whereabouts of Gwenyth and Renee Wells hadn't panned out. He wrote a thank-you response to the sender.

"Dad."

"Yes?"

"I'm sorry for being mean to Bea," Carly whispered.

Devin looked into her eyes. She meant it. "I appreciate the apology."

Carly toyed with the cereal floating in a bowl of milk. "I guess I should apologize to her, too."

"Yes, you should."

"I could go with you to work this morning and do it," she said.

"You're not missing school."

She offered up an exaggerated shrug. "I'm just trying to do things you and Mom raised me to do."

And she was trying to bargain like he'd done with his dad when he'd been her age. Carly was definitely his child.

Devin couldn't hold back a chuckle. "Nice try, Half Pint. Eat your cereal. We're leaving in twenty minutes."

LATER THAT AFTERNOON at the newspaper office, Devin multitasked at his desk, eating lunch and squeezing in a minute to work on his proposed schedule and co-parenting plan the mediator had suggested.

Carly staying with him this week was actually a bonus in helping him visualize his role as the primary parent.

His days would definitely be busier, but he could handle the changes. And Carly was old enough to take on a few more responsibilities—making her own breakfast, helping to keep the house tidy and learning to do the laundry, too.

His thoughts drifted back to that morning. He was glad that Carly had said she was sorry and wanted to apologize to Bea. That type of maturity showed she was growing up.

And it was a step in the right direction. If Carly and Bea could spend time together, he just knew they'd get along. Bea was fun-loving and patient, but she could also offer a firm guiding hand if needed. She doubted her ability to become a parent, but she was more equipped than she realized.

A few minutes later, Francis paced and sniffed in front of the closed door, signaling it was time for a break.

Done with his sandwich, Devin clipped the leash onto the dog's collar, grabbed a waste bag from a stash in the desk, and headed out from the office.

Late in the afternoon, only a few pedestrians were out, and an occasional car came by as he walked Francis to an open lot with a few bushes.

The Cowgirl Café was just down the street. A couple of staff members were being dropped off for work. He'd texted Bea that morning, checking on her before he'd gone to the office. But a message wasn't the same as hearing her voice.

As he waited for Francis to mark his territory, he phoned Bea.

She answered on the third ring. "Hey, Devin."

"Hey." Holding on to the leash, he followed the pup to the next bush he was curious about. "Francis and I are taking a short walk. Can you join us?"

"I really wish I could, but I have to finish taking inventory before we open. But I can pop out for a minute and say hi. Where are you?"

"Just down the street."

"Can you meet me in the parking lot near the side door in about ten minutes?"

He reached the café with time to spare. Francis alternated between sitting and walking near him. Most likely the dog was fidgeting around because he could sense his human's mood.

Devin crouched down and petted Francis. "It's okay. I'm just excited to see my girl."

My girl... As he thought about those last two words, contentment and happiness filled him. He couldn't help but smile. And as Francis wagged his tail, he seemed to be smiling with him.

Bea came out of the restaurant carrying two white paper bags. She held them up. "This one is for Francis. And this one is yours."

"That sounds confusing. Maybe this will help clear it up." Devin swooped in for a kiss.

As they started to ease apart, Bea's lips curved into a smile under his. "I hope it does. Otherwise you'll be eating leftover steak, and Francis will be enjoying your tartlets."

"I like tartlets, but I like the third option even more." He wrapped an arm around her waist and went back in for a longer kiss.

Francis threatening to lasso them with the leash brought it to an end.

Devin disentangled them.

"I should go back to work." Bea held out the bags.

He accepted them. "Before I forget, Carly wants to apologize to you for her behavior last night."

"Does she want to apologize, or did you tell her to?"

"She wants to." Bea's skeptical expression prompted

him to say more. "The only thing I mentioned to her last night was how disappointed I was in her behavior. She knows better. This morning at breakfast, she apologized to me and said she wanted to talk to you."

"Okay—if that's what she wants. I'll be free around eight tonight if she wants to call me."

He smiled at her. "I'll let her know."

As he took a step forward, the side door opened. A couple of the café's staff members came out for a break.

Reading Bea's body language, he took a step back. It wasn't about them hiding that they were together—she was the boss and wanted to keep certain boundaries in place. He could respect that.

"Thanks for the treats. Especially that third one."

She laughed. "You're more than welcome."

LATER THAT NIGHT, standing in the kitchen, Devin ate the last of the half dozen tartlets.

He and Carly had practically inhaled them after dinner.

Her animated voice floated in from the open sliding door. She was on the deck, talking with Bea over the phone. They'd been on the call a good fifteen minutes. The apology Carly was delivering must have been a huge one.

But the fact that it was taking so long was a positive thing, right?

The sliding door closed.

Carly breezed into the kitchen. "Bea wants to talk to you." She gave him his phone, then went back out through the other archway.

From her face, he couldn't gauge if Bea wanting to talk to him was a good or bad sign. Glancing at the screen, he was caught off guard to see Bea's image. From the background, she was in her office.

He hadn't realized it was a video call. "Hello."

"Hi." She tucked a strand of hair behind her ear. "So, we need to talk about something."

"Uh-oh, what happened?"

"Nothing bad." She laughed. "I've never heard you so serious."

"Well, Carly didn't give me a heads-up about how your talk went, so I'm not sure what to expect."

"It's all good. Or at least I think it is. Carly really liked the tartlets I gave you, and she wants me to help her make some for the bake sale. I wanted to check in with you first."

Devin leaned back against the counter. "I don't mind, as long as she's not infringing on your time. Did she tell you the bake sale is Saturday?"

"Yes, we can make them Friday afternoon. Carly said school is out an hour early for some reason?"

Was that this Friday? *Damn.* He'd thought it was next week. A sinkhole had opened up in a neighborhood the next town over, and he'd arranged to interview some of the residents.

"Yeah," he answered. "What time do you want to come by?"

"I was hoping Carly could come to my place. I'm not working on Friday. I'll already be at home. It would easier to do it there versus bringing everything to your house."

"That works." Devin calculated times in his mind. He could drop off Carly, go do the interviews, and be back around the time they were done. "Are you sure she doesn't need to bring anything? I'm happy to pick up the ingredients you need."

"No, that's fine." Bea met his gaze. She looked tired and pretty at the same time.

"Did you eat anything besides just tasting the entrees?"

"Yes. I had an entire chicken pot pie for dinner and a salad."

"I'm glad to hear that." He wished he could go see her, but it was getting late, and he couldn't leave Carly. "Francis really enjoyed his treat."

"I'm glad. And what about his foster guardian? Did he enjoy his?"

"Too much." Devin patted his stomach. "It's a good thing Francis is here to help me get some exercise."

"So I guess that means you won't be stopping by tomorrow for another bag of treats."

A grin broke through with his chuckle. "No, I will absolutely stop by, especially if more kisses are involved."

"I think that can be arranged." Bea's soft smile intensified his anticipation.

It grew so strong, in fact, that when he met Bea the next afternoon, he couldn't wait. As soon as she reached him, he took her in his arms.

When she met him halfway for the promised kiss, his heart leaped.

They eased back, and a soft smile even more beautiful than the one on her face last night lit up her eyes.

Taking it slow was impossible—he was already falling for her.

CHAPTER SIXTEEN

BEA DOUBLE-CHECKED THE BOWLS, utensils, and ingredients. The binder with her mom's recipes was also on the kitchen counter.

It was almost three o'clock. Carly would be arriving soon.

As the minutes ticked by, a sense of restless anxiety hit, and Bea resisted making sure everything was in place one more time. She and Carly were just making tartlets together. Why was she so darn nervous? Like *first day of school, wondering if she could make friends* nervous. But that was a weird take on the situation. Carly was thirteen, and she was a grown woman.

Still, she couldn't deny that she wanted Carly to see her as...what? She wasn't on the verge of becoming Carly's stepmom. She was just Devin's new girlfriend. And she would be the mother of Carly's half brother or sister. Whether or not she and the teen had a connection beyond that was yet to be seen.

Bea paced away from the counter. It would be so helpful to talk to Esme right now. But the newlyweds were on a warm, tropical beach enjoying time as a family. She wasn't going to interrupt them with her fears or her problems.

The doorbell rang, and she went to the door.

Devin and Carly stood outside. The teen had a backpack slung over her shoulder and held a bouquet of flowers in her hands.

"Come in." Bea waved them inside.

"These are for you." Carly offered her the bouquet of hydrangeas, roses, and lilies. "They're from Dad.

"No, they're from *both* of us," he interjected. "As a thank-you for your time."

"They're gorgeous and much appreciated." As she lifted the fragrant bouquet to her nose, her gaze landed on his mouth, and memories of kissing him yesterday afternoon flashed through her mind.

"Can I use your bathroom?" Carly asked.

Bea gave herself a mental shake and pointed. "Sure. It's down the hall, first door on the right."

The teenager dropped her backpack onto the floor, and as she hurried off, Bea turned toward the kitchen. "I better put these in a vase."

Before she'd taken a step, Devin looped an arm around her waist and brought her back toward him.

Just like yesterday, she met him for a kiss. This time, they didn't hold back. The slow drift and glide as he explored her mouth raised a moan out of her.

Bea laid a hand on his chest and nudged him back a little. "Carly…

"She took her phone with her," he murmured against her lips. "She'll be in there at least another couple of minutes. I have something important to ask you."

"What?" she asked breathlessly.

"Lauren's coming back early from her trip. She's picking up Carly later tonight. You could pack a bag and spend the night with me."

Sweet temptation curled inside of her. She wanted to… but what about them taking it slow? "I'll think about it."

"That's fair."

But the kiss he followed up with wasn't. It conveyed what would happen if she threw caution to the wind.

Caught in the spin of ever-deepening desire, she grasped a hold of the front of his shirt.

They really had to stop. Otherwise she wouldn't be able to concentrate on baking—all she would think about was him. Reluctantly, she slipped out of his arms.

Carly opened the bathroom door and came down the hallway. As she picked up her backpack, she gave them a curious look that paused on Bea. "What happened to the flowers?"

Bea glanced at the semi-squashed bouquet and the petals on the floor. "Oh…"

"She dropped them." Devin cleared his throat. "I should get going. I don't want to miss the press conference."

"Press conference?" Bea asked.

"Another sink hole opened up a few miles north of Chatelaine. The folks in that area are up in arms, and the county officials are making a statement. I won't be gone long. Just a couple of hours or so."

Carly snorted in disbelief.

"Hey." Devin playfully shot his daughter an admonishing look. "Behave. And do what Bea tells you. And make sure you save a few tartlets for me—I have to make sure they're fit for consumption."

"Whatever, Dad." Carly gave a small eye roll as she hugged him.

Bea walked him to the door. Before he stepped out, he gave her a wink. "See you later."

"Bye." Her heart was still fluttering in her chest as she and Carly went to the kitchen.

Fortunately, most of the flowers had survived being squashed, and they brightened the nook in the kitchen.

Moments later, she and Carly were both wearing yellow aprons and had pulled back their hair.

Bea pointed to a bowl of apples. "We're making apple

tartlets like we talked about, but I made some peach filling earlier today in case you wanted a variety."

"That sounds good." Carly picked up an apple. "So
we're peeling them?"

"Yes, but we're making the dough for the tartlet crust
first. It has to chill for at least an hour before we bake
them. I hope we can get everything done before your dad
gets back."

"We will. When dad's working on something for the
paper, he's never on time. Mom says she always has to
add an hour or more to when Dad says he's coming back.
He gets distracted and forgets what he's supposed to do.
We're used to it."

"Oh? That's…interesting." Was that really true?

Since she'd known Devin, he'd only been late once—
the day they'd gone to pick up Francis. Maybe Carly was
just parroting something Lauren had said a time or two.

Bea showed Carly how to make the dough for the crust.
She was a natural at it.

Next they peeled the apples. Once Bea had demon-
strated how to safely use the knife, she allowed the teen
to help cut the fruit.

The chop of the knives against their cutting boards
filled the silence.

Carly dropped diced apples into the bowl sitting between them on the counter. "Can I ask you a question?"

"Sure."

She hesitated an instant, then blurted out, "Are you and
the baby going to live with my dad?"

Bea carefully finished dicing an apple. It was best to be
honest, right? "Your father and I haven't decided on that."

Carly toyed with the peeled apple on her board but
didn't cut it. "There's only two bedrooms—mine and

dad's." A hint of color flushed in the girl's light brown cheeks. "His office was a bedroom…"

Bea put down her knife and turned her full attention to Carly. "No matter what we decide, you'll always have your room. No one's going to take that from you."

Carly gave her a quick smile and shrug. "I was just wondering."

Bea wanted to reach out and reassure the teen with a hug or pat on the shoulder, but they weren't at that stage yet.

What Carly had just asked was on the parenting questionnaire. Devin said they had time, but there were so many unanswered questions…including if his daughter was going to be living with him full-time. Should they wait on making any plans until after he and Lauren worked things out? Or should she and the baby be part of the conversation now?

A little over a couple of hours later, the finished tartlets were lined up on the counter.

They tasted them, and Carly's face lit up. "These are *sooo* good. Everyone's going to want one." Her smile faded a little. "Oh no—I messed up. I should have made a video or taken pictures of me making them."

"We still can. We have extra dough and filling. We just have to stage it a little."

They set up the prep area on the counter. While Carly made tartlet shells, Bea shot video clips and took candid photos. Like her dad, Carly had a good sense of humor, and it shined through.

In the midst of taking close-ups, strands of Carly's dark brown hair fell over one of her eyes. Flour was covering her hands, so she tried to blow her hair out of her face. She laughed. "It won't move."

"I've got it." On an impulse, Bea smoothed the strands behind Carly's ear.

Memories of her mom flashed in her mind, along with what she'd felt back then when she and her mother had cooked and baked together. A strong sense of caring hit Bea, and she knew what she wanted to be for Carly.

A guide. A teacher. An encourager. A protector if need be. And when she was older, a friend. She wanted Carly to know that with her, she'd always have a place to just be herself.

"Thanks." Carly smiled.

"You're welcome."

After the photos and videos were done, they cleaned up again.

Devin was still a no-show.

While Carly was in the bathroom, Bea sent him a text, asking if he was on his way.

He didn't reply.

The teen came back into the kitchen. She glanced at the phone in Bea's hand. "Did you hear from Dad?"

"No, not yet. But if you need to work on your homework... Oh, wait—it's Friday. Are you hungry? We could make dinner?"

"That's okay. Mom and I are picking up something on the way home."

"Your mom? Isn't she still on her way back from Corpus Christi?"

"Nope. She's here. I texted her your address, and she's on her way to pick me up."

Bea wasn't sure what to say. She wasn't going to stop Carly from going with her mom. "Well, we should pack up the tartlets."

They were almost finished boxing up the desserts when the doorbell rang.

"I'll get it," Bea said. Maybe that was Devin.

She opened the door.

Devin's ex-wife stood outside. With her hair pulled back in a ponytail, she was a pretty, adult version of her daughter.

She offered a hesitant smile. "Hello. I'm Lauren, Carly's mom."

Neither one of them had probably anticipated meeting this way, but it was happening.

Bea rolled with it. "Hi, I'm Bea. Come on in. Carly's still packing up the tartlets in the kitchen, but she won't be long."

Lauren walked inside. "Thanks for helping her with the bake sale." Genuine friendliness was in her tone. "I'm so tired from my trip, the best I could have done for her tonight was put sprinkles and chocolate chips on some store-bought cupcakes. I hope it wasn't too much trouble."

"Not at all. I enjoyed it. And Carly did most of the work. Come see what she did."

They went to the kitchen.

Carly showed her mom the tartlets.

"Wow!" Lauren exclaimed. "Those look amazing. Great job. They're going to sell out before the first hour of the bake sale."

"I know." Carly beamed.

"We'll have to be careful taking them home." Lauren handed the teen her car keys. "The thermal bag I use for groceries is padded. It's behind the back seat. Go ahead and put your backpack in the car now."

Carly left the kitchen.

The front door shut, and Bea and Lauren stood silently in the kitchen.

The dark-haired woman offered up a small smile. "I really do appreciate you helping Carly. I hope Devin didn't dump the task on you and leave."

"No, it was fine. He didn't need to be here."

"But he should have gotten back in time to pick her up. As soon as Carly told me he was working on a story, I knew what happened." Hints of exasperation filled Lauren's face. "When he's caught up in a story, everyone around him gets shut out. Nothing else matters."

Nothing else? On a reflex Bea almost laid a hand on her stomach, but she caught herself.

But not before Lauren noticed. Her exasperation morphed into a swift explanation. "I'm not saying Devin's a bad guy. He's just—"

The front door opened, and Lauren grew silent.

Carly returned, and Bea shifted her attention to helping her pack the bag.

As the three of them stood at the door, the girl looked from Bea to her mom as if unsure what to do next.

Lauren motioned to Carly. "What are you waiting for? Give Bea a hug and say thank you."

"Thank you."

"You're welcome." Bea followed Carly's lead into an embrace. Happiness filled her as the teen tightened her arms around her.

After Lauren and Carly left, she leaned back against the door. Happiness faded. Where was Devin? Was he okay?

He gets distracted and forgets what he's supposed to do. We're used to it...

When he's caught up in a story, everyone around him gets shut out. Nothing else matters...

Carly and Lauren's comments played through her mind. *I'm not saying Devin's a bad guy. He's just—*

He's just what? As Bea pondered the question, remnants of the doubt she'd felt years ago when she'd first noticed cracks in her marriage started to surface. *No.* This wasn't the same situation. She just needed to voice her concerns to Devin. He'd understand.

A rapping on the door startled her out of her thoughts, and she opened the door.

Devin's expression was filled with genuine remorse. "Bea, I'm sorry." He glanced down as he rubbed the back of his head. "Will you let me explain what happened?"

The first step in being able to voice her concerns was listening. Bea opened the door wider and let him in. After shutting it, she faced him, but she left her hand on the doorknob.

Devin held up his hands in surrender. "I realize none of what I'm about to say is a good excuse. I should have made it back when I said I would. But the press conference started late. And then I had people to interview. One of them gave me a lead on another story, and I made a stop to follow up on it. That side trip took longer than I anticipated."

"Why didn't you respond to my text and tell me that?"

"My phone was on silent." He grimaced. "It's a habit. When I was starting out as a cub reporter, my phone rang in the middle of an important interview. I lost the exclusive, and I almost lost my job. Ever since then, I've made sure that didn't happen again. Usually, I remember to change the setting back to normal, but I didn't until a little while ago. That's when I saw I missed your text as well as Lauren's."

He looked so sincere, but...

Devin took a step toward her. "Rather than texting or calling you back, I wanted to explain face-to-face."

Telling him what Lauren and Carly had claimed about him would sound like an accusation. And she wasn't trying to start a fight. This also wasn't about his ex-wife or his daughter—this moment was about them and their relationship.

Bea released the doorknob and walked closer to Devin. "I understand your work is important, but what if something had happened to Carly or me and we really needed to reach you? You can't go MIA like that. I was worried." Admitting that aloud made her heart constrict in her chest.

"In the future, I won't chase the next story." Devin took hold of her hand. "And I'll answer my phone. I promise."

Bea gave in to the need to be closer to him, and he immediately took her into his arms.

Kissing her temple, Devin's chest rose and fell with a deep breath. As she laid her head to his chest, their breathing synced.

He held her a bit tighter. "Thanks again for helping Carly. Lauren said she's really excited about showing off what the two of you made tomorrow."

"I'm glad," she murmured.

"I am bummed that I missed out on being the official taste tester."

The desire to be with him was undeniable, and Bea weighed whether to give in to it. "I still have ingredients left." She leaned away and looked up at him. "We can make them at your place."

CHAPTER SEVENTEEN

A LIGHT BREEZE blowing heat and a bit of smoke from the grill on the back deck at Devin's house brought him out of a happy trance. If he didn't keep his mind on what he was doing, the steaks he was cooking for him and Bea would burn.

But he couldn't stop looking at her through the window into the kitchen, where she was making salad to go with dinner.

He'd thought Bea wouldn't want to come back to his place after he'd shown up late. But thankfully, she'd forgiven him, despite how badly he'd screwed up. In the future, he would be more present. He had to find a better way to balance his duties to the newspaper and being there for everyone. Or he could lose Bea, and the chance to have more wonderful moments like tonight in the future.

The experience of preparing a meal together was even better than he'd imagined. From the moment they'd walked into his house, their actions had been synced. She'd instinctively known where everything was, or he'd anticipated what she'd needed before she'd asked. It was as if Bea had always been there…that she belonged in this house with him.

He finished grilling the steaks and went inside.

As Bea put the salad into bowls, Francis watched intently as if he was enamored with her. Devin chuckled to himself. He couldn't blame him.

Bea glanced over her shoulder. "Perfect timing. I made buttered toast. I tried to make garlic toast, but..." She laughed. "It's so weird to not be able to stand garlic anymore. Roasted garlic on the grill would have been great with the steaks. I feel like I'm depriving you of the good stuff."

Devin walked up behind her and kissed Bea on the cheek. "You're not depriving me of anything, sweetheart."

Bea leaned slightly into him. She was the perfect fit, and it took everything within him not to slide his arm around her waist and mold her backside to his front. He had the good stuff. Her—within arm's reach instead of miles away.

Devin set the platter with steaks on the stove, then opened the oven to grab the baking sheet with the golden-brown triangles of toast. "Everything's ready. Let's eat."

After dinner, while Bea made the tartlets for dessert, Devin took Francis on his last walk for the night. The anticipation of returning to Bea intertwined with a sense of contentment that she would be there, waiting for him.

Needing to express what he felt, he spoke to the dog, who was wagging his tail as they walked home. "Francis, I'm a lucky man."

And he hoped to stay that way by avoiding the missteps he made earlier. The last thing he wanted to do was hurt the people he cared about, including Bea. Today was a sign. He had to do better.

Back at the house, Devin came in through the garage. After washing up at the sink in the laundry room, he joined Bea in the kitchen.

The promised tartlets were on a platter, and she was topping them with whipped cream.

He joined her at the counter.

The sweet scent of vanilla wafted in the air.

"Ready for dessert?" she asked.

This time, as he slid his hand around her waist from behind, Devin gave in to the need of feeling her flush against him. "Uh-huh."

Looking over her shoulder, she fed him a peach tartlet, and the flaky, fruit-filled pastry filled his mouth.

"That's good..." he murmured.

"Was it worth waiting for?"

"Absolutely." Devin loosened his hold as she turned to face him.

Her gaze met his as she cupped his cheek. "Let me see." Bea briefly pressed her mouth to his, gently sucking on his lower lip as she eased away. "Oh, yeah—that's perfect."

She pressed his mouth back to his. Her teasing and slow, sweetly torturous kisses unleashed a hunger inside of him.

Devin cupped his hands to her butt, kneading her soft curves. Bea followed his lead as he lifted her up, and she wrapped her legs around him.

He wasn't just lucky. He was the luckiest man on Earth.

As DEVIN CARRIED Bea down the hall, she abandoned worry and doubt. No, they didn't have forever to make important decisions, but tonight they could wait. They could embrace time.

In his bedroom, removing each other's clothes became a slow exploration. Feather-light caresses and needy kisses followed each piece of clothing that fell to the floor.

When they were finally skin to skin on the bed, Bea longed so desperately to feel him inside of her, but he made her wait, exploring every inch, every sensitive spot on her body until she burned with erotic sensation.

Devin murmured near her ear. "You're beautiful."

And she truly felt beautiful and wholly desired by Devin as he worshipped her with more kisses and caresses that intensified her need for him.

Bea writhed and bowed up. "Devin...please..."

Holding her gaze, he slowly entered her. He moved his hips, igniting pleasure in places she'd never known existed. As she reached her orgasm, Bea felt as if every barrier, every wall of protection had splintered apart. All that was left was him. Wanting him. Needing him. Falling for him. Even possibly on the verge of loving him.

Afterward, wrapped in his arms, unease crept into her contentment. She'd trusted and believed in her ex-husband. And she'd overlooked his faults so many times, only for him to let her down? What if Devin was the same way, but she was blinded by how much she cared for him? What if she was wrong about him, too?

Pushing the thought aside, she snuggled up against him, searching for peace in the warmth of his embrace and the steady beat of his heart.

Soon, Bea fell asleep. She dreamed of holding a baby that resembled Devin in a room filled with friends and family. But he wasn't there. Suddenly the room was empty, and it was just her and the crying child.

Awakening in a sweat, she disentangled herself from Devin's arms and sat up.

Half asleep, he rasped, "You okay?"

"Yes, I'm fine." She slipped out of bed, threw on his T-shirt, and went into the bathroom.

After cooling her face down with water from the sink, she stared at her reflection in the mirror. "It was just a bad dream. I'm not alone," she whispered. "That won't happen."

But what if it did?

THE NEXT MORNING, fatigue and last night's dream hovered over Bea as she made her way to the kitchen.

Devin glanced over at her from where he stood at the

counter. While she was still wearing his shirt that she'd slept in, he was dressed in a gray T-shirt and black athletic shorts, looking sexy as ever.

"You're up. I was just about to bring you a cup of coffee and some tea." He held up two mugs. "I wasn't sure which one you wanted, so I made both."

Walking over to him, Bea swiped the remains of the dream from her thoughts. Worry was on overdrive in her mind for no reason. "Coffee, please."

He handed her one of the mugs, and she kissed him. "Thank you."

"You're welcome. Hey—when I came back from walking Francis, I heard your phone buzzing in your purse. It sounded like more than one text message coming in."

"Really?" She paused to take a sip of coffee. "Maybe it's Tanya."

"What time are you supposed to be at the café?"

"Around one."

"That soon…" Leaning back against the counter, Devin took hold of her waist and brought her closer. "We need to plan for an entire weekend together. Maybe an overnight trip. We could drive to Corpus Christi or even fly out to Dallas."

Uninterrupted time with Devin would be heavenly. "Either one sounds nice to me."

Her phone rang in the living room.

Sighing, Bea reluctantly stepped out of his arms. "I better answer that."

In the living room, she dug her phone from her purse. It was her brother. He never called…unless it was important.

She answered. "Hi, Asa."

"Hey—sorry to interrupt your morning, but did you hear the news?"

From his tone, it wasn't good. Her heart dropped. "Did something happen to Esme or Ryder? Or the boys?"

"No—as far as I know, they're fine. It's Wendell. He fell at the house late last night and was rushed to the county hospital. A group text went out about it."

"I haven't checked my messages yet." Worry trickled through her. "How is he?"

"Lily and I went to see him this morning. From what I've heard, he's going to be fine, but all the bumps and bruises he sustained are taking a toll on him. A simple fall can become a serious thing at his age. Everyone in the family has been asked to check on him."

"Okay, I will. Thanks for letting me know."

They said their goodbyes.

Bea looked through her text messages and found the one Asa had mentioned. She glanced at Devin standing in the archway to the kitchen.

"Everything okay?" he asked.

"No. It's Wendell."

Devin joined her by the couch. "What happened?"

"He fell last night and had to be rushed to the emergency room. He was admitted to the hospital. Asa and Lily went to see him this morning."

"I'm sorry to hear that." A concerned look came over Devin's face as he sat on the arm of the couch. "I really hope…"

"What?"

"The day we went to pick up Francis from the shelter, when we were in the car, I mentioned to you that I had visited Wendell at Fortune's Castle."

She frowned. "You did? I don't remember that."

"You had a lot on your mind. I made a joke about aliens from Venus just to get your attention. Anyway, when I went to see him, I asked him about Clint Wells, the foreman who'd worked at the silver mine during the accident. The conversation seemed to upset him."

"What did he say?"

Devin shook his head. "Nothing really. I've been trying to find someone who knows the whereabouts of Clint's wife and daughter. Wendell said he didn't."

The identity of the fifty-first miner. Edgar and Elias's part in the collapse of the mine. Now the foreman's family. Too many unanswered questions still remained about the silver mine collapse. But she also got the sense that Wendell knew more than he let on.

Bea stepped between Devin's legs and laid a hand on his shoulder. "I honestly don't think your conversation with Wendell put him in the hospital. He's been sick off and on for a while."

"Well, I hope he pulls through."

"I do, too. Everyone in the family has been urged to go and see him." She took a step back. "I'd like to drop by and visit him before I go to work. The hospital is across town from here. I should probably leave now."

"You should. That way you won't have to rush to get to the café on time." Devin stood. "I'll make you something to go for breakfast. What are you in the mood for? A smoothie? Some oatmeal?"

"A smoothie would be nice, but you don't have to make me anything."

"Yes, I do." He kissed her forehead and rested his hand on her stomach.

A sense of feeling wholly protected by Devin came over her. It would be so easy to get used to him taking care of her, but maybe she shouldn't. Yes, they were getting along, but there was still so much for them to figure out.

Still, she lingered until he let her go.

On the way to the bedroom, Bea paused. "The Wells family—have you found anything about them?"

"Just a bunch of dead ends." Resignation was in Devin's raised brow expression. "They don't want to be found. And maybe that's the way it should be."

CHAPTER EIGHTEEN

BEA STOOD BY Wendell's bedside in a private room at County General Hospital. As he slept, his breathing was steady, but he looked so frail, and his face had an unhealthy pallor.

She gently took his hand. "Hi, Wendell. It's Bea. I'm just going to sit here and visit with you for a bit."

The dark-haired nurse checking his IV glanced over at her. "He's doing well. He's on pain medication, so don't be alarmed if he doesn't wake up while you're here or if he wakes up in a daze."

"Thank you for letting me know."

"You're welcome." The nurse left.

Empathy filled Bea as she looked at Wendell. The poor man. It was too bad that he didn't have children of his own to look after his welfare. That made it even more crucial for her and the rest of the family to be there for him.

As she moved to sit down in the chair by the bed, Wendell's hand grasped her fingers.

"I'm sorry..." His eyes remained closed as he mumbled, "I should have done right by you. I should have done better."

"You have done right be me." She patted his arm. "It's okay."

"No..." As he shook his head, his breathing grew a little heavier. "I didn't. I should have acknowledged you publicly as my own instead of hiding from it."

The nurse's warning about him possibly waking up in a daze was accurate. He was clearly mixing her up with someone else.

Bea lightly squeezed his hand. "Wendell, I'm Bea, your niece. Bea Fortune."

Wendell's eyes opened, and he stared up at her with a confused look that became shadowed by a pained expression. "Don't hate me. I was just trying to do what I thought was best. I know you loved him, but he was destitute…a miner. I just wanted a better life for you…you're my child…"

His *what*? Was Wendell saying he had a daughter? Maybe an illegitimate one, from the sounds of it.

"Wendell…" She gave his hand another light squeeze. "Who are you talking about? What's her name?"

His eyes fluttered closed with a sigh, and as his hand went slack in hers, his breathing grew steady.

That was weird. Had she heard him right? No one had ever mentioned to her about Wendell having a daughter. Had he kept this secret from everyone…until now?

Moments later, sitting in the car, she struggled to make sense of what he'd said. In his dazed state of mind, maybe he had told this to someone else. Glancing through the names and numbers associated with the test message alerting the family he'd been hurt, she debated who to call.

Aunt Freya maybe? But what if she didn't know about him possibly having a child? This could potentially be a bombshell for her and maybe everyone else on the list.

One name caught her eye. Tabitha Buckingham. She was family via the twins, but she was also the most neutral party connected to the Fortunes. Talking to her might help. And Bea had been meaning to reach out to her anyway. She could squeeze in at least a half hour or so visit before she went to the café.

Bea gave Tabitha a call.

"Sure, come on over. I could use some adult company," Tabitha said. "But fair warning—I'm in the middle of folding laundry, so it's a little messy."

Bea arrived at Tabitha's house. Just as the young mother had claimed, stacks of folded laundry along with baskets of unfolded clothes took up most of the living room couch.

Tabitha's blond hair was tied back. Dressed in yoga pants and a T-shirt, she was in casual mom mode, and from the flush in her cheeks, she'd been busy.

Bea glanced around. "Where are the twins?"

"Napping."

"Oh…" She lowered her voice.

Tabitha waved her off. "You're good. When they're conked out, unless there's shouting, nothing wakes them up." She moved a basket of unfolded laundry and set it on the coffee table, before perching on the end of the couch. "Please have a seat."

Bea settled into the spot she'd cleared for her. "Would you like a hand?"

"I would love one."

As they started sorting and stacking bibs, blankets, socks, sleepers and onesies, Bea was reminded of the newborn-essentials checklist.

She'd emailed the checklist to Devin along with the parenting questionnaire, but he hadn't said anything about them. Maybe she should have reminded him? But shouldn't he have remembered their conversation and mentioned them to her or at least acknowledged he'd received them? He'd mentioned last night that he'd finished the parenting plan for Carly. Wasn't the parenting questionnaire for their baby just as important? Or was she being selfish…?

"This is a nice surprise." Tabitha added a folded bib to

the stack on the coffee table. "But from the look on your face, you have something on your mind."

Bea debated how to dive into the topic. "You saw the text about Wendell?"

"I did. But I have to admit, I've been so busy with the twins, I haven't even gotten a chance to really read it. Something about a fall?"

"Yes, he's in the hospital, but he's recovering."

"I'm so glad to her that. At his age, falls can be a scary thing. I wish I had time to go visit him now, but I'm behind on so many things, including the laundry, and I'm playing catch up. And then both Zach and Zane ended up with the diaper rash from hell. This week I wasn't sure if I was coming or going. And then…" Chuckling, she shook her head. "Sorry, I didn't mean to unload on you like that. You were saying…?"

Although she'd come here intending to discuss Wendell's dazed confession, after seeing Tabitha now, she had a change of heart. The young mom had said she'd needed some adult conversation, not speculation and gossip about things that weren't even on her radar.

Bea added a folded onesie to the stack beside her on the couch. "It's not important. So is the diaper rash from hell gone?"

"Yes, thank goodness! I had to remind my babysitter about sticking to the diapering routine. I need and appreciate her help, but it only makes it harder for me if she's not on board with my routines. It's tough."

"Other than managing the babysitter, how are you? And be honest. It's okay to gripe… I don't mind."

Tabitha's shoulders fell as she released a slow breath. "Honestly, what I wish I had and need the most is West." Her gaze strayed to the framed photo next to a baby monitor on the side table.

In the picture, the golden-haired couple were a striking pair. And they looked so happy.

Tabitha added. "But even if he was here, we wouldn't be together." Hints of sadness filled her tone.

"What? No—what makes you say that?"

"One, West never wanted children. And two, we broke up the night before he died. I had no idea I was pregnant at the time."

"But don't you think he would have wanted to know his children? That he might have changed his mind once the twins arrived?"

Tabitha gave her a slightly tremulous smile. "I don't know if his mind would have changed. He might have adapted to the situation, but West's job dominated his time." She sighed. "And honestly, I'm not sure I could have handled me and the twins coming in second or third to a never-ending list of trials or another tough case. And I loved him too much to make him choose. He might have done it, but he also might have resented me for it later on. I wouldn't have wanted to take that risk."

"So you might have chosen to be a single mom? It can't be easy."

Tabitha offered up a small shrug. "It's difficult to say. But I do know losing West the way I did was the hardest thing of all. I'm so lucky to have the twins. At least I have a part of him."

Bea's heart went out to the other woman, but she also admired her strength. "Yes, you do. And you're doing a great job raising them."

Tabitha smiled. "Thanks—I needed to hear that today. Sure, being a single mom is hard sometimes. But like I said, I've developed routines. I eat when they eat. I sleep when they sleep, or I catch up on laundry and housework. I make it work. And I have a network of friends that I can call on. But trust me, this isn't the most nerve-racking part of having kids." Humor filled her eyes. "Some people might think I've lost my mind by saying this, but I'll gladly take all of the chaos I have now over being pregnant. Now, that was scary. Unless you've been through it, nothing can prepare you."

"I know—I'm pregnant."

A shocked smile came over Tabitha's face. "You are? Oh my gosh! When did you find out?"

"Just recently," Bea admitted. "But you're the first family member I've told."

"Don't worry. I won't breathe a word to anyone. So are you happy, or are you..."

"Well... I'm definitely scared and..." A feeling Bea had never felt since finding out she was pregnant surfaced. "Thrilled?"

Tabitha laughed. "That's so normal." She quickly set the laundry aside. Moving closer, she took Bea's hand. "Tell me everything..."

Bea poured out her excitement and fears. Tabitha listened, answered her questions, and gave her advice on everything from how to handle morning sickness to pregnancy books to maternity clothes.

A cry from one of the twins came through the baby monitor. Then the second joined in.

"It's time to feed my boys." Tabitha tilted her head toward the hallway. "Do you want to see them?"

Bea hesitated. She really needed to head to the café soon. "I do."

In the nursery, Bea smiled and cooed at the light-haired twins along with Tabitha. She helped changed their diapers, and when Tabitha handed her a bottle, Bea settled into one of the rocking chairs with Zach in her arms.

Looking into his eyes, Bea saw her world in the future.

I'll have support. I won't be alone. But as scared as she was, she couldn't wait to meet her baby.

LATER THAT NIGHT in her bedroom, on a video call with Devin, Bea told him about her visit to see Wendell at the hospital.

She propped up the pillows behind her back on the headboard. "I'm really baffled by what Wendell told me. If he has an illegitimate daughter someplace, where is she?"

Devin was outside walking Francis. "That is strange."

"I don't know. Maybe I should ask someone if they know anything."

"Hold on a sec." Devin turned his attention from the phone. "Francis..." he said in a warning tone. "Sorry—someone else is walking their dog. What did you say?"

"I was wondering if maybe I should ask someone if they know anything."

"And if no one does, you're back at square one, trying to get answers from Wendell. And with his health the way it is, do you really want to broach that topic with him?"

"That's true." Her thoughts drifted to Tabitha. "I went to see my twin nephews today—Zach and Zane. They're a little over ten months old and so adorable."

"Really?" From the background change, Devin was entering his house. "Twins. That's a lot."

"Their mom, Tabitha, has a good routine. She says routines are important."

"Yeah, that helps." He propped up the phone on the counter as he took care of Francis.

"She gave me lots of ideas. And I love her nursery setup. She has a small refrigerator and counter space for a bottle warmer and feeding supplies. And on the other side of the room is the changing station. Seeing her setup inspired me, so I looked online and found a room design that I think will go well here. I'm sending you the page link."

"Sounds...nice." He picked up his phone again, but from the distance in his voice, something else was on his mind.

"And she hired a really good babysitter from Venus."

He gave her a lopsided smile. "I was paying attention. You like her nursery."

"You were *half* paying attention. Is something bothering you, or am I bothering you?"

"No, you're not bothering me." As he briefly looked away, he paused. "It's Lauren. She's postponing our next meeting with the mediator. We were supposed to present our co-parenting plans. We can't drag our feet on making this decision. And it feels like that's what she's doing." He blew out an agitated breath. "And I even told her that over the next two weeks, my schedule was going to be busier with Quinn taking days off one week and Charles the next."

Bea's excitement about her visit with Tabitha faded. She'd hoped maybe Devin would pull up the link on his laptop now so they could share ideas. "I'm sorry to hear that."

He shook his head. "As always with Lauren, it's complicated. I'm sorry for being so distracted. Next time we talk, I'll be in a better headspace. I promise."

They said good night, and as Bea pulled up the covers, unease settled in with her again.

Devin kept making promises to her. But what was that saying? The more promises you made—the more chances you took to break them.

CHAPTER NINETEEN

TANYA POINTED TO three plates of scrambled eggs on the table in the dining room of the café. She was perfecting the breakfast and brunch catering menus and wanted Bea's opinion. "The first plate is just eggs, butter, salt, and pepper. The second batch has cream added to it. The third has eggs, milk, butter, salt and pepper, and cheddar cheese."

"They all look good." Bea picked up her fork.

She tasted the food samples, but her thoughts felt as scrambled as the eggs on the plates. As much as she wanted to focus on this Wednesday-morning taste test, that past weekend and the last couple of days with Devin kept playing through her mind.

Since Saturday, he'd been distant and preoccupied. And his afternoon walks this week with Francis hadn't included a stop by the café. Although he had said he was coming by that afternoon. But when they did talk, the conversation always veered away from them toward the newspaper or issues with Lauren.

"So what do you think?" Tanya asked.

Bea brought her thoughts back to the task at hand, and she sampled the last plate. "I like plate number one and number three."

"Perfect." Tanya smiled as she got up. "Those two are the most popular with everyone who's tasted them, and they were my choice, too. The catering menu should be finalized in a few days. And the Belgian waffle makers I ordered are on the way. You know, chicken and waffles might be something to add to the dinner menu in the future."

"I like that possibility. We'll revisit that when the time comes." Bea added it to the notes on her digital tablet. Chicken and waffles wasn't an entrée her mom had made, but being open to new things would keep the menu fresh and interesting.

Bea returned to her office.

She and Tanya had also finished the new shelf diagrams for how the food should be organized in the walk-ins. They needed to be printed out. But her printer was out of paper, and the stash in her desk was gone, too.

Bea searched the storage room down the hall where they kept office supplies. But she didn't see a box of printer paper or reams stacked on the shelf. They couldn't have used all of the paper that fast. As she stepped back for a wider view, she spotted the packages on the top shelf out of reach.

Really? Bea let out a long breath. Putting the paper on a lower shelf made more sense, especially since they used it on a regular basis.

As she made a mental note to mention this to the stock person, Bea grabbed the small stepladder in the corner. After setting it up near the shelf, she climbed up, but she couldn't quite reach the copy paper.

A taller stepladder was in the dining room storage closet, but she just needed one package.

Raising up onto her toes, she reached up, and her fingertips grazed the side of one of the packs, knocking it askew. *Almost got it...* She stretched her arm higher and slid it out a bit further.

But instead of just one, a domino of reams broke free.

"No!" A package started falling toward her head, and

when she ducked out of the way, her foot slipped off the stepladder.

As she landed hard on the floor, horror consumed her mind. *The baby...!*

DEVIN SAT WITH Quinn in his office. He'd asked her to do some research on the Wells family, but the results were less than promising.

"It's like they disappeared." Quinn shrugged. "I searched birth and death announcements, real estate purchases, old addresses. Nothing is coming up for Clint Wells's family in the surrounding area. Do you want me to widen the search?"

Did he want to keep digging for answers? Devin was tempted, but the rabbit hole of searching for answers about the miners seemed endless. And the one person who probably knew the truth—Wendell Fortune—wasn't talking.

Devin shook his head. "We're going to have to press the pause button on this story for now."

She stood. "I don't blame the West family for disappearing after all they went through. If I were them, I would have gotten as far as possible from Texas and never looked back."

As Quinn left, Devin studied the document on his desktop screen listing the leads he and his assistant had checked into. All of them were dead ends. *And maybe that's the way it should be...*

That was what he'd told Bea. Quinn not finding anything could be a sign to follow that advice.

Devin closed the file on the Fortunes' silver mine, then opened the one he'd created with the co-parenting plan documents. He hadn't downloaded the newborn-essentials checklist and the parenting questionnaire Bea had sent him, but he still had plenty of time to get them done.

The checklist would be easy. He'd make sure Bea had

whatever she wanted for the baby. And the questionnaire probably resembled the one he and Lauren had filled out regarding Carly during their divorce mediation.

It had questions like, who would be your primary-care physician? Carly's pediatric physician was great. That would be his recommendation. Healthcare and medical expenses? Again, that was easy. He could take care of it all, or if Bea wanted to split the responsibilities, he wouldn't object. Which parent would be the child's "home base?" That was the most important question on that list.

A vision of him, Bea, the baby, and Carly living together as a family came into his mind. The possibility of that made him smile.

Carly and Bea had gotten along well making the tartlets for the bake sale. Maybe, despite his lingering doubts, his vision of a family wasn't as far off as it seemed.

A text from his ex-wife dinged on his phone.

Can we meet at my house in an hour?

Devin glanced at the clock on the screen. He'd left Francis at home today, but he'd told Bea he would stop by later that afternoon. Whatever it was, he could probably meet Lauren and make it back in time.

A follow-up text appeared on the screen.

It's important.

When *wasn't* it important with Lauren?

Meet you there.

Unease and frustration accompanied him on the drive.

He had no idea what Lauren had to tell him, but he sensed it wasn't going to be good.

When he arrived at the house and walked inside, Lauren's stubborn expression confirmed it.

Carly was at school, and the house was quiet.

The taps of his ex-wife's heels echoed as they walked into the kitchen and seemed magnified in the silence. Her keys, phone, and business tote were on the counter. From the looks of things, she'd come from work.

She faced him. "There's no easy way to say this, so I'll just be direct. They need me in Corpus Christi sooner. I wanted to work out a custody arrangement with you through a mediator, but I don't see the point under the circumstances."

He crossed his arms over his chest. "No, a change in your timetable doesn't change the circumstances of us coming to an agreement."

"That's not the circumstance I'm talking about. You're about to have a baby with another woman. It's a new responsibility."

"That has nothing to do with me taking care of Carly."

"It does. You can barely make time for her now. I have to fill in the gaps."

Devin's frustration broke through. "That's bullshit. You were gone practically a whole week, and we did just fine. In fact, Carly and I have done just fine anytime you've left town. You're just trying to come up with excuses for why you should take her to Corpus Christi."

"I don't need an excuse. And I think a judge will agree with me."

"A *judge*?" Disbelief made him pause.

His phone rang, and he took it from his pocket.

"See what I mean?" Lauren pointed at him. "You can't

even focus on a conversation about our daughter without distractions."

Not recognizing the number on the screen, he ignored the call, put the phone on silent, and tossed it onto the counter next to hers.

Irritation and calmness brewed inside of him. "You want to see me focused. I can build just as strong of a case. You'll be a single parent with a new job in a new city. You talk about filling in the gaps? Who are you going to call in Corpus Christi when you can't pick Carly up from an afterschool event or when you have to go away on a business trip?"

Lauren advanced on him. "You—"

"Stop fighting!" Carly screamed.

Startled, he and Lauren both looked toward the living room where their daughter stood.

Her face was pale, and her eyes were wide.

Devin's stomach plummeted. What was she doing home? Had she been here the entire time?

"Sweetie." Lauren rushed from the kitchen, and he wasn't far behind. "It's not what you think—"

Carly backed away from her mom. "We're *moving*? Why didn't you tell me?"

"I was waiting for the right time," Lauren began.

"So that's it?" Tears sprang from the teen's eyes. "You get to decide everything? What about what I want?"

Devin stepped ahead of Lauren "We know this is a surprise for you, but we just—"

"You and mom don't know anything!" Carly stormed past them to the back sliding door and left the house.

Devin looked at Lauren.

As she pressed her hands to her cheeks, she looked as stricken as he felt. "I didn't see her. I didn't look. I just assumed she was at school. She *should* be at school."

An accusation almost slipped out of him. Devin released a harsh breath as he massaged his neck. He couldn't find fault with Lauren's actions. He should have paid better attention when he'd walked into the house. They both should have—instead of going at each other.

"Her skipping school is the least of our worries," he said wearily. "We should go talk to her."

Lauren stalled him with a raised hand. "I can fix this now. I'll just turn down the job."

He was tempted to agree but knew that wouldn't be fair. "Taking away her right to decide by making a choice you don't want won't fix this situation. We need to listen to what she has to say."

They went outside.

Carly sat on the edge of the pool with her feet in the water.

Devin took off his boots and socks, rolled up his jeans, and Lauren kicked off her heels and rolled up her pant legs.

He sat on one side of Carly and put his feet in the water, and Lauren did the same on the other side of her.

Carly kicked up the water, soaking their legs.

As the long seconds passed, memories of playing games in the pool with Carly when she'd been younger, and of her infectious laughter floated through his thoughts.

"I'm sorry," Lauren said softly. "We should have told you. We were just trying to work things out with a mediator first."

Carly kicked the water harder. "You said you were going to a judge."

Lauren looked to him for help.

Devin replied, "That was something that came up today, but we started working with a mediator last Monday. He wanted me and your mom to make up schedules and parenting plans for either choice—if you stayed here with me or went with your mom to Corpus Christi."

She turned to Lauren. "You think Corpus Christi is better for me even though my friends are here?"

"I just want you to experience more opportunities. A bigger school with more activities would do that. But I can understand if you don't want to leave your friends."

Carly looked to Devin. "And you think I should stay here instead of doing new things?"

"No. I want you to try new things. But I know you were looking forward to going to high school here and playing volleyball or maybe joining the cheerleading squad. I didn't want you to miss out on that."

"Would the choice have been mine?"

Devin glanced at Lauren. From the look in her eyes, they were on the same page. "It is starting now. What do you want to do? Stay here, or go to Corpus Christi?"

Carly stared down at the water, then said, "And whatever I choose, you won't be mad at me?"

As Lauren wrapped an arm around her, she blinked back tears. "Of course not. Your dad and I love you." Resignation was in her eyes as she glanced over at Devin. And in that moment, he knew she wouldn't fight him about Carly staying in Chatelaine.

He nudged Carly's shoulder with his. "Your mom's right. We love you and we only want the best for you, whatever that may be."

Carly nodded. "Okay." She looked up and met his gaze. "I want to go to Corpus Christi."

Lauren's mouth dropped open in surprise.

Disappointment and disbelief pushed a sharp exhale out of him. He quickly recovered and forced a smile. "Then Corpus Christi it is."

"But I still get to come home and see you, right?"

Home... The reassurance that one word gave choked him up for a few long seconds. "Yeah, definitely. We'll figure it out."

"Can we talk about it now?" Carly asked.

"Sure. Just let me call Quinn and let her know I'm not coming back to the office."

Devin walked inside the house. Mixed emotions sat heavy in his chest. In the kitchen, he closed his eyes and breathed.

Lauren joined him. "I don't know what to say..."

"There's nothing to say. I just want Carly to be happy. And if that's in Corpus Christi with you, I can live with that." He picked up his phone. Noticing the missed voice mail, he listened to it.

"Devin, it's Freya Fortune. There was an accident at the café..."

CHAPTER TWENTY

"I'M FINE." BEA looked at Freya standing next to the bed in the treatment bay at the emergency room. "I stumbled off the step stool and twisted my ankle. That's all."

When she'd first landed on the ground, she'd been more afraid for the baby. But after a moment or two, she'd realized everything was probably okay with the pregnancy and that she'd just hurt herself.

"But you also bumped the back of your head on the shelf." Genuine concern filled Freya's expression. "It could be more serious than you think."

One of the kitchen staff had heard the commotion in the storeroom and found Bea sprawled on the floor. She'd convinced everyone not to call an ambulance, but the older woman had insisted on driving her to the county hospital.

The curtain opened, and the emergency room physician came in carrying an electronic tablet. "Hello. I'm Doctor Hanson. You're Bea Fortune?"

"Yes."

The dark-haired woman wearing a white hospital coat turned to Freya. "And you are?"

"I'm her aunt. And I'm not going anywhere." The look on her face dared anyone to tell her otherwise.

"As long as it's okay with Ms. Fortune."

Bea nodded. "She can stay."

Dr. Hanson consulted the tablet. "It says here that you experienced a fall in your restaurant and hurt your left ankle?"

"And she hit her head," Freya chimed in.

"But not that hard," Bea objected. As the doctor examined her ankle, she winced. "It's a little tender."

Dr. Hanson checked the back of Bea's head. "Have you felt dizzy or disoriented since the fall?"

"No. Nothing like that. Not even a headache."

The doctor took a pen light from the pocket of her coat. "Follow my finger."

Bea complied, looking left to right then up and down.

"If you're head does start to hurt or you feel dizzy, let us know." Dr. Hansen pointed to Bea's ankle. "Most likely you suffered a sprain. But I would like to take a couple of quick X-rays to be sure."

Alarm ran through Bea, and she placed her hand over her abdomen. "You can't."

"Don't be so stubborn." Freya scoffed. "It's a precaution. Why not be sure?"

"I'm not being stubborn. And I am being cautious." This wasn't the way Bea wanted to announce the news, but... "I'm pregnant."

Freya's eyes widened.

Dr. Hanson scrolled through information on her screen. "I was just about to ask you if you were. You didn't indicate yes or no on your form."

"In the midst of everything... I must have missed the question." Embarrassment sent a rush of heat into Bea's face. Did that make her a bad mom?

"How far along are you?" Dr. Hanson asked.

"Less than a month. I had a blood test to confirm it a couple of weeks ago."

An understanding expression crossed the doctor's face. "Have you set up an appointment to start prenatal care?"

"Yes."

"Good." She gave Bea a reassuring smile. "As long as

we stay away from the abdominal region, we can safely take a few X-rays."

The doctor left, and Freya looked to Bea. "Does Devin know about the baby?"

He had become a part of her life lately, so it made sense Freya would make the correlation. "Yes. We wanted to wait at least another month before telling anyone. Something happened, and we had to tell his ex-wife and his daughter. Otherwise they wouldn't know, either."

As a hospital aid arrived with a wheelchair, a thought popped into Bea's head. She grasped Freya's arm. "Were you able to get ahold of Devin?"

Bea's phone was back at the café. Earlier, before she'd been caught up in the admission process when they'd first arrived at the emergency room, she'd asked her aunt to reach out to him.

"I took care of it." Freya waved her on. "Now you just focus on looking after yourself and my great-niece or nephew."

On the way to get the X-ray, a small bit of anxiety gripped Bea. The fall hadn't hurt the baby, and the doctor hadn't been concerned. But what if she had? This visit to the hospital would have had an entirely different outcome.

Closing her eyes, she wished for Devin. Freya had called him. Undoubtedly, he was on his way. Surprisingly, tears threatened to well up as a sense of relief came over her.

Her climbing stepladders would now be added to the list of things he worried about along with her getting enough sleep and not skipping meals. And right then, she didn't care if Devin gave her a mini lecture when he arrived about taking better care of herself. She just looked forward to the hug and kiss he would give her afterwards.

Once the X-ray was done, she was wheeled back downstairs and taken to a curtained-off patient bay adjacent to the emergency area.

Freya wasn't there. Maybe she was outside meeting Devin?

A moment later, her great-aunt came into the patient bay alone. "There you are. It took two people to tell me where to find you."

"Hopefully Devin, won't have the same problem. I'm surprised he's not here yet."

"Oh, when I called the paper, he wasn't there. I had to convince them to give me his number. He didn't answer his phone, but I left him a message." She patted Bea's arm. "I'm sure he's on his way."

So Freya hadn't actually spoken to him? Had he gotten the message? But even if he hadn't, if he'd stopped by the café, someone would have told him what happened to her. Shouldn't he have already reached out to Freya?

Or had he lost track of time while caught up in a story with his phone off, again? Lauren had said when he was chasing a story, he shut everything out because nothing else mattered.

Bea closed her eyes, trying to erase doubt. But what Lauren and Carly had said about Devin loomed in her mind.

Dr. Hanson came into the patient bay. "Sorry for the delay. But I have good news—you're in the clear. You just have a small bump on the head, no concussion. As far as the ankle, you don't have any joint instability or serious bruising. The pain and swelling should resolve in one to three weeks. Rest, ice, compression, and elevation are all you need. Someone will be in shortly to wrap that ankle for you, and then you're free to go."

"Thank you," Bea said.

A short time later, as they prepared to leave the patient

bay, she stood by the bed trying to find her balance with a pair of crutches. Her thoughts about Devin were just as shaky and unsure.

As if reading her mind, Freya gave her an empathetic look. "Should I try to reach Devin again?"

"No."

"Are you sure?" Freya took her phone from her purse. "He's probably worried about you."

"If he was, he would have called—"

The curtain opened, and Devin rushed in. Concern filled his face as he went to Bea. "Are you okay?"

Instead of relief, despair assaulted her. She wasn't okay, and she got the sense nothing would be for a while. But she couldn't just ignore reality.

She sat back down on the bed and propped the crutches beside her. "Freya, would you mind giving us a minute?"

Her aunt gave a quick smile. "I'll be in the waiting room."

After she left, Bea responded to his question. "I'm okay, and so is our baby. Where were you? Freya called the office *and* your phone?"

"Something happened with Carly. My phone rang but I put it on silent to focus on the situation."

"Is she all right?"

"She overheard me and Lauren arguing about the co-parenting agreement and the move." As Devin stood in front of her, he took hold of her hands. "But right now my focus is you.

Until when? First his inattentiveness for the past few days, now this. If something serious had happened that put her or the baby in jeopardy, he wouldn't have been there for her.

Devin cupped her cheek. "Why don't you stay with me

for the next few days? I don't have stairs at my place. It will be easier for you to get around, and I can look after you."

Bea swallowed against tightness in her throat. The more she allowed herself to depend on him, the more promises he'd break. And honestly, she just couldn't face the same disappointment with Devin that she'd felt with her ex not being there when she needed him, no matter what the reason. She had to protect her heart. She had to protect *her baby*. He had obligations that didn't include them. And she did love him too much to make him choose. It was best to cut her losses now.

Bea took in a breath, but instead of air coming into her lungs, it felt like a flood of misery. She leaned away from his hand on her cheek. "I can't go home with you, Devin. Trying to turn our co-parenting situation into something else is a mistake."

Devin gripped her hand. "If this is about me not getting here right away, I'm sorry..."

As she glanced down at her still-flat stomach, panic warred with the conviction inside of her. She was scared, but she could do it. Bea met his gaze. "It's just not about that. You have other obligations in your life. But my primary focus is our child. And then the café. I need stability right now to balance everything. And I can't create that if I'm trying to be in a romantic relationship with you. But you're welcome in our baby's life."

Devin looked stricken. "Bea, don't do this."

"No, Devin, please—I've made up my mind." Swallowing hard, she slipped her hand from his. "I'm doing what's best for all of us."

CHAPTER TWENTY-ONE

LOSING CARLY, THEN Bea in the span of twenty-four hours was like a one-two punch, devastating enough to make Devin's head spin and almost knock him to the ground. He hadn't seen it coming.

Devin put a double-espresso pod into the coffeemaker, but he doubted there was enough caffeine in the world to take away the fatigue-laced pain and disbelief clouding his mind.

He'd hoped Carly would want to stay in Chatelaine. Did she want to leave because he was expecting a baby with Bea? But Bea thought he didn't have enough room in his life for her and the baby. Did Carly feel something similar—that she no longer had a place in his life as his daughter?

The questions he pondered late into the night still plagued him. But no clear-cut answers emerged.

Especially when it came to Bea. How had he messed up so badly that she didn't understand how he felt about her? She and the baby were important to him, and he was willing to do anything in his power to make her happy.

His gaze strayed to his phone on the counter, and re-morse pinged in his gut for breaking his promise of not ignoring his phone. If only he'd answered Freya's call or checked his messages earlier, he would be taking care of Bea right now instead of missing her.

The phone rang. It was Lauren.

He answered. "Hello."

"Hi." She paused. "How's Bea doing?"

Not wanting to get into it, he gave the simplest answer. "She's fine. What about Carly?" He and Lauren had talked briefly last night after he'd arrived home, but Carly had already gone to bed.

"She hasn't said much to me since last night. And she wasn't like herself when she woke up."

"What do you mean she's not herself?"

"She's fine now. She just seemed really sad. We talked and she's feeling better. I'm taking her to school this afternoon." Hints of concern still hung in Lauren's tone. "But I think she believes you're upset at her."

"Of course I'm not. If moving is what she wants, I accept that." But he couldn't deny the disappointment he felt.

"I know you do," Lauren said. "If it means anything, I was just as surprised as you were to hear that she wanted to move with me to Corpus Christi. She mentioned how excited she was about the baby... I thought she'd want to stay here with you and Bea."

Carly was excited about the baby? He'd missed that, too, along with everything else. "Should I come by?"

"Can you? I think it would help a lot if you talked to her."

"Sure." It didn't matter how dragged down he felt, his daughter needed him. He had to go.

An hour or so later at Lauren's house, Devin walked down the hall to Carly's room. He knocked on the closed door. "Carly. Can I come in?"

"Yes."

He opened the door. "Hey."

His daughter sat cross-legged with her feet tucked under her on the bed. Her attention remained on her phone. "Hi."

He sat on the side of the mattress beside her. "Can we talk?"

"Sure." Carly put her phone aside, but she still wouldn't look at him. She picked at the chipped purple glitter nail polish on her thumb.

"I'm sorry I had to leave before we finished our conversation about you moving to Corpus Christi with your mom. I had to go check on Bea."

"I know. Mom told me." Carly met his gaze. "Is everything okay?"

"Yes. She and the baby are fine."

"I'm glad." She paused. "So you're really not mad at me for not wanting to stay here?"

The trust in her eyes that he'd tell her the truth—he couldn't ignore it. "I'm really not mad about it. But is it hard for me to imagine you not being here? Am I sad that I won't get to see you play volleyball or cheer at a football game? Am I worried about not being there if you need me for something or just want to talk to me. Yes."

"I get it." Excitement and exasperation filled her face. "But hello, Dad, video calls work! We can talk every day, and if I make the volleyball team or the cheerleading squad, Mom can video call you then, too, so you can see me. It would almost be like you were there." She smirked. "And you and everyone else always said Corpus Christi was a straight shot from here. You can come there, or Mom can drive me here. And in a couple of years, when I'm sixteen, you can buy me a car and I can drive myself."

Drive? It was terrifying just imagining her driving, period. And he and Lauren would never let her travel between Chatelaine and Corpus Christi by herself.

But someday she would turn seventeen and then eighteen and beyond. Driving alone, going off to college, falling in love—it was all in her future. Pride, fear, and love gripped his chest. He wasn't ready for any of it.

"It'll be good, Dad." Carly reached out and took hold of his hand on the mattress.

For a fleeting moment, the vision of her holding on to his hand as she'd been learning to walk flashed in his mind. Back then, she'd grasped onto him with such certainty, knowing she was safe and he wouldn't let her go. He felt that same certainty in her now.

He angled his body more toward his little girl. "So, you really are looking forward to moving?"

"Yes." Her face lit up even more. "Corpus Christi is a city with more things to do. It will be fun. All my friends are jealous."

"So Bea and the baby have nothing to do with you wanting to leave?"

Carly shrugged. "Maybe a little. The baby's going to need you more than I do. And you'll need time to be a great dad for them like you are for me."

The earnestness in her eyes made a lump form in his throat. "Okay, then I guess it's settled."

"Good." She wrapped her arms around his neck and hugged him tight. "And since you're worried about not being there, maybe Francis could come live with me."

Devin chuckled as he hugged her tighter. She had all the answers, didn't she? "We'll see."

A short time later, Devin joined Lauren in the kitchen. Concern was etched on her face. "How did it go?"

"She's good."

"We really messed up by underestimating her, didn't we?" his ex-wife said quietly.

"Yeah, we did. But now we know better."

"We were so concerned about not stressing her out over our disagreement, but that's exactly what we did by not telling her the truth." Lauren huffed a wry chuckle and shook her head. "How did we get it so wrong?"

"I think we forgot we're on the same side. We may not be married anymore, but we want the best for Carly and each other."

"You're right. Let's make a deal not to forget that again. And instead of reacting, we'll focus on really hearing each other's point of view when it comes to Carly."

She held out her hand and Devin shook it. "Deal." Some of the heaviness he'd awakened with that morning lifted. "Before I forget—Carly wants to take Francis with her. It's up to you. I can adopt him, and he can stay here with the two of you before the move. If for some reason it doesn't work out, he can come back and live with me."

As reasonable as it all sounded, he couldn't ignore the pang of sadness echoing inside of him. He'd lost his daughter, the woman he loved, and he was on the verge of losing the dog who'd kept him company for the last few weeks. His life was starting to sound like a sad country song.

Devin dug his keys out of his pocket. "Well, keep me up to date on the details of the move. Let me know what I can do to help."

Lauren studied him. "Something's happened. What's wrong?"

I'm trying to wrap my mind around you taking my daughter. He could use that excuse. But giving her that answer wouldn't be the complete truth. And it would be unfair to lay that on Lauren.

"It's Bea."

"So she's not okay? Oh no—the baby..." From Lauren's expression she anticipated the worse.

Devin hastened to assure her. "They're both fine. It's just that..." Saying it aloud for the first time brought an ache to his chest. "Bea and I aren't together as a couple anymore."

Lauren looked stunned. "I'm sorry." She paused as if unsure of what to say. "Do you want to talk about it? I could make some coffee." Her genuine concern and empathy caught him off guard.

"Sure. I could use some caffeine."

Moments later, he sat on the stool at the kitchen counter with a cup of coffee in front of him.

Lauren stood on the other side of the counter, drinking tea.

The morning she'd told him she was moving to Corpus Christi crossed his mind. So much had occurred since then. Choices. Decisions…and losses.

"So what happened?" she asked.

Devin toyed with the mug on the counter. "Bea said she and the baby needed stability, and because of my devotion to the paper and other responsibilities, she doesn't think I can provide that." Lauren objecting to Carly staying in Chatelaine with him came to mind, and a harsh laugh escaped. "And I guess you probably agree with her."

Lauren took a sip of tea before responding. "You're a lot of things, but unstable or unreliable isn't one of them. But I can understand why she might feel that way."

He sat back in the chair. "I'm listening."

"Because she doesn't know you like I do. I have years of being married to you and us raising Carly together to back up that knowledge. Bea doesn't have time and certainty to erase her doubts."

"But I'm willing to put in the time," he protested. "I told her from day one that I'm not leaving her to handle the pregnancy or raising our child alone. Shouldn't that count for something?"

"I'm sure it does. But your choices are a big problem."

"I'm choosing her and the baby. How is that a problem?"

Lauren looked directly at him. "You need to choose *yourself.*"

He wasn't sure he'd heard her correctly. "You think I should choose myself?"

"Yes." Lauren stalled his forthcoming response with a raised hand. "And before you say that's selfish, listen to me. When your dad got sick, he had to come first. And the paper—it had been one of the top priorities, too, because it was one of the things that kept him going. After that, it was Carly and then our marriage and then you."

"My priorities couldn't have been different. All of you needed me."

"We did, but after your dad passed away, everything on that list changed or moved on, except you…until Bea showed up. She and the pregnancy forced you out of a rut. For the first time in years, you've been anticipating something new in your life, and I have to admit, it's been wonderful to see." She pinned him with a warning look. "But you'll lose it all if you don't fully embrace the moments that bring you joy—things like spending time with the people you care about and being a great father like your dad was. You've just forgotten how to do it. You've forgotten to be happy."

Devin tried to find something to object to in what Lauren was suggesting, but he couldn't. Those things did matter to him. And he had felt happy with Bea. And looked forward to helping her prepare for their child together.

As he studied Lauren's face something else became clear. Her choices. "The move to Corpus Christi—isn't about money or accepting a promotion. It's about choosing yourself, isn't it?"

"Yes—I had to. My time in Chatelaine is over. It would be easier to stay here and just go with the flow. You were right to stop me yesterday. It would have been a bad decision to turn down the job and stay here. What's best for me is moving ahead and trying something new. And those are the kind of choices Carly needs to see me making— and she needs to see that from you, too."

LATER THAT NIGHT, as Devin sat on the back porch reflecting on what Lauren had said, his thoughts drifted to his dad. Carl had been a hard worker, but Devin had always known that his dad had loved him and put him first.

When Carly had come along, his father had often put work aside, thrilled to hold and talk to his granddaughter. The way his dad had truly valued those moments had often made him pause. He could see now that Carl had been reveling in happiness.

Devin's memories shifted to his own moments with Carly. Her first cry as she'd entered the world, the first time she'd stared into his eyes as if she'd known him forever. First words, first steps, first hurts...he'd been there.

The vision in his mind morphed to Bea holding a baby. *Their baby.* And him not being a part of it. And worse, he'd no longer laugh with Bea, hold her, wake up with her, experience life with her. More images of all they'd miss out on together as a couple and a family flashed into his mind. His heart ached. He wanted a chance to build a life and a family with Bea. But would she give him another chance?

CHAPTER TWENTY-TWO

BEA TRUDGED TO the kitchen in her condo, flipping on lights along the way. It was before dawn, but more sleep wasn't in her future. She couldn't stop thinking about the baby and the future...and Devin.

Almost a week had passed since their breakup, and just as she'd requested, he hadn't contacted her. However, he had reached out to Esme to make sure she was okay.

It was good to have her sister back. Esme had been shocked to hear all that had happened since the wedding. But as expected, she'd been so supportive.

Bea went to the pantry and took out the box of lemon-ginger tea. It was the kind Devin had brewed for her the night she'd met Carly.

Once the hot drink was prepared, she sat down at the kitchen table. As she took a sip, comfort and warmth surrounded her, reminding her of Devin's embrace on the porch swing. She soaked it all in, wishing he were there. Heartache started to tighten its hold, threatening to unloose tears. No. She'd cried bucketloads over the past three days. It was time to stop.

Closing her eyes, she forced herself to breathe. "We'll be okay. Things might be a little bumpy at first, but I promise I'll figure it out."

It took a moment for Bea to realize she wasn't just talking to herself. She rested her hand on her stomach. Could the baby hear and sense what she was feeling? If so, she really *did* have to pull herself together, and go back to work. She'd been resting her ankle, and it did feel better. It was time to start adjusting to her new normal—being a single, pregnant business owner on her way to becoming a single mom. She also needed to really tackle the newborn-essentials checklist.

At some point, she should probably contact Devin about some of the things on the list. But designing and setting up the nursery was on her.

As the sun started to light up the sky, the doorbell rang. Who was stopping by this early? She checked the doorbell video camera.

It was Freya and Esme.

Bea answered the door, and as they walked in, each of the women gave her a hug.

Esme studied Bea's face before meeting her gaze. "You're not sleeping. Is it nausea or something else?"

Bea read between the lines about what "something else" meant. "No, I'm feeling okay." She and Esme looped arms as they followed Freya into the kitchen. "I just really miss my caffeine boosts in the morning. But coffee just doesn't taste the same."

"Cutting back on caffeine is probably a good thing." Her aunt dropped her purse onto one of the chairs at the kitchen table. "But food is important. When was the last time you ate?"

"Umm—yesterday." Freya's and Esme's pointed looks prompted Bea to confess. "Yesterday afternoon. I had some soup, but it was really filling."

"Soup?" Freya shook her head in disapproval. "No, you need a good meal." She went to the pantry. "Regular oatmeal. That's a start."

Esme perused the shelves in the refrigerator. "And

there's fruit. I'll cut some up. And if you don't mind, I'll take some oatmeal, too."

Bea got up to help, but Esme nudged her back to the table. "Sit. We got this."

A short time later, oatmeal, sliced apples, and toast with peach jam sat in front of Bea at the table.

Esme and Freya joined her for breakfast.

As Bea took a bite of toast with jam, her tastebuds perked up, and suddenly she was ravenous for more jam.

The memory of feeding Devin peach tartlets with whipped cream hit her at the same time that she sucked jam from her fingertips. Tears welled then spilled from her eyes.

"Oh, honey." Esme slid her chair closer and wrapped her arm around Bea's shoulders. "What is it?"

"Peaches…" Bea swallowed the words. "This is insane. What's wrong with me?"

"Pregnancy hormones." Freya patted Bea's hand.

Bea dried her cheeks with the napkin Esme handed her. "Am I going to do this every time I think about him?"

"Probably." Freya released a breezy chuckle. "The only way to make you feel better about it would be to have him here."

"No. We can't be together. It won't work." Bea looked to Esme for backup, but her sister wouldn't meet her gaze. "You agree with Aunt Freya?"

Esme offered up a delicate shrug. "From what you've told me and what else I've heard, you *were* happy with Devin."

"I was, but it's not just about me. As much as I care about him, I have to put our baby first. And part of that is not setting Devin up for failure by expecting him to be there. I know what it's like to be let down. I went through it with Jeff."

Her sister frowned. "You're comparing Devin to your ex? Is that fair? You said Devin *had* been there since the moment he found out you were pregnant."

"He was—as best he could. And I know he wants to do the right thing now, but..." Bea searched for the words to explain. "The newspaper is important to him. His daughter is important to him. I don't want to make him choose."

"Making choices are about learning to find balance. That's something you'll have to learn, too. And it doesn't happen overnight," Esme reminded her. "Ryder and I are still figuring it all out when it comes to us and the boys and our jobs. The one thing I do know is that finding the right balance as a couple takes practice and learning things along the way." She gently nudged Bea with her shoulder. "And allowing for mistakes. They happen. No one's perfect, especially as a parent."

"She's right," Freya said. "And relationships in general take a lot of work, and learning how to make things work takes time. And that's where love comes in." A nostalgic, faraway expression briefly came over her face. She focused back on Bea. "I saw you and Devin together. What you felt for each other was evident. You two were in love. And love makes all things possible."

The doorbell rang.

"I'll get it." Esme went to answer the door. A moment later, she came back with a cardboard box imprinted with a pink-and-blue design. Grinning, she handed it to Bea. "You've got a special delivery."

Bea studied the package. "Who's it from?"

Esme clapped her hands in encouragement. "Open it and find out."

Bea unsealed the box. Arranged in the colorful packing were an assortment of items: lotions and other pampering products and candles with a heavenly soothing scent.

She opened the envelope attached to the lid and read the card inside of it. "'Welcome to Well Mama Sunshine. Each month, you'll receive a box with curated items for moms-to-be.'" Happiness sparked a smile. "Did you two do this?"

Freya and Esme looked to each other, then shook their heads.

"But it's adorable," Esme said. "Oh, look. There's a stack of laminated cards with the votives. I think they're affirmations." She picked one of them up and smiled.

"What does it say?" Bea asked.

"Exactly what you needed to hear."

Bea accepted the card from her sister and read it.

I am loved.

OVER THE NEXT few days, more surprises from an anonymous source showed up: a spa bundle including monthly massages, an appointment with a personal stylist at a maternity store plus a generous clothing allowance, and a paid subscription to a grocery and personal-item delivery service.

Sitting at her desk at the restaurant, Bea finished the signup process for the latter. The subscription was a thoughtful gesture, just like the rest of the gifts. Despite eating many of her meals at the café, she still needed to stock her own refrigerator.

But who was sending her the gifts? She'd quizzed family and friends. It was easy to imagine them getting together to arrange this, especially to show their support and cheer her up after injuring her ankle. But they all denied involvement.

Was it Devin? Should she reach out to him to see if he was sending the gifts?

Her heart leaped at the possibility of him as the anonymous gift giver, but then she tamped down excitement.

What if she was wrong? What if he *was* respecting her wishes and staying away from her? Acceptance mixed with regret and sadness pinged inside of Bea.

She missed him so much. And it had become impossible not to think about him. One of the things that brought her comfort was the candles in the gift box. Their scent was so soothing, she couldn't resist lighting one the past few nights when she'd arrived home from work. And it was uplifting to read the affirmation cards at the start of her day. The message from the one she'd picked that morning had continued to stick with her.

By doing the best for my well-being, I am doing the best for my baby.

Since her talk with Esme and Freya, she'd debated what the best thing was when it came to her and Devin. They were right—Devin wasn't her ex-husband. And he probably was overscheduled. And she was in love with him. But what if love wasn't enough? If things didn't work out with Devin. She'd feel like...*a failure*.

Bea sank back heavily into the chair. Okay, she could admit it now. It wasn't so much about setting up Devin for failure. She didn't want to set up *herself* for failure. Her marriage ending with Jeff had hurt, but looking back now, she could see the commitment they'd shared had been a shallow imitation of a relationship. What she'd shared with Devin had been real. If they were together and it didn't work out...it would hurt much more.

A knock sounded at her open door.

A dark-haired, middle-aged man in a Western-style shirt and jeans peeked in. "Hello, Ms. Fortune. The person out front directed me to your office. I'm Milt—from Milt Handyman Services." He strode in and gave her a business card. "I was passing through this afternoon and just wanted to introduce myself in person. I was also hoping we could work out a time for us to discuss your project."

"Yes. Come in." Bea mentally went through her schedule. Esme had probably set up something with him and forgotten to tell her. "Which project are you referring to—is it something in the kitchen or the dining room?"

Milt looked puzzled. "I don't know anything about a kitchen or a dining room. I'm renovating a room that will be used as a baby nursery. I have the specs here." He took his phone from his pocket and tapped the screen. "Sea-green walls and ceiling. White trim. Bench seat for a window, and…"

"And a pocket door leading to the bathroom."

"Exactly." He grinned. "Whew. For a minute there, I thought I was talking to the wrong person. So mainly I just need…"

As Milt talked, Bea filled in the blanks. Only one person would know all of the details he'd described. Devin. She'd sent him the link to her dream nursery…and now he was making it a reality.

She wrestled with the surprise and happiness swelling inside of her. Was this his way of making amends for the mistakes he'd made? Was it enough? On some level, this wonderful, thoughtful action felt too big to ignore. It felt like an opening. A chance. A sign that what she and Devin shared could actually work.

Maybe this backed up Freya's claim that love made all things possible.

As Bea sorted through her thoughts, a question surfaced. The affirmation card she'd pulled that morning had stated she was doing the best for herself. But by not allowing for mistakes or another chance to make a relationship work, *was* she doing the best thing when it came to her and Devin and their child?

CHAPTER TWENTY-THREE

DEVIN SAT AT the head of the table during the late-morning meeting in the conference room. It was strange but also good to have another key staff member there besides just him, Quinn, and Charles.

Adele, the new assistant editor, had started three days ago and was already fitting in well with the team.

Having her there was especially helpful since Devin's mind was occupied with other tasks outside of the day-to-day with the paper. Absently, he grazed his thumb over a rough spot on his palm. A splinter—he thought he'd removed it last night, but part of it was still there. As aggravating as the damn thing was, the small discomfort was a happy reminder of the projects he was working on in the room adjoining his office and at his house. And strangely he had Lauren to thank for it.

He was also planning to tackle the newborn-essentials list and the questionnaire item by item, but first he was looking after Bea's well-being...anonymously.

In a week or so, he would reach out to her directly. Maybe by then, she would be open to seeing him, and he could show her what he'd been working on for the baby. They were just a few of the changes he was making—along with hiring more people to free up his schedule. He missed her so much and would give anything to be with her again or hear her voice. But he would give her what she'd asked of him. Time.

"I really think we need to move the article about the upcoming town council meeting to the front page," Adele said. The dark-haired Latina in her mid-thirties, studied her tablet with the draft of the upcoming newspaper on the screen. "Land zoning is current news. A lot of people are interested in what's going to happen with the upcoming proposal."

Charles nodded. "I agree, especially since it isn't just a hot topic here but in the surrounding towns, too. In fact, we might consider a series of articles on this. It would also be a good way for our new reporter at large to get acquainted with the area."

The other new hire joining the team in a week was relocating from San Antonio to Chatelaine.

All eyes turned to Devin. "Sounds good. Let's move the article to the front page. And as far as the series, write up a proposal with the angles for each of the articles, and we'll discuss it."

A chime sounded from the door in the reception area.

As Quinn went to see who it was, the group continued to discuss other changes.

A moment later, she returned. "Devin—Bea's here. She's waiting in your office."

"She is?" He immediately rose to his feet. Just as he reached the door, Devin remembered they were in the midst of a meeting. "Let's take a fifteen-minute break. But if I'm not back by then, keep going without me."

He strode to his office a couple of doors down. As soon as he saw Bea sitting on the couch, his heart thumped an extra beat in his chest.

"Hello." As Bea stood, a hint of anxiety reflected in her eyes. Just like that day in the parking lot when she'd told him she was pregnant.

Awkwardness and uncertainty. That wasn't what he wanted for their future.

Tamping down his own anxiety, he smiled back. "Hi."

As he shut the door behind him, Bea came closer. "You're working on the next edition of the paper—I'm sorry. I should have called. I won't take up too much of your time."

"No. You're fine." He couldn't stop his gaze from straying to the door leading to the other room. *Whew.* Good thing he'd closed it before going to the meeting earlier that morning.

"But aren't you on a deadline?"

"We are, but my staff can handle it."

They really didn't need him. The realization of that really hit Devin. For once, he didn't feel stressed out, trying to beat the clock. Hell, he could take the entire afternoon off. If he would have been able to do that weeks ago, maybe he and Bea wouldn't have broken up.

Regret needled him as he approached her. It was difficult not to reach out and touch her. "How are you?"

"I'm good. Really good. And so is the baby." Her genuine smile brought a glow to her face.

Words he couldn't stop just came out. "You look beautiful."

"Thank you." A light flush came into her cheeks enhancing her natural radiance. "I...well, like I said, I feel good." She glanced down as if gathering her thoughts. "A handyman stopped by my office earlier this morning. He said someone hired him to turn the guest room at my condo into a nursery."

"Really?" He injected surprise into his tone. "I wonder who set that up?"

From Bea's raised brow she already knew the answer.

Devin softly chuckled. "I guess I need to work on my poker face."

"Just a little. Actually, the handyman gave you away. He showed me the plans only you would know about." She stepped closer. "You didn't have to hire him. I don't expect you to renovate my home."

"I know..." Unable to stop himself, Devin reached out and took her hand. Pain shot into his from the splinter, and he immediately let go. He shook off the discomfort.

Bea frowned in concern. "What's wrong?"

"It's nothing. I just have a splinter in my palm."

She took his hand in hers. The sting faded as she gently caressed the red spot on his skin.

"You need to take this out."

The softness and concern in her gaze along with her scent were too alluring to ignore. Devin swallowed hard. "I will when I get home later tonight."

"Tonight?" Bea released him, and he immediately missed her touch. "No, this could get infected. Hold on." She went to her purse sitting on the couch and dug through it. A few seconds later, she pulled tweezers from a small cosmetic bag. "Let me see."

He walked over to her.

Bea firmly grasped his hand, inspecting the reddened spot. "The end of it is sticking out. I think I can get it." She probed his palm with the tweezers. "Sorry. I know this hurts."

"I'm good." The ache in his chest at the thought of losing her was far worse than his hand. He'd endure the pain a hundred times over if he could hold and kiss Bea again.

"Almost..." She held up the splinter with a triumphant expression. "I got it."

"Thank you. I'm lucky you were carrying around a pair of tweezers." On a reflex his hand tightened around hers.

Bea didn't pull away. "They came in the pregnancy pampering box I received the other day." She glanced down a moment. "If you're doing these things as an apology or because you feel guilty, please don't. It isn't necessary. I don't hate you or anything close to that."

Guilt? He hadn't realized Bea might see it that way. "No. That's not what this is about. Come with me. I need to show you something."

Devin led Bea to the side door to the adjoining room. Nervousness assaulted him as he gripped the knob. It wasn't finished yet, but hopefully she'd approve of what he'd done so far.

Holding his breath, he opened the door.

Bea gasped. "Oh, Devin…"

Glancing around the room with new beige carpeting and sea-green painted walls, he tried to imagine it through her eyes. He walked to the boxes stacked in the corner. "I bought three of the cribs you wanted—one for here, for the nursery at your condo once it's done, and the one I'm setting up at my house.

"The rocking recliner is from a store in Corpus Christi. It's really comfortable. I chose the leather one, but they have different upholstery options if you want one of those, too."

Devin turned to the wood cabinet connected to the wall. "I'm building another one of these with a changing table plus counter space for things like a bottle warmer. And the open space over here—that's where I'm putting the mini refrigerator. I'm almost done with the one at my house." As he saw the rooms completed in his mind, he smiled.

It faded as he spotted Bea, staring at the room with a shocked, weepy expression. Did he make a mistake or get something wrong?

He hurried over to her. "If you don't like what I've done—"

"No." She shook her head. "I love it. But when did you have time to do all of this?"

"I've made some changes. I hired two new staff members to lighten the load. And I'll bring in more people if I have to." As Devin faced her, he lightly grasped her shoulders. "Guilt or trying to make an apology has nothing to do with this. I want to help take care of our child. We both work, and at times, we'll have to use a sitter. But I can watch over them here, too, and you can come by during the day whenever you're free."

Visions filled his mind as he glanced around the room. "I'm looking forward to sitting over there and feeding our child. Or rocking him or her to sleep." He chuckled. "I'm even looking forward to changing diapers. I want a chance to embrace more of their precious milestones instead of missing them."

He took her hands in his and grabbed hold of possibility. "The one thing that would make it all complete would be a second chance with you. I know I disappointed you. And I understand—"

Bea pressed her lips to his, cutting off his words.

Devin slipped his arms around her. The yearning he'd kept in check for far too long short-circuited his thoughts, and he held her close, losing himself in the lush warmth of her mouth and her soft curves pressed against him.

But as much as he wanted to keep kissing her, he couldn't hold back on what else he needed to say.

Devin held on to her waist and eased out of the kiss. "You said you don't hate me, and I'm really glad about that. I'm sorry for not simplifying my life sooner—if I had, it would have prevented a lot of stress between us. The last thing I ever wanted was for you to doubt whether or not you could count on me."

Bea laid her hand on his chest. "You can't take all the blame. I added stress to our relationship, too. I gave in to focusing on my past experiences instead of what was standing right in front of me. You."

"I'm glad to hear that." Breathing away anxiety, he dived back in. "But there's something else you should know. I'm falling in love with you—and not just because we're having a baby together. It started the moment we danced at the reception."

"That's good to know." She met his gaze. "Because that's when I started falling in love with you."

Happiness fueled Devin's smile. Leaning away, he glanced down at her stomach. "Did you hear that? Your mama's falling in love with me."

Bea laughed. "If my growling stomach is the answer, they heard you."

"Then we should eat. Where do you want to go?"

"What about your place or mine? We can talk things through…and see where it leads."

The look of desire in her eyes made his heart leap. He brought her closer. "Should I clear my calendar for the rest of the day?"

Bea leaned more against him. "That's what I planned to do."

"I like that plan…a lot." Devin kissed her, grateful for a second chance at love and a bigger life.

EPILOGUE

Five Months Later

BEA WOKE UP to her back being spooned against Devin's front. As he stretched his strong arm around her, he curved his hand over the swell of her baby bump, enveloping her in a hug.

He brushed a kiss along her temple. "Good morning."

A contented sigh escaped from her. "Good morning." As she pushed back against him, instead of his bare legs and chest, she encountered clothing. "Why are you dressed?"

"I'm going downstairs to make breakfast with Carly. Do you need anything?"

Bea turned in his arms. As he rolled to his back, she rested her head on his chest. He wore a T-shirt and sweatpants. The softness of the fabric, his warmth, and the light, appealing fragrance of the aftershave lotion he used prompted her to snuggle against him. "Just you."

"Too easy, sweetheart. You've already got me."

His soft kiss to her forehead and the slight tightening of his arms around her suddenly made her want to cry with happiness and pee at the same time. Bea managed to hold back the water works on both ends, wanting another minute or two in his arms.

She'd never felt so cherished and cared for in her life as she had these past few months with Devin. He'd kept his word about cutting back on his schedule, especially on weekends. She looked forward to spending these early morning hours together.

"Do you want anything special for breakfast?" he asked. "We still have fresh peaches left over from yesterday. I can make pancakes with peaches and cinnamon again."

As much as Bea loved snuggling with him, hunger for food suddenly moved to the top of her list of needs. Her mouth watered. Pancakes sounded great but... "Is a breakfast pizza too much to ask for?"

He chuckled. "Not at all. Carly guessed that was probably what you'd want. She already made the dough. Eggs, cheese, and turkey bacon okay?

"Perfect."

Devin gave her a quick kiss, then went to the kitchen.

After taking care of the essentials in the bathroom, Bea headed downstairs.

Devin and Carly were talking.

"What about Baxter or a cool name like Hipparanamus?" he said with humor in his tone. "We could call him Bax or Harry for short."

Carly laughed. "Seriously, Dad? Those aren't close to cool names for my baby brother. What about Nick or Jaeden? Or Francis?"

The mixed terrier, who was now a permanent part of the family, barked as if he understood.

Baby brother... It was so good to hear Carly make that claim. Day by day they were growing closer, especially since she'd been spending the summer with them and was working at the Cowgirl Café.

Over the past few months, the restaurant had become popular not only in Chatelaine but also the surrounding area. So many good things were happening in their lives. Sometimes it felt like a dream, but it wasn't. This was her life now and Bea was grateful for all of it.

As she walked into the kitchen, Devin and Carly both looked up from where they were adding toppings to pizza dough in a pan on the counter.

Grinning, he pointed to the small, black dry-erase board on the front of the refrigerator. "You're just in time to give an opinion on the latest baby names to add to the list."

"I heard."

"So are you on board with Hipparanamus?" He wiggled his brows playfully."

"Yeah…no. I think I'm with Carly and Francis on this round. And I have another one to add."

As Bea made her way to the refrigerator, Francis followed. His tail thumped on the ground as he sat beside her.

"Hey, cutie." She gave him a head rub before sliding the marker from the holder on the door and adding *Nick* and *Jaeden* to the list plus one more.

Carly went to Bea. The teen smiled as she saw what Bea had written. "I actually kind of like it."

"I…" A small fluttering like butterfly wings spread just below Bea's belly button, and she released a surprised gasp.

"Are you okay?" Carly asked.

"Yes, I'm fine. It's the baby." Laughing, she took Carly's hand and placed it where she'd felt the baby kick. "I think he likes the name, too."

"I feel him." Awe and excitement filled Carly's expression. "Dad, come here—you have to feel this."

"On my way." Devin quickly put the pizza into the oven.

Carly glanced down at the dog who was fidgeting around them. "It's time for his potty break. Come on, Francis." She ushered the dog out the kitchen.

Devin reached Bea. He did a double take at what she'd written on the board. Smiling, he embraced her from behind. "Are you sure?"

The baby kicked again.

As Bea looked over her shoulder and met his gaze, her heart swelled with happiness and the same love she saw in his eyes. "I think it's decided. In a few more months, Devin Street Jr. will make his appearance."

Devin smiled. "I can't wait to meet him."

She turned in his arms to face him. "Neither can I." Bea met Devin for a kiss, excited for the future ahead of them…as a family.

* * * * *

The Doc's Instant Family
Lisa Childs

MILLS & BOON

New York Times and *USA TODAY* bestselling, award-winning author **Lisa Childs** has written more than eighty-five novels. Published in twenty countries, she's also appeared on the *Publishers Weekly*, Barnes & Noble and Nielsen Top 100 bestseller lists. Lisa writes contemporary romance, romantic suspense, paranormal and women's fiction. She's a wife, mum, bonus mum, avid reader and less avid runner. Readers can reach her through Facebook or her website, lisachilds.com.

Dear Reader,

You are cordially invited to a wedding—or maybe two—in Willow Creek, Wyoming. Maybe there'll be one at Ranch Haven, home of the legendary Sadie March Haven. She was already a legend for often retold stories of her fighting off wolves and breaking a car window to rescue a certain feisty Chihuahua. Now the multi-hyphenate (mother/grandmother/great-grandmother) is a legend for all the matchmaking she's been doing. But she worries her latest match between her grandson Dr. Colton Cassidy and lawyer Genevieve Porter has worked a little too fast and that people are going to get hurt. But with as much pain as the family has endured, they've also had joy and love. So it's no wonder that even though it isn't Valentine's Day in Willow Creek, Sadie has instigated a Valentine's Day in August to have the town decorated with hearts and flowers for another wedding she has planned...

I hope you've been enjoying all of Sadie's shenanigans as much as I've enjoyed writing about them. Sadie is one of my favourite characters. I'm not sure if she reminds me of someone or if she's who I will become in thirty years. She's definitely meddled with me as much as she has her family, stealing so many of the scenes I've written and my heart, and hopefully yours, too!

Happy Reading!

Lisa Childs

DEDICATION

With great appreciation for my editor,
Adrienne MacIntosh, for her great insight
and support and her incredible spreadsheets
that keep me on track with all my deadlines!
Adrienne, you've made my busy schedule
stress-free and fun. I can't wait to write many,
many more books with you!

CHAPTER ONE

COLLIN CASSIDY DROPPED heavily into the chair behind his desk, more from shock than exhaustion. He felt like he'd been sucker punched. A fist hadn't delivered the blow, though. The voice emanating from his cell phone speaker had. This wasn't the first hit he'd taken over the past couple of weeks, but it definitely struck him the hardest.

"Dr. Cassidy, did you hear me? Are you there?"

"Um... I..." Maybe he hadn't heard the social worker correctly. "Can you repeat that?"

"I found a foster family that will take Bailey Ann. Unfortunately they're in Sheridan."

That was more than an hour from Willow Creek, Wyoming—more than an hour from Collin.

"But that might be a good thing," Mrs. Finch continued. "It'll be close to the children's hospital where she had her heart transplant, and she'll be able to go back to seeing her doctors there."

And not him.

"Are you sure the foster family can handle her health care?" he asked. "If she doesn't get her meds..." Her little body could reject the heart that she'd waited so long to receive, the heart she'd nearly rejected once when another family hadn't been able to handle her care plan. That was why the seven-year-old was in the hospital now.

That was one of the reasons he didn't want her to go. The other...

"I've been wanting to talk to you about fostering or adopting Bailey Ann myself," he admitted.

A sigh drifted out of his cell speaker. "You've just recently moved to the area," she said. "And you've just started your job at the hospital. Are you sure now is a good time for you to be considering adoption or even fostering? Especially a child who has special needs like Bailey Ann?"

"That's why I want to do it," he said. Because she was so very special.

"So you have a home with space for Bailey Ann? Child care arranged for her while you're working what must be very long hours? Child care qualified to handle a child with her medical issues? You could do this with your schedule?" Mrs. Finch asked. "Because this other family is ready now to take her. They're a little older, so they've only agreed to a short-term placement."

He was losing her, just like he'd lost so many other people and places who mattered to him. "She's still regaining her strength after that last foster family didn't give her the antirejection meds correctly. She needs to be monitored for a week or maybe two yet at the hospital."

"I will make sure this family gets the proper training over the next two weeks," the social worker assured him.

A couple of weeks.

Was that enough time for him to prove himself capable and worthy of caring for her?

"We all want what's best for Bailey Ann," she said with that gentle tone that women had used when they'd broken up with him in the past. That whole "it's not you, it's me" thing when they were both well aware that it was really him, that because of his hectic schedule, he wasn't as available or attentive as they needed him to be. He wasn't enough for them.

He wasn't enough for Bailey Ann either. He wasn't

ready. Just as he hadn't been ready to help his own parents. He hadn't been able to take care of them, to save them. His mom hadn't survived. His dad had, but because of other doctors and surgeons and someone else who had unknowingly made the ultimate sacrifice.

That was how Collin felt about Bailey Ann, how hard he'd fallen for her. He was willing to make whatever sacrifices were necessary to be enough for her. Before he could say anything else to the social worker, to make his intentions clear, Mrs. Finch ended the call, as if the matter was settled.

Would she even give him a chance?

Knuckles tapped against wood, drawing his attention to the man standing in the doorway to his office. Looking at Colton was like looking into a mirror; they had the same dark eyes and dark hair, the same facial features and tall build. Colton, a firefighter, was a little more muscular than Collin, not that he would ever admit it to his twin.

And they weren't the only ones in the family who shared a striking resemblance. In addition to their older brother Marsh, they'd recently discovered they had cousins who looked almost as much like them as he and Colton looked like each other.

Colton's brow was furrowed beneath the brim of his black cowboy hat. He wasn't wearing his firefighter gear or his paramedic uniform. So, not at the hospital for work. At that moment, their expressions were probably alike: troubled.

They'd had a lot of troubles in the past few weeks, and it wasn't surprising that his brother was less upbeat than usual. The family ranch house had burned down, but they'd been about to sell it anyway. And fortunately nobody had been hurt in the fire. But what they'd learned after it...

All the family secrets their father had kept from them: a

grandmother and cousins they'd never known about. Even their last name. It wasn't Cassidy; it was Haven.

Collin was reeling, too, but he'd decided to focus on Bailey Ann, on making sure she was not alone. Like he usually felt.

"Hey, everything okay?" Colton asked him. "You look like you lost your best friend. And I know that's not possible since I'm right here."

They were identical twins, but they were really nothing alike. If they weren't brothers, they might not even be friends. Colton was easygoing and charming while Collin was intense and focused, so focused that he'd never really taken time to make friends. So Colton probably was his best friend.

"I just got bad news about Bailey Ann," he admitted.

Colton pressed his hand to his chest as if he felt the ache that Collin was feeling. "Oh, no, is her body rejecting her new heart again?"

A pang struck Collin, too. "No. She's actually improving a lot." She'd be ready to leave the hospital as soon as Mrs. Finch trained this other family in how to look after her.

He sighed. "I just got off the phone with her social worker. She found a placement for her."

Colton stepped farther into Collin's office and peered at his face, his dark eyes questioning. "That's a good thing, right?" he asked.

With his emotion choking him, Collin could only shake his head.

"Are you worried they can't handle her medical care, like her last foster family?"

He sucked in a breath and nodded. "But that's only part of it."

Colton's mouth curved into a slight grin, and he nodded, too. "You've fallen for her. *You* want her."

He nodded again, then released a shaky sigh. "But what can I really offer her?"

"Love," Colton said. "You love her. That's all that little girl wants. Someone who loves her and who will always be there for her."

Tears stung Collin's eyes, and he had to close them. "But I'm not ready. I would need a house and child care help for when I'm working, and I don't have enough time..." He hadn't had enough time to save his mom or help his dad. He'd had to get through school first and undergrad and med school and his residencies and fellowships. Everything took too long.

"We have somebody in our lives now who knows how to get things done," Colton said with a grin. "Sadie."

A grin tugged at Collin's mouth, too. Their indomitable grandmother that they hadn't even known they had. "She is a force of nature."

But because of that, Collin had actually been trying to avoid her. The old woman was intent on matchmaking, and he had no plans to get swept up in her schemes like his cousins and now even his twin had.

He cleared his throat and asked, "Are you here to see Livvy?" That was probably why Colton had showed up at the hospital in his casual clothes, looking more like a cowboy than the firefighter and paramedic he was.

Colton's whole face lit up with love at the mention of the ER doctor for whom he'd fallen so hard. But then his grin slipped away and he shook his head. "I actually came to see you."

"About what?" Collin asked.

Colton stood there for a moment, his hands shoved deep in the pockets of his jeans. Then he shook his head. "Never mind. It can wait. You need to focus on Bailey Ann so you can prove to the social worker that you're the right family for her."

Collin wasn't even sure where to start. Sadie? She really was good at getting things done, like setting up his twin and her friend's granddaughter so they couldn't help falling in love. Not that that was a bad thing, though, since Colton was happier than he'd ever been. But even with his happiness, something was weighing on him.

"I know something's been bothering you," Collin said. He'd been trying to get his twin to tell him what it was for the past couple of weeks. "So spill it."

Colton shook his head again. "Don't worry about it. It can wait. Bailey Ann can't. You need to focus on her. Get Grandma to help you."

Collin's stomach knotted at the risk of reaching out to Sadie Haven. "She's going to use it as an opportunity to set me up with whoever she has picked out for me. I don't have time for that when I have to focus on Bailey Ann."

Colton chuckled. "You think she has some kind of master plan for all of us? Like she's arranged a marriage for each of us?"

"Don't you?" Collin asked. "She had Katie for Jake. Emily for Ben. She brought Melanie back to Dusty after he lost her. And then Taye for Baker."

"Yeah, because she knows all of them really well. She raised them." Their cousins hadn't had easy childhoods either. They were young when their dad died, younger than Collin and his brothers had been when they lost their mom. "She didn't think Dad had even survived after he ran away all those years ago, and she had no idea we existed until a few weeks ago."

Collin continued as if his twin hadn't interrupted. "And she found Livvy for you."

Colton laughed and shook his head. "No, she didn't. We found each other right here at the hospital."

Collin snorted. "Yeah, so you think. But how'd you wind up working out of this hospital?"

"I got transferred to Willow Creek Fire Department from Moss Valley."

"And you know very well that Sadie was behind that transfer," Collin reminded him. "Just like we figured out she was behind Marsh getting the position of interim sheriff of Willow Creek when the sheriff suddenly decided to retire. Why do you think she wanted you to work here?"

"So that we would all be closer to Ranch Haven. She wanted to get to know us, to spend more time with us," Colton said.

Collin nodded. "To spend more time with us and to get us involved with whoever she's picked out for us."

Colton shook his head again but slower, more tentatively, and he murmured, "No..."

"That's why I've been staying away from her," Collin admitted. Marriage wasn't for him. He'd already lost too many people in his life, and he had no intention of ever risking his heart. And even if he thought it was safe to fall in love, with all his student loans to pay off yet, he was in no position to get married. These were all reasons that he should let Bailey Ann go to that foster home, but letting go of her was one more loss he wasn't sure he could handle. He had started treating her during his internal medicine residency. Despite all of her health struggles and all of the people who'd abandoned her because of them—her biological parents and numerous foster families—she was still so affectionate and optimistic. She was an inspiration for him.

He would have to do everything he could to get custody of her, even swallow his concerns and ask his grandmother for help. He'd simply be firm about not being able to give his heart away. He couldn't handle another heartbreak.

And it would break anyway if Bailey Ann was sent away. So right now, he had nothing left to lose.

GENEVIEVE PORTER HAD lost everything that had ever mattered to her—some things and people before she'd even realized they had mattered. She'd made so many mistakes in her life that had cost her dearly. The biggest mistake was in not realizing how short life could be for some.

Too short.

The second biggest mistake was in trusting people she shouldn't have. One was her ex-husband. The other...

"I'm sorry," Sue Masters said as she settled heavily into a chair across from Genevieve's desk. The gray-haired woman worked as a nurse in the Emergency Department at Willow Creek Memorial. "I thought that you wanted to make sure that your nephews were all right. That they were safe."

"Yes, but I just wanted you to let me know what you heard around town or if they had to go to the hospital," Genevieve said, with a pang of regret. "I didn't expect you to call Child Protective Services on the Havens."

After one of the boys had been injured in an accident, Sue had called CPS to investigate the children's safety with their current guardians. The case had, fortunately, been closed quickly, with the Havens being cleared.

Tears shimmered in Sue's usually frosty blue eyes. "I know. I made a terrible mistake."

"The mistake was mine," Genevieve said. Along with so many others she'd made over the years. "I should have been clearer about my intentions." The problem was that she wasn't even sure what her intentions were.

Not anymore.

Sue reached across the desk and patted Genevieve's clenched hand. "I can't imagine how you must feel over all of this. The fact that the Havens didn't even let you know…"

They had probably contacted her mother or at least tried, but Genevieve doubted Sue would believe that. Clearly she remembered Genevieve's mother as the sweet little girl she'd grown up with, not the bitter woman she'd become. Given the way Sue's face usually had a pinched look to it, like she'd just sucked a lemon, Genevieve's mother probably wasn't the only one who'd become bitter over the years.

Genevieve didn't want to become like either of these women, though she worried she had without even realizing it. "They may have tried to." Genevieve defended the Havens. "I've moved a lot over the years. And Mother and Father have as well."

"But surely there would have been a way to get them the news about the crash and…" Sue murmured.

"Have you talked to Mother lately?" Genevieve asked.

The older woman's face flushed. "No. But I know they're out of the country a lot."

Genevieve suspected the woman hadn't spoken to her old school friend in years. Once her parents had moved away from Willow Creek, they'd cut all ties to their hometown and had never looked back. Not even now…

Unlike Genevieve who, when she'd finally learned of her loss, had returned. But once she'd arrived in Willow Creek, just the thought of contacting the Havens had made her stomach clench. Her life had been one painful loss after another, and she couldn't face opening herself up to that again. So she'd done what she always did and had thrown herself into work. She'd joined a local law firm, the same one at which Ben Haven had worked before becoming deputy mayor of Willow Creek and now mayor. She didn't want to follow his political path, but she'd thought that he might come around the office from time to time.

He hadn't. And now she hoped he didn't. After the debacle with CPS, Genevieve hoped she didn't encounter any of the Havens. But her heart ached to meet seven-year-old Miller, five-year-old Ian and the toddler, Jacob. Her nephews.

SADIE MARCH HAVEN, soon to be Lemmon, was falling in love all over again with the little girl lying in the hospital bed. She understood now why Bailey Ann was Collin's favorite patient, and why Colton, who'd shared that tidbit with her, also spent so much time visiting the little girl. He must have been by today because the child was wearing his black cowboy hat. Since he was rarely without it, the little girl must have either charmed or manipulated him into letting her borrow it. The hat was so big it kept slipping down over her face so she pulled it off. With her sparkling dark eyes and dimpled smile, Bailey Ann was beautiful, but she was more than that. She radiated goodness, sweetness and hope.

All the things that Sadie, after all the tragedies in her eighty years of life, had learned to embrace, to hold on to with all her might.

"May I give you a hug?" she asked the little girl.

Bailey Ann threw back her covers and scrambled across her bed to wrap her arms around Sadie's neck. She patted Sadie's long hair. "You're pretty," the little girl said.

Sadie laughed. Nobody had called her that in a long time. If ever...

Not even her late husband.

Her fiancé, that old fool Lem Lemmon, said sweet things, and the way he looked at her made her feel pretty.

Made her feel like a young girl again instead of the old woman that she was.

"You're the pretty one," she told Bailey Ann as she pulled back and cupped the child's cheek in her hand.

Something about the child reminded Sadie of Jenny. And moisture filled her eyes at the thought of the grand-daughter-in-law she'd lost in the car accident months ago with her beloved grandson Dale. Gone, like so many other people she'd loved.

Bailey Ann's hands were in Sadie's hair, her fingers running through the long white strands. "Your hair is so pretty. You look like Mrs. Claus."

Sadie laughed again. "I guess I will be soon," she admitted.

Every year Lem dressed up like Santa Claus. He'd had white hair and a white beard for as long as most people could remember, and for the month leading up to Christmas, he wore his Santa suit and sat in a sleigh in the Willow Creek town square. Kids stood in line for hours to tell him what they wanted to find under the tree. And Sadie knew that if he didn't think their parents could afford to give them presents, he would make sure they got something to open on Christmas morning himself. Lem Lemmon was a good man. Once it would have killed Sadie to admit that, but now...

She wasn't sure that she could live without him. This was love. This was what she wanted for all her grandsons.

"Are you psychic?" a deep voice asked.

"No, Dr. Cass, she's Mrs. Claus," Bailey Ann said.

Sadie chuckled and turned her head to grin at her grandson who stood in the doorway. He arched a brow over one of his dark eyes, and a pang struck her heart again at how much he looked like his grandfather and his father. She'd lost his grandfather a dozen years ago, and she'd thought his dad was dead longer than that.

But, despite all the odds, Jessup was alive. He'd been living as JJ Cassidy on a ranch just an hour away from Ranch Haven.

"I haven't married him yet," Sadie said. But they couldn't wait much longer, not at their ages and not with the way they felt about each other. She leaned closer to the little girl and whispered, "And you have to keep it secret who he really is…" She pressed a finger against her lips.

Bailey Ann gave her a solemn nod before moving her fingers across her mouth like she was zipping her lips and throwing away the key.

Sadie couldn't resist. She had to hug the child again. "You are just precious," she said.

"Yes, she is…" Collin murmured, his voice gruff with emotion.

Clearly this grandson already knew something about love—a father's love for a child. This little girl wasn't biologically his. Colton had told her that whatever family she'd had once had abandoned her because she'd always been so sick. But Collin was sticking by her.

"Bailey Ann," he said. "Did you know that your visitor here is my grandmother, Sadie Haven?"

"Hi," Bailey Ann whispered.

"You seem to already know about Bailey Ann," he said to Sadie. "How did you…"

"I have sources everywhere," she said. Or at least she tried. But she wasn't always successful at getting the information she wanted. Collin's father was a good example. He'd taken off after high school and she hadn't been able to track him down. She hadn't even known where to look. That was because he hadn't wanted to be found. He'd been so sick, and he'd stayed away to avoid her overprotective-ness—and to avoid breaking her heart if he died.

Now that they were back in touch, she knew how much he regretted staying away. He understood well what she'd gone through because his oldest son, Collin's brother Cash, had disappeared after high school, too.

"My twin has a big mouth," Collin said.

"A family shouldn't have secrets," she said.

Collin snorted derisively. "Hmm… I wonder what my cousins would say if they heard you make that claim?"

Heat rushed to her face. She had kept secrets from his cousins—or at least one big secret. The cousins had no idea they had an uncle, and none of them, including her, had known about Jessup's sons. Cash, Marsh, Collin and Colton. The Cassidys.

"Well, a family *shouldn't* have secrets," she repeated. "That doesn't mean that they don't." She suspected his twin was keeping a secret, that something was bothering him. But now she could see that something was bother-ing Collin even more.

With the way he was staring at the little girl, with such longing and loss, it was clear what it was. "I'm not psy-chic," she said. "But I can tell that you need me."

Collin chuckled softly. "And I bet you love that."

"I love you," she said. "I want you to be happy."

And maybe that would excuse what she was about to do…

CHAPTER TWO

COLLIN HADN'T BEEN entirely joking when he'd accused his grandmother of being psychic. He and Colton had just been talking about her that morning and then a few hours later, there she was before he'd even had the chance to reach out to her.

But she wasn't psychic. She just had her sources, specifically his twin, and that was why she was so aware of what was going on in Collin's life. He hadn't even had to ask for her help.

She'd offered it anyway, in the form of a business card for a lawyer who specialized in family law, including adoptions. Genevieve Porter.

The woman worked out of a law firm on Main Street where too many people might see Collin walking into the two-story brick building. As a doctor just establishing himself in Willow Creek, he couldn't afford gossip about a visit to a law firm. He didn't need anyone wondering if he was hiring someone to represent him for malpractice.

So he helped himself to the black cowboy hat that his brother had left with Bailey Ann. She was all too happy to lend it, thinking it was hilarious that he could "dress up as" his brother.

He doubted the townsfolk would bat an eye over Colton visiting a law office. The firefighter was a hero without an enemy in the world. And no problems...

At least not until the last few weeks when he'd begun

acting as if something was weighing on him. Maybe Colton did have a reason to see a lawyer himself. Once Collin found out if he even had a chance of fostering, let alone adopting Bailey Ann, he would get his twin to tell him what was going on with him.

On his break, Collin put his plan in motion. Doctor's coat off, cowboy hat on, he headed to see Genevieve Porter.

For a moment, he wondered if she was part of his grandmother's matchmaking scheme. But no, he didn't believe Sadie would jeopardize a child's future. He had to trust that this Porter woman was a good adoption lawyer.

Once he stepped inside the reception area, with its exposed brick walls and high, coffered ceiling, he told the silver-haired receptionist his name and with whom he had an appointment.

The woman flashed him a smile and picked up her phone. "Dr. Cassidy is here for you," she said.

Given the short notice with which he'd gotten this appointment, he expected to have to take a seat and wait while the lawyer worked him in, but a door opened and a woman's voice called out. "Dr. Cassidy? You can come right back."

The silver-haired receptionist pointed to the open door just off the reception area. He assumed he was being pointed toward Ms. Porter's secretary or paralegal.

His patients often complained about the medical assistant and nurse asking them questions only to have him ask them again. Maybe lawyers were like doctors in that respect: they wanted to know the client's reason for showing up before they saw them. He hadn't really said much when he'd made the appointment, just that he needed to see her as soon as possible for some legal advice. And he was lucky enough to get in late that afternoon.

He walked through the open door and found himself

staring in awe at the woman waiting for him. With pale blond hair, bright blue eyes and delicate features, she was beautiful, but she also had an energy about her that would have been impossible to ignore. Intelligence radiated from her bright eyes, and she moved with such grace as she closed the door behind him and walked toward the desk.

The office was big with bookshelves lining the three interior walls and blinds covering the tall windows on the brick exterior wall. Most of the light came from the lamp on the big, mahogany desk behind which the woman took a seat after waving him toward one of the chairs in front of it.

"What can I help you with, Dr. Cassidy?" she asked.

"You're Ms. Porter?" he asked, just to confirm what he already suspected: her identity and the reason his grandmother had referred him here. As a setup...

She nodded and smiled. "Sorry. I didn't introduce myself. I must be getting used to how relaxed things are in Willow Creek."

"You're not from here?" he asked.

Color flushed her pale skin, and she looked away from him, as if she was uncomfortable. "Let's talk about you and your reason for needing my advice."

He'd vowed to focus only on Bailey Ann right now, even over his own twin. But something about her made him so curious that, despite Sadie's scheming, he was tempted to ask her more questions about herself.

But clearly she was more comfortable asking rather than answering questions. She picked up a pen and poised it over the legal pad on her desk. "What can I help you with?"

He settled into one of the leather chairs and clasped his hands together. The skin on them was still a little pink from the burns he'd sustained in the fire three weeks ago.

He and his family had lost their house that day. But they'd lost more than that. They'd lost even more than their material possessions and mementos. They'd lost their identities, too, and their family history as they'd known it.

"Dr. Cassidy?" Ms. Porter prodded him. "Are you all right?" She was staring at his hands as well, her blue eyes clouded with concern.

"I am," he said. But he wouldn't be if he lost Bailey Ann like he'd lost so much else.

GENEVIEVE WASN'T SURE why the doctor had wanted to see her. She wasn't a malpractice lawyer. Though she wondered, from the damaged skin on his hands, if he'd been the victim instead of the perpetrator of malpractice. Hilda, the receptionist, hadn't gotten any information out of him when she'd made the appointment. She'd probably figured Genevieve should just be grateful that she had a client, any client, given that business for her had been light since she'd moved to town a month ago.

"Dr. Cassidy?" she prodded him when he remained curiously quiet as he stared at his hands. "Are you sure you're all right?"

He leaned back in the chair and expelled a ragged sigh. "No. I'm not sure of anything anymore…"

"I know the feeling," she muttered softly enough that she hoped he didn't hear.

But he leaned forward again and stared at her with those strangely intense dark eyes. "Ms. Porter?"

"Genevieve," she said. That was something she liked about Willow Creek; it was so much more casual and informal than DC. "Call me Genevieve."

"I'm Collin," he said.

Collin Cassidy. He sounded and looked—with his black cowboy hat and dark eyes and long, lanky body—like he should be a rodeo star or country singer. But he was a doctor.

"Collin, then." She gave him a warm smile. "I hope I can help you, but if it's in regard to your job, I don't have any experience with malpractice claims."

"Fortunately neither do I," he said. "I was referred to you because you specialize in adoptions."

A cold chill rushed down her spine despite the suit jacket she wore over her sleeveless sweater. She'd only made that claim to one other person—a lawyer with another firm.

"Who..." Her voice cracked, and she cleared it before continuing, "Who referred you to me?"

"Sadie Haven," he said.

She should have known...

This was all going to blow up in her face, like so much of her life had. If only she'd been honest from the start.

She drew in a deep breath and resolved to tell him the truth. Or at least some of it. "While I have some experience with family law and have handled some adoptions, I mostly do estate planning now." That seemed to be the biggest need in Willow Creek. She'd specialized in other areas in DC.

He emitted a soft groan of disappointment or maybe frustration. "Oh, I should have known what she was up to," he muttered.

"She?"

"Sadie," he said again. "You know her, right?"

She shook her head. "I've never met Sadie Haven."

"Oh, I'm sorry then. I must have misunderstood," he said, his face flushing. "I was really hoping you could help me."

For some reason she wished she could as well. "Do you and your wife want to adopt?" she asked.

"No—yes," he answered with a slight head shake.

"Which is it?" she asked with a smile.

"*I* want to adopt. I don't have a wife."

She felt a strange rush of relief and nearly shook her head at herself. She had no business being attracted to anyone right now, least of all a client. Especially a client Sadie Haven had referred to her...

What was that about?

"Would it be easier if I had one?" he asked.

"One what?" she asked, and she glanced down at the blank page of her legal pad. She needed to start taking notes, needed to figure out what was going on...

"A wife," he replied. "Would it be easier for me to adopt if I was married?"

"Not necessarily..." She was intrigued now.

Dr. Cassidy shook his head. "It doesn't matter. It's not like I could find someone to marry me in two weeks anyway."

"Two weeks?" she repeated. "I don't understand."

"The little girl I want to adopt, my patient, is going to be leaving the hospital in two weeks," he said. "Her social worker found her a foster home, but it's only short term. I want to foster her instead and then adopt her to give her a home without any further disruption to her life."

"You can certainly petition to adopt her," she assured him.

"Her social worker wants to place her in foster care in Sheridan," he said. "She'll be so far away, and if this home is like the last one, and they don't follow her medical orders..." His deep voice got so gruff, he stopped and cleared his throat. "I just don't want to risk anyone else taking care of her. I don't want to lose her."

He wasn't talking about just losing custody or contact but of his patient losing her life. That struck her heart, and she felt concern for the child that she hadn't even met. "Are one or both of her parents alive? If so, we could see if they'll grant you legal custody," she said. That would be the easiest way.

But if they weren't alive…

Genevieve knew all too well the problems that could cause.

"No idea. They signed off their rights to her before I met her," he said. "She's a ward of the state and has been frequently moved from foster home to foster home because no one can handle her medical issues."

"What are those?" she asked.

"She was born with an enlarged heart, which eventually caused congestive heart failure, and she's just recently had a heart transplant," he said. "She's only seven years old."

That pang struck Genevieve's heart again. "Oh, that's so sad…"

But for some reason, Collin Cassidy smiled. "She's the happiest, sweetest little girl despite all the challenges she's had. And I want to give her a home that's safe and consistent."

"Do you have a foster care license?" she asked. "Because the adoption could take some time, but if you were licensed for foster care, we could get her placed with you while we filed the paperwork for adoption."

He shook his head again. "I didn't think… There's so much going on… I'm not ready…"

She bit her lip. "Okay. You said you're not married. You're right—that can be a barrier but it's not unworkable. Tell me about your home situation."

He glanced at his hands again and shook his head. "My family home burned down a few weeks ago, and we're all staying at someone's house here in Willow Creek."

While she was sympathetic to him, she also had to think of the child. "Are you sure then that she would be better off with you than the other foster family?"

He sucked in a breath as if she'd slapped him. "That other family isn't even trained yet in how to care for her and they don't want her long term," he said. "She's been my patient all through my residency and fellowship in Sheridan, which is most of her life. I know her. And I love her."

More than a pang struck her heart now; it was as if someone squeezed it. She could hear the love in his voice and see it on his handsome face.

"I… I would like to talk to her," Genevieve said. "I'd like to see what she'd like…"

"I don't want to get her hopes up," Collin said. "In case this isn't possible, in case I can't get licensed as a foster home or qualify to adopt her…"

"I understand," Genevieve said, and his consideration for the child increased her estimation of him. "But I'd still like to meet her."

"I don't want to get my hopes up either," he admitted. "Do you…" He stopped and cleared his throat again. "Do you think you can help me?"

She leaned back in her chair for a moment and studied him across her desk. He was so good-looking and obviously smart since he was apparently a cardiologist. But she'd learned the hard way to protect herself from handsome, intelligent men who were used to getting what they wanted. Like Bradford, her ex-husband, who had wanted biological children more than he'd wanted her. When she hadn't been able to give him those children, he hadn't wanted her at all anymore. Thoughts of her marriage usually hurt, but somehow, the pain didn't come.

Maybe she was over him. Or maybe she was as dead inside as Bradford had accused her of being, except that she was moved by the care this handsome doctor had for a little girl he wanted to make his own.

"I want to help *her*," she said. She wasn't sure if that

would help him or not. It depended on what was best for the child.

Instead of being offended, he grinned and nodded. "Thank you…" Then he muttered, "Sadie strikes again…"

She was pretty sure she wasn't meant to hear that. The chill rushed over her again, reminding her who had brought him to her specifically.

Why had Sadie referred this man to her? Was she sending a message to Genevieve that she knew she was here? Maybe that she knew what Genevieve had done, or at least caused…?

BEN HAD BEEN expecting and dreading this visit. While he loved his grandmother, he also knew that when she was on the warpath, there could be collateral damage. He didn't even know Genevieve Porter, but he felt a pang of sympathy for her that she was in Sadie Haven's sights.

He also felt a twinge of regret that he'd shared her name with his grandmother. But he'd been concerned that this lawyer had been asking questions about his nephews and who now had legal custody of them.

Why had she asked? Had she intended to challenge that custody for a client or for…?

He had a feeling he was about to find out. Since Ms. Porter worked out of his old law firm, Grandmother would probably have him investigate her.

His door opened, and he rose from behind his desk as Sadie walked in. She used to storm this office when Lem had been mayor. She'd loved giving him grief over how he managed the town. She only took Ben to task occasionally, usually when he deserved it like when he'd meddled in her love life like she kept meddling in everyone else's.

But she looked happy now, her face aglow with a bright smile.

And he tensed with suspicion. She'd been so upset over the lawyer call and most especially over that complaint to CPS.

"What's going on?" he asked, studying her through narrowed eyes.

"What do you mean?"

"You're not mad."

"Should I be mad?" she asked. "Have you done something to upset me?"

A smile tugged at his lips now. "When have I ever upset you? Did I upset you by bringing Lem around the ranch for dinner?" he asked.

She sighed. "Yes, you did, Benjamin Haven, and you know it. You upset my entire lonely, solitary life."

"You two really are getting married." He was still stunned at the success of his matchmaking. But maybe he shouldn't have been surprised; as everyone said, he was the most like Sadie.

Other people said it as if it was a bad thing, but he knew the truth.

She nodded. "Yes. Very soon. We're too old to wait."

He snorted his derision at her claim.

His grandmother and his deputy mayor were more vital at eighty than most people were in their thirties, which was another reason he was glad he took after her.

"So when's the happy day?" he asked.

"Soon," she said. "But I need your help."

"You want me to be your wedding planner?" Like he didn't have enough to do with running the town and helping his family with his nephews and the ranch. And with school starting soon, he wouldn't see as much of his fiancée as he wished either. Emily, as a teacher, would be back in the classroom instead of spending so much of her time at Ranch Haven which was an hour from town.

She snorted now. "I know how to plan a wedding," she said.

He chuckled. "I guess you do. You've been planning all of ours since you hired Katie, Emily, Melanie and Taye to help out at the ranch."

While her match making had worked out for him and his brothers, Ben wondered how his cousins were going to handle her meddling. She'd already been messing with their lives more than they might have realized.

Though thinking back to some of their visits to the ranch, he suspected they were well aware of her antics.

"Since we've had and are going to have so many weddings, I have a proposal for you," she said.

He chuckled. "I've already accepted Emily's proposal," he reminded her.

She reached out and smacked his shoulder. "I'm taken, too, thanks to you," she said. "To get everybody into the mood for romance, I propose that the town decorate for Valentine's Day, bringing out all the hearts and flowers and pink and red…"

"It's August," Ben said.

"So? We have Christmas in July. Let's have Valentine's Day in August."

"*We* don't promote Christmas in July," he said. "Retailers do to bump up their sales. What are you trying to sell, Grandma?"

"You have to ask?" she asked with a sigh of disappointment.

And he groaned. She was trying to sell romance, and since he and his brothers had already taken her bait, she must have come up with this plan to guide his cousins into falling in love.

"I thought you were going to be too busy for your matchmaking with everything going on with the boys."

"CPS closed the case," she said. "Lem's lovely grand-daughter made certain of that."

Dr. Livvy Lemmon hadn't appreciated someone saying that she'd failed to report when five-year-old Ian had come into the ER with bruises. She'd known that his falling in the barn had caused those bruises, not any abuse or neglect, and she'd made certain the CPS investigator had known that as well.

No wonder Ben's cousin Colton had fallen so hard and fast for the doctor. Still, his cousins Marsh and Collin were single yet...

And maybe his cousin Cash, but Ben hadn't met him. He'd figured Sadie would be looking for her runaway grandson even more intently than she'd looked for her runaway son.

She'd found Jessup, alive and with sons of his own, which was part of the reason she was so happy. Lem was the other part.

"What about Genevieve Porter?" he asked. "Don't you want to find out more about her?" Once the question slipped out, he bit the inside of his cheek. He'd probably fallen right into her plan for him to investigate the lawyer.

But she just smiled. "I have Collin handling that."

He wondered if Collin knew he was "handling" that. But before he could ask anything else, she was patting his cheek as she so often did.

"Just get those decorations up as soon as possible," she said. "I always wanted a Valentine's Day theme for my wedding."

He snorted again at the thought of Sadie wanting anything to do with hearts and flowers. But then her smile slipped a bit, and he wondered if she was thinking about her recent heart attack. He felt a twinge of regret.

Or maybe she really was a romantic. Maybe that was

the reason for all her meddling—that she loved love as much as she loved all her grandsons.

Or maybe she just loved meddling…

CHAPTER THREE

COLLIN STEPPED OUT of the law office into the late afternoon sun, squinting like he'd just woken up. But he couldn't wake up from this nightmare, just like he'd never been able to as a kid.

He didn't want Bailey Ann growing up like he had, with so much uncertainty about his life. His dad had had so many flare-ups with lupus that his organs had been affected. First his kidneys and then his heart. Collin had gone to bed every night worrying that his dad would be dead when Collin woke up again. The irony was that he hadn't worried about his mom, and then she was the one he'd lost to breast cancer.

Bailey Ann had already lost both her parents, not to death but to abandonment. And then there had been so many foster homes that had put her back into the system because the doctor's appointments, hospital stays and medications had been too much for those families to handle.

He'd been the most constant person in her life; she couldn't lose him any more than he could lose her. Had he made that clear to Genevieve Porter? Did she understand that this wasn't just about what he wanted?

He glanced over his shoulder at the law office, wondering if he should go back inside and try to explain it to her more clearly. But no, she'd had another client coming in, and she'd agreed to meet Bailey Ann after that appointment at the hospital.

She would talk to her and find out what the child wanted. He breathed a slight sigh of relief. Bailey Ann would want to stay with him. He was certain of it.

But how was he going to make that happen? Even if Genevieve Porter filed paperwork with the court for him, he still wasn't ready. He slept in the den at the property where his dad was staying until the insurance claim was settled on their burned house. He needed a place that was big enough for him and Bailey Ann and a live-in nanny who had experience caring for a child with medical challenges. And he'd need to accomplish all of that within two weeks and hope that Genevieve Porter agreed to help him, too.

He tugged down the brim of Colton's hat, blocking the sun, and as he could see more clearly, his eyes settled on Becca Calder's real estate office across the street. If anyone could find him a house on short notice, it would be Becca. Intent on talking to her, he stepped off the curb.

And a horn blared. Tires squealed. He stepped back and grimaced over his mistake. The truck hadn't been close, but Collin had upset the driver. The truck's box was piled high with plastic totes, and the driver pulled to the curb where he was standing.

He didn't have time to deal with an irate driver. But the guy just waved at him, motioning him to pass in front of his truck. Collin waved back, looked both ways this time and hurried across the street.

He didn't have an appointment, so chances were Becca would be too busy to see him. Or she might not even be in the office at all. But when he pulled open the door, she was right there in front of him in the reception area.

Collin hadn't seen her in years. He was struck by how different she looked than the girl who used to hang out in the barn with his older brother Cash.

Gone was the long, tangled hair; she wore the black tresses in a sleek cut that just skimmed her chin. And instead of worn jeans and an oversize sweatshirt, she wore a suit much like the one Genevieve Porter had been wearing, with a lightweight jacket, pencil skirt and heels.

While he was happy to see her, she did not seem as thrilled. She groaned and said, "Colton, stop badgering me. I am not getting into the middle of you and Cash and whatever has you so anxious to see him right now."

She'd mistaken him for his twin. The cowboy hat. He reached up and touched the brim again, pushing it back with slightly shaking fingers.

She focused on his hand, and her dark blue eyes narrowed. Then she groaned again. "You're not Colton."

His hands were definitely a giveaway. While Collin had sustained burns in the fire, Colton had been one of the responders, wearing his protective gear as he and the other firefighters fought to save the family home.

"No, I'm not Colton," Collin said.

Becca closed her eyes and sighed. "Forget what I said…"

"You and I both know that's not going to happen," he said. "What's going on with Colton and Cash? And do you still see him?"

"Colton's been by the office a couple of times," Becca said.

Collin shook his head. "You know I'm talking about Cash, not my twin."

"Collin…" she murmured.

"Yes, Becca," he said. "It's me." After mistaking him for Colton, she must have considered that he could have been Marsh, too.

"I heard you were in Willow Creek. That you're all in Willow Creek now," she said.

"Does that include Cash?" he asked.

Pink color flushed her pale skin. "Like I've been telling your twin, I'm not getting in the middle of that..."

"Of what?" Collin asked. "I still don't know why Cash took off like he did. Why he was so mad at Dad..." But he trailed off as he realized what his oldest brother's reason might have been. Maybe he'd learned the truth long before his brothers had. Maybe he'd found out about Sadie and the rest of their family that Dad had kept secret from them.

He bristled a bit as anger nagged at him. But as he'd done every time it had threatened to erupt before this, he reminded himself that all that mattered was that Dad was alive. He was doing well.

He needed to focus on that, on making sure that Dad kept doing well, which he might not if his sons expressed how angry they were with him.

Was that why Colton had come around Becca's office? Looking for Cash because he'd figured out why their oldest brother might have left?

But just as Collin needed to focus on Dad staying well, he needed to focus on making sure that Bailey Ann did, too. "I'm not here about Cash," he assured Becca. "I need your help with something else."

Becca's blue eyes narrowed as she studied his face with apparent skepticism. "My help?"

"I need a house," he said.

She groaned again.

"What's wrong now?" he asked.

She stepped back and waved him into her office. An older woman was standing up behind her desk, peering at them.

"Which one is this?"

"This is Collin. Dr. Cassidy," Becca said. "Collin, this is my mom. Phyllis Calder."

Phyllis smiled at him. "You look just like your brother."

"It's the hat," Collin said, pointing to the brim.

Mother and daughter both chuckled.

"Yeah, it's the hat," Becca teased. And it felt like they were kids again for a moment. But Cash had been gone seventeen years now.

And Collin wasn't certain they'd ever been kids, not growing up as they had with that constant worry and helplessness. Maybe that was why Cash had left and never looked back.

Collin couldn't really blame him. Even though he wanted to.

"So you want to buy a house?" Becca asked.

He nodded. "I need to. It has to be at least a three bedroom. And I need it within two weeks."

She chuckled again. "You must be joking."

That urgency he'd been feeling turned to panic now. Just as he'd already begun to suspect, he didn't have enough time to do what he needed to...to be able to keep Bailey Ann.

He was going to lose her, too.

ONCE HER CLIENT LEFT, Genevieve opened her desk drawer and pulled out the family portrait. The young couple, obviously so in love as they beamed at each other, the three little boys gathered around them on the bales of hay in a barn. This wasn't her family.

Genevieve had thrown it away just like her parents had because she hadn't agreed with her younger sister's decision to get married right out of high school to start this beautiful family that she'd had. Embarrassed that her daughter was marrying so young and worried that the town would think it was because she had to, Mother had insisted on moving away from Willow Creek.

Maybe she'd been worried that the town would compare

Jenny to her and remember how she'd had a child while she was in high school: Genevieve. She'd always wondered if that was why her mom and stepdad had named her sister Jennifer, like she was supposed to be a do-over of Genevieve, whose name was French for Jennifer. Like she was the legitimate daughter and Genevieve had been the mistake. But then that had given Jenny no room to make any mistakes, and that was what Mother and Jenny's father had been convinced she'd been doing. So they had sold everything and moved away and had never returned.

It had been even easier for Genevieve to cut off contact. She'd been in law school on the other side of the country, and as busy as she'd been, she'd barely talked to her sister. Jenny had been six years younger than Genevieve, so they'd never been in the same school at the same time or had the same friends. And feeling like she'd been the mistake and Jenny had been the wanted child, Genevieve had resented her a bit through no fault of Jenny's. And she'd avoided her so much, burying herself in her books, that they hadn't had much of a relationship growing up.

She touched her sister's beautiful face. She'd still looked like a teenager in that picture despite eleven years having passed since her high school graduation. She'd also looked so happy, happier than Genevieve had ever been.

So who had made the mistakes?

Not Jenny. She hadn't needed to get married; her oldest had been born four years after her high school graduation. She'd wanted to get married because she truly loved Dale Haven. She'd made a beautiful family. Something Genevieve hadn't been able to do.

She put the picture back in the drawer and pushed it closed. She couldn't look at her sister without tears burning her eyes.

She hadn't even known Jenny had died until a few

months after her tragic accident. Because of that, Genevieve hadn't been there for the funeral or for her nephews.

She'd failed them.

She couldn't fail any other children. So, like she'd told Dr. Cassidy, she needed to talk to his patient first. She needed to know what Bailey Ann wanted before she did anything else.

Drawing in a deep breath, she picked up her briefcase from the floor and headed toward the door. Hilda had already turned off the lights in the reception area, but the late afternoon sunshine streaked through the blinds.

At her former law practice in DC, people had often worked around the clock. Here in Willow Creek, they usually knocked off before five.

Genevieve usually stayed as late as she could because she didn't want to go home to the big empty house she'd bought when she'd first moved back to Willow Creek.

But this afternoon she didn't have to go home just yet; she was going to the hospital to meet Bailey Ann. She hoped Dr. Cassidy was the right choice for the little girl, that despite being unwanted by her parents and foster families, she was wanted now and forever, not just short term. Genevieve understood all too well how Bailey Ann might feel, how it felt to be unwanted. Her own mother had left Genevieve to be raised by her grandparents while she'd gone to college. Then her grandparents had simply given her back once Mother had her degree. The people who raised her hadn't even tried to fight to keep her.

And Mother had never let her forget that Genevieve was a mistake. They'd used her very existence as a case study for why her younger sister Jenny shouldn't marry out of high school.

Genevieve counted down the days until she could graduate from high school and leave Willow Creek far behind.

She'd doubled up on credits, graduated early and left for college. And she'd never intended to return...

But here she was. Now she stepped outside the law office onto Main Street. In some ways, it looked like nothing had changed. But the town was bigger than she remembered. There were more shops and restaurants. New buildings had been erected and old ones had been renovated.

It was not just bigger but nicer than she remembered.

And warmer.

She lifted her face to the late afternoon sunshine, but a shadow fell across her instead. Collin Cassidy towered over her, his black hat blocking out the sun. He was bigger than she'd remembered, too, even though she'd just met him an hour ago. The man was so tall and broad. Was he nice?

He'd seemed so, but Genevieve knew to be cautious. Even nice guys could be incredibly selfish.

"Were you waiting for me?" she asked with some concern. She'd told him she would talk to Bailey Ann after work, but she knew how to find her own way to the hospital.

"I'm not stalking you," he assured her. He turned slightly and pointed across the street. "I was just over there, at the real estate office, talking to Becca Calder." His broad shoulders sagged now, and his head was bowed, as if she'd given him bad news.

She could imagine what that was. "Still low inventory?" she asked.

He nodded. "Yes."

"When I bought my house, that was the case then, too." She and Becca had looked all around Willow Creek for something when the big house near town had miraculously popped up.

"She said there's very little on the market," he said. "And even if something came up, I wouldn't be able to close on the property with a mortgage for more than a month…if I even qualify for financing because of all of my student loans."

He was definitely feeling defeated. Genevieve understood that feeling all too well.

"I'm going to meet Bailey Ann now before visiting hours are over," she said. "Do you want to go to the hospital with me?"

A smile curved his lips, but sadness lingered in his dark eyes with that defeat. "I always want to see her."

"Introduce us," she said. "And then leave me alone to talk to her."

"I don't know if that's a good idea anymore," he said.

"You don't want her?" she asked.

He tensed. "Of course I do. But if it's not possible, I don't want to get her hopes up."

"I'll be careful when I talk to her," she promised, wishing that she'd been careful when she'd first talked to Sue about her nephews.

Wishing that she'd done so many other things differently…like being able to face the Havens. Every time she'd gone to pick up the phone or drive out to the ranch, she'd been filled with dread. What if they hated her for how she'd failed Jenny? She couldn't blame them. How could a person turn their back on their own sister? To not be there when she was married or when she'd given birth to any of her three precious children? To not be there when Jenny died, when she was buried, when those three boys needed her the most?

And what had she been doing? Trying to make the perfect life for a man who'd left as soon as it was clear she couldn't give him his own children. Those tiny lives she hadn't been able to bring into the world.

She closed her eyes for a moment, struggling to contain

her emotions. When she opened them, Collin was staring at her with deep emotions of his own in his dark eyes.

"I want to warn you that Bailey Ann is in hospital in the first place because of her last foster family," Collin said. "They didn't give her the antirejection medication in the proper doses. And she'd started..." His voice cracked now as emotion overwhelmed him. "She was very sick. And she's still getting her strength back."

She blinked against tears, both for her own difficult past and for the brave little girl this doctor was fighting for. "I'll keep that in mind and won't tire her out. Thank you for trusting me."

They shared a smile, and the tense moment passed. She looked around to clear her thoughts. Several workers were on ladders, hanging things from the streetlights along Main Street. She narrowed her eyes and stared in disbelief. "Are they hanging hearts?"

He tipped back his head and looked up as well. "Yes..."

And around the base of each lamppost, red, white and pink flowers had been planted.

"I don't understand," she murmured. "Are they decorating for St. Valentine's Day?"

Before he could reply, a banner swung across the street, tethered to a light post on either side.

It read: *Happy Valentine's Day!*

Collin chuckled, and the deep rumble of it raised goose bumps on Genevieve's skin despite the warmth of the summer day. "Okay..."

"Isn't it August?" Genevieve asked.

He chuckled again. "I'm new to Willow Creek," he said. "I don't know what all their traditions are, but apparently Valentine's Day in August might be one of them..."

He didn't sound any more convinced of that than she was, though.

"I wonder if Sadie has anything to do with this…" he muttered.

Sadie…

Why had Sadie referred him to her?

Jenny, in her letters, had always raved about her. She'd idolized and adored Sadie Haven. But Genevieve hadn't been gone so long that she'd forgotten about the reputation Sadie Haven had earned for being a formidable adversary. At least to the former mayor, Old Man Lemmon.

Did she know what Sue had done on Genevieve's behalf? Was Sadie her adversary now, too?

"GETTING OLD IS not for the faint of heart," Lem Lemmon mumbled to himself as he stared out his office window at the town square across the street. Balloon hearts and other heart-shaped decorations hung from every light pole, and flowers in pink, red and white were planted in every bed of the little park area.

"Oh, yeah?" Ben asked.

Lem turned around to find the mayor standing in his doorway. "I don't recommend it."

"You trying to tell me something?" Ben asked, arching a dark brow. "I'm just over thirty now, you know."

Lem chuckled. "And we both know I was talking about me."

"You're not old, Lem."

"I've been old a long time," he said. People had called him Old Man Lemmon for at least twenty years. Sadie had probably started it, as Sadie started most things. "I thought I was still pretty sharp, though, until I looked out my window and saw everything decorated for Valentine's Day. Isn't it August? Or have I missed the last six months passing?"

A pang of panic and regret struck him as he thought

about his late wife and how much time she'd lost and forgotten. She'd forgotten everything in the end. Everything but him.

What would she think of him and Sadie?

Somehow, he thought she and Sadie's late husband, Big Jake, would be laughing.

They would have gotten quite a kick out of him falling for Sadie, and probably an even bigger kick out of Sadie falling for him. No. Getting old was tough work, but if you got lucky, you might get to take another shot at love.

Especially when you knew how precious and short life was.

"You missed Sadie," Ben said. "She stopped in earlier." He pointed toward the window and all those decorations. "That was her."

Lem chuckled. "Of course it was. And you went along with it."

Of all Sadie's grandchildren, Ben was the most like her, and the most able to handle her. For example, knowing it was best to mobilize the town gardening crew to put up Valentine's decorations at Sadie's request for them.

Ben nodded. "I figured maybe I can get Emily to the altar a little earlier. And maybe Sadie suggested this to get you to the altar a little earlier."

Lem grinned. "We're not going to waste any time. Not at our ages..." And not after Sadie's recent health scare. But Sadie wanted to make sure her great grandsons were all right. That there was no threat against them anymore, like that call to CPS and to her lawyer.

He glanced back out the window at those decorations. At all the hearts and flowers...

"She's up to something..." he murmured. She hadn't brought him in on this yet, unlike her other schemes where she'd enlisted him.

"When isn't she up to something?" Ben asked.

"True."

But what was she up to this time? And who did she really intend to send a message to with this whole Valentine's in August thing?

CHAPTER FOUR

As COLLIN AND Genevieve rode the elevator up to Bailey Ann's floor, his stomach was in knots. Not over Genevieve meeting the little girl. Bailey Ann loved company, and Genevieve had promised that she would be careful not to raise the child's hopes. The knots in his stomach were because he had raised his own hopes for a moment, thinking that Sadie could actually work her magic. That somehow he would be able to foster and then adopt the child he loved like his own.

But there wasn't enough time. She would definitely wind up going to that foster home in Sheridan, and he wasn't certain if that family would be equipped to handle her care with such little training. And if her body rejected her heart again, she might not make it.

"You're so quiet," Genevieve remarked. "Have you changed your mind?"

"No," he quickly replied. "Not at all. It's just… I don't see how…"

"We'll talk about that after I talk to Bailey Ann," she said.

She was going to wait until then to tell him he was beyond hope?

Collin had had to give out that news to patients before. That they'd done all they could and there was nothing more…

He empathized with them because he'd received that

news himself. He'd lost his mother and, for so long, thought he was going to lose his dad, too.

But his dad had hung in there all these years, battling all the immune issues he'd had with lupus. Suffering through kidney failures and transplants and now his heart…

Collin barely noticed when the elevator dinged and the doors swished open. Genevieve touched his arm, and he felt a little jolt of awareness even through the material of his shirt.

"Are you okay?" she asked.

No. But not wanting to get into everything with her, he just nodded. "I appreciate you coming here to meet her," he said. "It's hard for her—not having any family to come see her—so she loves getting visitors."

Genevieve's long lashes fluttered for a moment as she blinked. "That's sad," she said, her voice cracking slightly.

"She's not sad, though," Collin said. "She's such a sweet, happy little girl. Here, you'll see." He reached out then, pressing his fingers against the small of her back to guide her in the direction of Bailey Ann's room. And again, even through her jacket, he felt that little jolt—a shock of awareness.

He couldn't remember the last time he'd reacted that way to anyone. He'd been so focused on becoming a doctor that the dates he'd gone on had never led anywhere serious. Everybody had wanted more time and attention from him than he'd had to give.

But things were different now. He was no longer a resident or a fellow. He was established. He would have more time for Bailey Ann. But could he convince her social worker and a family court judge of that?

Could Genevieve, if she agreed to help him?

His pace slowed as he neared the open door to Bailey Ann's room. And he lowered his head and his voice to whisper to her, "Just a short visit for now, okay? We don't want to tire her. Let me know if you need to speak with her again later."

"I understand," she said. "I won't stay too long." Genevieve nodded decisively, and he was touched at how seriously she was taking Bailey Ann's health before even meeting the little girl.

He hated leaving her alone in her room, hated leaving her at all. How would she handle leaving him? Would her foster parents tell her silly stories to help her go to sleep or hold her hand when she was scared? Or would she be alone again? He couldn't figure out a way for even the legendary Sadie Haven to stop her assignment to that foster home in Sheridan.

How was Genevieve Porter going to stop it? Would she even want to?

He drew in a deep breath as they neared the open door to Bailey Ann's room. Through it, he could hear the deep rumble of a voice that sounded eerily like his own. Colton...

He touched the brim of his hat. No doubt his twin had returned for that. Or more likely just to see Bailey Ann. Colton and his fiancée, Livvy, had started spending a lot of time with the little girl, too, at Collin's request. He hoped that his family would help her feel less alone.

Genevieve glanced up at him, her brow furrowed beneath the wispy strands of her pale blond hair. "She sounds an awful lot like you..."

"That's not—"

A high-pitched giggle cut him off. Then Bailey Ann's voice saying, "You're silly, Uncle Colton!" She sounded nothing like him, more like Tinker Bell.

"I thought she didn't have family," Genevieve said.

"She doesn't," Collin said. "That's my brother."

"Dr. Cass!" Bailey Ann called out; she must have heard him, too.

Warmth spread over him as it always did when she called for him with so much excitement and affection. He grinned. "How do you know it's me?" he asked as he gestured Genevieve into the room ahead of him. "I could be Uncle Colton." He pointed at the hat.

"So you're the one who took it," Colton said as he grabbed for it.

"Told you!" Bailey Ann said. "I didn't lose it!" But she looked away from him and his twin to focus on Genevieve. "Wow! You're so pretty! You look like one of my Barbie dolls."

With her pale blond hair and bright blue eyes, Genevieve really did resemble the doll that to some had represented unattainable perfection.

There was definitely something unattainable about the lawyer. Any time she'd seemed about to reveal something personal to Collin, she'd stopped herself and pulled back. Maybe she'd just been trying to remain professional, or maybe she was private. He'd been accused of being the same, though, so he wasn't about to judge her for it.

Except for Bailey Ann, Collin always tried to remain professional and a bit detached so that he could focus on his patients' care and not his own feelings. But it was impossible to stay detached from Bailey Ann.

Genevieve smiled at the little girl and said, "You are very sweet, just like Dr. Cassidy told me you are."

"Bailey Ann, this is my…" He didn't want to say lawyer, but he wasn't even sure if she would agree to represent him. To help him. "My friend, Genevieve Porter."

"I'm Dr. Cass's friend, too," Bailey Ann confided. She smiled warmly at Genevieve, then jumped up on her bed and threw her arms around Collin's neck. And as she did, Colton pulled off his hat.

"I'll take this back." He plopped it on his own head and turned toward Genevieve and held out his hand. "I'm Dr. Cass's far better-looking twin, Colton."

Genevieve shook his hand and smiled brightly up at Collin's brother. And for some reason Collin felt a little jab of something, but it couldn't be jealousy. Despite whatever Sadie's motives in referring him to Genevieve were, he wasn't interested in the lawyer for anything other than her legal help so he could foster and adopt Bailey Ann.

And he had to make certain that she was willing to help. Bailey Ann pulled away from him and reached for Genevieve. Instead of shaking her hand, she hugged her, too, wrapping her short arms around Genevieve's neck. And as she had with Sadie, she touched Genevieve's hair. "It's so pretty and soft..."

"I love your curls," Genevieve said.

"Did you come to visit me?" Bailey Ann asked as if awed. Maybe she thought Genevieve really was a doll come to life.

"Yes, I did," Genevieve said. "Is that okay with you?"

"Yes!" Bailey Ann exclaimed. "Do you want to play a game? I have Memory. And old maid. And checkers."

"And she cheats," Collin warned her. "So be careful with this one."

Genevieve gave him a slight nod.

She must have understood what he was really telling her: to be careful with Bailey Ann when talking with her as she tried to ascertain the little girl's wishes for her own future so she could decide whether or not she would help him. No. Help her. That was all she'd agreed to do, once she'd determined what was best for Bailey Ann.

He doubted she could determine that with one conversation, though.

Time to leave them to it—which meant it was also a good time to grill Colton about what was going on.

"You've got your hat back, brother. Say good-bye to Bailey Ann, and I'll walk you to the elevator."

Colton leaned down and kissed the little girl's cheek. "You be nice to Dr. Cass's friend. No betting on Memory and taking all her money." Bailey Ann had spent enough time with Collin's twin to know he was teasing and she giggled. Then Colton smiled at Genevieve. "Nice to meet you, Ms. Porter."

"Genevieve," she said. "And nice to meet you, too."

Colton's grin widened, as if he was thinking about flirting with her. But because he was madly in love with Livvy Lemmon, he would only do that to irritate Collin. Like Collin had probably consciously irritated him a few times when he'd talked to Livvy before Colton had known which of them the beautiful ER doctor had fallen for...

Collin had never had any doubt it would be Colton. Colton was the fun, lighthearted twin. Collin had always been too focused and intense for people to feel comfortable around.

At the moment, he needed to find his focus, though. He tugged on Colton's sleeve, pulling him into the hall with him. "Let's get out of their way so they can get to know each other," he said.

Once they were out in the hall, Colton started firing the questions at him before he could light into his twin himself. "How did you make a friend? Especially one who looks like that? And why would you be introducing her to Bailey Ann already? What's going on?"

Collin glanced through the open doorway where Bailey Ann was setting up her checkerboard on her tray. He tugged Colton farther from the doorway and whispered, "She's a lawyer. Sadie recommended her."

"Oh, she did, did she?" Colton chuckled.

"What?"

"Well, look at her. No, I don't have to tell you to do that. You haven't really taken your eyes off her." He chuckled again.

Collin felt himself flush. "Yeah, yeah, Sadie probably is scheming, but it's not going to work on me. My only interest in Genevieve Porter is her legal help so I can foster and adopt Bailey Ann."

Colton nodded, but there was still some skepticism in his dark eyes as he stared at Collin.

So Collin turned the tables on his brother. "So that's what's going on with me. What's going on with you?"

"What do you mean?"

"You wanted to tell me something earlier today," Collin reminded him. "I know it's about Cash."

Colton's dark eyes widened, and the color left his face. "How on earth—"

"I saw Becca today. She thought I was you."

"Because you were wearing my hat," Colton said in realization.

"Yep. What's your sudden interest in finding Cash?" he asked.

Colton shrugged. "You don't think he deserves to know what we just learned?"

"Are you sure he doesn't already know?" Collin asked.

Colton sucked in a breath. "You figure that's the reason he left?" He released the breath in a sigh. "I did consider that myself..."

"I don't know what to think," Collin admitted. About his family or about Genevieve Porter. "But I can't focus on anything but Bailey Ann right now. So I'll leave finding Cash up to you." And he would focus on trying to keep the little girl safe.

GENEVIEVE WAS GETTING her butt kicked by a seven-year-old. And she wasn't even letting Bailey Ann win. She was distracted though and kept glancing into the hall where the two men appeared to be having a serious discussion.

About Bailey Ann?

About her?

Collin's twin had certainly been curious about her, about their *friendship*. Obviously he knew they weren't friends.

"They look a lot alike, don't they?" Bailey Ann remarked as she slid her checker into a spot on Genevieve's side of the board.

"The checkers?" Genevieve asked, but she smiled to show she was joking. She knew the little girl had noticed her interest in the Cassidy twins.

Bailey Ann giggled. "No. Those mostly look like mine. Red."

"Yes," Genevieve agreed. "You're really good at checkers."

"Dr. Cass taught me," Bailey Ann said. "He's really smart. And funny."

"Funny?" Genevieve asked. She hadn't seen any hint of a sense of humor in him, but then he was incredibly worried about this young patient of his.

Bailey Ann giggled. "He tells really funny jokes. But the nurses and Uncle Colton call them silly dad jokes." Her smile turned wistful. "I wish he was my dad."

A little flutter moved through Genevieve's heart. "You would like for him to be your dad?"

Bailey Ann vigorously nodded, and her chocolate brown curls bounced around her shoulders. "Yes, he's like my dad because he's been around the most in my life. And he takes care of me. He reads books to me and tells me stories until I go to sleep. And he makes me feel better when I'm sick or scared."

That flutter was a pang of pain now. A doctor being the most constant person in the child's life was incredibly sad. But Bailey Ann didn't seem sad, just as Collin had told her.

Bailey Ann leaned closer and whispered, "That's why I call Colton 'uncle,' because he would be if Dr. Cass was my dad. I would have a big family if Dr. Cass was my dad because he has a grandma and brothers and cousins. I never had any family like that."

It was almost as if the little girl had figured out why Genevieve was there. Or maybe this was what she really wanted, and she told everybody. Or maybe she felt this instant connection with Genevieve that she felt with her.

"You really like Dr. Cass," Genevieve said.

"I love him," Bailey Ann said. "He takes the best care of me." Tears glistened in her big brown eyes. "I wouldn't be alive if it wasn't for him."

And now he wasn't just going to make her healthy but care for her as a father would his child. That was what she'd wanted to do for her nephews if their situation had been different.

"Is that why you love him?" Genevieve asked. "Because he takes care of you?" She might love all the nurses and surgeons, too.

But the little girl shook her head. "I love him because he's really nice and he spends time with me, playing games and watching TV, and when I'm scared he tells me this funny story about a bunch of little boys growing up on a ranch and doing silly things like playing tricks on each other with toads and grasshoppers. He asks me questions, and he really listens to what I tell him. Not like Mrs. Finch."

"And who is Mrs. Finch?" Genevieve asked.

Bailey Ann wrinkled her nose with distaste. "She's my social worker. She doesn't listen to what I want. She just puts me anywhere she thinks they'll take me." The little girl shuddered. "But those families are always so busy. And I'm just more work for them."

Parenting was a full-time, around-the-clock responsibility, but a child should never feel like a burden. And obviously this child felt like one.

Obviously Collin Cassidy didn't make Bailey Ann feel like a burden to him. Or had he coached her on what to tell Genevieve or the social worker?

Genevieve had learned at a young age, like Bailey Ann, to tell people what they wanted to hear. She'd wanted approval and acceptance but most of all, love, and so she'd tried to be what her mother had wanted, what her grandparents had, and her husband...

But she must have never said or done the right things because none of them had ever really loved her like Bailey Ann loved Dr. Cassidy.

And like he loved her.

He stood alone now in the doorway to Bailey Ann's room, his gaze on them, his body language tense. He was worried about losing the little girl. And not just to that foster family.

He was worried about losing her for another reason. For the big scar that peeked out of the top of her nightgown. The scar from her heart transplant.

DESPITE HAVING THE day off from the fire department, Colton had spent most of it around the hospital like he often did when he was working as a paramedic. Even after he took the elevator back down to the lobby level, he didn't leave. Instead he waited to see his fiancée, who was working in the ER.

Or waiting for a patient to come in as she hung out at the check-in desk. He grinned when he saw her, and warmth flooded his chest. He loved her so much.

"Hey, Doctor," he said. "I wonder if you could help me..."

"Are you feeling sick?" she asked with a smile because she knew he was flirting, as he always did with her.

"Lovesick," he teased.

A nearby door opened, and Nurse Sue poked her head through. He waved, which seemed to startle her. She quickly backed out.

His eyes narrowed. His family suspected that Sue had been the one who'd reported the Havens to CPS for an accident that had been Colton's fault. He should have been watching his young cousin better when five-year-old Ian had been in the barn at Ranch Haven with him. The little boy had let a wild horse out of its stall and it had knocked him over and momentarily knocked him out in the process.

It truly had been an accident. The boys were well cared for by Colton's family. But the unnecessary CPS investigation had upset the security the three little orphans had with their Uncle Baker and his bride-to-be, Taye, at the Haven ranch. They didn't know who it was, or what agenda the mystery person might have.

The boys were safe and loved. That was what mattered. Grandma had insisted that she would handle the matter of who had made that complaint to CPS, and he had no doubt she'd take care of things. Maybe he should tell her about Cash, too. Though he'd vowed to tell Collin first. But Collin was so worried about Bailey Ann that he really hadn't wanted to think about Cash.

And Colton couldn't stop thinking about him. He expelled a heavy sigh.

Livvy came around the desk to hug him. "Did you tell him?" she asked with concern.

He'd already shared with her what he'd found in the fire at his family ranch house. A family heirloom—his grandfather's silver lighter with the initials *CC* for Cornelius Cassidy etched in it. He'd last seen that lighter with Cash when he'd run away all those years ago.

But the lighter had turned up so Cash must have as well. To burn down the family ranch that his dad had finally agreed to sell?

"He knows I'm looking for Cash, but he didn't want any details. His total focus is on Bailey Ann right now," Colton said. "Her social worker found a temporary foster home for her."

Livvy waited, knowing him so well that she had to know there was more. And it wasn't the good news it should have been.

"In Sheridan," he finished.

And she gasped. "Collin must be so upset. And Bailey Ann…"

"She doesn't know yet," Colton said. And he hoped she never had to learn about it. "Grandma recommended a lawyer for Collin to contact, and she's upstairs with him and Bailey Ann right now."

"I hope she can help," Livvy said.

Colton hoped so, too.

CHAPTER FIVE

"Did you prep her?"

The question startled Collin, making him jolt like the elevator did as it started descending to the lobby. Prepping Bailey Ann in the past had entailed getting her ready for a surgery or a procedure, something no child should ever have to endure let alone all on her own.

"What do you mean?" he asked Genevieve.

"She told me all the right things, like a witness whose lawyer had prepared them to take the stand," she replied.

"I thought you were an estate lawyer," he said.

"I am now…"

She talked like she was an old hand at trial proceedings, so maybe she'd been a criminal lawyer or some other type.

He was curious but figured it probably wasn't worth it to ask. She wasn't as apt to answer questions as to ask them. Probably something else that came from being a lawyer.

"I had no idea you were going to want to talk to Bailey Ann today," he reminded her. "So I wouldn't have had the chance to prep her. I didn't even want to talk to her about this…if I can't actually foster or adopt her."

And he hadn't. But he wasn't sure what Bailey Ann and Genevieve had talked about alone, though when he'd re-joined them, she hadn't seemed upset.

Or overly hopeful.

She'd just seemed very happy and not just because

she'd beaten the lawyer at checkers. She also seemed to like Genevieve.

"She wants you to adopt her," Genevieve said.

And he sucked in a breath. "You weren't supposed to put that thought in her head—"

"I didn't," she interjected. "It's already there. That's why she calls your brother uncle. She wants you to be her dad."

A warm rush of relief and love flooded Collin. He'd hoped that was what she wanted, too, but he hadn't been certain. And he hadn't wanted to bring it up to her.

"I didn't know for sure," he said. "I didn't know if she would be happier with a family. A couple and other kids..."

"She wants you and your family," Genevieve said. "But she shared that Mrs. Finch doesn't listen to her."

"She must not," Collin agreed. "Because Mrs. Finch has yet to say a word about any of this to me." And in one short conversation, Genevieve had learned how the little girl felt about him.

Collin knew she loved him, like he loved her, but he hadn't realized that she wanted to be his daughter as badly as he wanted to be her dad. His legs felt a little weak, and he took a moment to lean back against the elevator's mirrored wall. Then the doors began to slide open, but Collin didn't move.

"Are you all right?" Genevieve asked, and she touched his arm.

And he felt that little shiver of awareness again. He nodded. "Yes..." Then he shook his head. "No..."

Her lips curved into a smile. "This again. So which is it, Dr. Cassidy?"

"I'm happy that she feels that way, but it's going to be even harder now if I can't adopt her or even at least foster her," he admitted. It was going to rip out his heart. And now he knew that it would upset her, too.

The doors dinged again and began to close, but Genevieve reached out and pushed her arm between them. "Are you going back up to see her?" she asked.

"Not yet." Although he usually stayed with her until she fell asleep, he needed some time before going back to her room. He might give away how he felt, how much he wanted to adopt her. "I want to talk to you first. Do you have time?" At her nod, he glanced through those doors, over to where his brother leaned over the check-in desk. "But not here…"

They'd driven here in separate cars, so she suggested, "Come on, you can follow me home. We can talk in privacy."

If she could help him adopt Bailey Ann, he would follow her anywhere.

If this was DC, Genevieve wouldn't have told a man she'd just met to follow her home. But this was Willow Creek, and the man was a cardiologist who desperately wanted to adopt an abandoned child.

He'd gotten to her just like Bailey Ann had. They belonged together. She knew for certain now that it was what they both wanted. The timeline was going to be tricky, though. While she could file all the necessary paperwork in this county and in Sheridan and hope that the case would move quickly through one of the family courts, she doubted she could stop that temporary foster home placement from going through. And if this foster family in Sheridan didn't take care of Bailey Ann any better than her last one had and her body started rejecting her heart again…

The little girl might not get her wish for the family she wanted. For Collin to officially become her father…

She might never get another wish.

Genevieve released a shaky sigh at the unfathomable

thought. She had to do something. Then maybe she would stop feeling so helpless because of all the things she hadn't been able to do.

All the people she'd let down.

Her sister.

Her ex-husband.

Herself.

She had to help Bailey Ann and Collin Cassidy. While she'd been playing checkers with the little girl, she'd been strategizing about how to get the cardiologist set up as a foster parent. That was the first step toward keeping Bailey Ann here in Willow Creek with him. And then they could get the adoption process started...

That was why she wanted to talk to him alone. So there would be no other witnesses, like Hilda or his twin, to overhear the strategy she was about to suggest.

Unfortunately her drive home from the hospital was so short that she didn't have much time to come up with an idea of how to make the suggestion to Dr. Cassidy. A mile from Willow Creek Memorial, she turned onto a side street with big lots and mature trees and sprawling homes. As she slowed to turn into the driveway, one of the three garage doors began to open at the approach of her SUV.

The house was set up with all the smart technology features Genevieve had gotten used to during her marriage. Bradford had always had to have the latest and greatest.

The car the cardiologist drove, an older model economy vehicle, turned into the driveway behind her. She stepped out of her SUV, closed the garage door and walked through the interior door to the house.

Wait until she told him the plan she'd come up with...

Her face heated just thinking about it.

She headed to the side door to let him in, remembering Bailey Ann and how she didn't think her social worker listened to her. Genevieve wanted the little girl to know that *she* had listened to her, that she understood exactly what she wanted. She opened the side door of the mudroom and stepped out onto the driveway.

He was leaning against his car, waiting for her. His vehicle was almost too small for a man his size, while she drove that tank of a sport utility vehicle. But she'd thought she might need those three rows of seats if she had needed to take custody of her nephews.

That assumption had been a mistake, like so many others she'd made. She hoped this wasn't another. But if it kept a little girl safe and made her happy...

"I hope you're not worried that I lured you here to murder you," she said.

"I wasn't thinking that..." he said. "Until now...because of course, if you lured me here to murder me, you wouldn't want me to think that."

She smiled. "Maybe Bailey Ann is right. Maybe you are funny."

His mouth curved into a slight grin. "She's the only one who thinks that."

"She loves your dad jokes," she assured him. Because she wanted him to be her dad...

Because she loved him. And he loved her.

Genevieve couldn't imagine how it felt to be loved like that. Wistful at the thought, she emitted a shaky sigh.

"Are you sure you're comfortable with me being here?" he asked.

"Doctors have to promise to do no harm," she said. "So I'm not worried about you murdering me."

"I am no threat," he promised.

She wasn't so sure about that. If she suggested her strategy...

She would just have to remind herself the reason for it:

Bailey Ann. She was doing this for the little girl, not for her handsome doctor.

"What about your husband?" Collin asked, with an arched brow, as if he was questioning if there was a husband. "Won't he mind you bringing your work home with you?"

"Not anymore," she said. "We're divorced."

"I'm sorry," he replied.

"I'm not," she said. Life was a whole lot easier, and her heart was a lot safer now that she didn't have to worry about disappointing someone she loved. She'd learned from the mistakes she'd made with Bradford, and she wasn't going to risk her heart again.

"Okay…" He glanced around at the house and the yard. "This is a kind of big place for just you. You have kids?"

A lump suddenly filled her throat, the one that always choked her whenever she thought of that, of the kids she hadn't been able to have. Even though she'd never had them, she missed them, or at least the idea of them, more than she missed Bradford. Swallowing hard, she could only shake her head. Then she turned back toward her house and held open the door for him.

He followed her inside the mudroom. He glanced around at the benches and lockers, washer and dryer, laundry sink and dog shower. "Should I take off my shoes?" he asked.

"Don't worry about it." She led the way into the kitchen, which had a large center island and granite countertops and windows that looked out onto the big backyard. A Crock-Pot sat next to the stove, the scent of chicken and garlic and lemon pepper wafting out of it. She'd put it on this morning and had nearly forgotten about it. "Are you hungry?" she asked.

"I wasn't until I smelled that," he said. "Smells a lot better than the hospital's cafeteria food."

"I'm not sure it'll taste any better," she said. "I've been trying out new recipes." She'd actually been trying to figure out what she liked since she'd gotten so used to making Bradford's favorites instead.

"I'm happy to be your guinea pig for this recipe," he said. "But I don't think that's why you had me follow you home."

"I really hate having too many leftovers," she said with a smile. She also wanted to stall before she shared her strategy with him. So she took her time making a salad and setting the table and dishing out the food.

He didn't just sit there and watch like Bradford used to, while sipping a drink and talking about his day. Despite her protests because of his still-healing hands, Collin insisted on helping her, taking care of washing, peeling and slicing the vegetables. Maybe he was stalling, too, with concern that she would tell him it wasn't possible for him to foster and adopt.

Clearly, from what he'd already said to her, he knew that he wasn't ready. That he didn't have the house or the stability that was necessary.

But she did.

SADIE STILL COULDN'T believe her eyes when she saw her oldest son. She always felt as if she was just dreaming, as she often had over all those years he'd been missing, of seeing him again. Of him being alive...

But he was alive, and he was doing well. Better than she'd thought possible.

"When are you going to get used to seeing me?" Jessup asked.

And she realized she'd been staring at him silently since he'd opened the door. "I don't know if I will," she admitted. "But I don't care, just as long as I can see you."

"Are you here to try once again to get me to move out to the ranch?" he asked.

"No, Collin made it clear that you need to be close to the hospital. That you should have been before…"

But he'd stayed out at the Cassidy Ranch until the house had burned down. He hadn't wanted to sell it, but with all his medical bills, he'd had no choice. She'd wanted to help him, had tried, but he'd refused.

Just like he'd refused to move back home.

"I should have been," he agreed. "Can't imagine where I got this stubbornness from."

She chuckled. "You come by that on both sides," she said. His father, Big Jake, had been stubborn, too, but not as bad as she'd been. As she sometimes still was.

"You don't often leave the ranch yourself," he said. "What are you doing in town?"

"I was at the hospital earlier—"

"Mom!" he exclaimed, and he reached out to grasp her shoulders. "Are you all right? I know you had that issue with your heart—"

"I was there to see Collin," she said. "And to meet that little patient of his that he's head over heels about…"

"Bailey Ann," Jessup said. "I need to meet her, too."

"She's a sweetheart," Sadie said, her voice a little gruff with the emotions rushing over her. A child shouldn't have to go through all the medical issues she had. And if that wasn't bad enough, she had no family. She'd had to do it all alone but for Collin. "Will be nice to have a little girl in the family with all the boys we already have."

Jessup's brow furrowed. "What do you mean?"

"Collin wants to adopt her."

"He what? I knew he was attached to her, but…how's he going to do that? He's so busy. And…" He trailed off as he focused on her and nodded. "*You*...you're going to help my son."

"Not me..." she murmured. But she hoped that the person to whom she'd referred him to would help him. And maybe that would help Genevieve Porter, too.

CHAPTER SIX

COLLIN WAS SURPRISED that he'd managed to eat, let alone enjoy it as much as he had. He was so on edge about the whole situation with Bailey Ann.

The sun was beginning to set outside now, leaving him one less day already in the two weeks he had left with her. He should have stayed at the hospital with her.

But if anyone could help him, he had a feeling that Genevieve Porter could. She was smart and empathetic, and clearly already cared about Bailey Ann.

While he didn't mind sharing a meal with her, he was worried that she was putting off talking about the situation. It probably meant that she couldn't help and she didn't want to disappoint him and now Bailey Ann, too. That the little girl wanted him to be her dad affected him so much, making him love her even more than he already had. He had to press his hand over his chest as if to hold it all inside him.

"Heartburn?" Genevieve asked. "I think I have some antacid."

"No, the food was delicious," he said. And meant it. "I usually eat at the hospital, so this was a real treat. I just... It's killing me not knowing if this is possible..." Something else hadn't even occurred to him until now. "And here you are feeding me and I haven't even given you a retainer yet. How much do I owe you for your time today?"

She waved a hand at him from over the sink where

she'd been washing out the crock part of her Crock-Pot. He'd wanted to help her, but she'd only let him load the dishwasher. "Consider this a free consultation," she said.

His heart, that had been so full just moments ago, felt as if it deflated, and he sucked in a breath. "So it's not possible, is it?" he asked. "There's no way I can get approved as a foster home let alone adopt Bailey Ann before the two weeks is up..."

He'd known it was a long shot, but when Sadie had recommended Genevieve, he'd thought that long shot might pay off.

"No," she said. "There's no way *you* can get approved in that amount of time. It took me more than a month here."

"You're a licensed foster home?" he asked. That might explain why she had such a big place for herself. And the SUV was big, too, with three rows of seats.

She'd said she had no husband anymore and no kids, but maybe she just meant she had no kids at the moment.

"Yes," she said, and that strange expression came over her beautiful face again, as if she was withdrawing behind some wall. "I was registered as a foster parent before I moved here. When I bought this house, I did it with kids in mind."

"I know Mrs. Finch is going to make sure that the foster placement she found for her has medical training but..." The thought of her being out of his care, out of his supervision, sickened him. Maybe he would need that antacid.

"You're worried," she said.

"She got so sick last time," he said. "And her body nearly rejected her heart, and she waited so long for one that would match, that would fit..." Emotion choked him, but he fought it, as he always had to when he thought about how much that little girl had already endured. "She can't go through that again."

"So let's keep her here," she said.

"In Willow Creek? Mrs. Finch said there were no suitable foster homes here..." But he glanced around her large kitchen. "But you said you're approved..."

"I just got approved here," she said. "I was approved in DC, too. But I haven't actually taken care of any kids yet, so I doubt that Mrs. Finch would consider me suitable for Bailey Ann."

"Then how... What chance do I have to take care of and adopt her?" he asked. "Just tell me how it is. I need to know what I can do, if there's anything I can do..."

"I do think there's something you can do to prevent them from moving her to that foster home in Sheridan," Genevieve said.

He waited, but she didn't continue. She just stared down into the sink, as if she was worried that it was a suggestion that he wasn't going to like.

"What is it?" he asked. "I've signed a contract with the hospital so I can't just quit—"

"I'm not suggesting you quit," she interjected to assure him.

"Then what are you suggesting?" he asked. "What can I do to keep Bailey Ann with me?"

She drew in a deep breath as if she needed to brace herself just to tell him.

And knowing that, he suspected her suggestion was going to be something he didn't like. "If this will help me keep Bailey Ann, I'll do it," he said. "I don't care what it is..." That little girl's health and her life were far more important to him than anything else.

Even himself...

"Please tell me," he urged her. But just in case he needed to brace himself, too, he drew in a deep breath as well.

Finally she released hers, but her voice was so soft and

raspy when she spoke that he wasn't sure he'd heard her correctly. Because it sounded a lot like, "Marry me."

SHE'D JUST WHISPERED the words, but her throat felt raw as if she'd shouted them at him. And he looked like she had, or that she'd struck him so hard that he'd lost his breath.

The expression on his face, how utterly appalled he seemed to be, made her laugh out loud. "I don't have any designs on you," she assured him. "I just want to help you. No, not you. I want to help Bailey Ann get what she wants. I want to show her that *I* listened to her. She wants to stay with you, and I think this is the fastest way to make that happen and so that she doesn't get moved to Sheridan."

"Marrying you is the fastest way to do that?" he asked, his dark eyes clouded with either skepticism or confusion.

"I already have a foster care license," she reminded him. "So you wouldn't have to start that whole process to get approved…" She didn't want to be insensitive, but he had to face the reality, so she continued, "…*if* you could even get approved."

He sighed. "Mrs. Finch made it clear that I would need my own house. And there's no way I can manage that within two weeks. Becca made that clear."

"I have a house," Genevieve said. "One that's already licensed for foster care."

"Why did you get that license?" he asked, his brow furrowing with confusion. "You said you haven't taken care of any kids yet, so what was your reason for…"

Tears stung her eyes, and she had to close them for a moment, to clear them, before she opened them again. "I… I wanted to foster…"

"But your husband didn't?"

"Ex-husband," she reminded him. "And no…but…" There was so much more to the story. To her story…about how hard she'd tried to get pregnant, the babies she'd lost and the kids out there who needed a home. She'd wanted some of those kids.

But this wasn't about her. This was about a little girl who had no one else in her life.

"Let's focus on Bailey Ann," she said.

"You do that every time you start to reveal something personal," he remarked. "You step back and shut down."

She flinched at the term Bradford had often used to describe how she'd dealt with all the disappointments they'd had, all those failed fertility treatments and rounds of IVF. And even in the ones that hadn't failed...

"You came to me for help," she said. "Not for my life story."

"I came to you for legal advice," he said. "I didn't expect this..." He gestured around the kitchen.

"Are you talking about dinner or..."

"What do you think?" he asked with the stunned expression he'd had since she'd uttered those two words.

She chuckled. "Oh, you're talking about the marriage proposal?"

"Are you the funny one?" he asked. "Is this all a joke?"

She could have used that excuse to save face. *I was just kidding...*

But she couldn't forget what Bailey Ann had told her. She shook her head. "No. I really want to show that little girl that I listened to her."

"She asked you to marry me?" Collin asked, his brow still furrowed with confusion.

"No. She wants to stay with you, though. She wants you to be her dad. I don't think we can get her into your care in two weeks, and even if that foster family takes good care of her, that could still be a problem. They might change their mind about caring for her short term and file to adopt her, too. And if they're already caring for her, that would give them the advantage with the judge."

Collin groaned.

"That's why we need to keep her here, with you," she said. "But if you marry me, then we can move Bailey Ann in here with us, into a foster care licensed home. And if her cardiologist is living here, always available to handle her medication care, how can her social worker refuse to place her in this home?"

"Because she would be placing her with two strangers who just got married in order to get custody of her."

"She can't prove we're strangers. I doubt she would think strangers would marry to foster a child with special medical needs," she said. "And if she does have doubts, we'll figure out how to deal with whatever questions she might have. Bailey Ann is the priority."

Collin nodded in agreement. "She is for me. But you just met her. And while I know how easy it is to fall for her, I still don't understand why you would do this."

She didn't know how to explain it to herself, so she wasn't sure she could explain it to him. "I want to help her," she said.

And maybe, in some small way, it would make her feel better about all the people she hadn't been able to help. The people she'd failed...

She didn't want Bailey Ann to be one of them.

"Again, you just met her," Collin said. "She's as much of a stranger to you as I am."

But was she? That little girl had had a heart replacement three or four months ago. Could it be her sister's heart?

No. Jenny had been an adult, albeit a petite one. Her heart wouldn't have gone to a child. But it didn't matter to Genevieve whose heart the little girl had.

"Bailey Ann needs help," Genevieve said. "And she doesn't have any family. She just has you."

Collin muttered something beneath his breath, something that sounded a lot like, "And I'm not enough..."

But maybe she just imagined that was what he'd said because she'd felt that way so many times herself. That she wasn't enough.

"If her social worker is wrong about this family like she was wrong about the last one, Bailey Ann could be in danger," Genevieve pointed out. "And if something happened to her, it would haunt me..."

Just like all the other mistakes she'd made haunted her.

JESSUP HAD BEEN uneasy ever since his mother had left. She was up to something. He'd known it even before Marsh came home laughing about all the Valentine's decorations hanging around town.

"In August?" Jessup asked.

Marsh nodded, then pushed up the brim of his white Stetson. "Yes, I asked Ben and Old Man Lemmon what was going on, and they both answered me with just one word."

"Sadie," Jessup said before Marsh could.

Marsh chuckled and nodded again. "Yup..."

Jessup groaned. "What is she up to now?"

"Hearts and flowers all over town, more than half her grandsons coupled up..." Marsh chuckled again. "I don't have to be interim sheriff to figure out that she's playing matchmaker again."

Tension gripped Jessup. While he loved his mother and was happy to be reunited with her, he was all too well aware of how overbearing she could be. That was why he ran away from her all those years ago.

Because he'd known that her desperate efforts to fight

his disease would have hurt them both emotionally and mentally. Was she going to do the same thing with his sons that she'd done with him?

Drive them away?

He'd already lost one. He couldn't lose any more of them.

"Don't let her get to you," he advised his second oldest son. "Don't let her bother you."

Marsh chuckled again. "She doesn't bother me," he assured his dad.

Marsh was the most like Jessup's younger brother. Michael had never let Sadie get to him. He'd just carried on with his life as he'd wanted to lead it, on the ranch. He had loved it so much. But eventually it had taken his life.

Tears burned Jessup's eyes as he thought of all the years he'd lost with his only sibling. But having Marsh was like having Michael with him yet.

Even Darlene, Michael's widow, had mentioned that over the years that she'd helped Jessup take care of his sons. She'd also taken care of Jessup when he'd been at death's door. And he'd spent so much of his time there, leaning against it, ready to fall through if it had opened.

But it hadn't.

He'd survived, and now he had a strong new heart. Although the donation process was anonymous, Jessup was pretty sure he had his nephew's heart, that he carried a piece of Michael with him always.

He didn't want to lose his son, though. "Are you sure she's not getting to you?" Jessup asked.

Marsh grinned. "The only person I'm falling in love with...is her. She's a hoot." He patted his dad's shoulder as he walked past him. "I'm going to take a shower." He walked off, muttering, "Hearts and flowers..." And chuckled again.

She wasn't getting to Marsh, but then Marsh had a sense of humor. So Jessup didn't need to worry about him. He needed to worry about Collin. And Cash...

He was never *not* worried about Cash, though. Just as his mom had never *not* worried about Jessup.

Collin, on the other hand, had always been so focused, so intent on his goals and working hard to achieve them. Jessup had never really worried about Collin either.

He didn't have a dangerous career like Colton—a firefighter—or his older brother, Marsh—a lawman. And Jessup always knew where he was: at the hospital.

The only danger Collin was in was of working too hard and caring too much for his patients. So Jessup did worry about Collin burning himself out.

The last thing the busy cardiologist needed was his grandmother messing with his heart and his head. Hopefully she'd been honest that she was just trying to help him adopt that little girl everyone had been talking about...

But with as much as Collin worked, could he really care for a child on his own? Would he at least open himself to asking for help? But Collin had always been stubbornly persistent on taking care of himself, on handling everything on his own. Had he asked Sadie for help?

Or had she just seen that he'd needed it?

Why hadn't Jessup noticed? Why hadn't he known about Collin's desire to become a daddy to that little girl?

Jessup feared that Collin was angry at him for all the secrets he'd kept.

The door opened and Collin walked in, his steps dragging, his gaze unfocused like he was shell-shocked. "Oh, my God!" Jessup exclaimed as he rushed over to grip his son's shoulders. "Are you okay?"

Had he been in an accident? Jessup glanced out the front

window, but night had fallen so he couldn't see Collin's vehicle, if it was even there.

"Collin? Are you okay?" Jessup repeated, his heart beating fast with fear.

Collin looked at him, finally, but his dark eyes were still unfocused. "I don't know..."

"What happened? Were you in a wreck?"

Collin shook his head, and finally he focused on his dad, cupping his shoulders in his hands as well. Hands that were still pink from the burns he'd suffered during the fire. Because Jessup had gone back inside, trying to find his home health aide's young son.

Thankfully the child hadn't even been in the house. But, once again, Jessup had caused his sons to worry and suffer. With his new heart, he'd hoped to put all that behind him. But instead...

It had opened everything up about the past, about who Jessup really was and who his sons were. Sadie Haven's grandsons.

"Is this about my mother?" Jessup asked. "She was here earlier this evening looking for you." And he'd known then that was a bad sign. But she'd explained that it was about Bailey Ann.

Collin shook his head again. "No, not Sadie..."

But it was about someone. "Bailey Ann? Is she all right?" Had something happened to the child Collin cared for so much?

"She's fine for now," Collin said.

That was the way it was for heart transplants patients. They could be all right for a while, and then their bodies could reject the new organ. That was why Jessup still had his home health aide; he didn't want to put the burden of his care on his family anymore.

"Then what's wrong?" Jessup asked.

"I think I'm getting married."

Unlike his brothers, who'd adamantly insisted they would never marry, Collin hadn't said much about it. But he hadn't had to; it had been clear to everyone, especially the women he'd dated, that Collin's first priority was his calling to be a doctor.

He clearly had no interest in being a husband. But until he'd gotten attached to his little patient, he hadn't had any interest in being a father either.

So he could have changed his mind. But Jessup had a feeling that it had more than likely been changed for him...by Sadie.

CHAPTER SEVEN

COLLIN WAS FOOLISH for even considering it, but what choice did he have? He stood in the doorway to Bailey Ann's room, careful not to get too close and disturb the sleeping child. He'd showed up at the hospital early, before she'd awakened, because he'd been awake. Pretty much the entire night...

He'd tossed and turned and not just because of the uncomfortable pullout couch in the den but because his mind wouldn't shut off. He was used to that and had spent much of his life awake, worrying about his dad and his mom and his brothers and about his studies and his school and residency and fellowship...

He'd worried a lot about Bailey Ann over the past years, too. But it wasn't just thoughts of Bailey Ann that had kept him awake last night.

He'd kept thinking about Genevieve Porter.

He couldn't understand why she was so willing to make such a sacrifice for strangers. He knew all too well how easy it was to fall for Bailey Ann, but Genevieve didn't know *him* at all. She didn't know that he was not good relationship material. While he would make time for Bailey Ann, he wouldn't have any left over for a wife or even a girlfriend. But she certainly hadn't fallen for him like she had the little girl. So why offer to marry him even if she thought it would help Bailey Ann?

It was still a huge risk for her to legally tie herself to a stranger and, especially, to invite him into her home. To live with her...

She'd joked about his oath to do no harm. But he knew a lot of doctors who were first-class jerks; he'd trained under some of them and worked with other ones, like the surgeon who'd done Bailey Ann's heart transplant. He'd cared more about the prestige of doing what he did than the patient.

Collin always tried to put the patient first. That was why he was actually considering accepting Genevieve's offer, but Bailey Ann was more than a patient to him. In his heart, she was already his child. He certainly loved her like she was.

He loved her so much that he would do anything for her. Make any sacrifice...

Maybe even marriage.

Was Sadie behind this? Was that why she'd referred him to Genevieve? But Genevieve had sworn she'd never met his grandmother, and she had no reason to lie.

He was so confused. He hadn't answered Genevieve last night. He'd told her that he needed to think about it. And that was all he'd done. He'd advised her to do the same, to make sure that she was really serious about this before they took any more steps and especially before they said anything to Bailey Ann or her social worker.

He hadn't been able to stop thinking about it, to stop thinking about Genevieve. And it wasn't just because of her unorthodox suggestion on how to foster and then adopt Bailey Ann. She was smart and beautiful and successful, yet he knew nothing personal about her. They'd only known each other a day, of course, but he felt like she had walls up, that she kept stopping herself from revealing anything personal, as if she didn't really want anyone to know her. Or get close to her...

Yet she was the one who had proposed to him.

Not that theirs would be a real marriage. It was just a way to help Bailey Ann. Genevieve Porter had the house, the foster license. She had everything he needed. Everything Bailey Ann needed.

She could probably go after custody on her own if he didn't agree to this plan. Would she do that?

He couldn't foster Bailey Ann right now on his own. But Genevieve could. And as she'd warned him about the other foster family changing their mind about keeping her, custody, even as a foster, would give her an advantage with the family court judge.

He didn't know anything about her, though. Even though he'd tried to find out more...

How could he marry her? And more importantly, how could he trust her with what mattered most to him? With Bailey Ann?

WELL BEFORE DAWN, Genevieve had given up trying to sleep. And because just being in her kitchen had reminded her of the night before, of her outrageous proposal to a stranger, she'd headed into the office.

But she could see Collin Cassidy there, too, sitting across from her in that black cowboy hat like some bull-riding champion. She'd thought then of how he even had the name of a rodeo rider. But while he looked the part, he had chosen an entirely different career.

A hard one that had required years of studying and training and sacrifice. Genevieve understood that—hard work and sacrifice. And she also understood the frustration of wanting to help someone and not knowing how...

And being too late to make amends like she'd been with her sister.

She could help Bailey Ann now. They both could. But her method was extreme. And probably foolish...

Genevieve felt like a fool. What had she been thinking to propose to a stranger?

Yet he hadn't said no. He probably would, though. While he wanted to make a home for Bailey Ann, that home he'd probably envisioned hadn't included a wife he hadn't wanted.

Genevieve should have been used to that, to being the wife that wasn't wanted. Had Bradford ever really loved her? In the beginning she'd thought so. But then she'd disappointed him...

And eventually whatever love he'd felt for her had gone away. But if there was no love to begin with, there was nothing to lose.

No way she could disappoint if there were no expectations for either of them. It would only be a legal union, not an emotional one. That was the only reason she'd proposed—because she knew she was in no danger of falling in love with Dr. Collin Cassidy, no matter how good-looking he was. She was not going to let herself fall for anyone ever again.

Like Bradford had said, she'd shut down after all their disappointments. She'd closed herself off. It was safer that way. She couldn't get hurt again if she didn't risk her heart.

Maybe she should have opened herself up some more to Collin, just enough to explain the reason she'd made that proposal. And to assure him that she had no ulterior motives.

She just wanted to help an abandoned little girl because she knew all too well how Bailey Ann felt. And because there had been other people in her life that Genevieve should have helped and hadn't.

She couldn't make it up to Jenny anymore. But she could pay it forward...

She could help out Bailey Ann.

A thought struck her. If Collin didn't think marriage was a good idea, that didn't mean Genevieve couldn't help. What if she did it on her own? It wouldn't give Bailey Ann what she wanted—Collin as a father—but maybe she would at least be able to keep her here in Willow Creek.

She checked the time, wondering if it was too early to call...

SADIE AWOKE WITH a start, then squinted against the light streaking through the blinds of her suite. A little sigh whispered out near her and she turned her head to see Feisty lying on the pillow next to her. The long-haired Chihuahua was a tiny ball of black fluff and attitude. And, at the moment, nerves. She licked Sadie's cheek, as if grateful that she was alive.

Feisty had been there the day that Sadie's heart had stopped, but the little dog had been shut outside the door, desperate to get inside the room with her. As if she'd known...

Her frantic barking was what had drawn the others. And Sadie's grandson Baker, a former army medic and paramedic, had saved her life with the help of Taye Cooper.

Feisty had saved her life, just like Sadie had saved her years ago from dying in a hot car. Her previous owners hadn't appreciated Sadie taking a crowbar to their Cadillac, but they were lucky she hadn't taken it to them for nearly killing this sweet creature.

Though not everyone knew she was sweet. She tended to bark and growl and even bite.

Feisty reminded Sadie of Lem, small but tough. Smart and loving with a heart of pure gold. They needed to go ahead and get hitched. They were too old to wait around. That was one of the reasons Sadie had wanted those hearts and flowers up all over town.

She would probably marry Lem where they'd met, where they'd gone to school together, where she'd terrorized him in city hall.

Her cell phone vibrated. And Feisty yipped. It was probably Lem calling as he did every morning.

Yes. They needed to get hitched soon, so he wouldn't have to call. So he would be here with her and Feisty.

She reached for her cell and saw it wasn't Lem's contact info on her screen. It was Jessup's. And according to her screen, she'd missed some other calls from him already.

Concern struck her that he'd called so early. He'd had to have a good reason...or an emergency. Either for him or his sons...

Her arthritic finger shook as she accepted the call. "Is everything all right?" she asked, her already deep voice gruff now with the fear rushing up on her.

"No," Jessup said. "Everything is not all right."

Sadie shot up in her bed, and Feisty yipped with concern. "What is it? Your heart?" Hers was thumping madly in her chest. She wasn't sure if that was a good thing or a bad thing, though. But wasn't it beating fast better than it not beating at all?

"Not mine," Jessup said. "You're messing with Collin's, though, aren't you?"

"What?" she asked, confused. She used to be such an early riser, but after her health scare, she needed more rest than she usually did.

"You're meddling too much," Jessup said.

"I don't know what you're talking about..." she murmured. "Bailey Ann? I want to help him adopt her." She just wasn't sure if she could.

But she hoped that someone else was able to help him.

"How?" Jessup asked. "By encouraging him to marry a stranger?"

"What? You're not making sense."

"Exactly!" Jessup exclaimed. "None of this makes sense. How do you think this scheme is going to work? He's going to be miserable."

"I don't know anything about a marriage," she insisted. "But I do know that he will be miserable if he loses Bailey Ann."

"I don't believe that you don't have anything to do with this," Jessup said. "It has your fingerprints all over it. This is one of your matchmaking schemes, probably why you cooked up this whole Valentine's Day in August thing."

Sadie nearly chuckled, but she didn't think her son would appreciate her amusement at the moment. She'd cooked up that celebration for herself, for the love she felt. But Jessup hadn't opened up his new heart to anyone, nor had he opened up his old one to anyone else since his wife had died.

He didn't understand how important love was. Sadie did. But even if Collin had managed to get an appointment with the lawyer already, he couldn't have fallen for Genevieve Porter yet.

But she couldn't think of anyone else he might be marrying. They would have just met, so this couldn't be for love. It had to be about Bailey Ann. But she couldn't imagine her practical, no-nonsense grandson coming up with this scheme.

No. It would have been Genevieve Porter's idea. Her scheme...

And why?

What was her ulterior motive in all of this?

Had Sadie made a mistake? Had she been so blinded

by her own romance that she'd been too understanding, too optimistic about other people's motives?

But now she was as worried as Jessup was. Worried that she'd made a terrible mistake...

CHAPTER EIGHT

BEFORE BAILEY ANN woke up that morning, Collin had been called down to the ER for a consult. And after that, he'd had to take his appointments in the clinic attached to the hospital. So he hadn't seen her yet that day, and it was already getting close to lunchtime. Maybe he would bring her down to the cafeteria with him. Or maybe even to the little café close to it since she was getting tired of staying in the hospital.

She could probably be out of it soon, if she had a foster home where she could get a lot of rest and supervision. That hadn't happened at the last one, and this one Mrs. Finch had found for her in Sheridan was just temporary and the family wasn't even trained yet.

The social worker had been so confident that she'd found her a safe placement last time. That one had been here in Willow Creek, but they hadn't managed her medications correctly and she'd been so sick when she'd been checked back into the hospital.

Thinking of that, of how close he'd come to losing her, he ran up the steps from the first floor clinic toward her room on the third. He was still in the stairwell when he heard her cry out, "No! No!"

She was used to needles so even if someone was taking her blood or giving her a shot, she wouldn't cry about it like he could hear her sobbing now. He ran up the last couple of steps and down the hall to the open door.

A woman was in the room with her. Not a nurse or Genevieve Porter. It was an older woman with dark hair and a weary-sounding voice. Mrs. Finch. Her back was to Collin, so she didn't see him.

And Bailey Ann had buried her face in her hands, so she didn't see him either.

"Bailey Ann, you know I've been looking for another foster family for you," Mrs. Finch was saying as if it had been a great burden, as if the child was a great burden. "So you should be happy that I've found one for you."

The little girl's shoulders shook with the sobs she tried to muffle with her hands. And Collin's heart broke.

He'd been worried about Genevieve building up her hopes yesterday. But he hadn't figured on Mrs. Finch coming to dash them all away—Bailey Ann's and his.

"I don't wanna…" Bailey Ann pulled her hands away from her face and saw him standing in the doorway. "I don't wanna leave Dr. Cass. I wanna stay with him!"

"You shouldn't want to stay in the hospital," Mrs. Finch said. "Other people, people sicker than you, need this bed and his medical attention."

Collin sucked in a breath, stunned at how insensitive the social worker was being with the child. But then she continued, "You need to go to school and make friends and live the life your new heart has enabled you to live." And he couldn't argue with that.

She'd spent more time in the hospital than out of it. As the social worker had just said, she needed to live the life her new heart had given her. And staying in the hospital was not really living, not like she should be.

Although it was still summer vacation right now, school would be starting soon. And she should be attending, making friends, learning…

"Why can't I live with Dr. Cass?" Bailey Ann asked.

She was looking at him when she posed the question, and the plaintiveness of her tone squeezed his heart.

Mrs. Finch hadn't noticed him yet, so she answered Bailey Ann instead. "He's not a foster parent," she said. "And he works so much that he wouldn't be able to take care of you—"

"He does here!" Bailey Ann interjected.

"With help," Mrs. Finch said. "He has nurses and medical assistants that are here around the clock. He can't take care of you on his own."

He wanted to call her on it, wanted to say she was lying. But she was right. He had to work; he couldn't take care of Bailey Ann on his own.

But he wouldn't necessarily have to do it alone if he accepted the proposal Genevieve had offered him last night. If she hadn't changed her mind...

He couldn't bring it up to Mrs. Finch or Bailey Ann until he knew if Genevieve was serious about it. And if she was...

He would take her up on her offer as soon as possible. He would do whatever he could to keep Bailey Ann with him. Even marry a stranger...one he found far too appealing for his peace of mind.

"Thanks for coming here," Genevieve said as she led Sue back to her office. She'd ordered lunch in since Sue had taken a break from the hospital to meet her. She would have met her in the cafeteria, but she hadn't wanted to run into Collin.

In case he didn't accept her proposal, which looked unlikely given his reaction the night before, Genevieve needed a contingency plan in place so that she could at least keep Bailey Ann here in Willow Creek. But he might be furious to find out she was going after the little girl without him. And if anyone else figured out that Sue had called CPS on the Havens because of her, a lot more people would probably be furious with her.

Unless someone had already figured it out…

But why would Sadie Haven have given her a referral if she knew and why wouldn't she have told Collin? Maybe Genevieve was just paranoid because she felt so guilty over the problems she'd inadvertently caused her nephews.

But she couldn't worry about that right now. She was already too worried about Bailey Ann.

"I was glad you called," Sue said. "I thought you were upset with me."

"I was upset with me, not you," Genevieve said. "You were only trying to help me." It had been sweet of the nurse to try to help Genevieve, a virtual stranger. Genevieve had left Willow Creek so long ago and her parents not long after.

"Yes, well…" Sue muttered. "I should have handled everything better. I didn't realize…"

"Your intentions were good," Genevieve said. She cleared her throat. "Sue, I need your help again."

Instead of looking put upon, like the woman had every right to be, she smiled instead and released a little shaky sigh. "That's good. That's really all I wanted to do, Genevieve. Your mother and I were so close in high school."

High school was a long time ago for the nurse, but Genevieve wasn't about to point that out to her. Not when she needed her.

"I appreciate your assistance," Genevieve said. "And I'm sure Mother does, too." Though Genevieve really had no way of knowing. She hadn't spoken to her mother in months. Not since…

She sucked in a shaky breath and reminded herself of the reason she'd asked Sue to come to the office for lunch.

"I hate to ask you to do anything else, but it's for a good cause." Bailey Ann had no one to help her but Collin.

Whereas her nephews had...all the Havens. CPS had assured Sue that the boys were very well loved and cared for. They didn't need Genevieve any more than anyone else ever had...except for Bailey Ann.

"I'm sure it is," Sue said. "I trust you."

Genevieve had done nothing to earn that trust. Sue didn't know her at all—unless she and Genevieve's mother had talked about her over the years. At one time, Genevieve would have cared, but she'd shut down about her mother just as she had about Bradford.

There was no sense in opening herself up again and again to more pain.

"I got my foster care license when I first moved here," Genevieve said. "And I'd like to open my house up to foster a child."

"That is a good cause," Sue said, but her brow furrowed slightly. "Are you talking about your nephews? Isn't that why you got your foster license?"

"They weren't the only reason." She'd also had her license in DC and back there she had never considered that she might have to foster Jenny's kids. She'd never thought Jenny would die so young. "I've always wanted to foster kids who needed a good home." She needed to be needed as much as they did.

"That's wonderful," Sue said with the pride and approval Genevieve had never received from her own mother.

"I want to foster a little girl who's in the hospital right now," Genevieve expounded. "She recently had a heart transplant."

Sue gasped. "You want to foster Bailey Ann?"

Genevieve nodded. "Yes. You know about her?" Sue worked in the ER, but Genevieve supposed the hospital wasn't that big. And Bailey Ann might have been in and out of the ER a lot during her short life and her heart issues.

"Everyone at the hospital knows Bailey Ann," Sue said. "How did you find out about her? Did her social worker contact you?"

Genevieve shook her head. "No. After I got licensed here, I had asked to wait awhile before taking any children…" Because she'd needed to find out what the situation with her nephews was. If they didn't need her, would they want to know her? Would they hate her for how she'd ignored their mother all these years? Or worse, would they be like so many other people and not care at all? That was why, in addition to her own shame and regret for how she'd treated her sister for so many years, she hadn't had the guts to reach out directly to the Havens. "No. Dr. Cassidy contacted me about Bailey Ann."

"Dr. Cassidy… You know he's Sadie Haven's grandson, don't you?"

Genevieve blinked. "Collin's last name is Cassidy."

"Long lost branch of the family. He is definitely Sadie's grandson," Sue insisted.

Genevieve's mind reeled. Why had Sadie referred him to her for help with the adoption? Especially if she knew who Genevieve really was?

It was past time that Genevieve summon the courage to reach out to the Havens and find out exactly what Sadie knew about her. And what about Collin?

Did he know who she was and what she'd done?

And if so, there was no way he was ever going to accept her proposal no matter how platonic it had been intended. Her only intent had been to help Bailey Ann, just as it had been with her nephews. She'd failed with the boys, but that didn't mean she had to give up. While they might not want a relationship with her, like so many other people hadn't, she at least owed them an explanation and an apology.

LUNCH TIME AT the ranch was so much chaos and so much fun with all the little boys running around the kitchen, trying to help Taye. Miller, Dale's seven-year-old son, had started taking cooking lessons from her first, and now the younger ones wanted to be like him.

Or at least, the brothers all did. Their new cousin, five-year-old Caleb Morris Haven, just wanted Taye's cookies. He snuck one now, and Sadie caught his gaze and wriggled her eyebrows.

He froze for a second, his hand literally in the cookie jar. But he wasn't afraid of her. He'd never been afraid of her like some kids were because she was tall and had a gruff voice and wasn't soft and cuddly like the usual grandmotherly type. And because she wasn't the usual grandmother type, she held up two fingers and mouthed the word *snickerdoodle* so he would know to steal her one of those. They were her favorite.

The chocolate chip cookies were Caleb's favorite. It was an ongoing debate between them—which cookie type was the best. He grinned and pulled out a bigger handful. He'd probably gotten her chocolate chip, figuring she would give it to him. At five, the kid was already a schemer; Sadie loved him so much. He slipped around the long, stainless-steel-topped island and over to where she sat at the end of the dining room table that was so big they could all sit around it, even as their family kept expanding.

When Jenny and Dale got married, Sadie had remodeled the old farmhouse to add a wing of bedrooms, this enormous kitchen and her suite to the main floor. Her other grandsons had teased her that it wasn't necessary to add on as much as she had because they'd been determined to remain single. But she'd been scheming even then... She'd just had no idea how it would all turn out.

Her and Lem?

That was ridiculous but it worked. They worked.

And now Collin and...

Genevieve Porter?

"You two are going to ruin your lunch!" Taye said, pointing her spatula at Caleb and Sadie. She was tall, like Sadie, with a long golden blond braid tossed over her shoulder and piercing blue eyes. She was fierce, fiercely loving and loyal and protective. She was the one—along with Sadie's youngest grandson, Baker—who was going to adopt Jenny and Dale's orphaned sons. Jenny would have loved her, just as she'd loved Sadie, because people often compared Taye to Sadie. Not that Sadie had ever been able to cook.

She popped one of the cookies into her mouth, savoring the taste of brown sugar and vanilla along with the chocolate.

"Hey!" Caleb exclaimed. "You don't like chocolate chip."

"I don't want you getting into trouble alone," she explained with a grin.

"He usually gets me in trouble with him," Ian said. Ian was five like Caleb and had welcomed the boy as his best friend when Caleb's widowed mother had first moved back to Willow Creek with her young son.

Caleb held up his small hands, which had smears of chocolate on them. "I wasn't with you in the barn the day you got knocked down. You got in that trouble on your own!"

Ian gave a little sigh and nodded. "And I got Colton in trouble, too." Colton had been with Ian in the barn that day and hadn't known yet how dangerous the horse was that Ian had been trying to show him.

Midnight was a beautiful beast, but he had caused as much trouble on the ranch as...

Sadie's cell phone vibrated in her pocket. Since lunch hadn't started yet, she pulled it out; otherwise she would have ignored her phone during a meal with the kids. But she didn't want to miss any more calls from Jessup, especially if he was still angry with her.

However, the number appearing on her screen didn't belong to either of them, but to a law firm. And it wasn't the one Sadie had always used.

It was the one she'd referred Collin to, which might have been a big mistake. Like trying to coddle Jessup all those years ago and driving him away instead. If she'd messed up with Jessup's son, she might push him away once again.

So maybe she shouldn't even take this...

Or maybe she better and do some damage control. "Hello?" she said, speaking over the babble of the kids around her.

She heard a gasp. Maybe her caller hadn't expected Sadie to answer her call or maybe she'd heard all the kids.

"This is Genevieve Porter," she introduced herself.

And Sadie sucked in a slight breath at how similar her voice sounded to Jenny's. She was glad, with Ian standing so close to her, that she hadn't put her cell on speaker. She wasn't certain how he would react to hearing someone sound so much like his mom.

But they'd grown used to Dusty being around the ranch, and as their dad's twin, he looked exactly like him.

"What can I do for you, Genevieve Porter?" Sadie asked.

"I'd like to talk to you," she said. "Is it possible to meet with you? You could come to my office or..."

"A lawyer calling *me* for an appointment? Shouldn't that be the other way around?"

"I understand I owe you for a referral."

"Collin."

"Yes. My payment is going to be an explanation, if you'll give me the chance…"

"Of course I will. And since I was in town yesterday, I'd prefer if you came out here."

"I can come to Ranch Haven?" she asked, as if she didn't believe her.

"You've always been welcome here, Genevieve," Sadie assured her. "Always."

A little quivery breath slipped out of the speaker as if the lawyer was about to cry. Tears burned Sadie's eyes too as she thought of how families hurt each other, and how sometimes they didn't get the chance to make up for their hurts.

She'd gotten lucky with Jessup. Hopefully she hadn't screwed that up with putting Collin in touch with this woman. But if Genevieve could help him…

"I have an appointment, but I can come out after that," Genevieve offered. "If that works for you…"

"Come out for dinner," Sadie offered.

"This… I'm not…" Genevieve floundered for the words. "I just…need to talk to you."

"I know. It's long overdue."

"Yes," Genevieve agreed. "It is…"

"So dinner then. You know your way here?"

"I'll find it," Genevieve said. "Thank you."

The line clicked off, leaving Sadie to wonder what the lawyer was thanking her for.

The invitation to dinner?

The chance to explain?

Or referring Collin to her?

CHAPTER NINE

COLLIN'S STOMACH HAD knotted itself so much that he was surprised he could stand up when he slid out from beneath the steering wheel of his car. He'd felt sick since he'd overheard Bailey Ann and the social worker. And while he'd tried to calm the little girl, he hadn't known what to tell her.

He couldn't make promises to her only to disappoint her as so many other people already had in her life. Because he knew that no matter how much both he and Bailey Ann wanted it, he couldn't foster the little girl on his own. And adopting her was going to be a lengthy process that would mean she would go into that foster home in Sheridan for a while.

And if their training to take care of her wasn't enough for them to do it properly, her placement with them could be a very short term, but she might not survive.

Before Mrs. Finch had left the hospital, he'd asked why she hadn't waited a bit longer to tell Bailey Ann about the placement. "And there's no foster home here in Willow Creek where you could place her?" he'd challenged.

She'd shaken her head. "No one with experience caring for a child with Bailey Ann's special needs."

He wondered at that. Did Mrs. Finch know that Genevieve was available? Was she considered unsuitable, and would that change if he married her?

At the moment he just wanted to talk to her. So as soon

as he'd been able to get away from the hospital, he'd driven over to her office. As he crossed in front of his vehicle, he focused on the building a few yards down from where he'd found the parking spot at the curb of Main Street where all those heart-shaped balloons and decorations fluttered in the faint afternoon breeze. The office looked dark inside, with no lights shining behind the blinds that were already pulled. He hoped he wasn't too late to catch her for the day.

But at least he knew where she lived.

He would knock on the office door first, just to be sure. As he started down the sidewalk toward the law practice, he noticed a familiar looking vehicle parked closer than his. That big SUV that had followed him first to the hospital before he'd followed it to her house.

Despite the SUV's tinted glass, she was visible inside, behind the wheel. Perfectly still. As if she was hoping he didn't notice her.

His stomach knotted more. She'd probably changed her mind about her offer to help him and Bailey Ann. And he couldn't blame her for rethinking it. He'd been a fool not to jump on her offer the moment she'd made it.

What other options did he have? Mrs. Finch definitely wasn't going to let him foster Bailey Ann without help.

He knocked on the side window, and she jumped and whirled toward him, making him realize that she hadn't even noticed him. Maybe she'd had her eyes closed. Meditating?

The window lowered, and she said, "I'm sorry. I didn't see you."

"You seemed a million miles away."

"Not yet," she muttered.

His stomach tightened more. "Are you leaving town?" he asked with alarm. What had happened between their dinner last night and now?

"Not forever," she said, "Or at least, I hope not."

"What's going on, Genevieve?" he asked. "Is everything all right?" He didn't really expect her to answer, though, since she'd successfully deflected all his personal questions the day before.

She peered at him, her brow furrowed slightly. Then she asked, "Why are you here?"

And he swallowed a groan of frustration. He would have pushed, would have pressed her to finally answer him, but he did have a reason for coming to see her—a really important reason.

"Bailey Ann," he said. "Her social worker told her about the move to Sheridan."

Genevieve's mouth fell open on a gasp. "Oh, no. She was upset."

It wasn't a question. She knew. From one meeting with the little girl, she knew her better than her ongoing social worker. Knowing how many cases the woman carried, Collin tried to cut her some slack. There was only so much she could do with the resources she had.

Collin hoped he had more. "Yes," he said.

"I'm sorry."

"I'm saying yes," he repeated. "To your proposal, if the offer is still open…"

Despite all the Valentine decorations dangling from the streetlights around them, there was nothing romantic about the situation. In the middle of the street, talking through her car window like a cop giving her a citation.

She released a shaky sigh. "I don't know if that's going to be possible any longer…"

"Because you're going away?" he asked. Was that why she'd changed her mind?

"Right now I'm just heading out to Ranch Haven," she said.

"You've been summoned?" He should have guessed. Sadie had referred him to Genevieve, so of course they had some connection. Though Genevieve had claimed she'd never met her.

Had Genevieve lied to him? And was she actually part of one of his grandmother's schemes? Was that why she'd really proposed? And if so, then he shouldn't trust her enough to marry her even if it was in name only.

"Not so much summoned. I actually asked to meet her," Genevieve said.

"You really haven't ever met her before?" he asked with skepticism.

Genevieve shook her head. "I know *of* her. I've never met her."

"She's definitely a local legend," Collin said. "I'd known *of* her long before I met her, too."

"She's your grandmother," Genevieve said.

He nodded. "I found that out a few weeks ago."

"I just found that out today," she said. "I didn't know that yesterday…"

"When you proposed?" His head began to pound. "Is that why you're changing your mind about your offer?"

She sighed. "No. But you might…or maybe she will… I don't know what she wants…"

"But you said you're the one who asked to see her." He was so confused.

She nodded. "I don't know why she referred you to *me*. I don't know what she wants from me."

So if Sadie had cooked up a scheme, Genevieve didn't know any more about it than Collin did. And at the moment he didn't really care. He cared only about Bailey Ann.

And maybe a little bit about this woman who was so generous and caring herself…

"I can go with you to the ranch," he offered. And he

reached for the door handle. But it didn't budge. While she'd lowered the window, she hadn't unlocked the door.

"You should be there," she agreed. "But let's drive separately."

"It's a long drive," he said. "Nearly an hour. We could..."

She shook her head. "We may want to leave at different times." ·

"Want or need?" he wondered aloud.

She shrugged. "I don't know." Her delicate features were tense as if she was as tied up in knots as he was.

"I'm sorry," he said, compelled to apologize for his grandmother despite having no idea himself what was going on.

She shook her head. "*You* don't owe anyone an apology, Collin."

His grandmother was stubborn. While he hadn't known her long or well, he knew that about her because she was so much like his dad. "But Sadie might not—"

"She doesn't owe anyone an apology either," she said. "I do." She exhaled a shaky breath. "And I better get to it." She turned on the ignition then and raised that side window before Collin could say anything.

As she pulled away from the curb, a soft pop rang out, and when she drove away, Collin noticed a balloon on the asphalt. It must have escaped from the light post, and her big SUV had run it over, leaving the heart shape flat and mangled on the asphalt.

Despite the warmth of the summer day, a chill raced over him. He'd been so worried about Bailey Ann this entire time, about her heart, but he hadn't realized until now that maybe he should be worrying about his own as well.

GENEVIEVE WASN'T SURE if Collin had decided to follow her or not. If he had, she'd not noticed him in her rearview mirror. She waited outside the enormous two-story farmhouse for a while, but he didn't show up. Sucking in a deep breath, she stepped out and walked up the steps to the front porch that wrapped around the house.

The house was big, and the property seemed endless with pastures and fields on both sides of the long drives and so many buildings. Ranch Haven looked more like its own town, with all of its barns and houses and even an old one-room school building.

Their parents had warned Jenny that she'd wind up living in poverty if she married her high school sweetheart. They'd underestimated the daughter they'd disowned and the son-in-law they'd never acknowledged.

The sister Genevieve had turned her back on…

Genevieve was glad her sister had known love and happiness. She wished she'd been able to find something like this for herself. She'd never been able to make that family of her own that she'd wanted with Bradford.

Now she had nothing.

Tears stung her eyes, but she blinked them back and forced herself to ring the doorbell. She wasn't going to wait for Collin to arrive; she didn't need or expect him to be her backup, not when the Havens were his family.

But some of them were also hers.

The door creaked open and one of them stood in front of her. He looked more like Dale with the sandy blond hair and hazel eyes. "Are you a CPS lady?" he asked.

And she sucked in a breath and shook her head. "No. I'm not."

He blew out a little shaky sigh and nodded. "Okay then, you can come in."

A twinge of guilt struck her. However well-meaning Sue's call had been to CPS, she'd upset these boys. And that was the last thing Genevieve had wanted to do. Although the child left the door open, she hesitated to just walk inside unless an adult greeted her. While she hesitated, something black and furry rushed onto the porch and bounced around her, yipping and snarling.

Even the dog didn't want her there.

Maybe he thought she was a CPS lady, too.

"Feisty won't bite you," another little boy said as he stepped onto the porch and scooped up the dog, which then licked his face. "She just wants attention." He looked like the last boy, just a little bigger. Probably Bailey Ann's age...

Seven. From the note on the back of the family portrait Jenny had sent her, Genevieve knew who they all were. This was Miller. Jenny had given him her maiden name. The name she and Jenny hadn't shared. Her stepfather hadn't offered it to her, to adopt her. She'd never been good enough. And then when Jenny had gone against their wishes...

She hadn't been good enough either. But she'd given her oldest child their last name. She'd still wanted a connection with her family, which was probably why she'd kept track of Genevieve and sent her letters and that family portrait. The last one they would ever take.

Miller cradled the dog in one arm. He held a spatula in his other hand, which he used to wave her into the house. He started off down the hallway.

Genevieve stepped inside and closed the door behind her. Then she followed the child down a wide foyer that separated formal rooms toward the back of the mammoth house.

Miller spoke to her over his shoulder. "Grandma told me to bring you back to the kitchen for dinner. Taye and I are just finishing cooking."

"He's my seven-year-old sous chef," a young woman

said as Genevieve stepped into the kitchen. The room was enormous, with a high ceiling, fireplace and wall of windows that overlooked a back patio. The many cabinets were stained a deep green that complimented the brick floor, backsplash and fireplace hearth and chimney. A stainless steel counter topped a long island. And on the other side of that, between the wall of patio doors, was a long table. A woman sat at the head of that table, her back to the unlit fireplace. Long, snowy white hair flowed around her gently lined face, and dark eyes studied Genevieve closely.

Genevieve couldn't meet her gaze, mostly because her attention was drawn to the toddler the woman bounced on her knee as he squealed and called to his great-grandma, "Horsey! Faster, horsey! Faster!"

Sadie obliged, bouncing him harder and higher, and he erupted with giggles. Tears glistened in the older woman's eyes for a moment.

And Genevieve remembered…

Sue had told her what the boys had gone through. The oldest one, Miller, had had to have surgery on his broken leg and physical therapy afterward to walk again. Ian, the middle one, had had a concussion that had affected his short-term memory, and he'd kept asking where his parents were, only to be told over and over about their deaths. And the toddler, who'd once babbled and giggled endlessly, had stopped talking except for when he woke up screaming from nightmares.

Genevieve wasn't sure where Sue had gotten the information, but Willow Creek, though bigger than she remembered, was still a small town. And everyone knew and talked about the Havens.

"I never get sick of hearing that," a man's deep voice drawled. He'd come up behind the woman at the counter and wrapped his arms around her.

She leaned back against him and smiled up at him with so much love, the same love he reflected back at her and then at the giggling toddler. Miller leaned against them both, as if confident they would hold him.

The man looked like Collin, tall and broad, with dark hair. His eyes were lighter, and he was younger. This was the one who wanted to adopt her orphaned nephews.

Ian had come back to her and now he tugged on the sleeve of her suit jacket. "Who are you?" he asked with curiosity.

She opened her mouth, but she wasn't sure what to call herself. And Sadie answered for her. "This is Genevieve Porter."

The kids didn't react to her name. Neither Baker nor the woman, Taye Cooper, reacted. They didn't know who she was then. But someone behind her let out a soft gasp, and she turned to find Old Man Lemmon standing behind her with Collin at his side. He knew who she was, but clearly he didn't know what she was doing there. Beneath the white strands of hair, his forehead furrowed in confusion.

"Genevieve is my guest for dinner," Sadie said as if she'd sensed everyone's unspoken question.

But she hadn't given them the real answer. Was she waiting for Genevieve to do that? To reveal who she was and explain herself?

She didn't even know where to start.

As if Sadie sensed that, she waved her over. "Come sit by me…"

The woman was as intimidating and compelling as Genevieve had been told. Despite every instinct in her body warning her to turn and run, she started toward that table.

But as if he didn't think she would find it on her own, a hand caught hers. A small hand. And Ian smiled up at her encouragingly. "Sit by me," he said.

"Are you a firefighter?" Baker asked with a chuckle.

Clearly, in her suit and heels, she wasn't dressed like a firefighter.

"He usually only wants firefighters to sit beside him," the former firefighter explained. According to Sue, Baker Haven had resigned from that position to take over Dale's job as ranch foreman.

He also wanted to take over Dale's position as father to these boys. Boys that Genevieve had also wanted...

"WHAT IN THE Sam Hill is that woman up to now?" Lem muttered.

"Which woman are you talking about?"

Lem glanced up at the man standing next to him in the entrance to the kitchen. Tall and broad and a little older than Michael's sons, it was one of the Cassidys. Lem wasn't adept at telling them apart yet.

"Either of them," the older man said. "Sadie's usually scheming. And that lawyer can't be trusted..."

The man's throat moved as if he was struggling to swallow something down. Then he rasped out the question, "She can't? Then why did Grandma tell me to contact her for help with Bailey Ann?"

Lem swallowed a groan, knowing that he'd screwed up. It wasn't Colton standing next to him but his twin, the cardiologist. He should have known that; Collin wasn't wearing the hat. But he wasn't wearing a white jacket or scrubs either like Lem's granddaughter Livvy usually wore.

"You'll have to have ask Sadie about that," Lem murmured. He was going to be in trouble for running his mouth. He needed to get his fiancée to the altar fast, before she changed her mind about marrying him.

CHAPTER TEN

WHY WOULD SADIE refer him to a lawyer who couldn't be trusted? It made no sense, but Collin couldn't get close enough to Sadie during dinner to ask her. He didn't get close enough to Genevieve to ask her either because the little Haven boys had gathered around her, Miller on one side of her and Ian on the other with his friend Caleb next to him. And the toddler, little Jake, had taken a seat on her lap. He leaned back and peered up at her, as if fascinated with her as she talked to his brothers.

She was beautiful, but it was something else seeing her with these kids. They were even more drawn to her than Bailey Ann had been, and she and the little girl had instantly bonded the day before.

This was even deeper than that...

He sat across from them, in one of the chairs in the middle of that long table, too far from Sadie to question her. So all he could do was mutter to himself, "What is it about her?"

"It's her voice."

He glanced at Katie, Jake Haven's red-haired wife. "What?"

"You've noticed how they've taken to her," Katie said, "even more so than they took to Colton."

"And you think it's her voice?" Collin asked. While Genevieve did have a sweet-sounding tone, he wasn't sure kids would make much notice of that.

Katie nodded. "She sounds exactly like their mom."

Collin felt a twinge of pain for what those kids had endured, for the tragic loss of both their parents. "Did Jenny have any family?" he asked.

Katie shook her head. "Not that she talked about. They disowned her when she married Dale out of high school."

They watched the kids and Genevieve for a while. Then Katie sighed. "Jenny was a sweetheart. She and Dale were my first accounting clients when I moved back to Willow Creek and opened my business. But they'd both taken accounting courses and really didn't need my help. They were just being supportive and kind."

"This town is certainly welcoming," he agreed. He'd found a place here. He wondered if Genevieve was finding her place, too. And he wondered why Lem thought she couldn't be trusted.

"They don't look anything alike, mind you," Katie mused, as she stared across the table at the blond-haired woman. "She looks more like Emily than Jenny…"

Emily was the schoolteacher whom Sadie had hired to come out to the ranch to homeschool the older boys and be the nanny to little Jake. She was now engaged to Ben, the mayor. Collin had heard that she'd been the one to propose, like Genevieve had proposed to him.

But he and Genevieve were strangers while Emily and Ben were clearly in love. They sat farther down the table, leaning against each other. Jake was on the other side of Katie, his arm wrapped loosely around the back of her chair. And Baker and Taye were sitting close together, too, on the other side of Collin. Somehow he'd gotten sandwiched between two of the three happy Haven couples.

There was a fourth couple that had been married the longest and would soon be expanding the family with a set of twins. Dusty and his wife were actually at Collin's family ranch. He'd been in the process of buying it when the house caught fire. Fortunately the barns and other out-buildings had survived, but they were in need of repairs, something Dusty had apparently started early to get his bronco horse out of the barn here at Ranch Haven.

The bronco had been responsible for Ian taking a trip to the ER with Collin. But he looked fine now as he stared with fascination at Genevieve.

Katie reached around Collin to tap Taye's shoulder. She sat on the other side of him. "And I thought you were the kid whisperer," Katie said to the cook.

"That was Emily."

"Was, when she first got here," Katie agreed. "But you took over."

Taye sighed. "Took me a while, though. It wasn't like it is with Genevieve."

"She sounds like Jenny," Katie said. "Doesn't she?"

Taye sucked in a breath, and her eyes widened. "Could it be…?"

"What?" Collin asked. "Could what be?"

"Is Genevieve Jenny's sister?"

"Jenny had a sister?" Collin was the one who asked the question since he hadn't grown up in Willow Creek. Had Genevieve?

"I think she did," Katie said. "Wasn't there a much older sister? She'd left town when Jake and I got to high school. I think she even had a different last name…"

The color suddenly drained from Taye's face, and she jumped up so fast that her chair would have fallen over if Baker didn't catch it. "Boys, want to help me with des-sert?" she asked. And she clapped her hands together and forced a bright smile, but it didn't reach her eyes.

"What's going on?" Baker whispered to her. Clearly he'd noticed her reaction, too.

"Ask your grandmother," Taye whispered as she headed toward the kitchen.

"You're going to love this dessert," Miller told Genevieve as he scrambled up from the bench.

"Do you really set the bananas on fire?" Ian asked with awe. He and Caleb swung their legs over the bench and chased after Miller.

And even the little guy crawled off Genevieve's lap to toddle off behind the older boys. Genevieve stared after them all with such an expression of longing and awe.

Could she be Jenny's sister? The boys' aunt? No one seemed to know her here, and that kind of secret-keeping concerned him.

He thought again of Lem's comment that she couldn't be trusted. What did the deputy mayor and Taye and Katie know about this woman? About Jenny's sister? Was she the one who'd called CPS? Was she the one who'd made trouble for the family? For Collin's family?

If that was the case, then Collin would be a fool to think she would help him. For a moment last night, during dinner at her house, he'd begun to hope that there might be a way for him to keep Bailey Ann in Willow Creek with him. But now he felt it all slipping away—Bailey Ann and his hope.

EVERYBODY WAS STARING at her, making Genevieve feel like she was having that nightmare—the one where she was arguing in court while naked. But this time, when she woke up, she was actually naked and vulnerable. The nightmare wasn't just a dream but her reality.

"Why's everyone so quiet?" Ian asked with naive directness.

He was a sweetheart. They all were. But then they were Jenny's kids, so of course they were. Jenny had been a sweetheart. Genevieve had overheard the red-haired woman saying that to Collin.

The red-haired woman... Katie Haven. She'd met them all before dinner. There'd been introductions around the table. But all Sadie had said was her name, not who she was.

Clearly they'd figured it out anyway.

But nobody probably wanted to address it in front of the little boys. Maybe the Havens didn't want the kids to know that she was their aunt.

She leaned closer to Sadie and asked, "Can I speak with you alone?"

Sadie nodded. "I think that would be wise."

"Grandma..." Baker began, his deep voice full of anger and confusion.

She shook her head. "It's not... It's fine... I'll explain later."

"I want to hear it now," Collin said.

"Can he join us?" Sadie asked Genevieve.

She nodded. That was why she'd wanted him to follow her out here. It was time to come clean about everything, including her role in the CPS scare with the boys.

She only hoped they would believe that she had never intended for Sue to call CPS. Genevieve had just asked the woman to find out what she could about them, to keep her apprised of what was going on with them. But from the way they were all staring at her, with such suspicion, Genevieve didn't know if they would believe her.

Looking for a sympathetic face, she focused on Old Man Lemmon—Lem, she reminded herself. Everyone here called him Lem. She wondered if he remembered her from Christmases so many years ago. He'd been the Santa on whose lap she'd sat.

He frowned at her, and she was reminded that he wasn't

Santa. There were no fairy tales, no happily-ever-afters, at least not for Genevieve. As she followed Sadie down the hall, with Collin behind her, she felt as if she was heading to court. But instead of defending someone else, she had to defend herself. Not that she had much of a defense.

Sadie opened a door and led them into a sitting room with two easy chairs and a television. The older woman settled into one of the chairs and pointed Genevieve toward the other. Was this the witness chair, and Sadie's the bench?

Collin shut the door and leaned back against it, as if blocking everyone else out. To protect her? Or to keep her from escaping?

He was the one who asked the first question. "So are you Jenny's sister?"

"Yes."

He sucked in a breath. "That's the first personal question you've actually answered."

"It's not something I'm proud of," Genevieve said.

"You're not proud of Jenny?" Sadie asked, her deep voice sharp with outrage.

"No! I'm not proud of myself," Genevieve said. "I'm not proud that I dropped out of her life when our parents disowned her. She and I were never really close..." She winced at the sound of her own voice, of her excuse. "But that was my fault, not hers."

"You're older than she was," Sadie said, as if giving her an excuse.

"A little over six years," Genevieve confirmed. Jenny would have been thirty this year. Genevieve was thirty-six, probably a few years older than Collin was.

"And you pushed yourself in school, graduating early, so you were gone from Willow Creek even before Jake got to high school," Sadie continued.

"How do you know so much?" Genevieve asked with wonder. Was Sue right about the woman?

"Your sister idolized you," Sadie said. "She talked about how smart and beautiful you are."

Tears rushed to Genevieve's eyes so quickly that she couldn't blink them away before one trailed down her cheek. She wiped it off with a shaking hand. "She was the beautiful one," Genevieve insisted. "The smart one." The child her parents had really wanted, not the unplanned one that Genevieve had been for her mother. The embarrassment...

"Jenny was beautiful," Sadie agreed. "Inside and out. She was just an angel, and now she is..." Tears trailed down the older woman's face now.

And Genevieve found herself reaching across the space between them to squeeze her hand. "Thank you," she said.

Sadie blinked furiously and asked, "For what?"

"For loving her like she deserved to be loved," Genevieve said. While her life had been cut too short, at least she'd had that: unconditional love.

"Nobody loved her more than Dale did," Sadie said with a wistful smile. "They were so close, so committed and so beautiful together. And they made three beautiful children."

Yes, even though it had been short, Jenny's life had been full. She felt a deep ache. Just as she'd resented Jenny for being the child her mother really wanted and not the mistake, she had probably been jealous of Jenny's happiness, too, because Genevieve had never been as happy.

That resentment was the real reason Genevieve hadn't kept in touch with her. The shame overwhelmed her now, and she began to shake. None of it had been her younger sister's fault.

Sadie turned her hand over and squeezed Genevieve's.

"Why didn't you contact me when you moved back to town?" she asked.

That shame overwhelmed Genevieve. "I didn't find out that Jenny died until two months after their funerals." Bradford's new wife had finally and almost gleefully passed on the letter that had been sent to Genevieve's old address. "I'd missed the funerals. I'd missed so much of my sister's life. I came here because I wanted to get to know the boys. To be available to care for them if they needed that."

The room was silent, both Collin and Sadie listening intently. It was finally time to own up to what she'd done. "The CPS investigation… It was my fault."

"You called CPS on them?" Collin asked, his dark eyes hard as he stared at her.

"She didn't call," Sadie said.

Sue was right. The Haven matriarch did know everything. Somehow she'd figured out who the anonymous caller was.

"No, I didn't call. But it was my fault," Genevieve said. "I'd reached out to the person who'd called—"

"To start trouble?" Collin interrupted.

She shook her head. "I just wanted to know how the boys were doing. If they were healthy and healed and safe." She blinked back tears. "I'm so sorry. I certainly didn't mean to cause them any harm. I can see just by watching them with the family how loved they are. That's all I could ever want for them."

"But why didn't you let any of us know who you are?" Sadie asked.

"I didn't know what Jenny had told them about me. She'd had every reason to hate her family for how she was treated."

"Jenny couldn't hate anyone," Sadie said. "Not with

that big heart of hers. But she was like me with Jessup, she stopped talking about what was too painful for her."

"So they don't know about me?" Genevieve said. She'd already guessed as much when the little boy hadn't recognized her when he opened the door. She hadn't sent Jenny family pictures because she'd had no family to take pictures of. And because of her law career with a high-profile firm, she hadn't even maintained a social media presence. And truthfully, she just always preferred to keep her private life private.

Sadie shook her head. "No. But we can tell them—"

Genevieve shook her head. "No. Let Taye and Baker decide that. I need to apologize to them, too." Another time; she felt more than naked now. She felt raw, like her skin had been peeled away. She turned her focus to Collin. "I need to apologize to you, too. When you told me Sadie had referred you, I should have explained right away how she might have known about me. But you didn't say she was your grandma..."

"Still..." Collin began, but he said nothing more. He just moved away from the door, walking farther into the room.

And as he did, Genevieve had a sudden, overwhelming desire to run. She jumped up from the chair and rushed out of the room. Then she ran down the hall and out the door as if someone was chasing her.

But nobody was. Not even that fluffy, feisty little dog. The only thing that chased Genevieve out of Ranch Haven was her own guilt.

SADIE STARED OUT the open door with shock. She hadn't realized the girl would run. And she was too old to chase after her. She left that for Collin to do, but instead he dropped heavily into the chair that Genevieve had so abruptly vacated. "Aren't you going to go after her?" she asked.

"Why?" he asked.

"Aren't you engaged? Your dad called me this morning yelling that you were going to marry a stranger and that it was my fault."

"This *is* your fault," Collin said. "You set me up. You used me as a pawn in one of your schemes."

The man was too smart for her to deny it, so she just nodded. "Yes."

Her affirmation seemed to drain the anger from him and he chuckled. "I was warned..."

"Who?"

"Pretty much everybody who's ever met or heard of you warned me," he said.

"You're exaggerating." It surprised her that he was capable. He always seemed so literal.

"Not much," he said. "You used me to find out more about her, about the threat to the little boys."

"She's no threat." Sadie knew that for certain now. Genevieve's tears had been real and ripped from her. She was suffering so much guilt and regret that Sadie's old heart ached for her. "And I really do believe she could help you get Bailey Ann."

He snorted. "By marrying me? Did you two cook that scheme up together?"

"I hadn't met her until today," Sadie said. And now she regretted that she hadn't reached out sooner—that she hadn't made sure that Jenny's family knew about her death so they would have the chance to attend the funeral, to see the boys and know for themselves that they were okay.

But in the beginning, in those first few months, they hadn't been okay. They'd all been struggling. Baker and

Taye had helped the boys, though. They were doing so much better now.

"So you don't really know anything about her then," Collin said.

She knew more than he realized—more than she'd remembered until recently when she'd had Ben check out the lawyer who'd called about the boys, and then she had realized who that lawyer really was. She knew that Jenny wasn't the first daughter her family had disowned; Genevieve had pretty much been the first. And it was clear to see she'd suffered for it and she was still suffering.

"I don't think it's a good idea to get involved with her," Collin said.

"Why not?"

"She obviously has a lot going on—a lot of pain and guilt and whatever—and I don't want to add to her stress or hurt her."

"What about you?" Sadie asked. She figured he was worried about getting hurt, too.

He sighed. "After how she conducted herself when she first got to town, how she didn't reach out directly to you or to the boys, how could I trust her?"

"Is Bailey Ann worth the risk?"

CHAPTER ELEVEN

COLLIN HAD ONLY had a few moments alone with Sadie in her suite before a bunch of his family had rushed in. They might have stormed in sooner if not for the smoke detector he'd heard pealing out along with smoke from the kitchen.

He had no intention of staying for dessert. So he snuck out past everyone firing questions at Sadie and slipped down the hall and out the door. Genevieve's massive SUV was gone. And he felt a flash of concern that she was driving, as upset as she was. Would she be able to see through her tears?

Worried that she might have gone off the road, he drove slowly along the route she would take home. And his heart hammered heavily with dread that he might find her the way Baker had found her sister and his brother, their small SUV twisted and turned over in the ditch after it had skidded off the icy road. He couldn't imagine how Baker had felt. Although he was a paramedic, he hadn't had his rig with him or backup. He'd struggled to keep his family alive while he'd waited for help to arrive.

Collin had felt somewhat like that the last time he'd treated Bailey Ann, when she'd showed up at the hospital so weak and sick. And before that...when they'd waited for a heart for her...

She was his family. And he was hers...

The only family she had. He had to find some way

to make that legal. And for that, he needed a lawyer he could trust.

Collin didn't think he could trust Genevieve. He had so much trouble trusting people. His own father had lied to him all his life.

Sometimes he felt like there was even more his dad hadn't shared with him. But he couldn't confront his dad like he wanted to; he wouldn't do anything that might risk his health. Although apparently he already had.

He'd told Dad last night that he might be getting married, and that had upset him enough to call and yell at his mother. Even though Collin hadn't told him who had introduced him to his bride, Dad had somehow known that it was his mother.

Probably because Sadie Haven was so notorious for her meddling. Collin hadn't been exaggerating when he'd told her that a lot of people had warned him about her. His own dad had and his cousins and most of the people he worked with at the hospital.

Sadie has a way of making people do things she wants. Sadie gets what she wants.

But Collin wondered about that. Yes, she had a way of making things happen, but she'd endured so much loss, too. His dad had been missing from her life for years. Her younger son had died. Then her husband and now her grandson and granddaughter-in-law.

Jenny. That made him think of Genevieve again. Apparently the sisters hadn't seen each other in years. Remembering Genevieve's tears and the misery in her voice, he focused again on the road, making sure that her vehicle hadn't veered off it. But there was no sign of the big SUV, not even in her driveway when he turned into it. Hopefully it was parked in the garage where she'd parked the night before.

Or maybe she'd just kept driving. When he'd talked to her outside her office, she'd made some cryptic comments, as though she might not stick around town. Had she thought Sadie would drive her out?

Or had she thought it would just be too hard for her to stay once everyone knew she was Jenny's sister?

She'd been so upset when she'd talked to Sadie, so apologetic, so broken...

He studied her house, the sprawling ranch with the brick and stone facade. The many windows shone no light. Was she inside? And if she was inside, why was she sitting in the dark?

His heart beat a little faster with concern for her. Needing to know where she was and if she was okay was more important right now than even expressing his anger with her for not being honest with him, as so many other people hadn't been honest with him.

How could he hold a stranger accountable when he had yet to hold his family accountable?

He shut off his car and stepped out, onto her driveway. Instead of following the sidewalk to the front door, he knocked on that side one she'd opened for him yesterday. There was no bell to push, so he knocked again, harder, hoping she would hear it.

If she was in the house...

But was her SUV parked in the three-stall garage, or had she just kept driving—right out of Willow Creek?

He wouldn't blame her if she had.

She had no family here now but her nephews. And who knew if Baker and Taye would even let her see them again...if they believed she'd encouraged that person to call CPS on them?

He could understand if they refused because they

wanted to protect children who'd already suffered too
much. That was why he wanted Bailey Ann. To protect her.

And because he loved her...

But he might have already lost her. Mrs. Finch was
clearly not going to give him a chance to foster if he was
on his own. But Bailey Ann wasn't the only reason he was
worried about Genevieve leaving. For some reason he just
hated the thought of her being so alone...and heartbroken.
And he wanted to make sure she was all right.

He knocked one more time, his knuckles chafing a
bit from the force of it. And finally the door rattled and
opened. She stood before him, her face red and puffy from
tears. But her chin was up, her body tense, as if she was
bracing herself for an attack.

He stepped inside the house and closed the door. Then
he wrapped his arms around her and pulled her trembling
body against his. And he held her as she cried.

GENEVIEVE LINGERED IN the half bath off the mudroom as
long as she could justify doing, before Collin probably
started to worry that she'd slipped out the side door and
run away again.

She was too embarrassed to face him. But more than
that, after sobbing all over his shirt, she was also unsettled.
She'd gone from crying in his arms to...

Feeling something she hadn't felt in a long while.
Aware...

Of his warmth, of his long, deceptively muscular body,
and of his gentleness and his empathy.

She hadn't felt so cared for, so protected, so seen in...
maybe ever. And that was scarier than showing up at
Ranch Haven to confront the intimidating Sadie March
Haven. Genevieve's intense fear was because she couldn't

give her heart to anyone, ever again. It just hurt too much when things ended.

And for her, they always seemed to end. It was more important that she focus on her job, on helping people she could help, on people who needed her help. Her nephews didn't need her; they had the entire Haven family.

And Collin didn't really need her either. But for a moment, while she'd clung to his long, lean body as he'd held her, she'd needed him. And she couldn't let herself feel that way again. Everyone she'd ever needed had wound up rejecting her. It was safer to shut down.

She leaned over the pedestal sink to splash a little more water on her face, trying to bring down the swelling and redness.

Not that she cared what she looked like; her looks had never gotten her the kind of attention and respect that she'd craved. So she'd learned to stop craving it.

She dried off her face with the hand towel, drew in a deep breath and opened the door. She could hear movement in the kitchen. Doors opening. A mug clinking. The whistle of the teakettle she kept on the six-burner gas range. Bemused, she stepped into the kitchen.

Collin didn't notice because he was behind a cupboard door, rooting inside the cabinet.

"What are you doing?" she asked.

He leaned back, closed the door and held up a tin. "I assumed you're a tea drinker."

He was holding one of her herbal collections while the teakettle continued to whistle. She shut off the burner and confirmed, "Yes, I am. If I don't have my cup of chamomile before bed, I can't shut off my mind."

"I thought I was the only one who couldn't do that," he said. "My brothers can go right to sleep, but I just lie there, thinking…" He shook his head a little and focused on her again, staring intently at her. "And speaking of thinking…"

She braced herself, waiting for the anger she'd expected when she'd opened the door to him.

"That you need chamomile tea to sleep is the first personal thing you've freely admitted to me," he said.

Something about him compelled her to tease him, like she had the night before. He just seemed so serious despite Bailey Ann thinking he was funny with his dad jokes. "Remember, I'm not charging you." She attempted a smile. "So everything I've said has been free."

"When will you start charging me?" he asked.

She narrowed her eyes to study his face now. His was not red and puffy; his was perfect. The man really was unreasonably good-looking. "What do you mean?" she asked. "I thought you came here to yell at me, not for legal advice."

"You thought I was going to yell and yet you opened the door anyway?" he asked.

"I already ran away once." And she regretted how she'd left the ranch, without even saying good-bye to her nephews. What if she never got to see them again?

And they'd been so sweet to her. Had they been drawn to her because she sounded like Jenny? It had almost hurt to hear that she and Jenny had shared the same voice. It was the only thing they'd had in common. They'd been so different, much more than six years and different fathers separating them.

Pride and resentment had also held Genevieve back from developing a real relationship with her sister. And now she would never have the chance.

Tears began to pool in her eyes again, and before she could blink them back, Collin touched her shoulder. "Hey," he murmured.

His touch, and that sympathy in his deep voice, jolted her. She shook her head. "I'm fine."

"Don't lie to me," Collin said, and he looked pained. "Please, don't lie to me."

"I didn't lie to you," she said.

"A lie of omission is still a lie to me," he said. "My dad never telling us that we're really Havens, that he's Sadie Haven's kid, that we had an uncle and cousins and grandparents..." His voice trailed off, gruff with what sounded like tears of his own. Or maybe it was just frustration.

She reached out to comfort him now and closed her arms around him. And he tensed within her embrace. She dropped her arms, and he stepped back.

"I just want openness and honesty from now on," he said. "No more lies, secrets...whatever..."

"I want to help Bailey Ann," she said. "That's the truth."

"Why?"

She released a shaky sigh then and forced back down the sobs that threatened to escape with it. "It's for selfish reasons," she admitted. "But that doesn't mean I can't do some good. I want to help that little girl because I didn't help Jenny."

"She died because of that crash," he said. "Baker was first on the scene, and there was nothing he could do. There's nothing you could have done either."

"I'm not talking about when she died," she said. "I'm talking about when our parents cut her off—when she chose to marry Dale. I could have stepped in, tried to change things, but I didn't. I was so caught up in my own life. In college and law school...and she kept reaching out but I never responded. Once I left here, I never looked back."

"What could you have done?" he asked. "Could you have gotten your parents to change their minds?"

She snorted. "No. Jenny's dad was my stepdad. He barely acknowledged me. And Mother never listened. But *I* could have been there for her. And I wasn't. I failed Jenny."

He studied her intently.

"That's why you came to Willow Creek. Why you bought this house and got your foster license here," he said. "You wanted the boys."

"I wanted to be ready," she corrected. "I didn't know what the situation was, just that my sister and her husband were dead. That's why I started asking around and preparing..." She released a shaky sigh. "And I should have just gone straight to the ranch and explained myself. That I thought her kids had been orphaned, and I know how hard it can be to get kids out of the foster care system. I thought if I had the job and the house and the license, I could take them if they needed me." And in some way she'd wanted them to need her; she'd wanted to be needed. "That's why I had...a friend of my mother's...check on them for me..."

"Nurse Sue?" he asked.

Maybe he was a bit like his grandmother. All-knowing...

"I should have just reached out myself," she said. "But I didn't know how the Havens felt about me, about my family, if they hated me for how we treated Jenny. And I couldn't face that because..."

"You hated yourself," he said.

He was definitely a lot like his grandmother.

She cleared her throat. "Collin, you have to believe me. I had no idea how loved they are. I didn't want to make trouble."

He nodded, still studying her. Did he believe her? "You had a foster license in DC, you said," he pointed out. "Why?"

She sighed. "That was for other reasons. Old reasons

that don't matter anymore. It has nothing to do with Jenny. Or the situation you and Bailey Ann are in. But if I can help you two… I want to be there for Bailey Ann. I know it won't make it up to Jenny, but maybe I'll feel like less of the horrible person I feel like I am now."

"So much so that you asked me to marry you," he reminded her.

And heat rushed to her face. "That was for Bailey Ann."

"I know. And that's why I showed up at your office this afternoon. I want to accept your proposal," he said.

She sucked in a breath, shocked that he would still consider it. "Even now?"

"As long as I know all there is to know about you," he said. "I can't handle any more surprises."

"But this won't be a real marriage." She needed to make that clear, for her sake more than his. She didn't expect him to fall for her. And she couldn't fall for him.

He nodded. "I know this is for Bailey Ann. But since she's going to be around you, I have to know that I can trust you with her."

After what had happened with the little girl's previous foster family, she understood. "Okay. You are going to have to help me with her medical stuff," she warned him. "And as for me…" She sighed. "I graduated high school early, intent on getting into college and law school, on becoming someone that my parents would be proud of, and I met my husband in law school. He came from a wealthy, prominent family that was all about carrying on their blue blood heritage. Of course we waited to start a family, making sure we did the travel, established our careers, bought our big house and joined all the country clubs. Maybe we waited too long."

"You're only in your thirties," he said.

She shrugged. "I struggled to conceive…even with IVF.

Every round failed. Except for..." Her voice cracked, the pain still fresh despite the few years that had passed. "A couple of times I got pregnant but miscarried."

"I'm sorry," he said. "That's why you got the foster license."

"I know there are a lot of kids out there who need homes." And she had needed a child. "I wanted to foster and adopt. My ex-husband wanted to carry on his lineage. After the IVF failed with us, he didn't even want to try using a surrogate. Now he has a new wife and toddler and another on the way."

A big, loving family in their old house. He'd kept that. He'd kept everything of the life they'd built together but her. Just like her parents had done with Jenny, he had easily replaced her with someone better, with someone who'd given him what he'd wanted.

At least he'd given Genevieve a generous cash settlement for her half of that old life. And that settlement had helped her set up here in Willow Creek.

She released a shaky, self-deprecating chuckle. "Was that more than you wanted to know?" she asked.

He nodded.

And she tensed.

"Because now I want to hurt your ex," he said. "And I'm not usually a violent man."

"I wanted to hurt him, too," she admitted. But she'd realized that she couldn't hurt someone who didn't care about her.

That was why she couldn't let herself care about anyone, especially not her next husband. Because that was the only way she could protect herself from getting hurt again.

LEM DIDN'T LIKE it when Sadie got upset. The last big upset she'd had was over Jessup, and her heart had literally stopped. He hadn't been there for her then. But he was here now, sitting beside her in her suite as the conversations finally wrapped up with her family. Once he would have felt like he was intruding, but now her family was going to be his, too.

Baker and Taye were the last to leave Sadie's suite, closing the door behind them. She'd assured them that Genevieve was not a threat to their plan to adopt the boys, but Lem wasn't as convinced as she was.

He waited until the door closed to ask, "Are you sure you can trust her?"

"Oh, yes," Sadie with that certainty and assurance that used to infuriate him. Her confidence that she always knew what she was doing had made him defensive, had made him feel as if he didn't know what he was doing.

Now it reassured him because of all the times she'd been proven right. But this time...

"You don't know her," he pointed out. "You don't know anything about her."

"She's Jenny's sister."

"Her *sister*," he said, and he reached across their chairs to stroke the back of her hand. "She's not Jenny." He knew how much she'd loved her first granddaughter-in-law. How much she missed her. Jenny Miller Haven had been a very special young woman.

"She reminds me of her, though," Sadie said.

"Her voice," he agreed. He'd noticed it, too. "But just because she sounds like her, doesn't mean that they have anything else in common. From what I remember, they weren't even raised together. Genevieve's grandparents raised her while their daughter finished high school and college."

"Exactly," Sadie said. "That's how I know I'm right about her."

He couldn't follow her line of reasoning, but maybe that was because his head was beginning to pound. Probably from the smoke in the air—the bananas Foster hadn't gone off as planned. Fortunately Taye had had a kiddie version of the treat that hadn't caught fire.

"Good thing she was gone," Baker had bitterly remarked to him. "Or she might report us again."

"I would still be careful," Lem advised Sadie now.

Her cell vibrated. He wasn't surprised. Maybe the Cassidys who hadn't been present had heard about who she'd referred Collin to... The enemy.

"Hello, Collin," she greeted her caller. As she listened to him, a grin spread across her face, crinkling the skin around her dark eyes. "That's great news," she said. "Don't worry about the logistics. Ben and I will help you with those." She disconnected the call and turned toward Lem to announce, "Collin and Genevieve are getting married."

And he nearly choked on his saliva. Feisty, sleeping on his lap, growled softly, probably annoyed at being startled. "Are you serious?" he asked.

She nodded.

"This is the fastest one of your match making schemes has worked yet," he said.

But her grin slid away and she sighed. "It hasn't worked."

"But they're getting married," he said.

"But they're not in love."

And he knew that was really what Sadie wanted for her grandkids: love. The kind of love she and Jake had shared. The kind of love she and Lem shared now.

He reached over and touched her hand again. "It took us a while to get there," he said. "But we did."

"Eighty years," she said with a slight chuckle.

"Hopefully they're not as stubborn as we are," he said.

She sighed again. "I don't know. He's my grandson. And Genevieve's been through a lot. She may not be open to love again."

"She was good with her nephews," Lem said.

The little boys hadn't taken to her like they had just because of her voice. She had been very sweet with them and had given them her undivided attention.

"Loving kids is easier than loving a significant other," Sadie said. "Kids don't hurt us like a lover can."

That was true.

It had taken a lot of courage on his part to open up his heart again after losing Mary. But part of his heart had probably always belonged to Sadie March.

CHAPTER TWELVE

A COUPLE OF days had passed since that night at Ranch Haven, and Collin had been waiting for the proverbial other shoe to drop. That night, he'd called Sadie and told her about his impending nuptials, and she'd mentioned getting Ben onboard. Though he didn't know for sure why just the mayor...

He'd expected her to also let everyone else know. And he'd expected his dad and brothers and even Darlene, who'd helped raise them after their mom died, to talk to him about it. To try to talk him out of marrying a stranger...

But he'd heard nothing about it. Either Sadie hadn't told them or she had and had somehow convinced them that he was doing the right thing. He wasn't as sure about that.

He wasn't even sure if it would work. But he parked his car outside Genevieve's office for the meeting she had called, the meeting to find out if their getting married would even make a difference in his quest to foster and adopt Bailey Ann.

He'd arrived early, hoping to spend some extra time talking to her. He hadn't seen her since that night. He hadn't even talked to her on the phone; she'd just texted him about the meeting today.

She must have been watching for him because she met him at the door.

"Good. You're here," she said, and she reached out

and tugged on his sleeve, pulling him along behind her to her office.

The white-haired receptionist didn't glance up as they passed her desk. Either she was preoccupied or totally uninterested.

"I'm glad you wore your white coat. That will look better to the social worker."

"Mrs. Finch sees me in this all the time," he reminded her. That was the meeting she'd set up, with the social worker.

"Yes, but you wearing the coat is a visual reminder for her that you have the medical expertise to deal with Bailey Ann's heart condition."

"She knows that."

"But she still hasn't considered you for adopting or even fostering her."

"Because I don't have a house of my own or the day care provider with medical care experience."

"I do."

"You do?" he asked with surprise. "I mean. I know about the house." And it was an impressive house with four bedrooms and three and a half baths on the main level with a big backyard. "But you have medical day care?"

"I have Nurse Sue."

He groaned. "She's the one who called CPS."

"Yes, but as well as being an ER nurse, she's also been a neonatal and pediatric nurse, and she's agreed to help us," Genevieve confirmed.

"Why?"

"She was a friend of my mom's," she said. "And for some reason, she wants to think she still is."

"But she isn't?"

"My mom doesn't have friends," Genevieve said. "She only has my stepdad."

Collin couldn't say much. As Colton had pointed out, he was probably his only friend. Collin had always been too busy with studying and work to sustain any relationships—friendship or romantic.

"Maybe the apple doesn't fall far from the tree," she said, "because I didn't make time for any friendships of my own. I didn't even make time for my sister." Her slender shoulders drooped beneath the heavy weight of guilt she seemed so determined to keep carrying.

"I never met Jenny," he said. "But from what I've heard about her, she was a very sweet person."

Genevieve blinked furiously, as if fighting back tears. "She was."

"Then I don't think she would want you to keep beating yourself up about the past."

Genevieve heaved a heavy sigh as she dropped into the chair behind her desk. "No, she wouldn't."

Instead of taking a seat in one of those leather chairs in front of her desk, Collin sat on the edge of the mahogany on the corner closest to her. Since holding her those couple of times a few nights ago, he was so drawn to her. He wanted to be close to her and touch her again and see if he reacted the way he had that night, with that little zip of awareness that had felt like electricity zapping him back to life. He hadn't realized he'd been dead to the world, so very focused on everything but himself.

"So stop," he said, but he wasn't talking just to her about her guilt but to himself about this attraction. He couldn't afford the distraction now. No. Bailey Ann couldn't afford it; she couldn't be separated from him, for her sake as much as his. She didn't want to go to Sheridan any more than he wanted to let her go.

Genevieve nodded so emphatically that a lock of hair fell across her face. Without thinking, he reached out and brushed it off her cheek. She was so beautiful. But she looked exhausted, too, with dark circles beneath her eyes.

"Are you sure you want to do this?" he asked.

"Stop beating myself up about the past?" she asked.

His lips twitched into a slight smile at her weak attempt at humor. "I meant marry me."

"I already asked you," she said, and she was smiling, too.

His heart did a little fluttery thing it had never done before. Maybe the stress was getting to him. "But are you sure?"

She glanced at the delicate gold wristwatch she wore. "We'll know in just a few minutes if it will make a difference to Mrs. Finch."

If it didn't, there was no reason for them to marry. Genevieve had been smart to request this meeting first.

This was all about Bailey Ann. Usually Collin wouldn't have had to remind himself of that, but...with his grandmother's penchant for matchmaking he was a little uneasy.

"How do we convince her that this makes a difference?" Collin asked. "Do we act like the engagement is real and we're madly in love?" And why did the prospect of pretending to adore her have that little fluttery thing going on with his heart again? If that kept up, he might need an EKG. Find out if it was an actual arrhythmia. Since Sadie had one, maybe it ran in the family...

Or maybe it was just stress, the same stress that must have been keeping Genevieve awake at night.

"I thought you were a doctor, not a thespian," she teased him. "A cardiologist, at that. You know how the heart works. So how do you pretend that you've given yours to me?"

He pressed his hand against his chest. "I would act like

it beats faster and harder every time I'm near you…" But he wouldn't necessarily be acting.

She snorted. "I don't think you're that good an actor, Dr. Cassidy, so we should probably just stick with our motto of being open and honest."

"With each other," he clarified. "I think it would be wiser to make Mrs. Finch think that we're actually marrying for the right reasons."

She snorted again. "What are those?"

He held up his hands then. "I don't know…" But he would have assumed love. "You're the one who was married before."

She sighed. "Yes, but I think I married him for the wrong reason," she said. "No. He married me for the wrong reason."

"So what is the right reason?" he asked.

"Bailey Ann."

He knew why she was doing it, that she was somehow hoping that helping Bailey Ann would alleviate some of the guilt she felt over her sister, brother-in-law and nephews. That helping Bailey Ann might somehow make up for how she felt she'd failed her family. "I appreciate your sacrifice."

"Marrying a handsome, successful doctor is not a sacrifice," Genevieve said with a flirty grin.

And his heart definitely had an arrhythmia, skipping at least one beat before hurrying up the ones that followed like an uncoordinated kid trying to play hopscotch. He sucked in a breath, leaning toward her, drawn to her beauty. Her eyes fluttered closed as she leaned in, too. He felt the imminent kiss, hanging in the air between them, and—

A throat cleared behind him, startling him. Mrs. Finch.

He realized Genevieve must have noticed her and had been acting for her benefit.

But he had a little flicker of concern over how easily she'd fooled him into thinking that she was really flirting, that she was really attracted to him. He would have to keep reminding himself that she was only doing this for Bailey Ann and for her sister.

FOR ONCE, Hilda had actually shown one of Genevieve's appointments back to her office. Of course she hadn't bothered announcing it, but fortunately Genevieve's ears were sharp and she'd heard them approaching.

Collin, on the other hand, had clearly been taken by surprise, nearly falling off the desk as he whirled toward the doorway. He seemed guilty, like they'd been caught doing something they shouldn't have been. But if they really were engaged, they should flirt. And more…

He'd been about to kiss her.

Had she wanted him to?

Her stomach tightened with nerves and frustration as she realized she had. She'd really wanted that kiss. She should have been glad that they'd been interrupted before that had happened, before she let herself start thinking this engagement was real. That the marriage, if they went through with it, would be real.

"Mrs. Finch is here," Hilda said, and she was smiling, which was probably the first time she had smiled at Genevieve. Despite the couple of months Genevieve had been with the law practice, the receptionist hadn't warmed up to her.

"Thank you, Hilda," Genevieve said with a smile of her own as she stood up. "And thank you for finding time to meet with us, Mrs. Finch. I'm sure you're very busy."

Hilda hesitated a moment before turning to walk out.

But she closed the door behind herself so it wasn't as if she'd been nosy about the meeting. It was almost as if she'd known what it was about…

Had Sadie spoken to her? Genevieve knew Collin had called his grandmother and confirmed their plan; he'd been with her, in her kitchen, when he'd called Ranch Haven.

Genevieve needed to call there herself, not for Sadie, but for Baker and Taye, to apologize and assure them herself that she didn't intend to fight the adoption.

"I am quite busy, as Dr. Cassidy knows," Mrs. Finch replied. "So I don't know why he's engaged a lawyer to talk to me, but I assume it's about Bailey Ann."

"It is," Collin said.

"But I'm not here as a lawyer," Genevieve added. "Collin isn't a client. He's my fiancé."

Mrs. Finch's brow furrowed. "You didn't mention that when you asked me about fostering Bailey Ann."

"I didn't want to speak for Genevieve," he said.

And that was probably quite open and honest of him. A smile twitched her lips. "Collin wanted to make sure that I was onboard for a child with special needs. I'm already a certified foster parent."

"I'm aware," Mrs. Finch said. She must have checked out Genevieve after she'd called her to meet. "But you haven't accepted any placements yet. We can't authorize your first one being a child with complex medical needs. You'd need more experience first."

Genevieve had expected this. "I'm marrying someone who knows everything about Bailey Ann's medical history and her current condition as well as her future needs," she pointed out, and she stepped closer to Collin.

He slid his arm around her waist, showing a united front. A unit. A couple.

She didn't know if she'd ever really felt like half of a

whole before. Her life and Bradford's had been so separate, so different.

"You're both busy professionals," Mrs. Finch said. "So who will be with Bailey Ann when you're working?"

"I have hired a nurse who will be with Bailey Ann when Collin and I are both at work." She was going to insist that Sue accept payment. "But I have a very flexible schedule and can do most of my work from home."

Mrs. Finch continued to study them with skepticism. "When will you be married and cohabitating?"

"As soon as we can get the license," Collin answered.

"This all seems very sudden," the social worker remarked. "How long have you been engaged?" And her dark eyes narrowed as she stared at Genevieve's bare hands.

Collin tensed and glanced down at Genevieve.

"The engagement is recent," she answered honestly. "But our history is long. My sister was married to his cousin. Jenny and Dale Haven."

The older woman gasped and shook her head. "I'm so sorry. Of course everyone in town knows about that tragedy." She glanced at Collin then. "I didn't realize you're related to the Havens."

He nodded. "Sadie is my grandmother." And instead of sounding exasperated, he actually sounded a bit proud.

Genevieve glanced up at him with a smile. "I'm sure your grandmother would be happy to talk to Mrs. Finch as well." Why not use the old woman's intimidating reputation?

Mrs. Finch shook her head. "I need to check with my supervisor and see if this is something he would even consider since we've already found a suitable placement for her."

It was clear that she didn't want to consider it, consider them. Collin must have picked up on that as well because his shoulders sagged as if with defeat while Genevieve bristled with indignation.

"That placement is only temporary," Genevieve reminded her. "We're moving up our wedding date, so that we can provide a safe and secure and permanent home for Bailey Ann."

Mrs. Finch narrowed her dark eyes, clearly suspicious of their relationship.

"We can also petition the court for immediate custody of Bailey Ann," Genevieve said. "I don't believe any family court judge would choose to put this vulnerable child into a home with strangers over a home with the one constant she's had in her life. Collin. If you ask Bailey Ann, I'm sure she'll tell you what she'd prefer."

"I'll do that," Mrs. Finch said. "We will also arrange for an inspection of your house, and we'll need your marriage license on file."

"That won't be a problem," Genevieve said. "As Collin already told you, we're getting married as soon as possible."

Before Collin could confirm, his beeper rang out. "I'm on call," he said. "I need to get back to the hospital." He sounded reluctant.

"Go ahead, dear," she said. "I think I can handle the rest of the meeting." And she rose up on tiptoe to press her mouth against his cheek in a soft kiss. He had a little bit of stubble, which tickled and made her lips tingle. Or maybe that was just the contact with him…

Collin glanced down at her once, his eyes dark and soulful as his arm tightened around her. Then he released her, almost as reluctantly as he'd sounded about heading back to the hospital.

"You go," she assured him. "I'm sure you're needed."

Bailey Ann needed them both. They had to pull this off for her.

But with the way Mrs. Finch studied them, with all that skepticism, Genevieve wasn't sure if they had fooled her or they should have even tried.

It was too late to back out now.

COLTON DIDN'T KNOW what was going on with his twin, just that Dad was worried about him. He knew that Collin was stressed over Bailey Ann, so that was probably it. And Colton didn't want to add to his stress but he also needed to share what he knew or at least suspected about Cash. And so, even though his double duty shift as a Willow Creek firefighter and paramedic had ended, he came back to the hospital. It was the one place he knew he could always find Collin. And usually the woman Colton loved, Dr. Livvy Lemmon, too.

It was because of her that he was here; he'd made a promise to her that he would stop shouldering the weight of this secret on his own. That he would share it with someone besides her; while she was happy he'd told her, she was also worried about him and didn't think he should try to figure out what to do without input from someone else. He couldn't tell Marsh or his dad.

He wasn't sure Collin was the best option either. The man was usually so black-and-white, so by the book. But if their dad was right, and Collin was considering marrying a woman he'd just met in order to foster Bailey Ann, then he was capable of stepping into a gray area.

Colton hoped Dad was wrong about that.

But the minute Colton stepped into his office, Collin dropped his cell phone and grinned. "I was just going to call you."

He sounded upbeat, but there was no spark in his dark

eyes. His hands, still pink from his burns, shook a little as he clicked off the cell and dropped it back onto his desk. He was standing, too, instead of sitting in the chair behind it...like he was all nervous energy.

That was sometimes how Collin was—always working so hard, never shutting off his mind or his drive. But there was something else to it tonight...something that had Colton, for once, feeling what his twin was feeling. That nervous energy gripped him, and he reached into his pocket for the lighter, wrapping his hand around it.

Then, almost impulsively, he pulled it out and dropped it onto Collin's desk, next to his cell phone. Collin stared down at it, and all the color drained from his face. His hand shook even more as he reached for and picked up the smoke-stained pewter lighter. With the finger of his other hand, he traced the letters. The two Cs that had been engraved in the metal so many years ago.

He'd been there with Colton, standing in their oldest brother's doorway, watching him pack his duffel bag to leave. They'd both seen him toss that lighter into the bag. "Where did you get this?"

"In the ashes of our family home," Colton replied.

And Collin sucked in a breath. "Cash was there? You think..." He swallowed hard as if he was choking on the accusation.

An accusation Colton didn't want to make either. He shrugged. "I don't know. And I don't know what to do with it."

"Tell Marsh," Collin urged him, and he dropped the lighter as if it had burned him. "Give it to him."

"He'll have to make it part of the record. And my boss—my former boss—already ruled the fire was probably just a result of the house needing major updating and repairs..." Repairs they hadn't been able to afford because of all of Dad's medical bills. "But the insurance adjuster is still investigating."

"And you're worried Dad might get blamed for this? It's even more of a reason to give that lighter to Marsh."

"He can't investigate the fire anyhow. He's no longer working for Moss Valley, and we're his family. If someone else gets involved, Dad will find out."

Collin sucked in a breath and dropped heavily into his chair. "Oh..."

"I'm not the doctor but I don't think that would be good for him—to worry about Cash any more than he already does."

Collin nodded. "You're right."

"So what do we do?" Colton asked the question that had haunted him for weeks.

"I don't know," Collin said.

And now Colton dropped into one of the chairs in front of Collin's desk. He was used to his smart twin having all the answers.

"I almost wish you hadn't told me," Collin murmured.

"You wanted to know what's been bothering me, and you guessed it had to do with Cash," Colton reminded him. He pointed at the lighter. "That's it."

"That's why you've been looking for Cash, bothering Becca..."

Colton nodded. "Yup. Were you calling me about that or..."

Collin shook his head. "I was calling to ask you to be my best man."

Colton released a shaky sigh and leaned back in his chair. "So you're really going to do it? You're going to marry a stranger?"

"She's not a stranger anymore."

"Do you love her?" Colton asked. Because he knew how

quickly someone could fall. He'd fallen that quickly for Livvy Lemmon, quicker than he'd even realized.

Collin shook his head. "It's not about love. It's about Bailey Ann."

"Of course it is," Colton said. "Everything you do is for someone else."

"What?"

"You became a doctor because you were trying to save our parents. When Mom was gone and Dad's heart started failing, you switched from renal failure to cardiology. *Everything* you do is for someone else. When are you going to start doing something just for you, Collin?"

"This is," his twin vehemently insisted. "I want Bailey Ann. I don't want to lose her."

That much was true. Colton could see that his brother loved that little girl. He loved her so much that he was willing to sacrifice his own happiness for her. And Colton had a horrible feeling that was exactly what he was doing, that this marriage of convenience was not going to make him happy at all.

CHAPTER THIRTEEN

COLLIN FELT LIKE he'd signed Bailey Ann out of the hospital to play hooky from school. But school wasn't starting for a couple more weeks yet, and medically she was doing so well now. The outing was going to be good for her.

Because, as he'd told his twin, Bailey Ann was his whole reason for doing what he was doing today: getting married. At the ranch...

Sadie had insisted on hosting their wedding at Ranch Haven. He knew she enjoyed getting all of her family out here, but he suspected she also wanted Genevieve here. To prove to her that her nephews were happy and healthy? To make sure that she wouldn't try to take them away from Baker and Taye? From the ranch?

She'd obtained her foster license and bought the house and vehicle specifically for those boys. For the sister she felt she'd abandoned. But now that she knew they were happy and loved, she had no intention of jeopardizing that for them. He believed that; he hoped the rest of his family did as well.

And he hoped that they appreciated what she was doing for him as much as he did. After parking on that circular drive, right in front of the steps leading up to the wraparound porch, he glanced across his console at Bailey Ann.

Her dark eyes were wide with shock. "It's sooooo big," she murmured in awe.

"Yes, it is," he said. Much bigger and nicer than the

house where he and his brothers had grown up. He still struggled with his dad's decision to keep their Haven heritage secret. But he also understood how sick his dad had been and how he hadn't wanted his mother to suffer with him like she had when he'd been growing up. Worse yet, he hadn't wanted to reconnect with her just as he was dying.

And there'd been so many years when it had looked like he wouldn't make it...

That panic struck Collin's heart as it always did when he thought of how it had been growing up like that, with that constant fear and uncertainty. He didn't want that for Bailey Ann. He wanted to make sure she was safe and secure with him as her dad instead of just her doctor.

"You ready?" he asked her. Because he was...except for one thing...

He and Genevieve had gotten the marriage license a few days ago, but they'd both been so busy that they hadn't really had time to talk. He hadn't had time to tell her about what Colton had shared with him about that lighter and the possibility that Cash might have had something to do with the fire that had destroyed his family home. And they'd promised to always be open and honest with each other...

But when they'd applied for the marriage license, he'd been more focused on their marriage and on making sure she drew up a prenuptial agreement protecting her assets. Making sure that she felt safe with their agreement.

Colton's truck was here, despite his misgivings about this situation, and so was Genevieve's SUV. She'd bought a dress for Bailey Ann and had texted him to bring the little girl to Sadie's suite when they arrived. The seven-year-old was the reason for the marriage, so of course they wanted her to be their flower girl.

"I'm ready for the wedding," she said with a big smile.

"For you to marry Genevieve and become my mommy and daddy."

His stomach flipped a little with concern. "Remember that Genevieve is just helping us out because we're friends. And she wants to make sure that you are taken care of the best way possible." That was how he'd explained it to her. That he had to marry Genevieve so that Mrs. Finch would let Bailey Ann stay with them.

"I know," she said. The little girl smiled at him with that look Sadie sometimes had, like she knew something no one else did.

"Let's go inside and find Genevieve," he said.

Bailey Ann quickly unclasped the belt from her booster seat and reached for the car door handle. She wasn't able to open the door on her own, though. It was too heavy for her, or she was still a little weak from her last ordeal.

He rushed around the front of his car and helped her out. When he would have picked her up, she shook her head. "I'm too old to carry," she said. She glanced shyly up the steps of the porch where three boys stood, all of them in jeans, Western shirts and white cowboy hats.

Caleb, the most outgoing of them, greeted her first. "Hi! Who are you?"

"I'm Bailey Ann," she said, and she hurried up the steps, panting just a bit from the exertion as she joined them on the porch.

"I'm Caleb, this is Ian—my best friend and cousin— and this is Miller."

Miller was seven, like Bailey Ann, so Collin had hoped they would bond. Bailey Ann needed friends her own age, but Miller just gave her a cool nod. Collin knew the kid had been struggling since his parents died, but he was doing better now. Though he'd had no problem with Genevieve, it might take him a little longer to warm up to another new relative.

Or at least Collin hoped Bailey Ann would become a new relative—that he would foster her with Genevieve and then he would be able to file for adoption of her, too.

The screen door flew open and a pudgy little boy toddled out onto the porch. He held up his hands to Bailey Ann as if he wanted her to pick him up.

"Hi, little one," she said, gushing with excitement, and she reached out as if she intended to pick him up.

Worried that the child was too heavy for her, Collin picked him up instead. Little Jake, as if to steady himself, reached for his tie.

"Watch out. He'll choke you," Ben warned as he joined them on the porch. "Trust me."

Collin wasn't sure he should; Ben seemed as much their grandmother's partner in crime as Lem Lemmon did, maybe more so. Although sometimes that was handy to have on your side. "You helped push our marriage license through," Collin said. "Thank you."

Ben shook his head. "Grandma thinks I have more power than I do." He was the mayor. "There was no reason to push it. We had plenty of time since she insisted on this big shindig at the ranch. You okay with that?"

Collin glanced down at Bailey Ann, who was smiling up at the little boy and making faces at him. She looked so happy. "Yes."

"What about your bride?" Ben asked. "She seemed a little nervous when she showed up a few minutes ago."

"That might not have anything to do with the wedding," Collin reminded him. She might still be worried about her place in the family; or, like him, she might be wondering if they were doing all of this for nothing, if Mrs. Finch refused to give them a chance. Maybe that was the reason for Bailey Ann's knowing look—because Genevieve had talked to her, too, about how they were already like family because her sister had been married to Collin's cousin. And that the wedding was just going to make it official so they could become her foster family. They'd wanted to be honest with her but not build up her hopes too much in case Mrs. Finch didn't approve them for the long term.

Ben reached out for Little Jake. "I'll take him. You take the flower girl to get ready."

"You're a flower girl?" Caleb asked.

Bailey Ann eagerly nodded.

"She's the reason we picked the flowers from the garden this morning," Miller reminded his younger relatives.

"It was fun ripping the petals off them!" Caleb exclaimed.

Bailey Ann's dark eyes widened with surprise. "Did you hurt them?"

Miller snorted. "Flowers don't feel anything."

"They're alive," the little girl pointed out.

Miller's hat slid lower as his forehead wrinkled with confusion.

Chuckling now, Collin took her hand and led her into the house. "We need to see Genevieve," he told her, and they knocked on the door.

"If that's Collin, you can't come in." That was Darlene's voice drifting through the door. "It's bad luck for the groom to see the bride before the wedding." She sounded almost desperate about it. Had she seen her husband before the wedding?

Darlene was Collin's aunt, though her identity had been another of the secrets he'd learned later in his life. He and his brothers had believed she was their mother's best friend. After his mother died, Darlene had lived with his family, helping care for them and their father. It turned out she'd been married to Jessup's brother, the one who had died in a ranch accident. Darlene had blamed herself for his death and decided to make amends to Sadie for costing her a son. So she'd set out to find the long lost Jessup and bring him home. But when she'd seen how sick Jessup was, she'd stayed and helped them instead, under the incorrect assumption that her own family hated her.

They hadn't. But Collin didn't know what he and his family would have done without her. He and Marsh probably wouldn't have been able to go off to college, for one thing.

"Darlene," he called back to her. "It's okay. I have Bailey Ann—"

The door opened but only enough to show Darlene, whose slight body still managed to block most of the room from his view. "Hi," she said to the little girl. "I'm so happy to meet you. I'm Aunt Darlene."

She was so much more than an aunt to him. "Or you can call her Grandma, like the boys do," Collin said. "She helped raise me and my brothers, so she's like my mom."

Tears filled Darlene's hazel eyes as she turned to him with surprise. Had she never realized how he felt about her? How they all felt about her?

He felt a pang of regret for not saying that sooner. For not thanking her more for all that she'd done for them. "She's a very special lady," Collin said.

Darlene stepped out into the hall. "Go inside, sweetheart. Miss Genevieve bought a beautiful dress for you." The little girl squeezed through the opening before Darlene pulled the door shut behind her. Then she hugged Collin.

He hugged her back tightly. "Thank you so much, Darlene. I don't think any of us would have survived without you."

She smiled but shook her head. "You're all so strong and smart. You didn't need me as much as I needed you."

That made him think of Genevieve. He knew she was doing this for him and Bailey Ann as a way to let go of her guilt over her sister. Darlene's story wasn't so different, and look how well that had turned out.

"I love you," Darlene told him. "But I'm not letting you in there to see her before this wedding."

"But I just need to talk to her for a moment. There's something I have to tell her."

"The wedding is starting soon," Darlene said. "It's going to have to wait."

With all the people around, it probably wasn't the best time to share such a major secret. Someone else might overhear—someone like Marsh, who would feel compelled to do something about it.

Then he heard Bailey Ann squealing with excitement from inside the suite. She was what was important right now. She was the only reason he probably ever would have agreed to get married. He'd never been able to make a relationship last beyond a few dates. He didn't have the time to give a girlfriend the attention she deserved; he certainly didn't have enough to give a wife.

But this wasn't a real relationship. It was just a marriage of convenience.

"This isn't real," Genevieve wanted to say. But she kept the words inside for Bailey Ann's sake. Not just because she was in the suite with her now, but because she knew Mrs. Finch would probably interview their family and friends about their union in order to make sure that their home would be secure for Bailey Ann.

People didn't necessarily have to marry for love, though. She doubted Bradford had really married her for love, or he wouldn't have divorced her when she'd been unable to give him the child he'd wanted. She would have been enough for him if he'd really loved her.

Although there certainly was love present. Collin and Bailey Ann loved each other, and Genevieve was already falling for her, too.

The girl twirled around in the dress Genevieve had bought. "Thank you for helping me pick that out," she told Becca Calder. She'd run into the Realtor in the boutique where she'd been trying to figure out Bailey Ann's size. "And thank you for coming here with me today."

Worried that everyone at the ranch might be hostile toward her, she'd wanted at least one friendly face with her. She and Becca had hung out a few times since she'd helped Genevieve find her house. The Realtor had a ranch and had even taught Genevieve how to ride.

"I wish your daughter could have come as well," Genevieve said. Bailey Ann needed friends her own age; she seemed so alone at the hospital. She was thrilled that Mrs. Finch had given her permission for Bailey Ann to join them today.

"She's...with a friend today," Becca said.

Rumor had it that her husband had divorced her before her daughter Hope was born. Genevieve had no idea what their custody arrangement was or if they even had one. Would Collin share custody with her if they were allowed to adopt Bailey Ann?

"But we'll get them together soon. How about you? Are you ready for this?"

No. And she had a feeling that Collin might have been having doubts, too. Was that why he'd wanted to talk to her? To call it off?

But he wouldn't have let Bailey Ann in the room,

wouldn't have let her get dressed, only to disappoint her. He loved the little girl too much to call off this wedding.

The suite was filled with women. Ones she'd met like Jake's wife, Katie. There was Emily, who was the schoolteacher engaged to the mayor, and Taye. It was Taye that she approached after Becca. The tall woman had a smear of frosting on her cheek. The other women had been gushing over all the food she'd prepared, including some pastries sitting on a tray in the suite.

"Thank you so much for all you've done," Genevieve told her.

"Miller helped with the cooking and baking," Taye replied with a small smile.

"I'm really sorry," Genevieve said.

"That he cooked?" Taye asked with a slight laugh. "He's getting better than I am. And Juliet, Melanie's mom, is a great cook, too. Everyone pitched in to help."

"I'm not talking about the food," Genevieve said. "Though I am grateful for that as well. I'm also grateful for how you've taken care of the boys. It's very clear how much all of you love them and how much they love all of you. And I'm very sorry that I did something that scared you into thinking that love was in danger."

"*You* didn't," Taye said, and her smile reached her dark blue eyes now, warming them. "Sadie told us exactly what happened."

Genevieve smiled, too, as she followed Taye's glance across the sitting room to the older woman who'd squatted down to Bailey Ann's eye level to talk to the little girl. "Sadie probably knows more than I do about that."

Taye chuckled. "Sadie knows more than everybody does about everything."

"I still feel responsible."

"Yeah, for a lot of things that you shouldn't," Taye said.

"I am marrying a man who does that. But he's working on it. You need to work on it, too, on letting go of the past and focusing on the present and future."

She wasn't sure of either right now. What if Collin had wanted to talk to her because he was having doubts? Was she going to be left at the altar?

She really didn't know him well enough to know if he would back out once he'd given his word. She definitely didn't know him well enough to marry him, if she were marrying for love.

But again she reminded herself that he wouldn't disappoint Bailey Ann. The little girl twirled again and reached up to touch the wreath of flowers Sadie had so painstakingly bobby-pinned into her dark curls. This was some amazing family Collin had. That Bailey Ann would have. Genevieve felt that pang of envy she used to feel for her sister. She'd wanted a family like this.

But she had to remind herself again that this marriage wasn't real. This family wasn't hers, and she would have to find a way, again, to deal with the disappointment and loneliness once Collin got custody and they ended their marriage of convenience.

LEM SHOULD HAVE been used to Sadie involving him in her schemes. This time he'd been tapped into service as the celebrant, the one actually performing the wedding. He'd done it before, several times, over his career as mayor and now deputy mayor of Willow Creek.

But he couldn't remember a groom and best man ever looking as grim as the twins standing on his left, out on the patio behind the kitchen. With the additional wings that had been added to the house, the patio was almost like a courtyard, with twinkle lights dangling between the wings. One side was open to a field of wildflowers behind it. It really was a beautiful place to get married.

He was surprised this was the first of the Haven weddings that had happened here. Jake and Katie had gotten married in the church in town. Dusty and Melanie had married in some chapel in Vegas before Melanie had even come to Ranch Haven. She'd come as Miller's physical therapist, though, not the rodeo rider's runaway bride. No one but Sadie had known they'd married. And Ben and Emily, while engaged, weren't getting married until her winter break. Then it would be too cold to get married in the courtyard. Maybe they'd get married in city hall.

Taye and Baker should get married here, but Sadie was afraid that would have Taye taking on too much of the work herself, as she had for today.

Where did Sadie want to get married? She hadn't told him yet, just that it wouldn't be at a tattoo parlor. He'd suggested it because he wanted them each to have their rings tattooed on. She liked the idea, but the artist would have to come to them. Where? Here? Was that why Sadie had had the wedding at the ranch? So that he would see how beautiful it would be?

She opened a patio door from the kitchen and made a gesture. The ceremony could begin. Marsh and Jessup started some recorded music that played out of the speakers mounted to the outside of the house. And Lem knew he should be turning to watch for the bride, but he couldn't take his eyes off Sadie.

She didn't often wear a dress. The few times he'd seen her in one, it had been black, for funerals. Today she wore a long pale blue dress that swirled around her boots as she walked to a seat at the front.

He wondered if he should ask her if she wanted to do it today. Get hitched here and now.

But he didn't have the tattoo artist yet. And this was Collin's day, despite how grim he looked about it.

Was he going to go through with it?

A little girl bounded through the patio doors, giggling as she tossed flowers everywhere. She skipped down the aisle toward Collin, and the grimness left his face. He smiled brightly at the little girl who stopped to throw her arms around his waist and hug him. Then she drew back and whirled around to take a seat next to Sadie.

The music changed, and they all turned toward the back.

Genevieve Porter appeared. She wore a simple cream-colored dress, and her blond hair was caught up with some pins and flowers. She looked nothing like sweet Jenny, but she was very beautiful. Did that beauty go as deep as Jenny's had?

Was that why she'd agreed to this marriage? For this little girl?

Or was Sadie wrong about her? He worried this was all a terrible mistake.

CHAPTER FOURTEEN

COLLIN HAD BEEN struggling with the burden of that secret Colton had given him to carry as well. He hadn't wanted to marry Genevieve without telling her. But then he'd seen Marsh and Jessup on the patio, and he knew he couldn't say anything where they might overhear it.

Then Bailey Ann had come bounding down the aisle like an exuberant puppy with so much love and joy...

And that love and joy had filled him. He couldn't lose her, not to Sheridan and definitely not to a worse fate than that. The fate she might suffer if the foster family didn't follow her medical orders exactly.

When she closed her arms around him to hug him, he knew that while he might not be doing the right thing, at least he was doing it for the right reason: her.

She pulled away from him to sit with Sadie, like they were already the best of friends. Or granddaughter and great-grandmother...

With this marriage, Bailey Ann was getting more than just him. She was getting an entire family. He hoped Mrs. Finch would see that.

The music changed and everyone turned toward the open French doors. Genevieve stepped out onto the patio, and the sunshine caught and shimmered in her pale blond hair.

"She looks like an angel," Bailey Ann murmured in awe.

She was certainly beautiful. One of the most beautiful

women he'd ever seen. But she also looked so vulnerable. Maybe it was his family and being here at the ranch intensifying all that guilt she carried over her sister that had her looking fragile.

Because he'd seen her strength; she'd shown it when she'd dealt with Mrs. Finch. She was strong and smart, but she didn't look as confident as she should have been.

Maybe that was his fault. He was the one gaining so much from this marriage of convenience. She might be doing it to ease her anguish over her sister, but that wasn't exactly convenient for her. Maybe she'd changed her mind.

After that first step onto the patio, she hadn't moved. She just stood there, staring down the short aisle at him. He braced himself, expecting her to turn around and run back inside, to run away like she had the last time she'd been at the ranch.

But her slender shoulders squared, and her chin came up and she took a step forward. She looked so alone, walking herself down the aisle. She'd had no one to give her away, but somehow that was fitting. She was her own woman and this marriage had been her idea.

The wedding, of course, had been all Sadie, but he and Genevieve hadn't argued with her about it. They needed as much evidence as possible to show CPS that their marriage was real.

Genevieve might seem fragile just now, but she was strong. Probably because she had never had anyone else she could rely on. So Collin met her halfway down the aisle and he walked those last few steps with her to the front.

While he had Colton standing up with him, she had no one on her side until Bailey Ann popped out of her seat and ran up next to her. She grabbed the small bouquet of wildflowers that Collin hadn't even noticed his bride was holding. "I'm the flower girl," she told Genevieve.

And Genevieve smiled at her. "Thank you."

"I wanna be fower grr..." Little Jake said, and everyone laughed.

Bailey Ann walked from the front to where Little Jake sat on Baker's lap in the middle row. And she gave the toddler a handful of petals from her basket. He clutched them in his pudgy fingers and grinned at her. And Bailey Ann grinned back, happiness radiating from her. She was loving this: the ranch, the ceremony but most of all the family.

Collin looked down at his bride and saw that she was watching the little girl, too, and she was smiling as much as the kids were. That palpitation struck his heart again, that strange flutter, and then a flood of warmth. He was definitely going to need to give himself an EKG.

Genevieve turned and saw him staring at her, and the smile left her face as it tensed. As she tensed...as if bracing herself... For what?

For marriage?

For him?

"Shall we begin?" Lem asked, and he stared at both of them as if making sure that they wanted to do this. As if he didn't think that they did...

Collin nodded.

Then Genevieve nodded, too, and some of that tension eased from her. Or maybe that was because Bailey Ann was back at her side, holding her hand again.

"All right then," Lem said. "Let's get these two married..."

His voice faded to a buzzing in Collin's ears. He couldn't focus on the words; he just had to focus on the intent. He couldn't pledge his love and commitment to Genevieve, not when he hardly knew her. This wasn't a love match. They shouldn't have had this wedding at the ranch. They should have just made a quick trip before the judge, just the two of them.

Colton nudged him, and the buzzing receded so that Collin could hear his name being called. He turned toward Lem. "Do you?" the older man asked, as if he was repeating the question.

He didn't need the whole question. He knew what Lem was asking, what was expected. He focused then on Bailey Ann, who peered around Genevieve to smile at him. And then he looked at his bride, whose smile was more uncertain, but who was here for him. For him and Bailey Ann.

Perhaps the choice of wedding venue had been a mistake, but the marriage? He was ready to go ahead with that. He nodded, then cleared his throat and said, "I do."

Lem turned toward Genevieve. "Do you take this man for your husband?"

There were no promises of love and cherishing. At least, not in her vows. Collin couldn't be certain what he'd pledged. But she nodded, like he did, and rasped out the two words as if she was choking on them. "I do…"

"I now pronounce you husband and wife," Lem finished.

Bailey Ann stepped forward and tugged on Lem's jacket. "You gotta tell them to kiss."

The little minx knew they were just friends. He'd made that clear to her but, once again, she reminded him of Sadie.

Lem glanced down at her and smiled. "You heard her," he said. "Collin, you may kiss your bride…"

He couldn't refuse, not without insulting Genevieve and disappointing Bailey Ann. So he leaned forward and brushed his lips across her cheek.

"Not like that," Bailey Ann said. "You're married now. You gotta kiss her on the lips."

Collin narrowed his eyes and studied the face of the child he wanted to officially make his daughter. "What do you know about kissing, young lady?"

"That's what it shows on the daytime soaps I watch with the nurse aides," she replied.

He looked to Genevieve for her consent and she gave him a sweet smile and nodded.

And Collin lowered his head again. This time instead of brushing his lips across her cheek, he brushed them across her mouth. Or at least that was what he intended to do, but that buzzing was back, not just in his ears but inside his body. It seemed to move through him like an electrical current, like he'd been shocked.

And he was...

And he found himself lingering over her mouth, kissing her longer than he'd intended. And he found himself wishing he never had to stop.

Genevieve hadn't known what to expect on her second wedding day, especially once she'd agreed to let Sadie host it at the ranch. The only thing she'd known for certain was that it would be uncomfortable.

For her.

Probably for Collin.

With the way he'd been acting since showing up at the ranch, wanting to talk to her before the ceremony, zoning out during the vows...

She'd feared he was going to back out. But then he'd said "I do." And she'd been compelled to say the same despite the sudden rush of nerves that had attacked her.

And this kiss...

Even the first brush of his mouth across her cheek had startled her, had started this tingling feeling...but now with his mouth on hers, kissing her deeply, she felt a rush of something more than nerves.

Then Bailey Ann tugged on her hand, pulling her back from him. "You're going to need to breathe," she warned them.

And everybody laughed.

Then Bailey Ann stepped between them. After looping her basket—with Genevieve's bouquet inside—over her arm, she grasped both their hands and tugged them down the aisle toward the open French doors. "Now it's time for cake."

"Yay, cake!" Katie's little boy, Caleb, exclaimed.

"You gotta see it," Miller said as he rushed out of his seat and followed them down the short aisle and into the kitchen. "I helped Taye decorate it." He took Genevieve's other hand, tugged her away from Bailey Ann and led her toward the kitchen counter where the cake had been set up with cupcakes and cookies around the base of it.

For as quickly as the ceremony had been thrown together, Genevieve had not expected all the flowers and decorations and food. And this beautiful three-tiered cake with buttercream icing and flowers in as many colors as the field of them out back.

"It's beautiful," she praised Miller. "Like something you'd see on the cover of a bridal magazine."

"Taye did most of it," he said bashfully. "She can do anything." There was such awe in his voice, such love for this woman who would be his mom now that Jenny was gone.

Tears stung Genevieve's eyes over the loss of her sister and over what she had lost. More than her life, she'd lost her children.

"Are you my aunt?" Miller asked suddenly, and his face flushed. "People are saying that."

Genevieve nodded. "Yes, I am. I am your mom's older sister. I've been gone from Willow Creek for a long time—longer than I lived in it. That why I was never around like I want to be now. That's also why I didn't know about the accident."

"It's okay," Miller said. "It was really bad then, but it's better now."

"You're amazing," she said. She'd been so broken after her divorce and all the other disappointments that had come before and after it. But he'd endured so much more than she had, and he was so young.

He smiled and shrugged. "Like I said, Taye did most of the work."

Taye came up behind him and slid her arm around his shoulder. "I couldn't do it without you. He's like my right arm now. He helped with the potato salad and the chicken salad, too."

"I can't wait to try it all," Genevieve said. But with the way her stomach was churning, she wasn't certain she would be able to eat.

She'd been nervous about coming back out to the ranch, about the wedding, about the marriage of convenience, but those nerves were nothing compared to how she felt about that kiss. She wasn't just nervous anymore; she was afraid. She did not want to start feeling again.

She'd shut down even before her divorce, and she wanted to stay that way, to not open herself up to a significant other. She didn't want to make herself vulnerable to love again only to be rejected when her husband realized she wasn't what he wanted. And Collin didn't really want her anyway. She was just a means for him to foster and adopt the little girl he loved.

She drew in a deep breath, reminding herself of that, of the real reason for this wedding, for this marriage…

Bailey Ann.

Who squeezed in between her and Miller now. The little boy jumped back as if afraid he was going to get cooties. "It's such a pretty cake," Bailey Ann said, oblivious. "Now you and Dr. Cass have to hold hands and cut it and then feed each other a piece…"

"I didn't realize there are so many weddings on soap operas," Genevieve mused.

Taye chuckled. "Oh, there are. When I worked at the diner in town, the owner always had her *shows* running on a TV in the kitchen. I have to admit I got a little addicted, too. Not like Caleb to my chocolate chip cookies, but…"

"Those cookies?" Bailey Ann asked, pointing to the ones arranged around the bottom tier of the cake.

"We should eat lunch first," Genevieve suggested. She needed something more solid in her stomach before she started in on the sugary treats.

"No, cut the cake!" Caleb called out from behind her. Then he began to chant, "Cut the cake! Cut the cake!"

And Ian joined in. Bailey Ann cast a furtive glance at Miller, then she quietly added in her voice. "Cut the cake."

Miller glanced back at her, then he added his to the chant, his just a little deeper than the younger boys.

Little Jake just yelled, "Cake! Cake!" And he finally released the handful of flower petals Bailey Ann had given them. He threw them up in the air, and since Baker held him, he was already up quite high. They rained down on Genevieve and Bailey Ann, Miller and Taye and the cake.

Somebody touched Genevieve's hair, plucking a petal from it. Not somebody. Collin. She instinctively knew it was him because her heart beat faster and her breathing deepened.

She turned to find him standing behind her. Close.

"I guess we better cut the cake, Mrs. Cassidy," he said. "Before we have a mutiny on our hands."

Taye smiled and handed over a cake knife. "Sorry," she said. "I could say that it's not usually chaos like this around here, but I would be lying." But she was beaming with love.

Genevieve didn't know how well her sister had known Taye Cooper, but she knew that she would have loved her and she would have approved of a woman like this, so nurturing and patient and sweet, as the mother for her children now that she could no longer be.

Collin leaned close to her and whispered, "I'm sorry."

She had no idea what he was apologizing for...

The chaos?

Calling her Mrs. Cassidy?

Or that kiss?

"THANK YOU, GRANDMA," Colton said as he leaned over and kissed her cheek.

He was wearing the black cowboy hat, but even without it, she would have known which twin he was. And he was not the one who'd just gotten married, although she wished he would do it soon.

He and Livvy Lemmon were so in love and so well suited to each other. But they weren't the only couple who needed to hurry up and get married.

She glanced around for Lem. But he was so short and her family was so big that she couldn't see him over or around all of her grandsons. Knowing him and loving him for it, Sadie guessed Lem was probably crouched down and entertaining her great-grandchildren. Children were so drawn to him. Not just children. She was, too...even when she'd thought she hated him.

She focused on Colton now, reaching up to pat his cheek. These Cassidy grandsons were as big or bigger than her Haven ones. "What are you thanking me for?" she asked. "I didn't think you actually approved of your brother getting married."

But he still had served as his best man, standing beside him, offering support or maybe urging him to run while he could. But while he'd seemed a bit distracted during Lem's service, Collin hadn't run. And when he'd kissed his bride...

It had seemed real for both of them.

Sadie had hoped that this would work out for them both and especially for Bailey Ann.

"I'm thanking you for helping me look for Cash like you promised," he said.

He'd asked her a couple of weeks ago with a strange urgency. What Colton had been carrying alone had something to do with his missing brother. Sadie understood that all too well, given all those years she'd been missing her oldest son while she'd kept the burden of that from her grandsons, choosing to focus on them instead.

But she'd never stopped searching for Jessup.

"I haven't done much yet to find him," she reluctantly admitted. She'd been distracted with her own engagement and then with Collin's.

Colton pointed across the room to his dad. No. Not to his dad but to the dark-haired woman standing next to him. "I thought that's why you invited Becca."

"No, she's Genevieve's guest." And the local Realtor. Sadie hadn't bought or sold anything recently, so she hadn't used the young woman's services.

Colton glanced at his new sister-in-law with interest. She was feeding her husband a slice of cake, but when his lips touched her fingers, she jerked back and nearly dropped it. There was definitely something there.

Something that neither of them, from the shocked look on Collin's face, considered all that convenient.

Sadie smiled.

"Becca was my brother Cash's best friend since they were little kids," Colton said. "If anyone knows where he is, she does."

Sadie already had an inkling of her own, especially after she'd learned about Cash's scholarship to a veterinarian program. But before she could focus on Cash, she had to make sure that Collin would be okay. That both he and Genevieve would be okay. No. More than okay. Happy.

CHAPTER FIFTEEN

COLLIN HAD LOST Genevieve for a while at the ranch when Miller had whisked her into the house. And during the party in the kitchen, after feeding him a piece of cake, she'd disappeared for a while. And now, even though she sat next to him, she seemed a million miles away instead of just a few cushions of the large sectional couch in her family room.

Bailey Ann sat between them, still wearing the flower girl dress that she wanted to wear forever, watching TV through half-closed eyes. An animated movie played, music humming from the surround sound speakers.

She was in awe of Genevieve's house. So was he, really. But it wasn't just the house. Genevieve had made popcorn with the popcorn maker in the corner of the family room. And with real butter drizzled over it, it tasted just like it did in the movie theater. Her TV was nearly the size of a movie screen, too.

She'd really gone all out for the nephews she thought she might need to shelter.

While Collin agreed with Baker and Taye adopting them and being their primary guardians, he hoped they would allow the boys to visit their newfound aunt. With the way they'd all taken to her, it would not be upsetting to them at all.

But he could tell it was upsetting for Genevieve when she saw them. Even though she smiled and laughed with them, there was such sadness in her beautiful eyes. Maybe that was why she was so quiet now.

Or maybe she was totally regretting what they'd just done even though it had been her suggestion. "Will it really work?" he wondered aloud.

And she jumped as if he'd startled her. Had she forgotten he was there?

She glanced at Bailey Ann whose eyes had completely closed now. Pieces of popcorn were stuck to her dress along with a few wayward flower petals. She smiled at the little girl. "It has to. She's so happy."

When they'd left the ranch, it had been midafternoon. Genevieve had suggested they come back here to rest for a while after the excitement of the day. Bailey Ann had been far more excited than they'd been and far more exhausted.

"Mrs. Finch authorized us having her for the day," he said. "But do you think she will extend that?"

"I'll work hard to make sure that she does," Genevieve said. "She had so much fun."

"Maybe too much," Collin admitted with concern. She'd gotten really tired at the ranch. And while she'd enjoyed the movie and popcorn, she'd barely been able to keep her eyes open. He needed to wake her up for one more dose of the drugs he'd brought along with them.

Genevieve's teeth nipped into her bottom lip as she stared down at her. "Is she all right?"

"Just tired." He touched her shoulder and the little girl grumbled in her sleep.

Genevieve smiled. "Hey, sweetheart, we need to hang up your dress so you can wear it again." She glanced at Collin. "Maybe soon, with all the engagements in your family."

"And she's the only girl," Collin said.

"She was already special without that distinction."

"All the kids are special."

"Yes, they are," she said with such raw longing in her voice that tears glistened in her eyes.

Sympathy flooded him. "Are you okay?" he asked. "Was today too much for you?"

She opened her mouth, as if about to speak, but Bailey Ann jerked awake and stared up at them. Her dark eyes were wide as if she was shocked to find herself with them both. "Did today really happen?" she asked. "Am I out of the hospital?"

"Yes, you are," Collin said. "And to keep you that way, we need to get your meds and get you to bed."

Genevieve jumped up from the couch and rushed off before he and Bailey Ann could move. "I'll get everything ready," she said over her shoulder, her voice drifting in as she hurried down the hall.

Was she just trying to help?

Or was she wanting to escape?

Once they got Bailey Ann settled, he would try again to get her to talk, to make sure she was okay and to share with her what he should have before they'd gotten married. No more secrets, they'd promised each other. That should have been part of their vows. Maybe it had been; he'd been so distracted that he hadn't been able to hear them.

And like Bailey Ann, he was not entirely sure anything had really happened. Was the little girl out of the hospital with him and his...wife?

He was married.

Or had it all just been a dream? It might as well have been because it wasn't real. And it couldn't be. They couldn't get their emotions involved and risk hurting each other or worse yet, hurting Bailey Ann.

"Sweet dreams," Genevieve whispered as she leaned over the race car bed and kissed Bailey Ann's forehead. The little girl was already back to sleep after her meds and her bath. A slight smile curved her lips.

"She looks like she's already having them," Collin remarked.

"Yes, she does," Genevieve agreed. Because the bed was so low to the ground, she'd had to kneel next to it to reach the little girl. Collin offered her his hand to help her up.

That feeling moved through her again—like a shiver but full of warmth and vitality instead of cold. She wanted to tug out of his light grasp and run away from him and from it. But she knew they had to talk about the plan with fostering Bailey Ann, how they could convince Mrs. Finch to let her stay for more than a day and a night. How they could keep her forever...

But then Genevieve realized she wouldn't have forever with her. She was just a means to an end, Collin's way to foster and adopt. But once he adopted the little girl, he wouldn't need Genevieve anymore. Bailey Ann wouldn't need her either. She'd only wanted a dad: Collin.

But of course, Genevieve had known that was what she was getting into when she'd made the offer. That was the only reason she'd made it, because it wouldn't be long term. Since her parents had already signed away their rights and there was no one to contest the adoption, it could happen in six months with approval from CPS and a family court judge. Six months...

Surely that wouldn't be long enough for emotions to get involved. She would be safe, invulnerable.

But she didn't feel that way now. And she didn't like it. Flustered and upset with herself, Genevieve turned away, which had his hands falling away from her shoulders. Then she slipped quietly into the hall.

He was right with her every step, his long legs keeping up with her. She didn't want to go to her bedroom yet, didn't want him walking her to the door and talking to her there.

And she knew he wanted to talk even before he said, "Can you give me a few minutes, Genevieve?"

She nodded and turned back toward the family room. "I should redo that room for her," she said.

"She picked it out of all the bedrooms you showed her," he said. "She loves it."

She'd decorated the three children's rooms with her nephews in mind. One bedroom theme with race cars, one with superheroes and the third with a cowboy theme. But little girls could like all those things, too. Still...

"You don't think I should change it to something more girlie?" She gestured at the animated cartoon playing on the television. "Like princess-y or something?"

"I don't think you need to change anything," he said. "I take it you decorated them for your nephews?"

She nodded.

"How are you feeling now, getting to know them, seeing them with the Havens?" he asked. She drew in a deep breath.

"I'm happy that they're doing well. That they're loved so much. But I have to admit that I'm also a little disappointed that they don't need me. I know that sounds incredibly selfish, but we agreed that being open and honest is the best policy."

He flinched now.

And she realized why he'd wanted to talk to her before the wedding. "I take it you haven't been..." A twinge of disappointment passed through her chest. She didn't know why she'd expected him to uphold their deal, though. She didn't even really know him.

And now she was married to him.

"Had you changed your mind?" she asked. "Did you decide not to marry me but went through with it anyways?"

He shook his head so vehemently that it tousled his dark hair. She wanted to reach up and smooth it back into place because Collin was always so put together, so calm and steady. He was exactly what a little girl, one who'd gone through all the medical and familial upheaval that Bailey Ann had endured, needed in a father.

Not that Genevieve had any experiences with fathers. She'd never met her biological one. Her mother said he left Willow Creek for college and never looked back. And her stepfather had made it clear that Jenny was his, but she was not. And even Bradford hadn't become a father until after he divorced her.

"No, this has nothing to do with you," he said. "I wanted to talk to you about my family."

"I know they're not exactly thrilled about your sudden marriage," she said. They'd all been so kind to her, but she sensed they were also cautious. They probably thought she was pretty desperate to propose to a stranger or that she was flaky.

Collin grinned. "They certainly never expected me to be the first one to get married," he said.

"Why not?"

"I decided long ago to never get married." He chuckled. "Guess that's a strange thing to tell my wife."

"I'm not really your wife," she reminded him.

"Legally you are."

"Not romantically, though." At least not for him. She was starting to feel all these things she'd vowed to never feel again. Attraction…

He shrugged. "It doesn't matter. I didn't intend to get married for any reason. I'm too busy with work and my family to have any time to see a girlfriend, let alone a wife."

"But you want to adopt a little girl," she reminded him.

"I will make time for her," he said. "And now that my dad is doing better, after his heart transplant, I don't feel the same urgency to work as hard as I once did."

She nodded. "I get that. I used to love being a lawyer. I did a lot of things in DC. I worked with big corporations. Politicians. I even considered running for office myself but when I couldn't have a child, it all seemed so empty." Like this house had until tonight, until she and Collin and Bailey Ann had sat on the big couch and watched the big TV. Then it had finally felt like a home.

"So...since you're my lawyer, does that mean you have to keep my secrets?"

She tensed and studied his face. "I didn't think you had any secrets."

"I didn't until Colton decided to share his with me," he said, then uttered a groan of frustration.

"Oh, that's different then," she said. "If your twin asked you to keep something secret, I don't expect you to tell me that. I just wanted us to be open and honest about things that mattered to each other and to Bailey Ann."

He clenched his jaw so tightly that a muscle twitched in his cheek. Whatever this secret was, it was troubling him.

"Is that what's had you so distracted today?" she asked. She'd been so certain that he'd changed his mind.

He nodded. "I just... It's big...and I know it's not a secret I should be keeping...or Colton should be either but I don't know what to do with it..."

She drew in a deep breath then. She'd intended for this marriage to just be temporary and impersonal with the focus on fostering a little girl who needed someone in her life she could count on. But now...

Now this was beginning to feel like a real marriage.

Not necessarily the marriage she'd had, but one in which the couple talked and shared their thoughts and feelings.

Or maybe this was just real friendship. Genevieve hadn't had many of those either. Just the superficial friendships she'd made at work and in the social circle she'd married into when she'd married Bradford. None of those people had reached out to her during her divorce or after her move, though, so they hadn't been real friends.

"Share it with me," she said. "And yes, it will stay confidential like all those legal agreements I drew up."

His lips curved into a slight smile then. "Should I have read those documents more closely that you had me sign?"

"You had me draw them up," she reminded him. And his insisting on a prenup to protect her assets had cemented for her that she was doing the right thing in helping him and Bailey Ann.

"Yes, but I can read medical journals, not legal jargon."

"Do I need to be concerned about legal ramifications with this secret?" she asked. His twin seemed as honorable a man as Collin was. She couldn't believe he had shared something with him that would have Collin this concerned.

"I'm not worried about me," he said. "Although maybe I should be since we're already under heavy scrutiny from Mrs. Finch."

"She has Bailey Ann's best interests at heart," Genevieve said, reminding herself as much as him.

He nodded and sighed. "I know. I just wish she could see that I'm in Bailey Ann's best interest."

"We'll make sure of that," she assured him. "And now that you've stalled, have you changed your mind about sharing?"

"I told you about my brother Cash, right? The one who ran away seventeen years ago?"

She nodded. "Becca's friend. Yes."

"I think he's back."

"You've seen him?"

"No, but Colton found a lighter that we both saw Cash take with him when he left."

"Okay. Where did Colton find the lighter?"

"In the ashes of my family home..." He stared down at his hands, at the skin that was still pink and new from the healing burns.

She gasped. "You think he started the fire? Is that why you're so upset?"

"We don't know what to think. Cash was so mad when he left, but that was so long ago. Plus, he had such an affinity for the ranch. If he knew Dad was selling it, he could have started it on fire out of spite..."

"Or there could be an innocent explanation—like he could have toured the ranch with a strange Realtor, or maybe with Becca, and dropped the lighter then," she said. "That it had nothing to do with starting the fire."

Collin expelled a heavy breath and nodded. "That makes sense. That makes so much sense." Then he reached out and hugged her. "Thank you. Thank you for making me feel better."

But with that hug, he'd made her feel worse because he'd made her feel, again, entirely too much. Blinking against the sudden rush of tears, Genevieve pulled back and forced a smile. "Call your brother," she said. "I'm going to head to bed. It's been a long day."

He nodded.

She hesitated before leaving him, though. "Do you need any help setting yourself up in a guest room? I can show you where the extra linens and towels are."

He smiled. "No. I already put my overnight bag in the superhero room."

"Of course you did..."

"Bailey Ann picked it out for me," he insisted, but his grin had widened as if he was as excited about sleeping there as Bailey Ann had been about her room. "Of course, the bed in there isn't nearly as cool as the one she has."

"You would have hung off the end of the race car," she pointed out. He was so tall. So handsome...

And now he was her husband. But he wouldn't be sharing her bed. So she hurried off down the hall toward her room and away from temptation.

"YOU DID WHAT?" Colton asked his twin. Then he lowered his voice and glanced around the mostly empty hospital lobby. He was waiting for Livvy's shift to end so they could spend some time together before she needed to go back to her grandfather's house and crash.

He definitely hadn't been expecting a call from Collin on his wedding night, but then he was aware that this wasn't a real marriage. So why had he told Genevieve about Cash and that dang lighter?

"She's a lawyer," Collin said. "And she's my wife."

Colton snorted. "She's a stranger. One who's already proved she can't be trusted. I still think you're making a mistake."

"I didn't call you about my marriage," Collin reminded him. "I called you about Cash."

Colton listened to his twin's theory about their oldest brother. No. Not Collin's theory. It was Genevieve's and sounded a lot like an excuse a lawyer would give in a courtroom for reasonable doubt.

The problem was that Colton doubted the theory more. "You think he came back to look at the ranch to buy?"

"Maybe he came over with Becca," Collin suggested, "when she was showing it to another client. Or...maybe there's some reasonable explanation for the lighter turning up that has nothing to do with the fire. Maybe he even gave it to Becca. They were close, remember?"

Collin was right about that, and as Colton had told his grandmother, if anyone knew where Cash was, it was Becca. Maybe he needed to show her the lighter and make her see how serious this was—especially if the insurance investigator deemed the fire an arson.

"This is your wedding night," Colton reminded him. "Your honeymoon. Shouldn't you be enjoying it?"

"I did…with popcorn and a Disney movie," Collin said. "Bailey Ann is so happy."

"What about you?" Colton asked. He knew how his brother always put himself last, and never more so than now when he'd married a stranger so that he could foster a little girl.

And he worried that if Collin kept sacrificing his happiness for others, he would never know true love and happiness for himself.

CHAPTER SIXTEEN

COLLIN DIDN'T KNOW how she'd managed, but somehow Genevieve had talked Mrs. Finch into letting them keep Bailey Ann on a trial basis. He'd heard her argument. Her house was close to the hospital. A registered nurse watched her whenever Collin wasn't home. And most of all, it was what Bailey Ann wanted. And then she'd put Bailey Ann on the call to confirm all of that and to plead.

He wasn't sure which of them had won over the social worker, but for the moment, Bailey Ann was allowed to stay with him and Genevieve.

His mind flashed forward to a day sometime in the future when he had adopted Bailey Ann. At that point, he and Genevieve could go their separate ways. He'd never be able to thank her enough for what she'd done for him and the little girl.

He worried, though, that Bailey Ann wouldn't be eager to leave. She was already attached to his faux wife, and she would probably plead with him one day to leave her here with Genevieve, like she'd pleaded with Mrs. Finch.

And then he would be alone again even if he was with his family. He had never felt as seen with them as he felt with Bailey Ann and even with Genevieve. She watched him, listened to him, comforted him like she had on their wedding night.

Surely she had to be right about Cash. He hadn't started that fire. But then she hadn't been there that day he'd run away, so many years ago; she hadn't seen how angry he'd been then. If she had, she might have considered it like Colton was.

Might have worried about it like Collin did when he let himself worry about something other than keeping Bailey Ann. She was doing so well. She was so happy.

He'd never seen her as happy as she'd been since the wedding. Even when he'd left to go to the hospital, she hadn't been upset. Probably because Genevieve had stayed home with her and Nurse Sue. It seemed the older woman had fallen for the little girl, too. Her sometimes icy demeanor had completely melted away with the child. And with Genevieve...

Sue had a great affection for his wife, which was probably why she'd gone overboard in her reaction to Ian getting hurt. She'd wanted Genevieve to get the boys because it was clear how much Genevieve needed children.

Genevieve was so attentive and sweet with Bailey Ann. He wondered at her ex-husband. Why hadn't the man encouraged and supported her in fostering children? Why had he only wanted a child with their DNA? DNA didn't matter to kids; only love mattered. And Genevieve had so much of it to give.

She seemed completely unaware of how wonderful she was, though. And at the moment, she was completely uncomfortable. "I know you have to go to work," she said, as if convincing herself as much as him. "But can you go in a little later...after Sue finds a replacement for herself?"

Sue had gotten sick, and she rightfully didn't want to put Bailey Ann's health at risk. The little girl was stronger now, but her immune system was being suppressed so that it wouldn't reject her heart. It wouldn't be able to reject a bug either.

He was actually a little nervous that Sue might have

already exposed her, and maybe that was why Genevieve was so on edge as well. He went over the medicine schedule with her again even though it was written down as well next to the automatic pill dispenser he'd set up for them. "You won't be able to forget," he said. "The alarm on this thing won't shut off until you take out the pills. You've got this."

Genevieve's teeth nipped into her bottom lip but she nodded. "Okay..."

"What's wrong?" he asked.

"I've taken parenting classes, but my time around kids has been limited," she said, and then lowered her voice to a whisper and continued, "and I've never been alone with one with a health condition."

"Bailey Ann is doing well," he reminded her.

"But what if she picked up Sue's bug?"

"She's fine," he insisted. "I checked her temperature and ears and nose. She's clear." And he prayed that she stayed that way.

Genevieve released a shaky breath and nodded. "Okay, that's good, and Sue said she would send someone over."

"You'll be fine," he said. Then he glanced at his watch. Thankfully her house was close to the hospital, just as she'd told Mrs. Finch. But still. "I'm going to be late..."

"Go," she urged him. "Like you said, we'll be fine." Then she glanced around nervously. "Where is she?"

"Right here!" the little girl said as she popped into the kitchen with them. "Are you going to work, Dr. Cass? Or can I call you Daddy now?"

Warmth flooded his chest. He wanted that so badly. But what if it didn't happen? He'd warned Bailey Ann about getting her hopes up, but his were up, too. And he didn't know what he would do if this all didn't work out.

"You and Genevieve are my foster parents now," she pointed out. "Can't I call you Mom and Dad?"

"Mrs. Finch only approved us on a trial basis," he reminded Bailey Ann and himself. After all the setbacks over the years with his father's health and even with Bailey Ann's, Collin had learned long ago not to get his hopes up too high. Not to expect too much...

"What's a trial?"

"You've been in them before," he reminded her. "Like when we tried drugs for just a certain amount of time to see if they would work. And then if they didn't we stopped them. That was a trial basis. To see if it worked, then deciding whether to continue or stop."

"But this is going to work," Bailey Ann insisted, her voice rising a bit as if she was on the verge of tears.

Genevieve hunched down and slid her arm around the little girl's shoulders. "It's not up to us to decide if it's working or not, though," she cautioned the child. "It's up to Mrs. Finch and her supervisor and eventually it'll be up to a judge."

Because this lawyer he was married to would take it to court if she couldn't convince the social worker and her boss. She was strong and determined, and he was so very happy she was on their side. He smiled at her. "Okay, ladies, I have to go to work or my patients will get mad at me."

"Not me," Bailey Ann said with a smile. She hugged his legs. And he leaned over and kissed the top of her head. "Kiss Mommy, too," she said.

"What?" Genevieve rasped out the word just as she'd rasped out her wedding vow, like she was choking. Her blue eyes glistened, too.

"I'm going to call you Mommy and Dr. Cass Daddy,"

the little girl declared with defiance. "And if Mrs. Finch says I can't, I'll do what she does to me. I won't listen."

Collin had to bite the inside of his cheek to keep the smile off his face. He didn't want to encourage her mutiny. "We need to be respectful of Mrs. Finch," he said. "She's just trying to help you."

"Then she'll let me stay here forever!" Bailey Ann said.

And longing tugged at Collin, not just for this special child but for what she wanted. Everything. The family...

He'd set her up for disappointment no matter if Mrs. Finch okayed her staying here or not. Because they couldn't stay forever, and he should have made that clearer to her from the beginning. He had told her that Genevieve was just a friend helping them out for a few months.

"Kiss Mommy," she urged again.

His beeper went off. He was already late. He didn't have time to explain to Bailey Ann what the situation really was. So he just brushed his lips across Genevieve's cheek.

"That's not like you did at the wedding," Bailey Ann said.

He smiled now and shook his head. "I don't have time. I'm late," he said. "I'll see you both later."

And he rushed out despite the guilt plaguing him. He didn't feel bad leaving Genevieve alone with Bailey Ann. He felt bad that he was letting the little girl believe that this was real and that it could last.

But maybe she knew better than anyone that nothing was guaranteed to last forever. Not family. Not love. Sometimes not even a heart.

FOREVER. THAT WAS how long it felt like Collin had been gone when it had probably only been minutes. Forever was what Bailey Ann wanted, not just with Collin but with Genevieve as well. And Genevieve wanted that, too.

But they had both tried, separately, to make it clear to the little girl that they were just friends. That they had gotten married for her to stay here, but that it wasn't permanent. Just like the social worker had said and Collin had repeated to Bailey Ann, this was just on a trial basis.

They hadn't wanted the little girl to believe that their marriage was a genuine love match. But clearly she'd begun to think that.

Maybe that was okay, though, because if the social worker questioned Bailey Ann about their relationship, the little girl would tell Mrs. Finch that it was real and not just for her.

But it was just for her.

And Genevieve needed to remind herself of that, too. That this wasn't forever. She just wanted to help Bailey Ann and Collin find their happiness because she knew how hard that was. She hadn't found her own. And even though Jenny had with Dale, that hadn't lasted.

So no one was guaranteed forever. She needed to make sure that Bailey Ann made it through today. This was the first time she'd been left alone with the child, and unfortunately Sue hadn't been able to find a replacement.

Genevieve had just taken Sue's call about it, and when she clicked off her cell and sat it on the counter, her hand shook slightly.

Bailey Ann reached across and clasped her fingers and squeezed. Sometimes it was so hard to believe she was only seven; she was so mature, as if she had an old soul.

Or maybe an old heart...

And again, Genevieve couldn't help but wonder...

Was it Jenny's?

"It's okay, Mommy," Bailey Ann said.

Longing squeezed Genevieve's heart. She'd wanted for so long for someone to call her that, but knowing that it wouldn't last was so bittersweet. And she was beginning to realize that everything about this marriage of convenience was inconvenient for her.

Especially these feelings...

And not just the attachment she was forming toward Bailey Ann and vice versa...

The attraction she felt for her husband was especially annoying. She'd shut down those type of feelings long ago; she wasn't supposed to have them anymore.

But whenever he touched her, like he had with his lips just brushing across her cheek, or sometimes when he even looked at her a little too long, she felt a zip of something moving through her. Almost like an electrical charge...

And she hated it. She hated feeling so alive and aware again. Because it scared her...

Like she was scared now.

Bailey Ann was so empathetic that she must have felt it, too. "You don't have to worry," she said.

Genevieve smiled and sighed. If only she could make herself believe that...

But she was getting so used to having a husband and a daughter.

What she'd always wanted...

But she wouldn't have them forever. And when she lost them she would be devastated, more so than she had when her marriage to Bradford had ended.

She would only have this husband and daughter until Collin could adopt Bailey Ann. Technically they would probably have to adopt her together and then she would award him full custody when they got divorced.

Maybe he would give her visitation, like they were a real married couple. Maybe he would see that it would be good for Bailey Ann to have Genevieve continue being part of her life. Or maybe, once his fake marriage was over with his fake wife, he would find a woman he really loved and wanted to marry. And this new woman would become Bailey Ann's mother just as Bradford had found a new wife and a real mother to his children.

Genevieve had only signed on to get Collin ready to foster and adopt. And that was all he wanted from her. That and to keep Bailey Ann alive.

She glanced at that mechanical pill dispenser that sat on the counter next to her cell phone. What if the batteries had run down? Shouldn't there be some kind of green light for her to know it was working? If the batteries weren't working, would she be able to open it?

The machine was designed for people with dementia who either took their pills too often or forgot to take them at all. It was intended to keep them from overdosing or underdosing. It was perfect for kids, too, but only if it was working. And if Genevieve was close enough to hear it.

"I don't know if I should trust this thing..." she murmured with a worried glance at it. She always struggled with trust...but somehow she'd won the trust of this little girl who was so sweet and straightforward.

"Trust me," Bailey Ann said. "Dr. Ca—Daddy has told so many people how I'm supposed to take these pills that I remember how." And she recited the names, doses and times as if she was reading from the paper that Collin had written out that lay on the counter next to the pill dispenser. Just in case...

He didn't entirely trust it either then. He might not trust anything or anyone either as well.

"That's impressive," Genevieve said. "It's like you read it off this sheet."

Bailey Ann shrugged. "I heard him say it so many times I think I hear it in my sleep sometimes. It won't be like that last foster family."

"That is what I was worrying about," Genevieve admitted. "I don't want you to get sick again because of me."

"I won't," Bailey Ann said. "I'll take my meds when you give them to me."

Genevieve tensed. "What…"

Bailey Ann's face flushed, and her shoulders sagged a bit. "Nothing…"

Genevieve could have dropped it. She sensed that she probably *should* drop it. But she was compelled to prod like Bailey Ann was a hostile witness on the stand. And they only got hostile when there was something they didn't want to admit. "What are you talking about?"

Bailey Ann shook her head. "Nothing."

"Dr. Cass—Daddy and I made a promise to always be open and honest with each other," Genevieve said. With each other. Not Mrs. Finch. "You need to be the same with us. Open and honest."

Bailey Ann looked up and studied her face for a long moment. "'Kay…"

"No secrets between us," Genevieve prodded again.

Bailey Ann smiled and then sighed, like Genevieve had earlier. "'Kay," she said again. "I didn't take all the pills Mrs. Morely gave me."

"Okay. Who's Mrs. Morely?"

"My last foster mom. I could call her Marcy, but I didn't want to." Her breath hitched a bit, and tears pooled in her eyes. "I didn't want to be there. I told Mrs. Finch that but she wouldn't listen."

"I'm sorry," Genevieve told her. "I know that it's frustrating when someone won't listen to you." She'd felt that way so often, with mother and stepfather, her grandparents and most of all Bradford. She hadn't chosen the other people in her life, but she'd chosen him. So that was her fault.

And it was also her fault that she'd turned away from

the one person who would have listened to her: Jenny. She blinked and focused on the little girl. "So tell me. I'm listening. What happened because you were frustrated?"

"I didn't take my pills like I was supposed to. I just pretended to when Mrs. Morely gave them to me."

Genevieve's heart was beating too fast. According to Collin, the child had nearly died because she hadn't been getting her antirejection meds. She cleared her throat and asked, "Why did you do that?"

Had she wanted to hurt herself? Dread rose up in her. She'd read so many books on parenting, preparing herself to be a foster mother. But reading about it...and actually trying to handle a situation like this...

"I wanted to go back to Dr. Ca—to Daddy. I wanted to be with him. And I knew if I got sick again, I would get to see him more."

Tears stung Genevieve's eyes now, hard. The little girl loved him so much that she'd sacrificed her health to be with him again.

But he loved her so much that that would have been the last thing he'd wanted. Unless...

"Did Dr. Ca—did Daddy know you did that?" Genevieve hoped not because then that would have meant he'd lied to her; he'd lied after promising to be open and honest with her.

Bailey Ann's face flushed bright pink and she shook her head. And now tears filled her eyes, too. "Do you have to tell him?"

Of course she had to. She wasn't sure if she could wait until his shift ended at the hospital. But then the doorbell rang, saving her from having to answer Bailey Ann at the moment. Maybe Sue had found someone after all—someone who could watch the little girl while Genevieve ran up to the hospital.

But when she opened the door, it wasn't a health professional standing on the step. Not even someone trying to sell something like replacement windows or magazine subscriptions.

She probably would have preferred that at the moment. No. It was Jessup and Sadie. Her new, temporary father-in-law and grandmother-in-law.

Grandmother-in-law... It struck her that Sadie had been Jenny's grandmother-in-law, too. Despite all the distance between them, here was one simple thing they shared.

"Ah... Collin isn't here," she told her visitors. Because she doubted that they were here to see her. But maybe Bailey Ann...

She rushed up behind Genevieve and shyly said, "Hi." And then, "Mommy, the machine is buzzing."

Genevieve's ears were, too. And she rushed off toward the kitchen, leaving the little girl to invite her grandfather and great-grandmother inside the house. She wanted to make sure the child got the medication she needed. But she suspected the little girl needed more help than that...

JESSUP SHOT A glance at his mother. So much for how wonderful she insisted his new daughter-in-law was.

She'd rushed off, leaving them standing on the front stoop until the little girl had stepped forward. She took one of his hands and one of Sadie's, like she had Collin and Genevieve's the day of the wedding at the ranch, and just as she had then, she tugged them toward the kitchen. He chuckled. She really was something.

He understood why his son had fallen so hard...for the little girl. Collin hadn't fallen for the woman; he'd only married her for Bailey Ann, so that he could foster and hopefully adopt her, too.

He knew his mother was hoping that this would become a love match, like all the matches she had made for Michael's sons and for Colton. But Colton was nothing like his twin. He was easygoing and relaxed while Collin was always so serious and focused, like Genevieve Porter.

They were probably the only two people who would consider a loveless marriage a convenience. Jessup wanted more for Collin than that.

"I'm sorry," Genevieve said when they stepped into her big kitchen.

"This is my first day without Nurse Sue to help me with Bailey Ann's medications," she said, her teeth nipping at her bottom lip. "I just want to make sure I get them right."

Bailey Ann released their hands to rush to her. "Mommy, don't worry. Remember I know…" She trailed off and glanced nervously at them. She took the capsule from Genevieve's palm with one hand and picked up a glass of water from the counter with the other.

Jessup felt a twinge of sympathy in his new heart. He was struck by this strange thing he shared with the little girl, the gift of someone else's heart to save their lives. He glanced at his new daughter-in-law. "Those capsules have a nasty aftertaste," he said. "Do you have an orange or applesauce?"

She nodded and rushed toward her commercial-sized fridge. She pulled out both and put them on the counter.

He reached for and peeled the mandarin orange for the little girl.

She'd cocked her head and studied his face. "How do you know how yucky they taste?"

He tugged on the top of his shirt, pulling it down far enough to show the top of his scar.

And she gasped. "You have a new heart, too?"

"The best heart," Sadie said.

"My heart is good, too," Bailey Ann said.

"I'm sure it is," Sadie agreed.

"Sometimes I wonder…" Genevieve began, but she trailed off with a wistful sigh.

"You think…?" Sadie asked, silently communicating with this woman who was essentially a stranger to them.

But his mother was like that. She could bond easily with people she'd just met despite how intimidating she could be. Or maybe it was because she was so intimidating; the only people who truly impressed her were the ones who could speak easily to her.

It seemed like her new granddaughter-in-law didn't even have to speak and they understood each other.

But then, Genevieve was Jenny's sister. Of course there was a bond already there between her and Sadie.

Between bites of orange, Bailey Ann asked him about his medications and his surgeries and how many times he'd been in and out of the hospital. It was like they were old war buddies. But he was nearly sixty and she was just seven. She shouldn't have been through everything that she'd gone through.

And he wasn't sure how much more she would be able to handle.

She was already calling this woman, Genevieve, Mommy. But Collin had no intention of staying married to this stranger; he'd just intended to be with her until he adopted Bailey Ann. But what happened then?

Had any of them considered that?

CHAPTER SEVENTEEN

COLLIN FELT LIKE a coward over how he'd rushed off, leaving Genevieve to deal with all of Bailey Ann's expectations on her own. As if she hadn't been nervous enough about being solely responsible for her medical care...

Seeing his brother walking around the ER, all decked out in his firefighter gear, just served to remind him that Colton was the hero. His twin was the one who rushed into burning buildings all the time. Collin had done that only once, and it wasn't something he was likely to repeat.

Especially after the lecture Colton had given him over it, over the risks of going into that situation without the proper equipment. Colton was wearing it now, and so was the other firefighter he was helping into one of the ER bays. "You don't have to worry. The best doctors work in this ER."

Collin knew his twin was talking about Livvy. Not him. He was just finishing up the notes for the consultation he'd been paged for—a young woman having a heart attack. Fortunately it hadn't been that. She was a mom with young kids and she was also a daughter with aging parents. With all her obligations and stress, she'd been having a panic attack. Understandably...

He felt a little panicky himself, and he knew that Genevieve did, too. So he wasn't surprised that he got a text from her: We need to talk tonight somewhere that Bailey Ann can't hear us.

This wasn't just about Bailey Ann's medications; this was about the little girl's expectations. The same thing that worried Collin. They definitely needed to talk about how to handle her calling them Daddy and Mommy and her belief that this arrangement was going to last forever despite how much they'd both warned her that it wouldn't.

Once he adopted her—if he even could—his marriage would be over. That was the deal. Genevieve hadn't wanted to get married again, and she'd only done this when she saw a child in need.

That was fine. He didn't need this marriage to have a happily-ever-after, but part of him actually wished it was possible for him to stay married to this amazing woman who was so selfless and generous and beautiful. Maybe that was all that Bailey Ann was doing, wishing, and maybe she figured if she wished hard enough, her wish would come true.

If only such a thing was actually possible...

But his wish for his mom to stay alive hadn't come true. Or his wish for his oldest brother to come home...

Or had it?

He had to focus on Bailey Ann. He had nearly lost her once when that foster family hadn't administered her meds correctly. And with heart transplants, there was always a risk of complications, of another failure...

He didn't want to take away Bailey Ann's hopes and dreams for a future, though, even one that included both him and Genevieve. But he couldn't hold Genevieve to a marriage she'd only agreed to until he could adopt Bailey Ann. No matter how much he might want that himself. Too many people had already discounted Genevieve's wants and needs. She deserved more.

His head throbbed, and he reached up to rub his temple. "Bad consult?" Colton asked.

Collin shook his head. "No. Not the one I'm here for." The one he needed to have with Genevieve probably would be. He gestured toward the curtain. "How's your coworker?"

"Some smoke inhalation. Best doctor in Willow Creek is working on him, though." He grinned. "No offense."

Collin chuckled. "None taken. Livvy is good."

"Yes, she is," Colton said with a dopey grin. The man was hopelessly in love.

Collin had once pitied, and mercilessly teased, his twin over how hard he'd fallen for Livvy, but now a twinge of envy struck him. He ignored it to rib his brother again. "I only question her judgment when it comes to you…"

Instead of being offended, Colton nodded. "I know. She could do better."

Collin shook his head. "No. You've both done well."

"How about you?" Colton asked. "How's your marriage going?"

"It's only been a few days," he reminded his twin. But he had three days of memories, not just of the wedding at the ranch but of watching movies and eating popcorn with Bailey Ann and Genevieve. And the board games they'd played and the walk they'd taken into town, where Bailey Ann had delighted in all the Valentine decorations, insisting that they were for them. Because they'd just gotten married…

Despite all the times they'd told her they were just friends, she thought their marriage was real and this was going to last. Knots clutched his stomach that he hadn't handled all of this better.

Colton pitched his voice low and leaned closer to ask, "That bad?"

For his brother to ask that, he must have already been grimacing, but with the acrid smoke from Colton's uniform burning his sinuses, Collin grimaced again. It reminded him of the fire, of nearly losing his dad again.

"No. It's not bad," he said, all the memories of the past few days tumbling through his mind. "It's almost too good."

Colton pushed back his fire hat as if he needed to see him better, because now he was staring intently at him. "Too good? You falling in love with your wife, Collin?"

He felt that jolt he felt whenever he touched her or even sometimes just thought of her.

"I meant with Bailey Ann," Collin demurred. "It would just be hard if this doesn't work out how it's meant to..." Or if it did and she was still unhappy when he and Genevieve divorced.

"Just on Bailey Ann?" Colton asked.

"No. I want her to be happy and healthy."

"What about Genevieve?" Colton asked.

"She wants her to be happy and healthy, too. She was so worried about being alone with her today and not giving her the medications correctly." He glanced down at his phone. But her text wasn't about the medications; he knew that. It was about the little girl's expectations.

"That's not what I meant," Colton said.

He glanced up at his brother. "What?"

"I was wondering if you want Genevieve to be happy and healthy."

"Of course," he said. She'd been happy the past few days, happier than she'd been that first time they'd gone to the ranch together and she'd fled in tears. "I hope she's feeling less guilty about Jenny and the boys." But even if she was, he had a feeling that she'd replaced the guilt over them for guilt over Bailey Ann. Would she consider giving their marriage a real chance? Or had she been too hurt to ever risk her heart again, especially on someone like him who'd never had a real relationship before? "Do you and Livvy have plans tonight?"

Colton shrugged. "Our shifts don't always line up, so we usually play it by ear. But we *are* both supposed to be off this evening."

"Do you mind watching Bailey Ann for a bit? Genevieve and I need to talk without her being able to overhear us."

"So you're not trying to set up a double date with us?" Colton asked as if he was teasing, but there was concern and sympathy in his dark eyes.

"Genevieve and I need to talk about Bailey Ann's feelings if this doesn't work out," he admitted. "If we can't continue to foster her…"

"Do you ever worry about yourself?" Colton asked.

The question startled Collin. "What? Why?"

"This whole marriage of convenience thing…" He shook his head. "I can't imagine not marrying for love."

"That's because you're in love," he pointed out. Something he'd never been. "And I did marry for love."

Colton's eyes widened with shock. "That fast?"

"I'm talking about love for Bailey Ann."

"I know why you did it," Colton said. "I just wish that you would do something for you and not just for everyone else."

"Not this again."

"Your career, this marriage…" Colton sighed. "I worry about you, and I'm sorry I dumped that whole Cash thing on you, too."

"I'm glad you did," Collin said. "No more secrets."

"You're saying we should tell everyone else?"

"I don't know what there is to tell," Collin said. "It could have been nothing, just like Genevieve said. Becca had the lighter or Cash toured the house. We don't know that it was anything more than that. And until we know what it was, it doesn't make sense to say any more about it."

Colton grinned. "So you're kind of selective with this whole secret thing?"

Collin sighed and smiled. "Yeah, I guess…" Because he and Genevieve were lying to Mrs. Finch, or at least not being completely honest. And Collin couldn't help but wonder whether he was being completely honest with himself…

Because he wanted to go out with Genevieve and not just to talk about Bailey Ann.

"Will you babysit for a while?" Collin asked.

Colton nodded. "Of course. Since meeting our little Haven cousins and Bailey Ann, I've realized I like kids a lot more than I thought."

Collin grinned. "They have that effect on you." And he remembered the effect they'd had on Genevieve. She wanted a child so badly.

And Collin wanted her to be happy. But he was worried that they were all headed for disappointment and heartbreak.

BAILEY ANN HAD insisted on helping Genevieve pick out a pretty dress and heels for her *date* with *Daddy*. That was what Bailey Ann had called it. But that wasn't what it was at all.

Genevieve knew this, whatever *it* was, wasn't going to last. She just wanted to make sure that Bailey Ann did, that she fully understood how dangerous what she'd done with her medication had been. But first Genevieve had to talk to Collin about it. Alone.

She'd probably been so distracted during Sadie and Jessup's visit that they thought her unwelcoming since they hadn't stayed long. Or maybe they just figured she was in over her head in caring for a child with the medical needs that Bailey Ann had.

And she was...

Because she didn't want to upset the little girl, she played dress-up for a date with her husband. She and Bradford had done date nights, but usually at the country club where he'd left her sitting alone while he just had to say something to someone for a minute that had turned into far longer.

This wasn't a date. This was a meeting between two people who had an arrangement. She needed to remember, especially when she heard the creak of a door opening, and her pulse quickened in anticipation.

No. Anxiety. She wasn't sure how to tell Collin what Bailey Ann had told her.

"Perfume," Bailey Ann said. "You need to smell as pretty as you look." She picked up one of the bottles from the vanity table in Genevieve's bathroom and spritzed it, liberally, on her. So liberally that they both sneezed and Genevieve's eyes began to water.

She wiped off what had hit her cheek, but unless she washed her hair, she couldn't get rid of all of it. The doorbell rang now, leaving her no time to shower unless she wanted to keep Collin's family waiting and Collin. She'd waited long enough to tell him what she'd learned that morning.

Bailey Ann ran out of the room, maybe to escape the fumes, maybe to greet their guests. But then Genevieve heard, "Daddy! Daddy! You're home! Mommy looks so pretty. Wait till you see her! And she smells pretty, too!" She sneezed.

And Genevieve smiled as she walked down the hall and joined them in the kitchen. "I smell a little too pretty,"

Genevieve said. "I think Bailey Ann could get a job as a mall perfume tester."

She'd hoped everyone would laugh. But Collin just stared at her, as did his twin and the woman who'd come with them. "I'm sorry," she said. And she held out her hand. "I'm Genevieve."

"Livvy," the petite woman replied. "I'm sorry I missed your wedding. I was on call at the hospital."

Right, Colton's fiancée was an ER doctor, and if Genevieve recalled correctly, she was also Lem's granddaughter.

Genevieve flinched, remembering the trouble the CPS call had caused. Livvy had been the doctor who had checked out little Ian. "I'm sorry," she said. "I never intended for Sue…"

"I know. She explained it, and she apologized," Livvy said.

"Doesn't Mommy look pretty?" Bailey Ann prodded Collin.

"Yes, she does," Collin said, his voice a little gruff.

"She insisted that I dress up," Genevieve said, making it clear that the dress—*blue, like your eyes*—and the heels hadn't been her idea. "Like the ladies on the soaps do when they go out."

"Where are the flowers, Daddy?" Bailey Ann asked.

"Yes," Colton said, his mouth curving into a grin. "Where are the flowers?"

Livvy bumped his shoulder. "Stop teasing your brother. And you need to pick up our dinner." She smiled at Bailey Ann. "We ordered pizza."

"Pizza!" Bailey Ann exclaimed, clapping her hands together.

"She's not going to miss us at all," Collin remarked. But he was grinning.

He had no idea how much she'd missed him.

Bailey Ann hugged Collin's waist. "I will, but you and Mommy need a date." She released him to hug Genevieve next. Then she pulled back and said, "You can go now. And get her some flowers, too."

Collin pointed at the medication dispenser and the note and said to Livvy, "You don't need me to explain any of that to you."

She shook her head. "No. Colton and I can handle this one...unless she challenges me to a game of checkers. Then I'm in trouble."

"Mommy has all kinds of games," Bailey Ann said. "And movies, too. And she even gave me some polish for my nails." She held up her fingers with the bubblegum pink polish on them. "Can I do your nails?"

"I've been wanting a spa day," Livvy said with a chuckle.

"Make sure you do Uncle Colton's when he gets back," Collin said. "He wouldn't want to be left out."

Everyone was so happy and upbeat that Genevieve's stomach churned with dread. But she had to tell Collin. "We should go," she murmured to him.

Bailey Ann waved at them before taking Livvy's hand to tug her off down the hall.

"Yes, let's go," Collin said, and he sounded as if he was bracing himself, as if he knew that she wasn't as happy and upbeat as everyone else. "My car's in the drive—"

"Let's walk," she said. She needed the fresh air, especially with the strength of the perfume burning her eyes.

"In those heels?" Collin asked, his gaze sliding down her legs to her shoes. And his eyes seemed to get a little dark, his face a little tenser.

"I lived in the city for years," she said. "I'm used to walking in heels."

Unlike Bailey Ann who'd nearly wiped out. But she was

only seven. That was why she hadn't understood how serious what she'd done was.

They walked out through the mudroom and outside. They only had to walk a block before heart-shaped balloons and decorations and pink and white and red flowers sprang up all around them.

"I feel like I'm walking through a kid's Valentine's party," Collin remarked as he glanced around them. Then he looked at her. "So, what's up?"

"I'm sorry," she said. "I didn't know how to explain to Bailey Ann that this was not a date. I don't know how to explain anything to her." Not the way he would need to.

"None of that is your responsibility," he said. "I'm sorry I had to leave this morning without talking to her about her expectations."

None of that is your responsibility...

She should have been relieved. But instead those words just reminded her that all Collin really wanted was to adopt Bailey Ann. If he could have done that without marrying her, he definitely would have.

But she'd known that from the beginning. They were strangers, after all. Maybe Bailey Ann wasn't the only one who'd started having unrealistic expectations...

COLTON HAD HOPED the date night with his wife was a good sign for his twin, that maybe Collin and Genevieve had more in common than Bailey Ann. Especially with the way Collin had looked at her when she'd appeared in the kitchen, looking more like a model than a lawyer.

Collin had seemed to lose his voice entirely when he saw her. And he must have stayed just as hypnotized, since he hadn't noticed Colton drive past them as they'd walked along the sidewalk to town and he'd driven back with the pizza. But when they returned to her house not long after they'd left, he had a sick feeling in his stomach. They both looked so grim.

And Bailey Ann was so happy.

He'd figured this marriage was a mistake for so many reasons, but Colton really wished he'd been wrong. For all their sakes...

CHAPTER EIGHTEEN

ONCE GENEVIEVE HAD told him what Bailey Ann had confessed to her that morning, Collin felt too sick to eat. And she must have sensed it as well because she'd suggested they cut the evening short.

Very short and just skip dinner altogether.

He doubted she would have been able to eat either; she'd looked as sick as he felt when she'd shared Bailey Ann's secret with him.

How hadn't he known?

How hadn't he guessed?

The foster family had sworn that they'd correctly administered her meds, but he'd been convinced that they were lying to cover up their negligence.

But instead the negligence was his. He should have known. Should have made it clear to Bailey Ann how serious her condition was. He had to do that now, and he hadn't wanted to wait another moment. So he got rid of Colton and Livvy quickly, promising that he would explain later.

Colton had been reluctant to leave but Livvy had tugged him out the door with her. "He'll tell you later," she said. She knew Collin well enough to know that he would keep his promise.

Once the door closed behind Colton and Livvy, he turned toward the little girl. "We need to talk, Miss Bailey Ann."

Her shoulders slumped and she sighed. Then she shot a slightly resentful glance at Genevieve. "You told him…"

"I had to," Genevieve said. "He's your doctor. He needs to know how you really wound up in the hospital last time."

Collin's empty stomach flipped with the memory of how sick she'd been. And he'd been so angry at those foster parents…

"And we've promised now to always be open and honest," Genevieve said. "It's not nice to keep secrets from people we love."

Tears sprang to Bailey Ann's eyes and trailed down her cheeks. "I'm sorry," she said, her voice shaky. "I just missed you so much when Mrs. Finch sent me to live with the Morelys. I didn't want to be there. I wanted to be with you!" She threw her arms around Collin's waist, holding tightly to him.

"I missed you, too," he said, patting her head. While Bailey Ann was sweet, he was also beginning to see that she was used to getting her way and as stubborn as every Haven or Cassidy he knew. She was a bit of a mini Sadie. God help them.

He unhooked her arms from around his waist and lifted her up into his arms. So that she had to face him. The tears were real. They were making her face red and her lips were quivering with sobs. His heart ached, and he wanted to just hug her and let it go. But it was too important.

Any other child he might have coddled. But he had to be straight with Bailey Ann. Her life depended on it. "I would have missed you even more and forever if your body rejected that new heart because you weren't taking your medicine. You have to remember how long it was before we found one that would work for you." He braced himself, knowing that he had to be blunt with her. "Somebody died for you to get that heart, Bailey Ann. And you were in a line with a lot of other people waiting for it. If you don't take care of it, it's not fair to the person who died, and it's not fair to the other people who could have taken it."

She began to shake now, the sobs wracking her. "I'm sorry, Daddy. I'm so sorry..."

Regret and guilt gripped him. He hadn't known how else to get his point across and ensure that, no matter what happened, she would never pull something like that again.

"Your life depends on doing everything right, Bailey Ann," he said, even as he realized all the things he'd done wrong, too. "And your life is all that matters. Even more than I want to be your daddy, I want you to be alive. So, if for some reason we can't be a family...or stay a family... I want you to promise me that you will take care of yourself and that heart."

She nodded, then—in a quivery voice—she said, "I promise."

He clutched her close against his chest, feeling her heart beat against him. But he wasn't reassured as he'd been in the past when he'd felt that beat after her heart replacement. Now he was scared that she might not keep that promise, that she might do what she'd done before when things hadn't worked out how she'd wanted them.

She might stop taking her medication. Then she would lose more than him and this makeshift family they'd formed; she would lose her life.

THE TEARS AND emotions must have exhausted Bailey Ann, who'd fallen asleep in Collin's arms. While he'd carried her to her room and tucked her into her race car bed, Genevieve had tried to grapple with all the emotions pummeling her. She felt raw and exposed when he stumbled back into the kitchen.

He looked as exhausted as the child he'd just carried to

bed. Genevieve knew that she should encourage him to go to bed himself, in that superhero bedroom that had never seemed as fitting as it did now after he'd had to have such a difficult conversation with the little girl who adored him. So much that she'd risked her life to be with him again.

But she could tell that what had exhausted him most wasn't the conversation but the guilt. His shoulders bowed with it. She understood that guilt all too well. "I'm sorry," she said.

He shook his head, and his throat moved as if he was struggling to swallow. Then he cleared his throat and said, "Don't be. None of this is your fault. And I'm glad you told me."

"Are you?" she asked. Sometimes ignorance was better. When she hadn't known that Jenny was dead, she hadn't missed her as much. When she hadn't known how unhappy Bradford was with her, she'd thought they'd had a chance of making their marriage work.

But then she sighed with the acknowledgment that it was better to know the truth, even if it hurt, because then you could figure out how to go forward. If you could go forward...

She hoped to find a way to do that with Bailey Ann. "She's mad at me for telling you," she said. The look of betrayal the little girl had shot her had hurt. But she would have hurt more if she hadn't said anything to Collin and something happened to the child.

"You did the right thing," he said, offering her assurances when he looked like he needed them more. "I had to know. I made such a mess of things."

She shook her head. "No. You didn't. Trust me. I know how to make a mess of things. This isn't it."

"But she could have died." His body shuddered with revulsion at the thought. "And I had no idea."

"Who would suspect that she would do something like that?" She'd been so shocked when Bailey Ann had made the confession.

"Mrs. Finch," he said. "She was certain that that foster family wouldn't have messed up. I just thought she was covering up her own negligence over trusting the Morelys with Bailey Ann's care."

"We need to tell her," Genevieve said.

He groaned.

"It's not fair to that family," she pointed out. "And it's not fair to the children who might not have been placed with them because of what happened. There is such a need for foster families everywhere. It would be a shame if what happened with Bailey Ann meant CPS didn't place other kids with that family."

He groaned again, louder, and closed his eyes. "Oh, God, I told Mrs. Finch that she shouldn't leave kids with them that had medical needs." He rubbed his hand over his face. "I could have ruined someone else's family, someone else's health, all because I hadn't known what had really happened. And I'd assumed the worst, just like I did with Cash until you'd pointed out that it could have been innocent."

She sighed. "I don't know that it is. I just presented another possibility."

"Just like when you proposed," he murmured. "I thought I was going to lose Bailey Ann and then you presented another possibility..." His throat moved again, and his voice was gruff when he continued, "But I still might lose her."

"We'll explain to Mrs. Finch that she's so young she didn't understand what she was doing."

Collin groaned again. "I think she understood exactly what she was doing."

"She didn't know it would hurt the Morelys or other

children who might have been taken from them or placed with them," Genevieve said. "And they should have made certain she took the medication. That was covered in foster parenting classes—to make sure kids take their meds."

"I should have made it clear to her how important they are," he said.

"She knows that now," Genevieve said. "She has a good heart. She just wants that heart to be with you."

His shoulders were still slumped, his face taut with stress. She stepped closer to him and touched his tightly clenched jaw. "Stop beating yourself up," she said.

"Why?" he asked. "You do it to yourself all the time over your sister."

"And it doesn't do any good," she pointed out. She didn't feel any less guilty about not staying in contact with Jenny and not getting to know Dale and the boys.

Without thinking, she stepped closer to him. "Would a hug help?" she asked.

A strange look passed over him, and then he wrapped his arms around her.

She felt that current move through her again, heating and unsettling her. But instead of pushing him away, she wrapped her arms around him, too, and hugged him back. "Do you feel better?" she asked.

He sighed. "Yes."

Then he touched her jaw and tipped her face up to his. "A kiss might help even more…"

Despite the heavy evening, she found herself smiling at that, and rising up on tiptoe as he lowered his head. Their lips met. Caressed. Held. The kiss deepened.

She felt so much…but she wasn't sure if it was better or worse. Because she had a feeling she was making a horrible mistake…that she was starting to fall in love with her husband.

BECCA CALDER WAS a single mother with a thriving career. She was one of those people who did it all, did it well and mostly did it alone...except for some help from her parents.

Sadie didn't know the young woman well, but she was impressed with her. And she now understood that Becca was probably the key to finding Cash.

Sadie sat in the Realtor office's reception area, across from Becca's mother, Phyllis. Phyllis covered the front desk for her.

Becca came in a moment later. Competent and beautiful, she had not a hair out of place or a wrinkle in her summer suit as she swept into her office, despite her long day.

She glanced at Sadie, who sat in the reception area waiting for her, and tensed.

Sadie smiled. Becca knew why she was there.

"Colton sent you." It wasn't a question. She knew.

Sadie stood up and smiled wider at her. "I like you."

"I'm not sure if that's a good thing or not," Becca said, but she was smiling, too.

Phyllis sucked in a breath, probably worried that Sadie would judge her for her daughter's manners. Sadie laughed instead. She always respected other strong women. And a woman had to be strong to take on a Haven.

Like Genevieve Porter. She was stronger than she thought she was, stronger than Jessup thought she was. He'd been worried after their visit today. Something had definitely been bothering Genevieve, but she hadn't asked them for help. Sadie knew she had Collin to lean on.

They had each other now and given some of the things the little girl had said to her and Jessup, they were going to need each other.

"I need your help," Sadie told Becca.

"You looking to sell the ranch?" Becca asked.

And Sadie laughed hard. "I really like you."

"Will you if I don't do what you want me to?" Becca asked.

Her mother gasped again, her head swiveling back and forth between them as if she was watching a tennis match. Instead of being embarrassed, the woman should be proud. She'd raised a strong daughter.

"What do you think I want you to do?" Sadie asked.

"We both know it's not to list the ranch or find you a house, so you must be here looking for the same thing Colton has been..."

"Cash," Sadie confirmed. "I'm looking for Cash. It's time for him to come back to his family."

CHAPTER NINETEEN

COLLIN HAD A bad feeling about the upcoming meeting with Mrs. Finch. He and Genevieve had called her and informed her about what had happened with the Morelys, not wanting them to be denied a child who needed them because of what Bailey Ann had done.

The social worker had been concerned about them, too. But she'd been even more concerned about Bailey Ann. She needed to talk to her supervisor and a child psychologist and then she would meet with them again. When she'd texted Genevieve the meeting time, she hadn't said what she'd decided.

They had to wait another day to find out, and since he'd had the day off, he'd decided they needed an outing. Or maybe he'd just needed to get out of that beautiful house of Genevieve's.

He probably needed to get away from her, too. After he'd been so foolish and kissed her a few nights ago, he'd found his thoughts occupied by her. It didn't help that Bailey Ann insisted that Daddy needed to kiss Mommy whenever one of them left the house either.

But in front of Bailey Ann, he didn't kiss Genevieve like he had that night. Like he'd never wanted to stop kissing her. If the little girl hadn't cried out with fear from her bedroom, scared because of a nightmare, he wasn't sure if he would have stopped.

Confused about his feelings for Genevieve and on edge

about the meeting the following day, Collin had proposed a trip to the ranch. Bailey Ann had wanted to wear her flower girl dress, but Collin had insisted that nobody was getting married that day.

Knowing Sadie, though, he couldn't be sure. She might have manipulated another one of his brothers or cousins into marriage. He hadn't seen Marsh in a while.

But that wasn't exactly an accident. He wasn't sure he could see him and not tell him about Cash and that dang lighter. And Marsh, being a lawman, probably wouldn't think of the innocent reason that Genevieve had. Collin couldn't deal with that now. He was most concerned with Bailey Ann.

And she was concerned with him, staring at him with suspicion. "You really know how to ride a horse?" she asked as he carried her into the big barn. After Ian had gotten hurt there, he was determined to make sure she stayed safe for as long as he could.

"I grew up on a ranch," he told her.

"What about you?" she peered over his shoulder at Genevieve who walked behind them. "Do you know how to ride horses, Mommy?"

If she'd been upset with Genevieve over telling him what she'd done with her medications, she wasn't upset with her any longer. Or maybe she was just desperately trying to hang on to her happiness because she sensed the same thing he did...

That something was going to go terribly wrong. Maybe it already had.

From one of the stalls came a horrible sound, more than a whinny. It was a kind of frenzied screech, and hooves kicked against the wood. This was why he'd carried Bailey Ann and maybe why Genevieve walked behind them.

They'd heard about that bronco. The one that had inadvertently injured Ian.

As well as hiring some "horse whisperer" to work with the animal, Dusty had intended to move him to the barn that was still standing at the Cassidy Ranch, but it had needed repairs, not from the fire but from all the years the ranch had been neglected. He felt a pang of the guilt he always felt when he thought of the ranch. But Dad's health and medical bills had been and were still more important.

"I didn't grow up on a ranch," Genevieve answered Bailey Ann, collecting herself after the bronco's awful whinny. "But I've ridden horses before. Just a few weeks ago I went for a ride at Miss Becca's ranch."

Collin turned to her. "Becca has a ranch?"

She nodded. "Yes, with a really beautiful barn and some horses." The bronco kicked that stall door as it reared up inside it, and she flinched and added, "Some very gentle horses."

"We have gentle horses, too," a little blond-haired boy said as he ran into the barn. He clutched a bunch of carrots in one hand and a small plastic bag in the other. Caleb. He was the blondest of the boys.

Ian and Miller followed him in; they both had sandy hair. And Miller still had a slight limp to his gait.

Bailey Ann wriggled down from Collin's arms as if embarrassed that he'd been carrying her. He caught her shoulders before she could follow the others to the stall where the horse thrashed around inside.

"You shouldn't go near him," Genevieve warned before he could, her voice cracking with fear.

"None of them are allowed without an adult with them," Baker called out, his voice loud with authority as he trotted in behind them with Little Jake propped on his hip. While he was the youngest of his brothers and his cousins, Baker had chosen to take on the most responsibility by adopting his late brother's and Genevieve's sister's kids.

"I know! I know!" all the boys called back to him.

Baker glanced at Genevieve, as if checking to see if she believed him. He still didn't entirely trust her.

Collin did. He wasn't sure why after so many other people he cared about had lied to him. But for some reason he did.

Maybe because she'd been so quick to share with him what Bailey Ann had confessed to her. Part of him wished she hadn't told him because now he blamed himself—and they also had to meet with Mrs. Finch.

"And we do indeed have gentle horses," Baker assured Genevieve. "Nobody rides Midnight but Dusty."

"Did he really win him in a bet?" Collin asked, wondering about this new branch of his family that he was still getting to know.

"Yes!" Caleb exclaimed. "The owner bet Dusty that he couldn't ride him eight seconds, and Dusty stayed on even longer than that. He thinks Midnight let him do it, though, because he wanted to be with us. He's my best friend."

"I'm your best friend!" Ian indignantly declared.

"You're my best human friend," Caleb assured him. "Midnight is my best animal friend."

"What about Feisty?" Ian asked.

"She's Miller's best animal friend."

"She's Grandma's dog," Miller said as if embarrassed that the little dog had been dubbed his friend. His face was a bit flushed, too, and he looked away from Bailey Ann who'd come up next to him.

"Who's your best friend?" she asked him.

He shrugged. "Uncle Baker."

Baker made a sound in his throat, and those pale brown eyes of his glistened a bit in the shadows of the big barn.

"Or Miss Taye," Miller said with a slight grin, as if he was teasing his uncle.

"They're grown-ups!" Caleb snorted.

"Grown-ups can be your best friends!" Bailey Ann hotly defended Miller. Then she added, "Dr. Cass was my best friend before he was my dad. And Miss Genevieve, too, before she was my mom. She listens to me." She glanced at Genevieve and sighed. "Sometimes too much."

Collin nearly laughed, but he held it together…until his gaze met Genevieve's. She could have been upset with the comment, over what could happen tomorrow when they met with Mrs. Finch. But there was amusement twinkling in her blue eyes.

Bailey Ann was as cute as she was maddening. He loved her so much, even though he realized now that she'd been playing him a bit. All the time she'd spent in and out of hospitals had made her somewhat precocious. Or maybe she was just a lot like a Haven—stubborn and intent on getting what she wanted.

Miller actually looked right at her then and he nodded. "Yeah, grown-ups can be your best friends." But he wasn't talking to Caleb. He was agreeing with her.

Collin smiled. Both of these kids could use a best friend their own age. And they understood each other from the harrowing experiences they'd lived through, better than even the grown-ups in their lives probably did.

"Do you know how to ride a horse?" Miller asked her.

Bailey Ann looked away from him now and shook her head, embarrassed. But then she touched her chest. "I couldn't. I had a bad heart my whole life. I just got a new one a little while ago."

Maybe someone had told the kids about her already because none of them seemed all that surprised. In fact Miller just nodded. "I haven't been able to ride for a while because of this." He touched his leg. "It was messed up really bad. But it's better now, so I'm just starting back up. I'm a little rusty."

Collin stepped back to whisper to Genevieve. "I think we lost our best friend."

She had pressed a hand against her heart, and she nodded now. "I think we did."

He was joking, but after tomorrow's meeting, would they lose her for real?

GENEVIEVE'S HEART FELT like it was breaking for so many reasons. Maybe just because it was too full of love. For the kids...

Just the kids...

She wasn't falling for Collin. At the moment, clutching the saddle horn and the reins, she was just trying not to fall off the horse. Bailey Ann rode in front of Collin, and Genevieve felt a flash of envy for the little girl. But then she knew it wouldn't have been smart for Genevieve to sit that close to Collin. She would have been so on edge that the horse would have felt her nerves.

The one with him and Bailey Ann on it was plodding calmly along; the one with her on it had stopped moving entirely.

"You're pulling so hard on the reins that Peanut Butter thinks you want her to stop," Baker pointed out. They were now heading back to the barn, along the route he'd already taken them around the ranch. He was at the rear with Little Jake now instead of the front.

Heat flushed her face. She should have known that; Becca had given her a quick riding lesson that day. She knew how to ride, but she was so distracted over that meeting tomorrow with Mrs. Finch. Not to mention Collin. That kiss they'd shared kept replaying through her mind, keeping her awake, making her want something she had no business wanting anymore. Love.

Though she didn't want to open herself up to that pain and disappointment again, it didn't matter what she wanted at this point; she had a feeling that it was coming anyway.

She eased her grip on the reins a bit to urge the horse to move again, but Baker reached out and caught her reins, holding them up.

"I've been wanting to talk to you alone," he said.

She glanced at Little Jake, who was riding in front of him. But Little Jake's eyes were closed, his body slumped. The movement of the horse must have rocked the toddler to sleep.

She braced herself, expecting Baker to blast her over the ordeal with CPS. While Taye had forgiven her, Baker might not be as compelled to do that. He was obviously very protective of their nephews. "I'm sorry," she said. "I really never meant to cause any trouble for them. I only wanted to make sure they were okay."

"They weren't...for a while," Baker admitted. "Neither was I."

She remembered what Collin had told her. Baker had been first on the scene of that horrific accident. She shuddered, thinking of what he must have seen, how hard it must have been to treat his family. No wonder he'd quit being a firefighter and paramedic and had become the ranch foreman, which was what Dale had been.

"I'm sorry," she said again, her voice cracking with sympathy for them all.

"Don't be," he said. "I believe you had their best interests at heart."

"But I don't know them—not like you do," she said. "I can see how much you and Taye love them."

Baker cuddled Little Jake closer. The toddler had the

dark hair and eyes of his uncles. And his mother. Jenny had had dark hair and eyes; she'd been so beautiful.

"We all love them, but…" His voice got so gruff he had to clear his throat. "I really believe that it's best for them to have one set of guardians instead of all their uncles and aunts trying to raise them."

Realizing he was telling her to butt out, she flinched. "I understand…" And she really did. She could see how Bailey Ann had played that foster family to get what she'd wanted: Collin. Kids with divorced parents often took advantage of the situation and played them off against one another. If so many people tried to act as their parents, the kids were going to be confused by the rules and lack of rules.

"I want *everyone* to be involved in their lives," he said. "But as uncles and *aunts*."

Wait. She drew in a shaky breath. He *wasn't* telling her to butt out; he was inviting her in. "I want that, too," she said. "That's all I wanted."

He pushed back his hat and arched a dark eyebrow. "Really? Colton told me about your house…"

Heat flushed her face and it wasn't just from the sun beating down on them. "I wanted to be prepared in case they needed someone to take them." She reached out now and touched his arm. "But I realize you and Taye are all they need."

"I didn't believe that in the beginning," Baker said, and his topaz eyes glistened a bit. "Miller hated me."

"But he said you're his best friend…"

"We came a long way," Baker said, "with the help of a child psychologist and Taye. We're going to get married soon. As soon as Sadie and I can figure out where we can set it up without Taye doing all the work."

"Like she did for my wedding."

"Miller really does help her, and Dusty's mother-in-law, Juliet, does, too. But I don't want her to even have to think about anything but us."

"I'll do whatever I can to help."

"Help us adopt the boys."

"Sadie has a lawyer working—"

"We want you," he said.

She smiled. "I can't fight it if I'm facilitating it?"

His mouth curved into a slight grin. "That might have been part of it. But we've also seen what you're doing for Collin and Bailey Ann. The sacrifice you're making for them."

Sacrifice...

It didn't feel like that now, with both of them living with her. But when they weren't...

Her stomach dropped at the thought of it, of going back to that empty house, that empty existence.

She shouldn't have waited for Bradford to come around to the idea of fostering. She should have just done it on her own. And she could have when she'd moved to Willow Creek, but she'd been using her nephews as an excuse to wait.

But she hadn't even sought them out. She'd been so scared of being hurt and disappointed again. Of feeling again...

Bradford had been right about one thing; she had shut down during their marriage.

"We don't know yet how that's going to work out with Bailey Ann," she said. She and Collin hadn't told anyone else what had happened yet but Mrs. Finch. She was tempted to tell Baker because she was so worried.

But he had enough on his plate right now.

"If you're too busy..." he said, giving her an out.

She shook her head. "No. I'll never be too busy for you and for them. I'll get right to work on it."

"Good," he said. "Grandma's lawyer is nice and all but he's probably older than she is and has a tendency to nod off during appointments."

She laughed. "I know who you mean. He has nodded off on me a time or two. I was hoping it was just a brilliant strategy on his part."

Baker laughed, too.

"Mommy!" Bailey Ann called out.

Genevieve and her horse both jumped a bit, the horse's hooves pawing at the ground. Baker reached out to steady her as Collin came up alongside her.

"Sorry," Collin said, apologizing to her. "We came back to make sure you were doing okay." He glanced at his cousin, as if worried that he'd been giving her a hard time.

Bailey Ann looked worried, too. The child was so empathetic that she'd probably picked up on their fears over that meeting with Mrs. Finch, that they might take her away from them. They'd wanted to reassure her that it wouldn't happen. But they just didn't know...

If they lost her, Genevieve wouldn't just lose Bailey Ann; she would lose Collin, too, because the little girl was the only reason he'd married her.

LEM WATCHED SADIE watching her family as they all crowded around the island in the big kitchen at Ranch Haven. Just back from a long horse ride around part of the extensive property, the kids were *starving* for cookies of course. He'd managed to sneak a couple himself before they'd burst back into the house.

The cookies were good, especially the snickerdoodles. The taste of nutmeg and cinnamon lingered on his tongue.

But the look on Sadie's face was what gave him the most pleasure. Happiness and love.

She loved all her family so very much. Then she glanced over at him, and that look stayed on her face. She loved him, too.

He was a lucky man. He kept thinking that he needed to marry her as soon as possible, but with her family—their family—still a bit unsettled, he wasn't sure if now was the time to push her. He knew she'd met with that pretty Realtor, trying to get information out of her about Cash.

And that she was concerned about Collin and Genevieve, too. And, most of all, that sweet little girl…

They all seemed so happy, like Sadie's plan was working. Of course she'd denied that she'd had a plan when she'd referred Collin to the lawyer, to Jenny's sister, but Sadie didn't ever *not* have a plan.

He needed her to tell him what the plan was for their wedding. Since the tattoo parlor was out, did she want to get married here? On the ranch?

Or did it hold too many memories of Big Jake for her? She'd remodeled and built on to it so much since Jake had passed that it wasn't the same place they'd shared.

It was a place Lem felt comfortable sharing with her now.

Despite being old and set in their ways, they'd managed to adjust to suit each other.

He loved her so very much.

She looked away from him to where Collin and Genevieve stood at the counter with Bailey Ann. Her brow furrowed, and he followed her gaze to see what had concerned her.

They looked so happy, but there was also something a little off. As if they were trying too hard to look happy for the little girl…

Something was wrong.

He had no doubt that Sadie would find out what and would come up with some way to try to fix it. But she'd learned the hard way, the same way he had through the loss of ones they'd loved, that some things were beyond even their control.

CHAPTER TWENTY

YESTERDAY HAD BEEN a fun day. Maybe too fun because it had been hard for Collin and Genevieve to get Bailey Ann settled and asleep that night. Or maybe, despite their efforts to get their minds off the meeting with Mrs. Finch, she'd felt their anxiety.

Their fear...

And from the grim look on Mrs. Finch's face, it was obvious they'd had every reason to be fearful. She'd just come out of Bailey Ann's bedroom where she'd insisted on having a private conversation with the little girl while he and Genevieve had paced around the island in the kitchen.

"Can I get you anything, Mrs. Finch?" Genevieve asked. "Coffee? Tea?"

He didn't know if she was being a gracious host, or if she just wanted to put off whatever bad news Mrs. Finch was about to give them. And from the look on her face, he doubted it was anything else.

Even Genevieve, who seemed to work hard to find the positive in a situation, didn't seem as if she'd found one now. Not like she had with Cash's lighter. And Sadie's lawyer. He'd overheard the conversation she'd had with his cousin, how she'd considered Sadie's lawyer was deliberately using a strategy instead of accidentally falling asleep. Genevieve Porter was so many things. The smart and savvy lawyer. The woman who carried such guilt over her sister and nephews. The generous optimist...

"I am very disappointed," Mrs. Finch said. "I had hoped this would work out."

"It will," Genevieve insisted.

Mrs. Finch shook her head. "I was concerned that there was an unnatural attachment between Dr. Cassidy and his young patient, and this proves it."

Collin sucked in a breath. "What are you saying?"

"That's why I was hesitant to place her with you and why I considered it might be better to move her to Sheridan."

"Collin and Bailey Ann are like father and daughter," Genevieve said. "And they should be father and daughter."

"Not if it puts her health at risk."

"*Not* being with him put her at risk," Genevieve said in his defense.

But was that accurate? He could almost understand what Mrs. Finch was thinking.

"That was because she wasn't taking medication so that she could see her doctor again," Mrs. Finch. "That's why it's an unhealthy attachment for her—when she would put her life in jeopardy like that."

Collin's knees shook a bit, and he had to lean against the countertop or he might have fallen. Mrs. Finch was right about that.

"They should have been making certain she was taking her medication," Genevieve said. "In my training to become a foster parent, I learned that some kids put their meds under their tongue and spit them out later, especially their ADHD medications."

"Nobody expected a child who'd been through everything that Bailey Ann had would risk her life like that, especially after her new heart gave her a chance at having a normal one. She needs some psychological evaluations," Mrs. Finch said. "That's where I'm taking her today."

Collin tensed. "Where specifically are you taking her?"

"The child's ward of a psychiatric hospital. I have her packing now—"

"No!" Collin said. "She'll be terrified in a place like that."

"It's necessary," Mrs. Finch said. "What she did was so extreme. What happens if she doesn't get her way again? Will she deliberately sabotage her health until she gets what she wants?"

"I talked to her," he insisted. "She understands how dangerous what she did was. She won't do it again."

"I need to make certain of that," Mrs. Finch said.

Genevieve cleared her throat. "So what is this? Some kind of test? You'll see if she takes her meds away from him and if she does, she can come back to us?"

Mrs. Finch tensed. "I don't know. My supervisor and I will consider the psychiatrist's evaluation and make our determination on her placement."

Collin's heart rate quickened, his pulse racing. He was losing her. Just as he'd feared...

"THIS IS YOUR FAULT!" Bailey Ann cried as Mrs. Finch tugged her toward the front door.

Genevieve flinched, guilt weighing heavily on her because the little girl was right.

"This is your fault! You had to tell!" Bailey Ann shouted, tears streaming down her face.

Tears were streaming down Genevieve's, too. "I didn't mean for this to happen..." she murmured. She hadn't wanted Collin to lose her. She hadn't wanted to lose her.

Collin stepped around her. "Mrs. Finch, wait a moment please," he requested, his voice gruff.

The social worker stopped, her body stiff with resistance.

Bailey Ann threw her arms around Collin's neck. "I don't want to leave you, Daddy. I don't want to leave you!"

"Hey, hey," he said gently. "This isn't Genevieve's fault."

Bailey Ann's face tensed with displeasure and she glared at Genevieve over his head. "It is! I shouldn't have told her the truth!"

"Yes, you should have," Collin said. "You should always tell the truth. No matter what. I know you wanted to see me, but you put your health at risk."

"I won't ever again. I promise!"

Genevieve squeezed her eyes shut at the pain in Bailey Ann's voice.

"It's not just that," Collin said, still holding her gently. "Right now, the Morelys aren't allowed to take care of kids who have medical needs. That's not fair to them or to the kids who might need them. Do you see that?"

Though to some extent, Genevieve mused, they did deserve a mark on their record.

Tears trailed down Bailey Ann's face. "I didn't think about that…"

"You need to," Collin said. "I know you've been in this little world that revolves around you and your health, but there are other people out there, other kids like you who need good homes and need help—"

"I need you!"

"I need you, too," Collin said. "But we need to do it the right way. We don't want to play tricks or cause problems. That's not the right way to do things, especially when other people get hurt because of it."

Like the way Genevieve had hurt the Havens because she hadn't been straightforward about her relationship with her nephews and her concern for their well-being.

"I made a mistake like this," Genevieve said. And she knelt down next to Collin to face the little girl. "I was worried about Ian and Miller and Little Jake, and instead of finding out for myself how they were, I was being sneaky.

I was asking other people to help me find out. And they got reported to CPS."

"CPS?" Bailey Ann asked. As angry as she was with Genevieve, she was still curious...probably just because it was about the boys.

"Child Protective Services," Mrs. Finch explained for her. She was watching this scene unfold closely.

"And they could have been taken away from the ranch, away from the Havens, and they might have even been separated," she said. "And I was wrong. I should have just been open and honest and they never would have had to worry." And she was going to push that adoption through as fast as she could to make sure they never worried again and that they had the security they deserved.

Bailey Ann deserved it, too.

"I made a mistake," Genevieve said. "Just like you did. Everybody makes them." She glanced up at Mrs. Finch. "It doesn't make us bad people...unless we don't learn from those mistakes. We need to always try to do better. To be better. But just because you made a mistake doesn't make you bad or wrong. It just makes you human."

Did the little girl understand what she was trying to tell her? She didn't want her blaming herself for this. Genevieve would much rather have Bailey Ann blame her. "You're a good girl," she said, as those tears continued to roll down her face, "and I love you very much."

Bailey Ann didn't say anything. She just closed her eyes and more tears rolled down her face. She probably hated Genevieve.

Genevieve stood up and stepped back, then turned away because she couldn't watch Mrs. Finch take the little girl out of the arms of the man Bailey Ann considered her father.

She braced herself as the door opened and closed. They were gone. And when she turned around, so was Collin.

She waited for a long while in that empty hallway, in that empty house, but he didn't come back. Bailey Ann wasn't the only one who blamed her. Apparently Collin did, too.

Genevieve had lost them both.

JESSUP GLANCED UP as the door opened. It was early for Marsh to come home. And Darlene, Sarah and her son were already here. Mikey was playing in the backyard while Sarah and Darlene made dinner.

He should have been doing something. For so many years he hadn't had the strength or the energy. But now, with his new heart, he was stronger. Healthier...

He jumped up now from the chair where he'd been reading and walked toward the front door. Collin was the one who'd opened and then closed it—with his back, apparently, since he leaned against it.

He was pale and shaky, like he'd seen a ghost. Like Jessup had felt for so many years. Like a ghost of himself. Of the father he should have been to his sons.

"Collin, what's wrong?" he asked with concern. "What happened?"

Jessup stepped closer, surveying his son for injuries. He looked fine except for his face. His expression of such...

Devastation. He'd only looked like that once before that Jessup could remember. When his mother had died...

No. Twice.

And when Cash had run off...

"You're scaring me," Jessup said. "What's going on?"

Collin blinked and roused himself, worrying now about Jessup. "I didn't mean to scare you," he said, his voice gruff. Almost as if he'd been crying.

Collin had always made it a point to never cry in front of anyone. Ever since he was a kid...

Jessup had figured at first that it was because he hadn't wanted his brothers to tease him about his tears. But even when they'd cried, he hadn't. It wasn't because he hadn't cared or he'd been too proud; it was because he hadn't wanted to worry anyone.

He wanted to take care of people, not have anyone take care of him.

That was why he'd become a doctor. Jessup knew all that. And he knew, too, that all those times he hadn't cried in public, he'd cried alone. Because Collin's voice had sounded then how it did now, raw and vulnerable, as he continued, "I just didn't know where else to go."

Jessup stepped forward and reached for his son, closing his arms around him as Collin gave into the sobs that wracked his body. He could barely understand what he said through his tears. But it sounded like, "They took her away. They took Bailey Ann away."

CHAPTER TWENTY-ONE

COLLIN HADN'T WANTED Genevieve to see him cry, so he'd just kept going after he'd walked Bailey Ann and Mrs. Finch out. He'd gotten in his car and driven off. And now he didn't know how to undo what he'd done...

With Bailey Ann.

Or with Genevieve.

Why hadn't he realized what the little girl had done? Why her body had been rejecting her new heart? He should have talked to her. No. He should have done what Genevieve had done. He should have listened.

Hopefully Genevieve hadn't listened to what the little girl had said in anger, how she'd blamed her. Genevieve already took the blame for too many things that weren't her fault.

Too many mistakes...

What she'd said to Bailey Ann was so much better than anything he or Mrs. Finch had told the little girl. Genevieve had done her best to make sure the little girl didn't blame herself for anything. She was an incredible foster mom. An incredible person...

An incredible woman.

She was his wife.

But that had only been for Bailey Ann. Now that Bailey Ann was gone...

It would have been awkward for him to go back to that

house without the little girl. Without the reason he and Genevieve had gotten married in the first place...

But he had another reason now. He'd started to fall in love with his wife. And he missed her as badly as he missed Bailey Ann, and it had only been one night, one night spent lying awake in the den of his dad's rental house.

Jessup couldn't buy it yet, not until the insurance settled his house fire claim and the sale could close on the ranch. Collin wondered if settlements like this usually took so long. Was the insurance company investigating the possibility of arson? Of Jessup's involvement?

He couldn't believe it of his father. He had nearly died while he'd tried to find the nurse's son. His dad wouldn't have put anyone else in danger. He wanted to believe that Cash wouldn't have either. Cash had been so gentle with animals and with their mother when she was sick. But the Cash that had left their house had been so angry...

So full of rage.

Like Bailey Ann had toward Genevieve. He should have stayed after the little girl and social worker left. He should have comforted Genevieve. Instead he'd run home to his dad, to his comfort.

And he'd left Genevieve all alone.

And she was. She had no one.

He had his family. While he hadn't sought comfort from them before, somehow he'd always known they would be there when he needed them.

When Genevieve had needed someone, he hadn't been there for her. If he'd really been her husband, he would have been a lousy one. He needed to talk to her. To apologize...for his own behavior and for Bailey Ann's.

His cell vibrated in his pocket, startling him with the movement and the fact it hadn't died. He hadn't even plugged it in last night. He probably hadn't even brushed his teeth. After falling apart on his dad, he'd slunk away to the den and dropped onto the foldout bed. As exhausted as he'd been, he hadn't been able to sleep. Instead he'd kept imagining where Bailey Ann was, worrying that it was terrible and then wishing that Genevieve was there to force him to look on the bright side.

That the little girl needed to talk to someone, just as Dale and Jenny's kids had needed to talk to a child psychologist in order to deal with their parents' deaths. He'd been so concerned about Bailey Ann's medical care that he hadn't seen to her emotional and psychological care.

Mrs. Finch was doing just that. And chances were that she wasn't going to trust him with any care of Bailey Ann again. She might even move the little girl back to Sheridan so that she could see the specialists there.

His phone vibrated again, with a voice mail, and he realized he hadn't even answered it. He grabbed the cell from his pocket, anxious to see if it was Genevieve calling or Mrs. Finch. But it was the hospital.

He was needed for a consultation.

What about Genevieve? He should have called her and at least texted her. But she hadn't called or texted him either.

Had she needed him last night? This was why he hadn't wanted emotions to enter into their relationship. He never seemed to live up to what other people needed from him. He'd feared he'd end up hurting Genevieve, that she deserved more than he would be able to give. And his worst fears were coming true.

WHEN GENEVIEVE FINALLY gave up on sleep and rolled out of her bed the next morning, she felt the way Ian must have when that bronco had knocked him down.

Ian had just gotten a few bumps and bruises from his fall, though, whereas she felt like the thing had stomped all over her. She ached all over.

Mostly her heart.

All night she'd lain awake worrying about Bailey Ann and Collin. She'd only wanted to help them, but instead she'd hurt them.

Bailey Ann had been so upset with her. And Collin...

Obviously he hadn't wanted to be with her. He'd never come home last night. She'd lain awake all night with her head cocked, listening for any sound.

But there had been no creak of hinges, no soft snap of a door closing. She'd been alone in the house—more alone than she'd felt in a long time.

Probably since she'd lost one of those babies she'd carried for such a short time.

This disappointment over losing Bailey Ann was nearly as sharp as the disappointment and devastation she'd felt when she'd tried to conceive. When, month after month, she'd found she wasn't pregnant. And then, when the IVF had worked, she'd lost the babies anyway.

But she hadn't been able to do anything about those losses. With Bailey Ann, maybe there was hope. She wasn't gone forever.

This time Genevieve could fight. As her foster parent, she had rights. She had to...

SADIE HAD GOTTEN another early morning call from Jessup. This time he wasn't angry with her. He sounded too upset and frustrated to be angry.

She understood how he felt—how much it hurt when one of your kids was hurting and you were no help. And he knew she understood because she'd felt that way about him so often; she felt that way even now.

Because she wasn't sure how much she would be able to help…

But she'd had to do something. So instead of going back to sleep with Feisty, who'd grumbled over the call, she'd gotten up and driven toward town. She didn't go to Jessup's, where Collin was staying. She didn't go to her grandson. He had Jessup and his brother and Darlene to support him.

Sadie went to the person who had no one.

Genevieve opened the door to Sadie and, her voice so soft and so much like Jenny's, said, "They're not here."

"I know," Sadie said. "That's why I'm here."

Tears pooled in Genevieve's blue eyes, rimmed by dark circles. She looked exhausted and vulnerable. But then she blinked back those tears and straightened her shoulders. "I'm not giving up."

"Good," Sadie praised her. "What are you not giving up on? Fostering Bailey Ann or your marriage?"

"My marriage isn't real," Genevieve said, but her voice cracked slightly. "What I need to fix is this situation with Bailey Ann. It was my fault Mrs. Finch took her away for that evaluation." Her voice cracked again, and she cleared it. "I have to make sure she comes back here after it."

"But Collin isn't here," Sadie said.

Genevieve sucked in a breath. "Did you talk to him? Do you know how he's doing? Does he blame me like Bailey Ann does?"

"No. His father called me," Sadie said. "And he didn't really understand what had happened. Just that Bailey Ann had been taken away. I don't know why. Did Mrs. Finch suspect the marriage wasn't real?"

Genevieve shook her head, and her tears pooled again as she told Sadie how the little girl had sabotaged her own health to leave her last foster family.

"You had to tell Mrs. Finch about that," Sadie assured her. "And her getting help is good. The boys needed that, and I wish we would have gotten it for them sooner. But it was so chaotic after the accident..."

Genevieve flinched, and her slim shoulders sagged even more with the weight of all that guilt she kept carrying. Sadie gripped those shoulders in her hands and turned her toward her.

"You didn't know," Sadie told her. "You didn't do anything wrong, Genevieve, with your sister or with Bailey Ann."

The tears brimmed over and ran down her face. Sadie pulled her in for a hug. And Sadie wasn't really much of a hugger.

Genevieve clung to her for a moment before pulling back. "Thank you. Thank you for coming over to check on me. Thank you for caring."

"I don't think anyone cares as much as you do," Sadie said. The woman was a really good person. "You remind me so much of your sister." And her chest ached over that loss.

Genevieve smiled but shook her head. "It's the voice."

"It's the heart," Sadie said. "You both have big ones."

Genevieve's teeth nipped her bottom lip for a moment before she mused aloud, "Sometimes I wonder if Bailey Ann has Jenny's heart. She got it around the same time of the accident. But her surgery was in Sheridan—"

"All transplant surgeries for anyone in this area are done

there," Sadie said. "The hospital here isn't set up for them. I've wondered the same thing. I like to know that something good could come out of something so horrible. I'm pretty sure that Jessup has Dale's heart."

"Oh... I'm sorry. I'm so sorry about Dale, too. I keep thinking of Jenny and the boys but Dale..." She shook her head. "I didn't know him. I didn't know my brother-in-law."

"He was so much like Jenny. If there really is such a thing as soul mates, they were it. It didn't matter how young they married, they would have made it for the long haul."

"Our parents were wrong," she said. "And they missed out on so much and keep missing out. Those little boys are the only grandkids they'll have."

"You won't have any?"

Genevieve snorted. "Not biological ones. And those are the only ones they'll consider theirs, just like my ex-husband. Some people don't understand that a child can be yours even if you don't share the same DNA. Collin understands that."

And Genevieve understood and cared about Collin. Why hadn't he stayed here with his wife?

"I'm going to fix this," Genevieve said. She lifted her chin. "I'm going to make this right for Bailey Ann and Collin."

"And what about what's right for you?" Sadie asked.

Genevieve shrugged. "It was always about them. I only agreed to help Bailey Ann." She sighed. "And instead I hurt her..."

"She's not the only one who got hurt," Sadie said.

"I know Collin is hurting."

"You are, too," Sadie said. But Genevieve only seemed

to care about others, not herself. Somebody needed to love
this woman like she deserved to be loved. Hopefully he
already did; he just didn't know how to show it.

CHAPTER TWENTY-TWO

COLLIN WAS GRATEFUL that he'd had a reason to get up and out of the house. He was also grateful that he'd been able to help the person who'd come into the ER with what he'd thought was an anxiety attack.

It wasn't. And it could have been so much worse if his wife hadn't insisted on bringing him into the hospital. Fortunately Collin, with his interventional cardiology fellowship experience, was able to quickly assess and get the patient to the cath lab where he'd inserted a catheter and removed a blockage that could have killed the young husband and new father.

He was so glad to help that family. A real family, not like what he'd tried to cobble together. Genevieve didn't love him; he knew that. Love wasn't part of their marriage. Only Bailey Ann was and now she was gone.

His office door rattled, knuckles striking the wood. He glanced up from his desk and saw that those knuckles were swollen with arthritis but the hand, and the woman to whom it belonged, was strong. "I'd like a consultation, Dr. Cassidy," she said.

He shook his head. "You know I can't treat you anymore now that we know we're family."

Which was why he probably shouldn't have been treating Bailey Ann either, once he'd gotten so attached to her. Because she'd become family to him then and he hadn't been able to be objective with all of his emotions involved.

"I'm not here for a medical consultation," Sadie said.

He leaned back in his chair and arched an eyebrow. "My dad called you."

She nodded. "He's worried about you."

His stomach knotted. "I don't want to talk about this..." His throat already felt raw from last night, and he hadn't talked much. He'd cried instead. And he'd felt like he hadn't cried just for Bailey Ann but for all his other losses and disappointments over the years.

In some ways it had been cathartic. In other ways it had left him as raw as his throat. And vulnerable...

"I'm worried about you, too," she said. "I know how hard you studied and worked to become a cardiologist. I know you're not a quitter. So I don't understand why you're giving up now."

"Giving up?" he asked. "I have no rights to Bailey Ann."

"What about your wife?"

"Genevieve is really her foster parent," he said.

"She is going to fight for Bailey Ann," Sadie said.

"How do you know that?"

"I just talked to her," Sadie said. "She's determined. She actually thinks Bailey Ann might have her sister's heart." She cocked her head and studied his face. "Is that possible?"

He shook his head. "No. It's not Jenny's heart. Is that really what Genevieve has been thinking?"

"It's crossed her mind," Sadie said. "It's crossed my mind, too. The little girl just feels like she belongs with all of us."

"She deserves a family of her own," Collin said. "One that loves her for her." Not because of someone's body part they might have.

"Genevieve deserves the same thing," Sadie said.

He furrowed his forehead as the pounding in his skull intensified. "What do you mean?"

"Jenny talked about her big sister a lot," Sadie said. "She probably felt as guilty about Genevieve as Genevieve feels about her."

"Why? Everybody has said how sweet and kind and loving Jenny was." Which was maybe why Genevieve had thought Bailey Ann had her heart.

"She was. And she felt like it was her fault—the way her parents treated Genevieve. Her mom got pregnant with Genevieve in high school and dumped her on her grandparents so that she could live her own life. She probably would have left Genevieve there, but when she got married years later, her parents made her take her daughter back. It was as if nobody wanted responsibility for her. Nobody wanted her."

His gut wrenched with sympathy for her. "That's terrible. I knew it wasn't a good family situation, that her stepdad didn't really want her." But he hadn't realized that her mother and grandparents really hadn't either.

"That's why she wanted to help Bailey Ann," Sadie said. "Because she knows how it feels to have nobody want responsibility for you."

"I want responsibility for Bailey Ann," he said. But he wasn't sure he deserved it when he hadn't figured out what had really happened with her medications.

"What about your wife?" Sadie asked.

"She didn't want this to be permanent. She was just helping us out." While she might have fallen for Bailey Ann, he doubted she'd fallen for him. And even if she'd started developing feelings for him, he'd probably ruined his chances with her over how he'd left her after Bailey Ann had been taken away.

Sadie sighed and shook her head, as if she was disappointed in him. "Despite all your education and training, you just don't get it."

"Get what?"

"Life. Love. You've spent so much of time studying that you haven't spent much living, have you, Dr. Cassidy?"

He stiffened, getting defensive like he had whenever his brothers had teased him about never doing anything but studying and working. But they'd understood why; he wasn't sure that his grandmother did.

She walked around his desk and reached down to lay her hand against his cheek. "Your father is doing well. And Bailey Ann, despite this issue, is doing well. You can stop worrying about everyone else for a bit, Collin, and worry about yourself. What do you want?"

"Bailey Ann." And Genevieve. He wanted his wife, too, but he was afraid to admit it, afraid that he didn't have a chance with her. She'd made it clear that she'd never wanted to get married again. He'd appreciated that she'd been willing to marry him anyway for Bailey Ann's sake, yet he found himself wishing that it had been for another reason. Wishing he'd been the man she'd married for love.

"Kids are wonderful," Sadie said. "But they grow up and move away. Or they run away before they grow up. They don't grow old with you. And you don't want to grow old alone." She moved her hand from his face, and she suddenly looked very old—her shoulders sagging, and the lines around her mouth and eyes deepening a little.

He thought she and Lem Lemmon were engaged. Had something happened?

"Are you okay?" he asked her with concern.

She nodded. "Yes. Just realizing that everything doesn't always work out how I intended…"

"Did you have a matchmaking scheme in mind when you referred me to Genevieve?" he asked.

"I did," she admitted. "But I realize now that throwing people together isn't enough...not if they're not willing to risk their hearts..."

Was she talking about him or Genevieve?

GENEVIEVE HAD GONE into her office, figuring that calls coming from a legal practice might bear more weight than calls from a scared foster mom. So she sat at her desk, calling Mrs. Finch and the psychiatrist and Mrs. Finch's supervisor, and she pleaded her case to every one of them.

She was just looking up the number for family court when her door creaked open. It was probably Hilda, who'd been very supportive this morning after acknowledging how tired Genevieve had looked.

She wasn't just tired. She was exhausted. Physically and emotionally. So when she looked up and saw that it was actually Collin standing in her doorway, she nearly groaned. If he was angry with her, she couldn't deal with that emotion right now, not on top of all the others pummeling her. "I'm working on trying to get her back," she promised. "I've been on the phone all morning..."

But she had no idea if Mrs. Finch had listened to her any more than she listened to Bailey Ann.

"Why?" he asked.

"Why what? We can't leave her in a psych ward or let them move her somewhere else..."

"No, I mean, why do you care so much?" Collin asked. "Is it because you think she has Jenny's heart?"

She sucked in a breath. "You talked to Sadie."

"So did you," he said. "I didn't realize you thought that."

She shrugged. "Just a couple of times in passing. I didn't think it was actually possible."

"It wasn't," he said. "She doesn't have Jenny's heart.

But I know that someone got it who desperately needed it. A part of Jenny still lives on."

She sucked in a breath and nodded. "That's good."

"I hope that gives you some comfort," he said.

"I've accepted that I can't change the past," she said. "Like I told Bailey Ann, I can't make up for those mistakes that I made. I can just make sure I don't make them again."

"That's why you won't marry for love again? Because it didn't work out the first time?"

A bitter chuckle slipped out. "It more than didn't work out. It destroyed me. The IVF, the miscarriages, the disappointment...being the disappointment..." She was right; she was too full of emotions to deal with his right now. To deal with him at all.

She pointed toward the door now. "You can leave, like you did last night. The only thing we have in common is that we both care about Bailey Ann. You can question my reasons for caring, but that doesn't change that I care. Unless you'd rather I not get her back? Unless you'd rather she went to someone else other than me?"

Bailey Ann might not want to come back to her since she blamed her for all of this, just as Collin was probably blaming her.

"Genevieve, that's..." His throat moved as if he was struggling to swallow. "I didn't mean it like that..."

She shrugged as if she wasn't hurting as much as she was. "We both know we were only together for Bailey Ann. So of course, you'd leave when she did. I didn't expect anything more from you."

She hadn't expected it, but she'd wanted it. She'd wanted his support. She wanted him. But clearly his only interest in her was to help him get Bailey Ann.

Suddenly very weary, she dropped into the chair behind her desk. "We can get this marriage annulled. We can end it now."

"Is that what you want?" he asked.

No. It was the last thing she wanted. But she also wanted to be wanted for herself, not for the babies she was supposed to give birth to or as a means to anyone's ends but her own. She wanted happily-ever-after; she wanted the love that Jenny had found with Dale.

She sighed. "You know... I'm still jealous of my little sister like I was when we were growing up. Even though she ultimately lost everything...even her life...she and Dale had it all."

Love was everything.

"Genevieve, I don't understand..." Collin murmured.

"No, of course you don't," she said.

"What do you want to do?" he asked.

She wanted to love and be loved, but she was done begging for it, like she had with her mom and stepdad, her grandparents. Even at the end, she'd begged Bradford as much as her pride had allowed.

"I want some time to think," she said. Because at the moment, all she could do was feel, and it was too much.

"Genevieve..."

She shook her head. "No. Please, just go."

He didn't argue with her. Didn't fight for her. He just turned and walked away like he had the night before when she'd needed him. Instead of coming together to support each other, he'd just left her alone.

She was sick of getting left.

LEM WATCHED SADIE's face as she finished up her call. It had rung the minute she'd stepped inside his office, so they hadn't had a chance to even greet each other. And he'd missed her...even though he'd had dinner at her house the night before. But because he'd had a morning meeting, as Ben's deputy mayor, he'd left right after dinner. He didn't like leaving her anymore.

She clicked off her cell and closed her eyes and sighed.

"What's wrong?" he asked with concern. "Who was that?"

"Hilda Feltman from Genevieve's office."

He nodded. "Oh, so you have a source at Genevieve's office."

"Yes, and I don't like what she just told me. Sounds like Genevieve and Collin are done. She overheard them fighting." She shook her head. "And that's my fault. It's all my fault." A tear trailed down her cheek.

And Lem rushed around his desk to kneel in front of the chair she'd dropped into when she'd walked into his office. "Oh, Sadie…"

"Go ahead," she said. "You warned me. Go ahead and say I told you so."

"I love you," he said instead.

And she snorted, then laughed. "You never do what I expect you to do, Lem Lemmon."

"That's why you love me," he said.

"Yes, it is," she agreed. "Even like now, you're on your knees again after telling me when you proposed that was the last time you were getting down on the floor."

"I know you'll help me back up," he said. "Just like you did last time. And I want to help you, too, with Collin and Genevieve. But what I want to do most of all is to stop worrying about our families and just think of ourselves for once. I want to marry you, Sadie March Haven."

"You already proposed," she reminded him. "And I already accepted. Though technically I did propose first…"

"And I was a fool for not accepting right away," he said.

"You're proud. That's why I haven't…"

"Haven't what?" he asked.

"Haven't pushed for a wedding date."

He stared at her. "I haven't pushed for a wedding date because I thought you wanted to wait until Ben and Emily and Baker and Taye got married."

She snorted. "They're young. They have time. You and me... We shouldn't wait."

"I agree."

"I guess there's a first time for everything," she said with a chuckle.

"You know you always get me to come around to your way of thinking..." He chuckled now, remembering all the times she'd charged into city hall to confront him with something or other about the town. "Let's get married here or in town square," he said. "Like as soon as we can get the license and a tattoo artist booked."

She laughed. "You're serious about those tattooed rings."

"I'm serious about you," he said. "And I want everyone to know that. So will you marry me as soon as we can make it happen?"

She nodded. "I didn't want to push you, but I was hoping that you'd take the hint when I talked Ben into putting up the Valentine's decorations."

"Those were for me?" He was so touched.

"I am for you, Lemar Lemmon, and you are for me," she said. And she leaned forward and kissed him. "As long as we have each other, we can let the rest of them sort themselves out for once."

He touched her forehead. "Feeling okay, woman?"

"Never better," she said and kissed him again.

CHAPTER TWENTY-THREE

JUST WHEN HE'D thought he couldn't have made a bigger mess of things with Genevieve, he had. First he'd taken off the night before without saying a word to her. She'd probably thought he'd blamed her like Bailey Ann had.

And now he'd left her again. Sure, this time she'd told him to go. That she couldn't deal with him. That was why he'd walked out of her office and out of the practice. But now...

He stood on the street, watching the heart-shaped balloons and decorations flutter around in the slight breeze. It was as if it was all mocking him. As if love was mocking him.

He'd gone and fallen in love with his wife. And instead of fighting for her, for them, he had walked away again. She'd talked to him before about shutting down, and he realized now that was what he'd always done. He'd buried himself in his studies because it was easier than dealing with his fears over his dad's health and losing his mom and Cash.

He'd run away instead of dealing with his problems. Not that Genevieve was a problem...

The only problem was going to be if she didn't feel about him like he felt about her. If she hadn't fallen for him, too...

But he wasn't going to know until he asked, until he put his heart on the line first.

GENEVIEVE WONDERED IF she was going to need a new heart someday. Hers felt like it had been broken so many times, ever since she was a little girl, that she wasn't sure how long it would last.

She was smart not to risk it again. That had been her decision after her divorce. That had been the reason why she'd thought it so smart to just have a marriage of convenience, where there would be no messy emotions involved. No expectations. No disappointments.

But when Collin walked out of her office, that disappointment settled heavily on her again. She'd told him to go, so she had no reason to be upset with him. She should have been upset with herself.

She was the hypocrite who hadn't been open and honest with him like she'd promised they would be. She should have told him what she really wanted. A real marriage. She should have told him how she felt about him, that his kisses—even the innocent ones against her cheek—affected her. He affected her.

And his leaving had her putting her face in her hands and fighting to hold in tears, wishing that he would have fought for her...

For them.

A knock rattled her door. This time it had to be Hilda checking to see if she was okay, like she'd checked on her right after Collin had left.

She was actually very sweet. Like Sadie...

But Genevieve kept her face in her hands. She knew if she saw that look of concern and sympathy on Hilda's face that she would probably cry again. And she was already all cried out. Over Bailey Ann and over Collin.

"I'm fine," Genevieve said. "You don't have to worry about me."

"What about me?" a deep voice asked.

Collin.

He'd come back.

She tensed but lifted her face as he stepped inside her office again and closed the door.

"What about you?" she asked. She'd been worried about him last night; she'd known he was devastated when Mrs. Finch had taken Bailey Ann away.

"I'm not fine," he said.

"I'm sorry about Bailey Ann."

"That's part of it," he said. "I don't want to lose her. But I don't want to lose you either, Genevieve. I know this marriage isn't supposed to be real, but to me, it is. I have fallen for you."

She shook her head, unable to understand what he was saying. "You don't really even know me."

"We promised to be open and honest with each other," he said. "And I'm being open and honest. You impress me so much with your determination and your strength and your generosity."

She snorted. "Most of it's out of guilt."

"You shouldn't feel guilty," he said. "You haven't done anything wrong. But the fact that you do feel guilty proves what a good, caring person you are. You're so amazing that it's no wonder I've fallen in love with you."

"Really?" She couldn't believe it, couldn't believe what he was saying...

"I didn't realize what it was at first," he said. "I've never been in love before. So I didn't understand it, and I was terrified. I left yesterday because I was falling apart, and I didn't want you to see me like that."

"I know it hurt to have Bailey Ann taken away like that."

"It hurt you, too, and you were so strong for her, for

me, but I couldn't do the same for you. I don't deserve you, Genevieve."

She sucked in a breath. "That's the way I've always felt, like I wasn't good enough to deserve love. That I wasn't enough."

"You're more than enough. You're everything," he said. "And even if we can't get Bailey Ann back, I don't want an annulment. I want you. Forever." He tensed then, as if bracing himself for rejection.

It was good that he'd braced himself because she jumped up from her chair and ran toward him to throw her arms around his neck, to hold him close, to hang on to him forever. "I love you," she said.

He stared down at her, as if in awe of the words. "I love you."

She and Collin were so much alike in how they'd dealt with their emotions, in how they loved, that it was no wonder they'd fallen in love. She'd found her soul mate in him. Or maybe Sadie Haven had found them for each other.

COLTON HAD FOUND a mobile tattoo artist for the ceremony. After all, the tattooed rings had been his idea. Now he just had to find his brother.

Grandma and his dad had told him about Bailey Ann, about how the social worker had taken her away from Collin and Genevieve a couple of nights ago. So he'd expected to find Collin burying himself in work at the hospital. But he hadn't been there.

He hadn't been at Dad's either. So Colton pulled his truck to the curb outside Genevieve's sprawling brick house. Collin's car was parked in the driveway next to her big SUV. Maybe they'd gotten Bailey Ann back. Feeling hopeful, for so many reasons, he ran up to the door and knocked.

Long moments passed. So long that he knocked again. Then he noticed the doorbell and rang that. Chimes played out inside the house. Just the sound of chimes, though.

Maybe they'd gone for a walk. He turned away from the door, but then it creaked open. When he turned around, his mouth dropped open. Collin stood in front of him. His usually perfectly combed hair was tousled, and his face looked more relaxed than Colton had ever seen his twin.

"Are you okay?" Colton asked. "I heard about Bailey Ann being taken away."

"We're trying to get her back," Collin said, his expression tense.

Colton narrowed his eyes. "We?"

"It's not a marriage of convenience anymore," Collin said, and despite his concern for the little girl he loved, he grinned. Colton saw happiness there, too, which helped to temper his fears.

Colton had to believe, with Collin and Genevieve working together to get her back, they would win. They had to win.

"That's why I'm here," Colton said. "I'm supposed to get you to a wedding."

"I'm already married." Collin's eyes widened. "Wait, are you getting married?"

He shook his head. "Not yet. Grandma and Lem are getting married at city hall. And she wants us all there ASAP. I guess they figure at their ages, they don't want to wait another minute to spend the rest of their lives together."

"That will be a long time," Genevieve said as she joined them at the door. She looked like she was ready for a wedding in the dress she was wearing.

He grinned. "Grandma called you," he suspected.

She nodded. "She wanted to make sure we were all there." Tears glistened in her blue eyes. "All the family..."

Colton felt a twinge of regret for the doubts he'd had in the beginning about his sister-in-law. Clearly Grandma had been right about her and Collin. She was usually right about these things.

"Come on then!" he urged. "I have to make sure the tattoo artist gets there."

"The what?" Collin murmured.

But Colton was already heading back to his truck until a faint whiff of smoke stopped him. Reminded him...

Of the fire at the ranch. The lighter...

The destruction of not just the house they'd grown up in but their lives as they'd known them. But they'd gained more than they'd lost.

CHAPTER TWENTY-FOUR

COLLIN TRIED TO find a place to park, but the street in front of city hall was pretty packed. "We should have taken my car," he said. "It would have been easier to squeeze in somewhere."

"There," Genevieve said, her hand over his as she pointed him in the direction of a side street.

Collin turned and parked. Then he got out on the driver's side to go around and open her door. But she was already out and leaning in to the open back door. She pulled out something wrapped in a plastic dry cleaner bag, dangling from a hanger.

"What's this?" he asked.

She was already dressed in a soft blue dress that swirled around her legs when she walked. He was wearing a suit, too. They didn't need extra clothes.

"Sadie asked me to bring it," she said.

"Sadie can't wear anything of yours." His grandmother was six feet tall. Genevieve was probably only five feet four or five inches tall.

Those tears, that he'd glimpsed back at her house when she'd told him and Colton that Sadie had called, glistened in her eyes again. And his heart began to get that feeling again—a palpitation.

A flicker of hope...

Whatever was in that bag was too small for Genevieve to wear, too.

And he realized what she'd really meant back at the house. "She wants all her family here for her wedding..." he murmured.

"Go. Bring it to Lem's office on the third floor," she said. "He's getting ready there. They're getting married in Ben's office, since that was Lem's for a long time when he was mayor. And Sadie used to barge in and tell him how to run the town."

Collin chuckled. "Imagine that..." And he could. His grandmother was fierce. And somehow she must have pulled off what he'd thought impossible. She got Bailey Ann back. Maybe it was just for the wedding. Just for the day.

But for the moment, all that mattered was seeing her again. "Come with me," he told Genevieve.

She shook her head. "You need a moment...just the two of you."

She slipped away into a big room where music played softly and he headed to the closed door with Lem's name on it. He was half-surprised it didn't say "Old Man Lemmon" instead since that was what most people in Willow Creek called him.

He raised his hand to knock, surprised that it was shaking slightly. It opened quickly and he was tugged inside—that strong hand, despite the arthritis, wrapping tightly around his. "Hello, Grandma," he greeted her. "Are you getting cold feet?"

"Not at all. I can't wait," she said. "For this." Then she urged him forward to the little girl who spun away from the woman doing her hair. Taye.

"Daddy!" she exclaimed. "Daddy! I missed you!"

He really needed that EKG; there was so much going on with his heart, so much love swelling in it. "Oh, sweetheart! I am so happy to see you!" He lifted her up, hugging her close.

She kissed his cheek and pulled back. "Did you bring my flower girl dress?"

"Genevieve did."

She peered around him. "Where's Mommy?"

"She thinks you're mad at her."

She blinked hard. "I was mean to her. I need to tell her I'm sorry and I love her so much. Where is she?"

He nodded. "She's in the room where the wedding is going to happen."

"Let's get you dressed and you can go see her before we start," Taye suggested.

"Only girl in the family, she's going to get this gig a lot," Sadie warned him.

"Is she?" he asked, his voice cracking a bit.

She nodded. "This isn't just for today."

"You got her back for us?"

Sadie shook her head. "Not me. Your wife did that."

"I am a lucky man," Collin said. Then he focused on his grandmother again. "No. Luck had nothing to do with bringing me together with Genevieve. It was all you."

She shrugged. She was wearing a long blush-colored dress in lace. It was so soft and feminine, so unlike Sadie, but she was different around Lem. She was so in love.

And because of her, so was Collin.

"Want to give me away?" she asked him.

"No. I intend to keep you forever," Collin assured his grandmother.

"I'll give her away," Jessup said.

"I'm sure you will," Sadie said with a chuckle.

Jessup hugged his mother. "I don't want to get rid of you."

"That's good," Sadie said. "Because I'm not going anywhere but down the aisle. Took Lem and I too many years to get here to not spend as many years together, driving each other crazy, as we can."

Collin had never met his grandfather. He'd only heard stories about Big Jake Haven. But there was something about Lem Lemmon, something that made Collin think the short little Santa-like man might have been his grandmother's true soul mate all along.

GENEVIEVE HAD FOUND a seat next to Becca on what was probably the Haven side of the room. Chairs had been put into rows on either side of a makeshift aisle. And some of those decorations from outside had found their way in here, like the balloons dangling from the ceiling. Her nephews, wearing those little white cowboy hats again, tried to reach the dangling strings of them. When they jumped to reach them, their hats slid down over their eyes. She chuckled at how cute they were.

"They're adorable," Becca said.

Genevieve smiled at her friend. "I'm surprised to see you here. I didn't know you and Sadie were that close."

"We're not," Becca said. "I'm kind of a plus-one."

Genevieve leaned forward and noticed the tall blond man sitting on the other side of Becca, next to the wall. Genevieve had left a few chairs open between her and the aisle for Collin and...

"Mommy!" a little voice exclaimed. And short arms wrapped around her neck, pulling her in for a hug.

Genevieve wrapped her arms around the little girl holding her close. "Oh, I missed you so much..."

"I missed you, too, Mommy."

"I thought you were mad at me," Genevieve admitted. That was why, when Mrs. Finch and her supervisor had authorized Bailey Ann to return to her care, she'd asked them to drop her here instead of right at her house. She'd wanted to surprise Collin, too, as much as he'd surprised her with his declaration of love.

"No. I know it's always the best to tell the truth and be open and honest," Bailey Ann said.

"Wow, you're one smart little girl," said the guy on the other side of Becca. He leaned around his date now. "How'd you get so smart?"

"From my mom and dad," Bailey Ann said, hugging Genevieve again. "This is my mom. She's a lawyer, and my dad is a doctor. A heart doctor." She touched her chest, but her scars were hidden beneath the lace and satin of her flower girl dress. "He fixed my heart."

He had fixed Genevieve's, too, opening it up for love again. For love to give and for love to receive.

"There's my daddy!" Bailey Ann exclaimed.

"You have to get back to Grandma," Collin said, "so they can get started. Can't start without the flower girl."

"Nope," Bailey Ann agreed as she rushed back down the aisle.

Collin dropped into the chair next to Genevieve, and he looked a little shaken. "I'm sorry I didn't warn you," she said. "I just wanted to surprise you."

"With Cash?"

"With Bailey Ann," she said.

"But Cash is here, too," he said.

"Where?"

He pointed toward the man sitting next to Becca. Then he repeated her question to his brother. "Where have you been?"

"I've been here," Cash said. "In Willow Creek."

SADIE COULDN'T REMEMBER a time that she'd been happier, and it wasn't just because so much of their family was here. Jessup. His boys. Michael's boys. Dale's.

Even Livvy's brothers had made it to their wedding. And Cash...

The infamous Cash Cassidy. But he didn't call himself Cassidy. Or she would have known who he was all this time...

She would sort all that out later, though.

For now she just wanted to savor this day. To savor the moment she became Sadie March Haven Lemmon.

And the ring on her finger, tattooed on as an infinity symbol, would be there forever. A testament of her love for the person she'd called an old fool for more years than he'd been old.

A person who'd challenged and infuriated her and always made her better. Those were the vows she spoke to him, and his were the same, about how she'd pushed him to be a better man. And how sometimes she'd just pushed him...

Just as she was pushing all of her great grandsons to find their soul mates, like she'd finally found hers in Lem even though he'd been here all these years.

* * * * *

Don't miss the stories in this mini series!

THE FORTUNES OF TEXAS: DIGGING FOR SECRETS

Follow the lives and loves of a complex family with a rich history and deep ties in the Lone Star State.

MILLS & BOON

WESTERN

Rugged men looking for love...

Available Next Month

The Maverick's Thirty-Day Marriage Rochelle Alers
A Cowboy For The Twins Melinda Curtis

Fortune's Lone Star Twins Teri Wilson
Her Temporary Cowboy Tanya Agler

LOVE INSPIRED

Safe Haven Ranch Louise M. Gouge
A Cowgirl's Homecoming Julia Ruth

Keep reading for an excerpt of a new title
from the Special Edition series,
MATZAH BALL BLUES by Jennifer Wilck

Chapter One

"Caroline, this will be the trip of a lifetime."

The owner of The Flighty Mermaid Travel Agency handed Caroline Weiss brochures with beautiful color photos of Croatia, Bosnia and Herzegovina, and Greece. Deep blue ocean water, blinding white buildings, Moorish Revival architecture, arched bridges, and craggy mountains beckoned. Caroline's heartbeat quickened. She'd waited eight years for this trip. It was supposed to be her college graduation gift, when her life plans included an athletic scholarship to a Big Ten university. Instead, she'd taken classes from home as a part-time student, while taking care of her mother, who died of cancer three years ago. Now that she'd finally paid off the last of the medical bills, her trip was in reach. The next few months, until May and the day of her departure, couldn't come fast enough.

"Thank you, Georgia," she said. Her voice shook with giddiness. "I can't believe I've organized this trip. Part of me keeps waiting for the other shoe to drop."

The purple-haired woman gave her a motherly hug around the shoulders as she accompanied her to the front door of her office. Georgia's bangle bracelets jingled and her colorful boho skirt swayed with every movement. "I know, honey. But your airline tickets and hotels are booked, your transportation in-country is reserved, your tours and tickets are set, and nothing will get in the way of your dream. Trust me."

Caroline waved goodbye and strode down the street of

Browerville, NJ, on her way to work at the Jewish Community Center and nodded at the people she passed on Main Street. Midmorning on a weekday, young parents pushed strollers on the sidewalks and retirees enjoyed the brisk spring sunshine. Some paused to gaze in shop windows or entered or exited various shops and offices. The town Caroline had spent her entire life in was pretty, if predictable. Rose-colored buds covered the trees, ready to sprout into new green leaves. She inhaled. The first hints of spring tickled her nose and teased her with the new growth to come, as if imitating the approach of her new life as well. Her feet flew over the pavement in her excitement. She couldn't wait to explore the new cities she'd visit this summer.

But first, she needed a quick stop at the grocery store. The JCC's little juice bar with refrigerated energy drinks was running low, and she liked to keep it stocked in case any of the seniors needed an energy boost during class. She made a beeline to the health food aisle. Music played over the loudspeaker, something from Mamma Mia. Didn't that take place in the Greek Isles? What were the odds?

As she sang under her breath, she passed a man pushing a grocery cart. The little legs of a toddler swung into her view. Something about men with babies or little children warmed her heart. She turned down the correct aisle and filled her cart with some of the more popular drinks before she maneuvered her way toward the cashiers. The store was filled with morning shoppers, and she cut through the diaper aisle to skirt traffic. Ahead of her, another cart entered the aisle from the opposite direction.

The man with the toddler.

A few more steps, and she froze.

Jared Leiman.

An older, taller, broader, and harder version of the boy she'd dated in high school. She hadn't seen him since he broke her heart the summer after their sophomore year of college. Her mouth dried, and she shut it. Mouth breathers were unattractive. Jared, however, wasn't. He was gorgeous.

And he has a kid.

Chocolate-brown hair brushed away from his forehead. When she dated him, it had been unruly, always falling across his forehead. Deep blue eyes. They turned gray when he was angry and more midnight blue when passionate. Square jaw. It was less defined when he was younger. Broad shoulders, broader now and which her five-foot-five frame reached, as opposed to in high school, when she'd come up to his ear. He'd had a growth spurt. Large square hands gripped the cart as he stopped at the last second before he crashed into her.

"Sorry." He winced. "I was looking at the diapers. Didn't see you."

"Clearly."

He cocked his head to the side before his expression brightened in recognition. "Caroline Weiss. Wow."

Those three words oozed arrogance and sex appeal, made her knees tremble, and irritated her to no end. You know what else irritated her? His daughter. Not her, specifically, but her existence. Despite all rational thought that told her otherwise, the only thing she could think of at this moment was that he'd chosen to settle down and have a family with someone other than her. Guess his claims that he didn't want to be tied down with responsibility meant he didn't want to be tied to *her*.

"How are you, Jared?" A sliver of pleasure that she could still maintain her composure when her ex-boyfriend confronted her slithered along her spine.

"Out of my depth. I don't suppose you know anything about diapers?" he asked, a helpless look on his face.

"Sorry, no."

"How have you been?" he asked. "I cannot believe—"

His daughter fussed at the same time his phone buzzed. His eyebrows gathered in. "I'm sorry, I'd love to catch up, but…"

Caroline shook her head. "I've got to get to work anyway. Good luck."

Before he could say anything else, she made her escape. Of all the people to run into, it had to be him. Thoughts of Jared dulled Caroline's earlier excitement about her vacation as she arrived at the JCC. She entered the staff locker room and stripped down to her workout clothes—pink-and-black-striped leggings and a matching bright pink tank top—and twisted her light brown hair into a ponytail. She checked herself in the mirror and wondered what Jared saw when he looked at her. The lines of sadness—caused by her mom's illness—had faded. For the first time in ages, she looked happier. Not that Jared would notice. She doubted he'd noticed much about her.

With a quiet groan, she made her way into the bright workout room and put on some upbeat music as her clients entered. If anything could get her mind off Jared, it was this class. Most of her clients were in their seventies or older, looking to improve their health with moderate activity. They attended her workout classes every week, as much for the socializing as for the exercise.

"Hi, Hildie. Hey there, Artie." She greeted them by name as they entered, made sure they brought filled water bottles, and asked about their day.

"Caroline, doll, you look beautiful today," Martina said as she entered.

"Thank you. You do as well."

"Eh, I always do." She winked. "Got a new man?"

Caroline paused. "I've sworn off men."

"Ladies never swear, dear."

Caroline turned to an older gentleman. "Bob, how's the back?" she asked.

"A little sore, but much better."

"Please be careful and modify anything you need. Exercise is good, but I don't want you to get hurt."

She started her class with light warm-ups before she moved into the regular exercise program. When the routine ended, everyone hung around to schmooze before they returned to their homes. Once it cleared out, Caroline sank to the floor and leaned against the cinder block wall. Jared Leiman. In high school, she'd been head over heels in love with the guy. They'd discussed marriage, but that was before he'd shown his true colors. After two years at his fancy college, he'd changed his mind, telling her his dreams were too big to waste on Browerville and he didn't want to settle down. She could have understood that if he'd kept his promise of staying in touch and maintaining their friendship. But he'd ghosted her, never asking how she was or if he could help during those darkest days when her mom was sick.

Although the hurt had faded, and only a trace of its bitter aftertaste remained, her curiosity returned in full force. Jared had a baby! There was so much more she wanted to know.

What kind of guardian forgets diapers?

Berating himself for his lack of preparation, Jared Leiman pushed the shopping cart with his two-year-old niece along the diaper aisle and pocketed his phone. He scanned the brands. Although the store offered several choices, it didn't carry what his former nanny favored—some organic, biodegradable, granola brand, exclusive to California—and he was at a loss as to which replacement to get. Caroline wasn't any help, not that he'd expected it of her.

He groaned in exasperation. What kind of person didn't recognize his high school girlfriend? He shouldn't have been surprised to run into her, yet the sight of her threw him. The last time he'd seen her, his sophomore year of college, he hadn't treated her well. She'd grown more beautiful. He was used to his actress clients whose entire lives revolved around their careers and their artificial looks. Somehow, Caroline's appearance was fresher, more natural.

He pulled out his phone once again, ready to dial the nanny for advice, but paused. She'd quit and wouldn't be any help. Besides, he'd graduated top of his Ivy League university, number one in his law school, and was the most sought-after entertainment lawyer in LA. One small human's diaper needs weren't beyond him, were they?

His niece grabbed his hand and squeezed his finger. He looked at her, and she gave him a smile.

His heart pounded in panic. "What do you need, little one?"

Although he'd been her guardian since his brother and sister-in-law's deaths a year ago, this was his first trip alone with her. He'd left most of her care to the nanny he'd hired, and he was clueless. He scanned the aisle for someone to help him out, but no one was around. What kind of town had an empty diaper aisle in the middle of the morning? Did no one run out of diapers?

If his colleagues could see him now.

If his colleagues saw him now, they'd steal his clients away from him, confident he'd lost his edge. He shuddered at the thought. He hadn't lost his edge, he'd just… He didn't know what. But sometime between his brother's death, his niece coming to live with him, and his nanny quitting, he'd lost his ability to juggle responsibilities. He couldn't focus on work, didn't understand how to be a father-uncle, and for the first time in his life, he'd panicked. So, he'd taken an extended time off and come home to regroup, even if he didn't tell anyone else his reasons. Let his parents think he was here for a much-needed visit. Let his office think it was a long-overdue vacation. He'd spend time with his family for Passover, figure himself out, and return to LA better than ever. Or he hoped.

Speaking of LA, someone in his extensive client list must have children. He scrolled through his contacts. Angelina Jolie had six, she'd know what diaper brand to buy. No, her kids were too old. Alec Baldwin had a boatload of little ones. He scrolled, ready to hit dial when a woman with a baby came down the aisle.

Thank God.

"Excuse me," he said.

She looked up, a wary look on her bare face until she noticed Becca. "Yes?"

"I need diapers, and well…" he shrugged.

She nodded in sympathy, her messy bun bobbing. "It can be overwhelming, I know. Your wife didn't tell you what brand to buy?"

He was about to explain he didn't have a wife, but then he'd have to explain about his brother and sister-in-law. His chest tightened. It never occurred to them to fill him in on their diaper preferences.

"No, unfortunately."

"Hmm." She glanced at Becca, asked her age and weight, and reached for a box. "Why don't you try these? We like them."

"Thanks, I will."

With a sigh of relief, he paid for the small package and returned to his car. This time, it took him three tries to strap Becca into her car seat, plus the four extra checks he made to ensure she was protected. At the airport rental-car office, it had taken him a half an hour. Progress.

As he drove the tree-lined streets to his childhood home, he thought once again about Caroline. Babbling from the back of the car made him glance in the rearview mirror. Becca's blue eyes met his.

Caroline's eyes were also blue, but they were lighter than Becca's dark blue ones, and there was depth to them, as if he could see into her soul if he looked hard enough. He'd ended things during college. At the time, he wasn't ready for a long-distance commitment, especially when the trajectory of their lives was different. The amount of responsibility she had for her mother scared him. He hadn't been ready, and the more he'd talked to Caroline, the more afraid he'd become of losing his career goals. Now older and more mature, he realized what a selfish jerk he'd been. He'd failed her when she needed him most. Although she probably couldn't care less about him, he wished he'd talked to her longer today, if for no other reason than to apologize.

He pulled into the driveway of his parents' two-story colonial house and sighed with relief to have reached his destination. He left his luggage in the car, unstrapped Becca, and took her out of the car.

"Let's go see Grandma and Grandpa."

The house sat at the end of a quiet cul-de-sac. Budding, mature oak and maple trees surrounded it. The grass was still dormant from winter, and there were small piles of snow which had yet to melt. The brisk air made him wish he'd brought a heavier jacket, and he added it to the list of things he'd have to buy for Becca. Although she was wrapped in four blankets, he didn't want her to catch cold.

She strained against him. "Down, down!"

If he put her down, she'd be cold. With that in mind, he strode up the porch steps, eager to get inside where it was warm. "Knock, knock," he yelled as he opened the door.

Jared's mother, gray hair pulled into a ponytail, rushed into the foyer. "Oh my goodness, what a *punim*!" She stroked Becca's cheek as he held her, reverting to Yiddish as she did whenever she grew emotional.

Her gaze pierced Jared and her green eyes misted. "She's the spitting image of Noah."

Grief stabbed him, as it often did when he looked at the mirror image of his brother. Usually, he avoided thinking about what he'd lost by turning Becca over to the nanny and burying himself in work. But not this time. His throat clogged.

"Yeah." He forced out the single syllable.

Becca stared wide-eyed at her grandmother before she grabbed a stray lock of her gray hair. Jared jumped, ready to pull her hand away before she could tug, but his mother waved him away. She took her granddaughter in her arms and loosened the toddler's grip.

"It's soft, isn't it?" she asked Becca, her voice gentle.

"Soff," Becca echoed.

She stroked Becca's hair and ran her perfectly manicured hands through her brown curls. "Like yours."

As if she understood, Becca touched her grandmother's hair and then her own hair before she rested her head on her grandmother's shoulder.

Jared stared. "Smart like Noah, too," he whispered.

The smile on his mother's face took the edge off the pain when he thought about his brother. It had been too long since he'd seen it. They all still grieved.

"Come sit," his mother said. "How was your trip? Dad ran out to buy a few things I said we needed, but he'll be home soon. In the meantime, let's get this one settled."

Leading the way into the living room, she sat on the sofa. The gray-painted room with white curtains and deep blue furnishings was homey. Soft throw blankets rested on each armrest, family photos decorated the walls, and favorite biographies and historical fiction filled the shelves. The brick fireplace was unlit, but logs were arranged inside, as if waiting for a match. Jared remembered family game nights in front of that fire, where he battled with his brother for dominance. His chest tightened. No matter how often they'd argued, he'd never wanted to be an only child.

"Uneventful, considering I traveled with a toddler." His phone buzzed with a text, and he frowned before he put it aside.

His mother clucked in sympathy. "I'll bet it wasn't what you're used to."

He thought about the private jets he flew, owned by either his law firm or his clients, and marveled how much his situation had changed since he left home. Even first class on a commercial flight was a new experience.

"I'm glad you're here." His mother held Becca on her lap on the sofa.

She didn't squirm like usual. His niece was content, and the part of him that was hyperalert to her every breath relaxed.

He eased into the upholstered chair next to them. "Me too. I'm sorry it's been so long."

His mother grasped his arm. "Since the funeral." She looked away and swallowed. "You don't have to apologize. I know how busy you've been. But it's nice to see you two. Spending Passover together, well…"

He reached over and squeezed her hand. His brother and sister-in-law died a year ago, but he hadn't returned for any of the holidays. Instead, his parents flew out to him. Guilt wracked him. He'd avoided long trips home as much as possible, forgetting about how his parents might have needed him here.

"I'm sorry," he said, again. It wasn't enough, but it was all he could manage right now.

His mother nodded. She jiggled her knee and made Becca giggle. "This little one is the cutest!" She kissed her granddaughter's neck.

Jared marveled at Becca's reaction to the grandmother she hadn't seen in months. She was more at ease with his mother than she was with him.

His phone buzzed again, and he glanced at it before he returned his attention to his mother.

"I thought we could go to the playground later today," she said. "And they have toddler programs at the JCC we can check out while you're here. Dad and I have memberships there. It's not a problem."

"Sure. Lucinda takes her to the playground near our home all the time."

His mother raised an eyebrow. Uh-oh. He remembered that look from when he was a kid. It was directed at either him or Noah, rarely their dad. Probably because his dad was too smart to become the object of her disappointment. He and his brother got the look whenever they fought about something stupid—like something being "unfair"—and a lecture always followed. What had he done now?

"Lucinda? Your nanny? What about you? Don't you take her to the park?"

"I work, Mom. My clients expect me to be on call for them whenever they need me." He glanced at his watch.

"So does Becca."

His hackles rose. "You think I'm a bad guardian?"

His mother bit her lip. "How are the adoption papers coming?"

He swallowed. They were at home on his desk. "They're coming."

This time, his mother raised her other eyebrow.

"Priorities are like a deck of cards, Jared. Sometimes you have to shuffle the deck to play the hand you're meant to have."

He reached for Becca's legs and squeezed her chubby thighs, eliciting another squeal from her.

What if the deck was stacked against you?

Later that evening, Caroline let herself into her house, toed off her sneakers, and shuffled through the mail. Although she'd paid off all her mother's medical debts, she still held her breath every time she made her initial scan of the postal delivery. Some habits would never disappear.

Her phone rang as she cooked dinner.

"Hey, Sarah, how did you know I needed to talk to you?"

Sarah Abrams was a high school friend who returned to

Browerville after ten years away. Now their relationship was stronger than ever, and Caroline considered her one of her best friends.

"Psychic, I guess. Or Aaron mentioned he'd seen you in town. Nothing's wrong, is there?"

Aaron, her boyfriend, owned the most popular deli in town.

"Not in the way you mean, no. But life is crazy. My trip, running into Jared Leiman, planning programs for the dementia patients—"

"Wait, you ran into Jared? Tell me what happened!"

Caroline grabbed a package of frozen wontons and poured oil in a small pan.

"There's not much to tell—" okay, she was a liar "—I want to hear about your conference."

"Fascinating, exhausting. But I won't let you change the subject on me. Where did you see him?"

"I don't want to change the subject, either. Did you learn anything related to the JCC?" Sarah worked for the Jewish Federation, which oversaw the JCC.

"Ugh, you're driving me nuts. Clearly, we have to get together to discuss everything, which is tricky because with budget season, my hours are ridiculous."

With the oil heated, Caroline added the wontons to the pan and covered it. "That reminds me, I need to turn in my list of equipment for the gym before the budget is finalized, as well as whatever else I need for next year's senior programs."

Sarah cleared her throat.

"Uh-oh," Caroline said. "Did you hear something about funding?"

"Rumblings," Sarah said. "You know how it is at this time of year."

"I hate this part of the job."

"You and me both. Let's put something on the calendar

before my schedule blows up. Do you want to come over and order takeout?"

Sarah was notorious for her inability to cook. "Oh, different takeout menus from mine. That'll be a treat."

Sarah laughed. "Come over around six thirty."

When they finished, Caroline's wontons were ready.

She turned on the TV as she sat to eat. Scanning the channels, she paused on a dance competition reality show before she continued. A crime drama enticed her, but then she discovered a documentary on Greece.

"Perfect timing," she muttered. Reaching for her laptop, she pulled up her notes on her vacation and settled in to watch.

The host of the show interviewed the owner of a small hotel, and Caroline stared. She couldn't decide which was more beautiful—the immaculate hotel, steps away from the Acropolis, or the dark-haired man who owned the place. He laughed at something the documentary host said, and Caroline's memory flashed to Jared.

The Greek hotel owner was shorter and stockier than her ex, with jet-black hair and gleaming white teeth. Jared was taller, with broad shoulders and wavy dark hair. But the cut of their jaws and their bearings were similar.

"Ugh!"

Why did thoughts of Jared pop into her mind now? She shouldn't waste any more time on him. If she'd learned anything over the last ten years, it was he didn't care about her in the same way she'd cared about him. On the nights when she was scared and alone, he'd been out with friends, or doing whatever one did in college. He'd called a few times, but never caught up with her in person, although he'd said he would. She'd nursed her mom, dealt with insurance and unpaid bills, and mourned her mom's death while he'd studied, partied, and built his future. Without her.

She mentally poked the wound and found it didn't hurt the

way it used to. If she hadn't run into him today, she wouldn't have thought about him at all. Returning her attention to the TV, she listened to the tour guide describe an olive farm. She'd waited for so long for this trip. At times, it had been the one thing keeping her going as she dealt with the responsibility of caring for her mom. A twinge of guilt hit her. She loved her mom and cherished the time they'd spent together. But as her sole caretaker, with no one else to help her, she'd sometimes wished it wasn't just the two of them. Was that wrong?

"I'm sorry, Mom," she whispered. "I love you."

She straightened her spine. No more guilt about her mom, and no more thoughts of Jared.

For once, she was going to focus on herself.

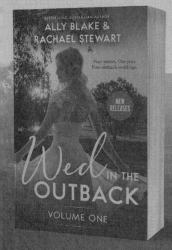
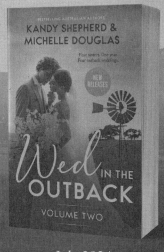

Subscribe and fall in love with a Mills & Boon series today!

You'll be among the first to read stories delivered to your door monthly and enjoy great savings.